"**W**alter J. Boyne has put his considerable talent on the line once again. The result, TROPHY FOR EAGLES, is perfect summer reading. . . . It is against the rich tapestry of recent world history that Boyne unfolds his saga. . . . Sparkling."

The Washington Post Book World

"Boyne's TROPHY FOR EAGLES spans a good chunk of aviation's Golden Era. . . . What makes the novel fly is its careful attention to the giant technological leaps that aviation made in that 10-year span."

St. Louis Post-Dispatch

"Awesome . . . TROPHY FOR EAGLES is unrelenting in its pace—translating the grandeur of history into a human story that is magnetic and spellbinding. Walter Boyne is the dean of aviation writers."

Payne Harrison
Author of *Storming Intrepid*

"Brilliantly weaves the personalities of a few unknown pilots with the lives of some of our legendary aviators and aviatrixes."

Jeana Yeager

Also by Walter Boyne:

Nonfiction

THE SMITHSONIAN BOOK OF FLIGHT
THE SMITHSONIAN HISTORY OF FLIGHT
PHANTOM IN COMBAT
THE LEADING EDGE
DE HAVILLAND DH-4: From Flaming Coffin To Living
    Legend
BOEING B-52: A Documentary History
THE AIRCRAFT TREASURES OF SILVER HILL
MESSERSCHMITT ME 262: Arrow To The Future

By Walter J. Boyne and Steven L. Thompson:

Fiction

THE WILD BLUE*

*Published by Fawcett Books

TROPHY
FOR
EAGLES

Walter J. Boyne

IVY BOOKS • NEW YORK

To Jim and David Nagle,
who loved aviation

Ivy Books
Published by Ballantine Books
Copyright © 1989 by Walter Boyne

Library of Congress Catalog Card Number: 89-1138

ISBN 0-8041-0529-4

This edition published by arrangement with Crown Publishers, Inc.

Publisher's Note: This is a work of fiction. The characters, incidents, and dialogues are products of the author's imagination and are not to be construed as real. Where the names of actual persons, living or dead, are used, the situations, incidents, and dialogues concerning those persons are entirely fictional and are not intended to depict any actual events or change the entirely fictional nature of the work.

Manufactured in the United States of America

First Ballantine Books Edition: July 1990

PROLOGUE:
DEATH FROM THE AIR

Guernica, Spain/April 26, 1937

The old priest was in pain, his side aching from the unaccustomed effort of a twenty-minute run. Inside his thin leather black boot, the homemade patch had built, then burst a blister on his heel. In great sobbing gasps he gathered wind for the dash down the arid hillside into the church of San Juan. The rising drone of aircraft engines gradually drowned out the anguished tolling of the bell—his bell. Helpless, he watched Generalissimo Franco's Nationalist bombers drift from their standard V-formation to become a blasphemous oncoming cross, their bellies disgorging tumbling black dots that straightened into keening pointers of death.

Stopping at a twisted hedge, too late to join his people in the church, the priest saw the line of bombs reach toward the sun-baked houses, Basque-built back-to-back at the edge of the village. With drill-press precision the red-tiled homes disappeared into holes punched into the ground like fingers into dough. Then they erupted, spewing their poor contents in black-and-red fountains that built a smoky staircase pointing back toward the next wave of bombers. His rough sleeve wiped away tears as the string of destruction marched across the city center. He wondered how God could let the Germans build such airplanes, with their pretty butterfly-blue wings and propellers glinting in the sun, only to permit them to bomb this poor Basque village.

Explosions masked the sound of the hotel facade slumping into the street, a dusty cascade of rubble blotting out the familiar double-door entrance. He made the sign of the cross as the bombs two-stepped across the square, turning cobblestones into cannonballs in a rising storm of smoke that blotted out everything behind. Despite the inexorable churning destruction he was sure that it would stop in the square. God wouldn't permit anything to happen to the praying people crowding his church. He staggered and his mouth went slack in horror as the insensate blind bombs continued to fall.

The impossible happened. The front wall of his church dissolved from the bottom up, the bell tower easing noiselessly earthward like a child on a slide. The priest burst forward through the smoke toward the screams welling up as the engine noise trailed away.

The first wave was gone, leaving only a single angular monoplane, a red Messerschmitt Bf 109 V5, above the city. It turned constantly to shepherd the oncoming second *Staffel* of *Jagdgruppe* J/88, twelve Heinkel He-51 single-seat fighters.

Circling and dipping like gulls following a fishing boat, they were part of the Condor Legion, mercenaries sent by Hitler from first-line Luftwaffe units to help Franco. The young Germans flying the bobbing fighters were relaxed, reveling in the liquid-smooth roar of their twelve-cylinder BMW engines, pleased to be on a carefree escort mission instead of doing their usual risky ground strafing. They had come to Spain as tourists in civilian clothes, eager to win promotions in an easy war against a crumbling government Hitler had labeled "Red." But then the Russians had sent counterparts in better airplanes to help the Loyalist government, changing the war from easy to deadly. For the moment they were happy, glad to loaf in the sun, waiting for the pampered bomber pilots to finish their work.

To the south, a line of the clumsy trimotor Junkers Ju-52 bombers from *Kampfgruppe* K/88 bored in at 130 miles per hour, one thousand feet above the ground. These were the Condor Legion's workhorses, aging Luftwaffe bombers that could not defend themselves against an aggressive fighter attack and were totally dependent on their fighter escort to protect them. They were simply dump trucks of the sky, emptying explosives on passive targets, an act without passion or skill. The Ju-52s came in just high enough to avoid the blast effect, low enough for the bombardiers to obliterate the undefended village economically, for bombs were expensive and in short supply.

The casually planned bombing attack was an almost perfectly mindless act of war: innocent people slaughtered in a target without value. No one noted the irony that the bombing helped the Loyalists more than it helped the advancing Nationalists. The German commanders had determined quite by accident to destroy territory about to be surrendered, territory that was already earmarked for destruction by the scorched-earth policy of the retreating Loyalists.

The northern front was crumbling; there was no way to resist Franco's forces as they squeezed the Loyalists, kilometer by kilometer, into the Bay of Biscay. Yet the intractable Basques were inveterate warriors, refusing to surrender. Even as Guernica burned, they launched their last two planes. The snub-nosed Russian-built fighters, their gritty green paint broken only by wide bands of red behind the cockpits, raced toward the columns of smoke, the grass from the Bilboa polo field, their airdrome, still spinning on the wheels snugged up in their fat bellies. The pilots—one a Spaniard, one an American—had known each other for only a few weeks, but combat had made them old comrades. They climbed in loose formation as they turned to get the sun behind them to attack the oncoming bombers.

The American crouched in the open cockpit, sheltered from the slipstream. He banked swiftly, checking his rear and then glancing down on the sea-bordered rolling hills reminiscent of the California landscape he missed so much. As he scanned the strange Cyrillic markings on the instrument panel he wondered at the imponderable turns of fate that put him, a pacifist at heart, in the cockpit of a Russian airplane, killing for an alien cause. When he was a boy, his father had had to force him to hunt, goading him with taunts about buck fever when they needed food for the table. In Spain his squadron leaders had dealt with his misgivings by threatening to kill him if he didn't kill the enemy.

It was difficult for an American in the air or on the ground. The Spanish civil war, even though expected and feared for so long, had exploded with an unreasoning savagery that lusted to settle all accounts, political, clerical, familial, racial. A vicious paranoia gripped the land, sparing no one. The enlisted men, the townspeople, the priests, the farmers—all were worn so hard by the bitterness of the war and their own passionate beliefs that they suspected everyone. Even the indispensable camaraderie usually found in every fighter squadron in every air force was missing, replaced by an agonized tension of mutual distrust. There had been only one exception, the other man leading their pathetic last-gasp two-plane formation.

They flew as one, the American one hundred feet to the right and to the rear—not one hundred and one, not ninety-nine, but one hundred feet. It was close enough to see every detail of the leader's plane, the oxide coating trailing out behind the exhaust slots around the broad cowling, the quiver of the ailerons as he caressed a turn, the tips of the 20mm ShVAK cannon protruding from each wing, the bulge of the two machine guns in the nose. His tired engine was weeping oil in a thin film that made what was left of the paint glisten in the sun.

They had saved each other's lives more than once. At the battle of La Coruña, in the bitter January cold, the Spaniard had burst from nowhere to shoot a German off the American's tail. At Guadalajara, he had repaid the favor. Now each knew exactly what the other would do in any circumstance. It was a curious saving grace to being there at all, a compelling human purpose when all the rational ends of duty had lost their meaning.

He understood how the Indians of the Old West must have felt, sad survivors in a changed world. He and the Spaniard were the last remnants of the Loyalist government's air force in the north, sent by the harassed leaders in Madrid to stem somehow the remorseless flow of Franco's forces. But it was not an air force, just two tired veterans flung against long odds, flying airplanes they had never flown before.

In the south he had grown familiar with the Russian Polikarpov I-15, a sturdy biplane that had surprised the Germans and the Spanish with its speed and agility. For the trip to the north— a suicide mission, the Spaniard had called it—the government had given them two of the scarce I-16s, the best and fastest Russian fighter in Spain. A stubby, fat-winged monoplane, affectionately called the Mosca—"fly"—it was as difficult to maneuver as the I-15 had been easy. Yet it had to serve in this last attack.

In isolated unison, the two pilots pulled their goggles down, tightened their harnesses, set the arming switches, automatically performing a precise precombat ritual. The American felt his energy surge, and he was eager to attack, indifferent to the usual twelve-to-one odds. The Spaniard's customary stoic calm was replaced with a fierce burning indignation. He was fighting for more than his homeland; he had been born on a farm outside Bilboa and spent many a market day in the little town square now consumed by flames and smoke. His orders were to ignore the fighters and get the bombers. It suited him. With full tanks, they could make at least three passes before disengaging. Three passes could mean six bombers and many lives saved on the ground.

The German fighter squadron commander in the red Messerschmitt saw the blunt fleeting shapes of the two enemy fighters and shook his head. Where had they sprung from? The last Loyalist fighters in the north were supposed to have been shot down the day before. He waggled his wings and pointed, and the Heinkel biplanes shimmered into little buzzing packets, flying in the newly adopted finger-four formation, each pilot performing his own precombat litany. The two Russian planes were fifty miles per hour faster than the Heinkels, fifty miles per hour slower than the red Messerschmitt. The Heinkels could only meet the Russian I-16s head on, then dive to catch them after the attack.

The priest, standing now at the edge of the square, cheered the flaring sweep of the Moscas' attack. The two green fighters dropped in a knife-edged dive, turning through the Heinkels, and he could hear the clatter of their guns as they attacked the Junkers. Flames immediately broke out from one bomber as the lead Mosca fixed it in a spray of fire before disappearing into the center of a midgelike swirl of fighters.

The American swept up in a wide, twisting arc. He glanced down at his comrade, admiring the finesse with which the Spaniard slammed his fighter through hard uncoordinated maneuvers, forcing his Mosca into attitudes for which it was not built, using the brute forces of acceleration and gravity to slide out from under the guns of one Heinkel and then send his own bullets hammering through another. The American wished he could have this on film to show students how a master worked against the odds.

A check of his instruments and he peeled off in a headlong diving attack. He brushed past the uplifted noses of the Heinkel fighters, their tiny 7.9mm MG 17 machine guns winking on their cowls, to fasten his sights on the rough corrugated skin of a trimotor. The target, camouflaged in the surreal antic angles of a World War destroyer, blossomed in his sights like an onrushing freight train. He knew that inside the pilot would be grimly holding formation, watching for the signals from the bombardier, humped over the bombsight. The rear gunner could see the Mosca coming, and fired a long burst in vain before watching Russian bullets stitch through the cockpit into the wing. The Junkers blew up above the American as he pulled out of his dive into another soaring climb, trying to see where the Spaniard was.

He shrugged as half the remaining Heinkels raced to the north to cut the two Loyalists off from their base. It was a textbook move, designed to ensure that they could not break away, but it probably didn't matter, for the battle would be decided here and now, in the columns of smoke roiling up from battered Guernica below.

The American, his mouth dry and neck tired from swiveling, glanced for an unbelieving instant as the Messerschmitt opened fire from behind and below at his comrade. The Spaniard jinked, trying to turn away from the stream of lead being poured from the two cowl guns. The Russian plane staggered, then spun away, belching black smoke, the Heinkel fighters jabbing at it like magpies attacking a crow.

The American cursed. It could not be, not after so many battles. He prayed that the Spaniard was faking, that his spin was an escape maneuver. Anguished, he dove headlong, firing at the whirling Heinkels, knowing he was too far away to be effective. He pressed the trigger button until the clatter of the gun blocks moaned that he was out of ammunition. Almost out of sight, his friend's plane, tumbling erratically like a drop of water running down a window, stopped in midair, exploding in a crimson splash.

For a moment he was lost, drowned in the thought that one more friend had died flying. There had been so many, in peace and in war. He banked vertically, pulling back on the stick so that the G forces buried him in his seat as the Mosca turned on its wing, white vapor trails flaring from its tips. He strained to see if there was someone on his tail, waiting to touch a button that would end him.

A thin line of bile surged in his upper throat, a sour mixture of fear and melancholy that suddenly disappeared in the thought that this was his last battle too. A strange exalted sense of deliverance coursed through him, a knowledge that he would fight no more, lose no more friends, kill no more.

Expectant, he turned again: there was no one behind him. The fevered happiness grew. He wondered if anyone was looking down, anyone of all those men and women he had known so well and whose love of flying had taken them early to their deaths. Now he was ready, eager. If the Spaniard had to go, so would he, but he'd take someone with him.

Bullets came from behind, punching whistling holes in his windscreen, smashing instruments. His engine shuddered and oil spurted from his cowling to smear back over the windsceen in a greasy black blanket. He forced his head outside the open cockpit against the wind, wiping his goggles with his scarf. Blood from a ragged wound on his hand ran down his sleeve.

His exaltation ebbed with the blood's flow, and the old dual response to grasping fear raged back. He felt his guts and knees turn to the usual uniform vat of shivering clotted jelly, even as his brain became alert, detached, and observant. The mind fought on, telling his hands and feet what to do to survive, ignoring the whimpering cry of his body to lose all control, to curl into a corner of the cockpit and fall to the ground. As distinctly as he had seen the Spaniard fighting his last battle, he saw himself jerk the stick against the side and pull back, turning vertically to head due north, in an attempt to disengage before the shuddering engine jerked out of its mounts.

Ahead, he saw the Nationalist formation of Heinkels in two layers, one at three thousand feet, one at five thousand feet above him. Like a trapeze artist swinging down from his loft, the lone red Messerschmitt, already once a victor in this battle, curved south to attack him.

He knew only too well how fast and how deadly the Messerschmitt was. There was time still to admire its angular nose, blunt-tipped wings, and even the St. Andrew's cross insignia. The thin black streamers from the low-slung exhausts showed that the airplane was pulling maximum power. As it closed in the curving dive that would place it at his rear, the American saw it also bore a personal marking, one he had seen long ago.

He had no doubt in his mind who was flying that slanting red killing machine, and the knowledge washed him in a fierce warrior's joy. He would revenge the Spaniard or join him.

PART ONE

====================

GAMBLING FOR GLORY

1

New York's nightlife saved Frank Bandfield. Broadway-baby lights down below turned the gray meringue covering Manhattan into a luminescent signpost to Roosevelt Field. Sandbagged by fatigue, he'd drifted far off course, rousing to find himself hurtling westward back into the same storm that had battered him for the last three hours. He flew directly over the city's center at two thousand feet, above the jagged points of skyline floating like islands in the fog. A nudge of the rudder set a descending course for Long Island, the slowly turning propeller cutting phosphorescent slices from the clouds.

Earlier he had flown with his customary tenderness, fingers sensitive to the stick, the plane responding like a bride passionate to please. Lashed by hours of wind and rain, the compliant bride had turned shrewish, fighting his control and bounding off in directions of her own. From Columbus on, sleep had dimmed his senses as implacably as the cold turned his gasoline-soaked fingers into ice. A copper fuel line, routed through the cabin in the frenzied improvisation at the factory in Salinas, had developed a long crack that sent a fan-shaped film of fuel spraying into the cockpit. He'd spent the last hour with his hand clamped over the line, gloves wet through, damping the vibration to prevent a complete break that would cut off fuel flow to the engine.

Clamping the stick between his knees, he blew futilely on his hands, one at a time, to summon feeling.

Six hours into the flight, he'd begun to bite his lips to stay awake. Now they were raw and swollen, but sleep still assailed him. He was hungry and thirsty, his guts rumbling in protest against the unaccustomed neglect. Waiting for the prelanding adrenaline to course through him, Frank Bandfield rocked back and forth in his seat, trying to ease the cramps, letting the sharp handles of the fuel cocks at his side prod him awake. He was alone in the sky; he needed a little help from the ground.

He prayed someone was there. He might have flown across the country to a field empty of his competitors! What if Byrd or Lindbergh had already taken off, was halfway across the Atlantic? The Orteig Prize was $25,000 for the first airplane across— nothing for second place. Yet the prize was the least of it: the headlines and the future would belong to the first pilot to land his plane in Paris. Whatever came after would be an anticlimax.

His usual optimistic manner came back with the rush of the wind. Christ, if they were gone, he'd turn around and head west to California, maybe make the first flight to Hawaii or even Australia, if there were enough islands in between. He'd do what had to be done, whatever it was.

Twenty minutes later, his wingtips trimming gray shreds from the clouds like whiskers from a beard, he ducked below the last layer to see a long L of lights flicker on at Roosevelt Field. They'd believed his estimate, and were waiting for him. Elated, he thought, Goddam, Slim must have turned out the whole National Guard.

He dropped, curving through the patchy mist to meet the field's east-west layout, sideslipping to bleed off altitude. Tired eyes sought to pick out Lindbergh against the cars parked a hundred yards apart along the field's boundary. The sleek little monoplane's tail skid cut through the soaked grass, sluicing a rooster tail of moisture to glisten in the yellow headlight halos. Bandfield turned off at midfield, the field's potholes bobbing the wings up and down in a Swedish exercise rhythm. He taxied toward the tall, lanky figure who was waving a flashlight and shouting at him.

"Bandy, great to see you! But, you rat, you beat my record!"

The pilot climbed out of the cockpit, his legs stiff and his back aching.

"Good to see you, Slim! The record's not official. I didn't .

log off from St. Louis. And thanks for the lights. I really needed them.''

"I was afraid you wouldn't see the dinky little string of boundary lights in the fog. Too bad it's too early for the reporters—you made one hell of a landing."

He helped Bandfield walk to get the circulation going. As they circled, the airplane steamed and gurgled like a winded horse, the hot engine and exhaust manifolds crackling in the misting rain. Lindbergh's bird-quick eyes took in the smooth finish of the plywood fuselage, the cantilever wing. His old flying-school roommate had a first-rate airplane.

Bandfield saw the glance and laughed.

"It's a doozy! And it flies as good as it looks, Slim."

"It must if you got across the Alleghenies in this weather." He switched subjects. "Do you have anybody here to help you?"

Bandy looked at him blankly. It had taken every dime he and his partner had to get him here. There was nothing left over for a support crew. If there was work to do, he'd do it.

"No, I'm on my own. I'll be okay."

"I'll give you a hand when I can. We'll talk about it in the morning."

Bandfield thanked the mechanics who had parked the cars to illuminate the field and were now pushing the airplane into a battered hangar, little more than a garage, three hundred yards from the main buildings. Lindbergh yawned and said, "When Dick Byrd heard you were inbound, he said you could use this."

Bandfield looked anxious. "How much will it be? I'd planned on just tying the airplane down."

The tall pilot laughed. "No charge. Byrd is very hospitable."

Lindbergh knew from experience that all Bandfield could handle now was a cup of coffee and some sleep. He handed him a Thermos as they drove in a borrowed Essex to a shack where a folding cot and two Army blankets waited. "Not the Plaza, Bandy, but you'll need to get some sleep before the briefing tomorrow. The latrine's around the corner. Tomorrow, if you want, I'll get you a room where I'm staying. See you in the morning."

Bandfield awoke six hours later, champagne corks popping through his sinuses and muscles tightened like a sardine-tin lid, head pounding from the engine fumes. He had two hours before the meeting—plenty of time to check the airplane, get some breakfast, and do some thinking.

Back in Salinas, his old friend, partner, and mentor Hadley

Roget would already by elbow-deep in another project, probably tinkering with the racer, cracking his stream of tired jokes. As much as they had argued building the airplane, Hadley would be as confident that Bandy had made Long Island as he was that he would make Paris.

It seemed incredible that the two of them had rolled his airplane out of the hangar for the first time only four days earlier. Working around the clock with pick-up help, they had built it in just eight weeks of calico cat/gingham dog fighting. It was a battle between Bandfield's hard engineering practice and Roget's inventive genius. Clarice, Hadley's wife, would bring them coffee, wincing at their swearing. They argued and yelled even as they built, but no matter how angry or frustrated they were, the hammering and the gluing never stopped. As a result, Bandy had the sleekest airplane in the world, powered by a 220-horsepower Wright Whirlwind engine and fueled by an enormous note at the bank.

If he won, the Orteig Prize would pay off the bank, and there would be a little left over to build some airplanes, improved versions of what he was flying. He loved Hadley Roget like a father, but next time, he had said, the airplane would be built his way, according to sound engineering practice, and with no cockamamie unproven ideas like Hadley's full-span flaps and single-strut landing gear.

The fuselage-building process that Bandfield had invented was radical enough. They had made male and female molds out of concrete, then used heat and a vacuum bag to mold plywood into any shape desired. He had the vision, and Hadley was enough of a master craftsman to make it work. The fuselage was a shell of plywood strengthened with formers, and when the big tanks needed for the ocean hop were removed, capable of carrying the pilot and four passengers in relative comfort.

Their biggest argument had come over the cowling and wheel covers that Bandfield had insisted on. Roget swore that the engine would overheat and that mud would catch in the covers. Bandfield had worked it all out on a little wind tunnel he had built out of a packing crate and an old fan. His lungs still ached from sucking on the big White Owl cigars to get smoke to blow through the tunnel. The flight confirmed the test results; he'd averaged 125 miles per hour coming out, the engine running cool all the way.

In the end, all the arguments had ended in a draw, for he'd been wrong about Hadley's flaps. They worked like a charm, cutting his takeoff distance by about a third, and making the approaches easier. But the single-strut gear still worried him—he still hadn't made a takeoff with the full fuel load he'd need to get to Paris, and he had a vision of the plane sitting in a Fatty Arbuckle pratfall, gear spread wide.

Their final argument had been about the airplane's name. Roget wanted to call it the *Bandfield Bullet*; Bandy insisted on the *Roget Rocket*, and the older man graciously gave in.

It was too expensive to telegraph, let alone telephone, the coast to confirm his arrival. He carried six $5 bills, three in his wallet, three in his shoe, and they had to last all the way to Paris and back. The nest egg he'd built up so painfully during his years in school, repairing and souping up cars, had been wiped out by his mother's final illness, an excruciating bout with failing kidneys that left her wracked with pain and drenched with sweat day after day. Even after selling the truck he and Hadley had converted into a mobile repair shop, he was still in debt for the funeral bills and the airplane. Anyhow, no news would be good news. Every paper in the world was reporting on the New York–Paris race and would be quick to pick up on a crash.

There had been time for only one short test flight before he headed for Long Island, the last of the contestants to arrive. The premier pilots in the world were in competition for the Orteig Prize, and he felt lucky to be with them. Except for the fractured fuel line and the failure of the new artificial horizon just out of St. Louis, the flight out had been uneventful. Bandfield had flown the rest of the way on needle and ball, accepting as ordinary working conditions a cabin so cramped that they'd had to build a recess in the firewall for the rudder pedals. For twenty hours, the engine's heat had roasted his feet while the rest of his body froze.

He opened the small valise that he'd tucked between his seat and the big tank that filled most of the cabin area. A clean pungent odor ghosted through the usual gas-and-grease aircraft smell. Nestled among the clean shirt and two pairs of BVDs and socks was a bar of Fels-Naphtha soap, so strong it made you feel clean just sniffing it. Clarice must have slipped it in, knowing he'd be doing his laundry in the sink. He was content; between the valise and the thirty dollars, he had all he needed. If he got to Paris, there'd be plenty of money to buy anything he wanted. If he didn't, he wouldn't need what he had.

He sanded the back of his hand on his stubble and decided to risk the cold water and shave. Lindbergh was going to be introducing him to some famous people, names he'd read about for years. He wondered how he'd be received, an unknown pilot in an unknown airplane.

The asphalt road to Roosevelt Field disappeared in the murky rain, merging anonymously with the roadside bushes, the glaucous yellow reflection of the headlights running everything together like dried paint on a palette. They could have been traveling in any direction, any dimension. The long black car, high gear groaning at the twenty-mile-per-hour pace, entered a lane of trees, and the reflections seemed to shift their route of travel from horizontal to vertical, as if they were falling straight down a well shaft. His stomach protested the drop until the horizon was restored suddenly by the subdued glimmer of light from the open doors of a hangar.

The gloomy, foreboding precipitation had the same granular texture he remembered from storms along the Baltic coast, where sea and sand mixed with the gritty industrial effluvia to produce a textured rain. Bruno Hafner rolled the window down and thrust his hand out, gathering moisture to cool his brow.

He was tired and bored. Flying in peacetime was so different from, and in many ways more difficult than, flying in war. Even late in 1918, when there were shortages of fuel, oil, tires, everything, there was still a mechanism to get things done. If an airplane needed repair, crews worked all night to have it on the line, ready for its pilot in the morning. And the flights were short; one might have to fly four or five times a day, but only an hour at a time. Now he had to attend to things personally, not to win victories for King and Kaiser, but to face the broad Atlantic in a flight that would last more than a day. He told himself that it was worth the work and the risk—if only they could get on with it.

"We're here, boss." Murray Roehlk's gravelly voice seemed to reach up in apology from his toes. In the back of the Marmon town car, Hafner placed the cashmere lap rug tenderly around the portly dachshund asleep next to him. He got out to stretch. As he tried to untie his muscles and clear his brain, he suppressed his usual unreasoning anger with Murray, forcing a civil tone.

"What time is it, Murray?"

"Six. You can wash up and I'll go get us some breakfast."

Hafner's stomach barrel rolled at the word *breakfast*. Last night he'd been drinking Johnny Walker Black Label "straight off the boat" at the Club Vendôme on 56th Street, confident that there wouldn't be any flying in the morning. The Vendôme was "his" speakeasy, where the owner was pleased to have a distinguished flyer as a guest. He was the club celebrity and rarely had to spend a dime.

His control slipped, and he glared at Murray, bellowing, "Scram." Then, the oversight dawning, he said, "Make sure you take Nellie for a walk. I've got something for her to eat when you come back."

Murray nodded, and slipped from behind the wheel with the dog's leash. Hafner sober was no prize; hungover he was a man to avoid.

The big German slipped back into the car and spread his bulk out over the backseat, looping his legs over the Marmon's mohair upholstery, knowing he had to go through his ritual of self-hate to bottom out his mood, to get functioning again. He thought about searching for a flask, but decided against it, swearing for the fourth morning that week that he would stop drinking, cut out all the habits that gave such intense transitory pleasure that the rest of life was pallid.

Lately, it was taking so much longer to get drunk, and even longer to recover. He remembered the old days, back in France, indiscriminately sampling the captured wines and cognacs, drinking whatever was poured. A few glasses of Bordeaux at dinner, a drink or two afterward, and he was out cold. But he'd be on the line before dawn, checking over his Fokker, joking with the other pilots, eager to get airborne. Now he had to drink all evening to feel it. His hangovers lasted till noon and were different, depressing. With the *Staffel*, a hangover was something to laugh about, a trophy like a victory. Now it clung like a stinking black octopus around his shoulders, reproaching him for all he did and didn't do.

Even at the end of the war, when his scoring string was brought to a halt by the Armistice, he hadn't felt the same bone-devouring depression. People were always saying that everything was relative. Nothing was. In 1918, he was being shot at every day, didn't have a mark in the bank, no time for romance except for quick tumbles with the local unwashed farm girls, and he was completely happy. Less than ten years later, no one was shooting, he had become wealthy selling surplus arms around the world, and he enjoyed a beautiful rich blond wife as well as a string of young girlfriends. But he was totally miserable.

He walked himself painfully through his analysis, working to get to the pit of his self-reproach, to worry his secrets like a terrier, and then to bound up, ready for the day. The reasons for his self-pitying black moods were paralyzingly simple. The first was good, one he could talk about to anyone. In 1918, he had lived in an ordered world in a powerful Germany he believed in, and where he was famous as the youngest ace to win the Pour le Mérite. His squadron mates liked him, he had dined with the crown prince, his face appeared on postcards, and he was courted by the airplane manufacturers when he flew in the fighter competitions. He had scored forty-five times in aerial combat. The official records credited him with only twenty-seven, because he had given away eighteen victories to grateful young pilots to build their confidence.

Giving away victories was unusual. The reason he had done it was tied to the puzzling, unsavory second cause of his depression, an evil appetite he could admit only to himself, an appetite for killing even more than for victory. He remembered his first realization of his obsession precisely, on May 10, 1918, when he was engaging a Royal Air Force Bristol fighter. He could see it now, its drab brown colors overlaid by the blue-white-and-red cocardes, the curious lower wing slung on struts below the fuselage, a tiny red-haired man in the backseat who played his twin Lewis guns like an organ. They had fought for twenty endless minutes, and as Hafner's brand-new Fokker D VII picked up bullet hole after bullet hole, his lust to kill grew. A snap shot, hanging on his prop, through the bottom of the Bristol's fuselage had killed the enemy rear gunner. On his next attack he closed to within fifteen meters, the big Bristol filling not only his sights but the prop disk. He could see the gunner hanging slackly in the Scarff ring turret, blood spraying in a mist from a face wound, the pilot whipping quick glances back over his shoulder, pounding on his jammed forward-firing Vickers machine gun. Hafner closed his eyes to picture the scene precisely, remembering how he had mashed the trigger lever, spraying the Bristol till his ammunition belts ran empty. The pilot fell forward and the flame-precursoring wisp of white vapor streamed out. He dropped back to watch the Bristol spin, gently at first, then more quickly and steeply until it disappeared in an exploding circle of smoke that sent small drifting bits of men and machine to litter no-man's-land below.

The excitement was beyond the sexual. He had experienced no erection, no orgasm, no genital sensation at all, but no caper in bed had ever given him the same wild rush of pleasure. It had been a cerebral release, a mind-clearing exaltation, a searing soul-cleansing mixture of triumph and survival that he had never felt before but knew that he must experience again.

After that, ordinary honors were bland, even the notice that he'd won the Blue Max. At first, he'd tried to talk to his colleagues about his feelings, confident that they must have felt something of the same. They were embarrassed. They had no idea of what he meant, but were uncomfortable in the suspicion that whatever it was, it was unnatural. So he never again mentioned that he found that his real enjoyment was simply in killing. What had begun as a patriotic keen-edged hyper-hunting experience became an addiction, a thirst that he assuaged every flight, either in a fight against another airplane, or in a quick sweep behind the Allied lines, looking for staff cars, marching troops, anything on which to spend his bullets. Goering had reprimanded him officially for needlessly risking his life and a valuable airplane. It made no difference. He couldn't help it, and it gained him a reputation for wild bravery that was totally unjustified. He knew he was brave enough, but the exploits, the balloon-burning, the wild dives down the trench line, were compulsion, not courage. And he'd come to learn the hard, blinding rules of a compulsion to worship destruction.

Without it, life had no bite. When he first came to America, the differences, the challenge to succeed, had temporarily replaced the urge to kill. It had passed, and he tired of the continual posing, the sham of playing the good-natured German nobleman who enjoyed nothing better than competing with American pilots. The Berlin charm he turned on like beer from a spigot was devastating to American women; he had only to kiss their hands to feel their underclothes dropping with their inhibitions. Even American pilots had come to have some sort of inverse appreciation for him as a German ace. He couldn't understand it. Maybe it was because they had won the war, and wanted their opponents to have been worthy.

He felt his black mood turn the corner. Once he forced himself to think about the killing, to realize how much he missed the feeling, he could gather the energy to bound out of the car and again assume the well-paying role of a tennis-playing knight of the air.

Murray came back, with Nellie prancing on the end of her leash. Hafner took the bit of steak he had wrapped the night before and bent down. A tender look suffused his face. "Roll over, Nellie. Even you must work for your supper."

The battery acid that passed for coffee at the field café finally jolted Bandfield awake. He paused at the door of the tiny operations shack to check the weather. Long Island's verdant greens amazed him; spring had already faded from the hills around his Salinas, California, home. A single deceitful ray of sunshine bled through the rolling gray clouds, brightening the pale green crayon stippling of new growth on the trees lining the field before drowning in a fresh drumroll of rain. A transparent veil of water peeling off the wings of a big trimotor was clear evidence that there would be no flying today. He eased the door open and entered self-consciously, as if this were his first day in school. In a way, it was.

Inside, he straightened his shoulders to a good military carriage and stretched to his full six-foot height. Lean at 165 pounds, a shock of curly black hair showing no sign of the combing he'd just given it, the twenty-two-year-old Bandfield looked tired and worn. He sat down, tight muscles creaking in harmony with the fragile squeaking wooden rungs of the chair, tilting back to survey the room. He had breathed better air in his dad's smokehouse, but in all the world this was the best and only place to be, surveying his competition. The stale odor of cigarettes, unwashed bodies, and oil-stained leather jackets underscored a salty sporting tension. Four men were already dead in this game, and the two Frenchmen, Nungesser and Coli, were missing, probably lost at sea. It could happen to some of the others here.

The low-ceilinged room was fifteen feet wide by twenty-five feet long, its bare-stud walls decorated in standard ops-shack style with old calendars and oil-company advertisements. Sprawled on wooden chairs and boxes were the handful of men who were the fulcrum on which the entire American aviation revolution balanced.

For a decade after the war, pilots and aeronautical engineers had watched everyone else—stockbrokers, radio repairmen, car salesmen, bootleggers—make money. One cynic, with fifteen years invested and no return, mused that there was plenty of money in aviation—he'd left all of his there. Another quipped that the only real danger in aviation was starvation. Bandfield's casual walk to the operations shack convinced him that east or west, it was the same: too many men scrambling for too few jobs in flying. Aside from some trainers, the only signs of activity were the planes gathered to compete for the Orteig Prize. Half the buildings were empty, fading signs lamenting famous names of long-gone aviators, optimistic victims who thought they could make a living flying. All across America, in every other industry, the economy was booming and the sky was no limit. In aviation, the sky was a sure pathway to bankruptcy. Cal Coolidge said that the business of America was business. It didn't apply to flying. And it was Coolidge who had suggested that the Air Service buy only one airplane and let the pilots take turns.

But it wasn't Silent Cal's fault that the profession was torn by a never-ending battle between cost and revenue. Airplanes were expensive, and sometimes lasted only a few weeks or months. Crashes were common, and hangars were usually ramshackle tar-paper buildings littered with oil-soaked rags, easily victim to casual cigarettes or faulty wiring. The investments of many a lifetime had gone up in smoke. Insurance was costly and hard to come by. Maintenance costs were high, and neither passengers nor cargo yielded profit.

Inevitably, management sought economies in pilots' salaries and the workplace. Pilots who complained were ruthlessly replaced. Youngsters were always coming up, glad to subsidize the company—manufacturer, air-mail carrier, no matter—for the privilege of gaining a few hours of flying time. Every airfield office Bandfield had ever seen had been just like this one, inadequately furnished, poorly heated, an offense to the eye. A masochistic glee hung over the whole discipline of flight, a perverse reasoning that if you really wanted to fly, you wouldn't mind being miserable. It was a price most pilots gladly paid, trading ten hours of labor on the ground for every hour in the air.

Even the Orteig race planes, supposedly the best in the business, confirmed his view. He knew the problem was the same he'd had with Hadley Roget—a lack of engineering discipline. Airplanes were designed by people who loved them blindly without targeting what they were supposed to do, never realizing that it was pointless to build the best-looking airplane in the world if it couldn't earn its keep. They were all going to try to fly the Atlantic, and if they all succeeded, it still wouldn't prove a thing. What the world needed was safe airplanes that could make money, airplanes like his own.

There were so many hazards, from engine failure to losing

control in a storm. Few of the airplanes had decent instrument systems, and fewer pilots had any experience with the sort of weather they'd find over the North Atlantic. Bandfield glanced around, estimating that the sea might claim half of the men in the room. They all knew it, but not one of them would have been anywhere else in the world.

He watched Lindbergh's strong, slender fingers tear up an orange crate and hand the bits of wood to tiny Richard Byrd, who stuffed the splinters into the gasping coal stove as carefully as if staving off an arctic wind. Last year, the slightly built Navy commander had been the first man to fly over the North Pole; this year he intended to be the first across the Atlantic. Neither man spoke, each preoccupied with thoughts as bleak as the weather.

Lindbergh noticed his old friend and came over to introduce him.

Bandfield thanked Byrd for the use of his hangar. The explorer smiled and said, "Glad to do it. I looked in this morning; you've got a nice-looking airplane."

Bandfield flushed with pleasure. "It's the best thing I've flown, sir. I'd be glad for you to fly it sometime."

Byrd's smile faded like ice in a cup of coffee. Little worry lines appeared on his brow as he murmured, "No thanks. Not until I'm back from France, anyway."

Bandfield realized that his plane had shifted the warmth just as it had the odds. Before, Byrd had clearly been the leading contender; now the race was up for grabs. As Lindbergh introduced him to the other pilots, the same feather edge of resentment surfaced. It was understandable. He was a wild card flying a slick airplane, and the record time he'd made across country, just under twenty hours, had superheated the competitive tension already searing the room. The other planes—a Bellanca, a Ryan, and a Fokker—were roughly equal to one another in performance, and the race could have been won by the first one off. The rotten spring weather that had kept them grounded was the only thing that had made it possible for him to compete. If it had broken even slightly in the last week, they would have leaped off on the flight to Paris, and he would never have left Salinas.

Bandfield sat down again, balancing on the back legs of his chair, his head braced against the rough wall. He wished that Hadley could see him, meeting pilots they'd only read about. Shaking hands had hurt the raw red creases that split his knuckles into a map of pain. The only thing that would get hands clean was a corrosive mixture of gasoline and Spic and Span cleaner that removed the skin along with the grime and turned nail-brushes into medieval instruments of torture. He needed some Jergens or vaseline, but he knew he wouldn't get any, and that his knuckles would still be sore on the next takeoff. It was an occupational hazard to be ignored, like missed meals, lost laundry, and empty pockets. Still, the barren room seemed cozy compared to the interminable night flight from St. Louis. A sudden burst of warmth from the stove, seen rather than felt, helped him transform past fear into present pleasure. He blew his breath down into his plaid flannel shirt, recycling warmth back into his system, listening to the sharp staccato chatter of the men he was going to beat to Paris.

The aviators were as different in backgrounds as in builds, alike only in their gut desire to hammer out a living in a profession in which it was easier to earn death than a dollar. Bandfield smiled as he tried to analyze their personalities. Though most had things in common—wrinkled clothes, no glasses, and quick reflexes—each man was unique, and each one somehow resembled the airplane he flew.

Take good old Slim, whom he'd known only too well in flying school. Despite his serious, almost worried demeanor, Lindbergh was always playing wild practical jokes, from lacing a canteen with kerosene to putting itching powder in the first sergeant's shorts. But he was a professional pilot, shy despite an obvious competence. Lindbergh was a born leader, and definitely a contender to be first across. He could have been a success in anything—medicine, law, even following his father into politics—but he'd given his life totally to aviation. Like most of them, he was broke, in hock to his backers. He was tall, lean, and gawky, somehow handsome in spite of it, just like his airplane, the *Spirit of St. Louis*. Aesthetically, the silver Ryan's wing seemed too long for its stubby fuselage, and the windowless nose had a blind, salamander look to it. The landing gear was joined to the wings by a wild Erector Set of struts, yet it looked capable.

Richard Byrd was entirely different, compact and contained, with a handsome face lit up by a smile he switched on and off like a light bulb. He viewed his real profession as exploration. Flying was only a tool that let him leapfrog over older, more famous competitors. Bandy had read endlessly about the Virginian, whose generosity with the hangar had made him a friend for life. Byrd was an enigma, adored by the public and yet treated with frosty reserve by those who should have known him best. A patrician, he'd chosen the equally elegant Fokker tri-motor, a big airplane to suit a big ego, one he wouldn't fly but would command.

Byrd had selected two crew members noted for their capabilities and frailties, neither one of them likely to accept orders easily. The first was tall, mustachioed Bert Acosta, a wild man irresistible to the ladies and a superb pilot—as long as the sky was blue. The other was the popular Norwegian Bernt Balchen, quiet, handsome, and an excellent instrument pilot. A good combination, and hard to beat, given that they had an excellent airplane.

An important member of Byrd's team hovered in the background. *The* Tony Fokker stood quietly by the coffeepot stoking himself with granulated sugar licked from a spoon. It was an addiction; the soft-featured Dutchman often ate a bowl of sugar for dessert, and nipped at it constantly during the day. In 1914 Fokker had sold his services to Germany, and by 1918 had created the war's best fighter, the coffin-nosed D VII. At the Armistice, the twenty-eight-year-old multimillionaire fled to Holland with trainloads of planes and engines. After a booming success in the Netherlands, he expanded his operations to the United States. Self-trained, willful, and as much a pilot as any man in the room, Fokker preferred others to make the record flights, as long as they made them in his planes.

Bandfield couldn't understand why Byrd, with his superior airplane, had not yet departed for Paris. Nor, apparently, could Fokker, who didn't bother to conceal his disapproval of the famous explorer.

The door burst open, a barking dachshund preceding a blond giant with a hundred-watt smile that seemed to light up every corner of the room. There was a chorus of "Bruno!" as he apologized for being late.

"I was helping a young lady start her engine"—an obviously familiar line that set the other pilots hooting and rolling their eyes.

"Come meet our newest entrant, Bruno." Byrd looked like Jeff steering a husky Mutt as he guided the huge German to Bandfield's side. "Mr. Bandfield, Captain Bruno Hafner, late of the Kaiser's air force, now a well-known junkman about town."

Bandfield stuck out his hand. Hafner's precisely measured hesitation in returning the grip was exactly long enough for a jagged electric charge of mutual dislike to streak between them. Bandfield had seen the look before in the eyes of the fraternity men at Berkeley whose cars he'd fixed, vapid John Held caricatures who tendered him the ignition keys as if their fingers were tongs. Hafner marked Bandfield down as the troublesome sort of enlisted man, the smart noncommissioned officer whose "sirs" were always a half beat away from courtesy and who always had to be reminded of his place.

The big man nodded abruptly and turned away, leaving Bandfield standing, once again a green freshman embarrassed by what he was wearing, how he looked, and where he was from. In a single glance Hafner had charted the difference between haves and have-nots, nobles and commoners, the adept and the maladept.

If the chemistry had been different, Bandfield would have told Hafner that in flying school he had learned all about the German's wartime career, and had even seen him in person once before. The Germans had evolved a unique "star" system in which the most promising young aces gravitated to *Jagdgeschwader* I, a conglomerate of four *Jastas*—squadrons—that formed the great aerial flying circus of Baron von Richthofen. Hafner had been summoned after his first fifteen victories; he had quickly gained five more to earn the *Pour le Mérite*.

The guns on the Western Front had scarcely fallen silent when a Hollywood promoter had gone to Europe searching for "authenticity" in his war films. It hadn't taken much talking to bring Hafner back, along with the French ace Charles Nungesser, now missing over the Atlantic. They had made a few two-reelers in the early 1920s, then toured the West Coast, flying fake dogfights out of country pastures, drinking homemade wine, and screwing the local women. In the beginning they had used planes like those they'd flown on the Western Front, Nungesser in a Spad XIII and Hafner in a Fokker D VII. By 1923, when Bandy had leaned across the barbed-wire fence to see them in Salinas, both warplanes had crashed and the men were flying Jennies. Nungesser's white JN-4 was decorated with wartime French cocardes and his macabre personal insignia, a black heart illuminated with a skull and crossbones and mourning candles. Bandfield remembered vividly the roughly painted oversize black iron crosses on Hafner's Jenny, an odd contrast to the almost delicate rendering of a white winged sword.

Hafner began speaking quietly in German to Tony Fokker. Bandfield sat back down, swallowing a rage he didn't understand, angry with Hafner for the snub, but more with himself for caring. Covertly he studied Hafner, whose square-cut face was dominated by a huge jaw, along which ran a thin white scar. Hafner's bushy eyebrows occupied the high ground of the ridge that ran across his forehead like a small visor. An aquiline nose was poised sharply over his fleshy lips. As he watched, Bandfield saw that all the separate elements of Hafner's face operated independently of his emotions; his lips could smile without any trace of humor in his eyes, or he could frown while seemingly amused. On either side of his mouth were small dimpled lines which acted as signals for his feelings. If he was going to smile, the little dimpled lines would react first, their ends pointing up. If a frown was coming, the little lines would become an inverted V.

Watching Hafner cooled Bandfield's anger, and he resumed his inspection of the competition. Dusty Rhoades was at his left. Of medium height, with wavy russet hair, Rhoades leaned against the wall, his left leg tucked up for support, a target for the rolled-up *Aviation Age* nervously drummed against it. Arrow-collar handsome, he could have been cast as the hero in a Western. He wore a uniform of his own devising, an exotic cross between an RAF tunic and a state trooper's motorcycle garb. A year ago he had flown with the marines in Nicaragua, using an ancient DH-4 to dive-bomb General Sandino's troops in the jungle. Rumored to be a great pilot and an even better mechanic, Rhoades led a charmed life, surviving more bailouts from airmail planes than even Lindbergh. Bruno Hafner had picked him from a dozen candidates to fly as copilot/mechanic in his airplane, the Bellanca *Miss Charlotte*. Once again the pilot/plane physical comparison held true. Giuseppe Bellanca was an Italian, but his airplane was as Teutonic as Hafner, square-cut wingtips and tail disdaining any effort at streamlining, cutting through the air on brute power and lift.

Bandfield watched Hafner's copilot closely, to see if he was infected with his boss's arrogance. Bandy had heard that Rhoades was terribly underrated, a brilliant pilot whose natural manner kept him out of headlines, but who could be counted on to do the work. By all appearances, Rhoades was the most relaxed man in the room, humming an off-key version of "One Alone." Yet Bandfield sensed a quiet, desperate tension revealed in the grimaces Rhoades made as he repeatedly glanced out the window to check the weather.

All the other men were legends to Bandy. He wanted to become a legend to them. He had more to gain. They could all use the $25,000 from the Orteig Prize; he needed the fame. There would never be enough flying jobs to go around, but if you were first across the Atlantic, you would always have work.

Byrd strode in front of the group, taking command as if it were a natural right. As he talked his right hand, index finger crooked, kept time, waving an invisible conductor's baton.

"You've heard that a reward has been offered for anyone who locates Nungesser and Coli. If we were ready, we'd begin a search mission today, but there are some more tests I want to do." Tony Fokker glowered in the background.

There was no reaction; they were here to compete, not to fly rescue flights. Besides, most of them had written the Frenchmen off as fish food. Byrd changed the subject. "We'll need a little wind to dry the ground. I walked it yesterday, and it's just like last September." The explorer's Southern heritage came through clearly in his soft voice.

Bandy asked, "What happened in September?"

Byrd's icicle eyes speared him. "That was when Captain Fonck crashed."

Bandfield felt stupid. Fonck, the Allied ace of aces with seventy-five victories, had been the first to compete for the Orteig Prize. He had been trying to lift his overloaded Sikorsky off from the same wet field when a jury-rigged auxiliary wheel collapsed. Digging in like a scraper blade, it sent a protesting spray of mud that screamed to stop the flight. The stubborn Fonck pressed blindly on with the takeoff until the big biplane lurched over a gully to crumple and burn not half a mile from where they sat. Fonck and one man got out; two others did not, the first in a procession of victims in the quest for the Orteig Prize.

Byrd stepped back from the stove, a slight limp adding to his distinction. He reached down and flicked a spot of ash from his polished high laced boots, and then tugged his spotless windbreaker around him. His manner was a stippling of contradictions. Apparently instinctively modest, he nonetheless frequently alluded to his Arctic experience as if it confirmed his right to be there.

"Somehow, I never get warm enough anymore." He flushed, as if this were an unseemly personal revelation. Byrd raised his voice and went on. "The weather bureau called—someone will be along in an hour to give the latest report. There hasn't been much change. Fog from here to beyond Newfoundland, rain all the way.''

Fokker's expressive snort said the weather was adequate for the flight. Always a businessman, he now regretted selling the airplane to Byrd. They had agreed that Balchen was to be the pilot, and fog was no problem to him. Yet Byrd was too cautious to leave, and Fokker fretted that his big trimotor would be beaten across by the single-engine Bellanca, or worse, by Lindbergh's Ryan. Bandfield's fast airplane presented a new threat, and he was nervous.

Fokker's Dutch accent came through as he said pointedly, ''For some people, the fog wouldn't be any problem. My airplane is designed to fly through weather like this.''

Byrd busied himself breaking up another box for the fire, ignoring Fokker as he ignored all critics.

Lindbergh circled around to stand between Rhoades and Bandfield. Rhoades spoke: ''If we hadn't had a fuel leak, the Baron and I would already be in Paris, counting our twenty-five grand.'' Hafner looked over, smiling—he wasn't a baron, but felt he should have been. Rhoades knew how to keep him happy.

Balchen tossed him a pack of cigarettes. ''Here's some Twenty Grands. That's about as close as you two will get.''

At the beginning of the month, only Hafner's Bellanca had been ready to try for the New York–Paris race. Then it developed a fuel leak that couldn't be found until they'd disassembled the entire fuselage tank, working night and day while the weather changed from good to bad. Now there were four planes ready, and the weather kept them all on the ground.

The room was quiet. Lindbergh signaled with his eyebrows to Balchen. Yawning and pretending to stretch, Lindbergh swept his foot in an arc to knock the legs of Bandy's chair out from under him, flopping him on his back. Laughter broke the tension.

Lindbergh doubled over, holding his sides, saying, ''Bandy, if you spin in like this in a chair, what will you do in an airplane?'' Fokker looked the other way, chuckling. Balchen threw his head back, braying.

Only Byrd moved to help him up. ''You must be careful, Mr. Bandfield. It's quite a problem for us to get insurance.''

They laughed again. It was the first joke Byrd had ever cracked.

Bandy grinned weakly at the roughhouse acceptance ritual. He was now one of the boys. Flying humor was never subtle.

Byrd turned serious. "Shall we all meet back here at one to get the full weather report?" The men nodded, and Byrd walked out, followed closely by Fokker. Tony intended to do some nagging.

The others left to check their aircraft one more time. Lindbergh grabbed a chair, turned it around, and straddled it, his eyes crinkling with good humor. "Sorry, Bandy, but I couldn't resist." He had just a trace of a polished Scandinavian accent, which gave his rather high voice a ministerial tone. "It's been a long time."

The two men looked at each other, remembering their days together at flying school. Lindbergh cleared his throat. "I never felt right about the way they washed you out. It could just as well have been me."

Bandfield nodded, pensive. It had been three years since he had slunk away from flying school, a failure in the only thing he'd ever really loved to do. The depressing smell of the San Antonio station came back to him, its rolling clouds of steam-laden coal smoke matching his utter dejection. It had been the most miserable day in his life, the end of his dreams, the end of his flying. Or so it had seemed at the time.

"What the hell happened, Bandy? I was as much at fault as you were."

"Banana oil, Slim!" Bandfield knew exactly what had happened, having lived through it in memory hundreds of times since then. He and Lindbergh had been flying single-seat S.E.5s in a practice diving attack against a solitary DH-4 observation plane. Lindbergh had disappeared beneath the target plane as Bandy sent an imaginary line of machine-gun bullets through it.

A jolt had turned the roaring noise of wind and engine into sudden silence. Twenty feet away, Lindbergh had stared wide-eyed across their locked wings. The two S.E.5s had collided, noses whipping together to splinter the propellers and stop the engines, crumpling the spirited fighters together like grotesque mating dragonflies. Pounding noise had given way to a silence flawed only by the broken-bone grating of the interlocked struts. He could have called to Lindbergh, but instead gestured with his thumb toward the ground. They had leaped into a welling terror, relieved at once by the groin-wrenching jerk of the parachutes opening.

"Slim, I already had two strikes against me. You only had one."

Lindbergh knew about his own strike; his outrageous practical joking had earned him enough demerits to keep him walking tours on weekends.

"What were your two strikes, Bandy?"

"You remember that the Cadet Squadron commanding officer, Captain Westerfield, was the presiding officer on the elimination board. He'd had a complaint about me from a girl's family in town. I had a tough session with him the day before the board met."

Lindbergh smiled. "Ah, María. I'll never forget her, Bandy, she was the prettiest little Mexican girl I ever saw. I always wished I had enough nerve to ask her out."

Bandfield knew that Lindbergh had never dated while he had been there; he wondered if he had later.

María worked in headquarters as a sort of roving secretary, backing up with her typing skills the generally pathetic hunt-and-peck efforts of the typical squadron clerk. You could tell when she was coming or going by the ripple effect on the soldiers, and it had become a gentle custom for any marching body of troops to be given "eyes right" if they happened to be passing her. She ignored all equally and democratically, keeping her pleased brown eyes straight ahead, content just to be aware of the train of admiration in her wake.

"Westerfield thought so too. He'd been trying to make time with her for almost a year."

Lindbergh shook his head vigorously, and his voice went up half an octave. "No, he wouldn't have risked it! As career-crazy as that old mustang was, he wouldn't have fooled around with anybody like María."

"You didn't know María very well."

"Bandy, I still can't believe he'd wash you out for that. He was an iron-ass, but not a bad guy."

Bandfield's tone took on a sudden bitterness. "No, Slim, there was something else, a typical stupid goddam military balls-up, something I should have been smart enough to avoid. Westerfield asked me which of us—you or me—I thought was the better pilot. I was honest and said you were. He got all over me, saying that I would never make a good pursuit pilot, that a pursuit pilot always had to be convinced that he was the best in the world. He gave me the same stupid fucking spiel that every dumb-ass would-be Rickenbacker gives at every officers'-club bar in the world. Half of them couldn't fight their way out of a morning report, but they've got to act like they are killers."

Lindbergh was plainly surprised by the sudden vehemence. "Well, he asked me that too, but I knew what he wanted. I told him that I was the best in the world. I really thought you were, but there was no sense in telling Westerfield that. But I still can't believe that he'd wash you out about that, either. He was a dumbass, all right, but that wouldn't have done it."

Bandfield was somewhat mollified. "No, except that I got mad, and I told him that if the average pursuit pilot's brains were dynamite, he couldn't blow his nose."

Lindbergh laughed. "That would do it. But it still wasn't fair."

They were quiet a moment. Bandfield was painfully aware of the character flaws that made life difficult for him. He had a reckless drive to prove himself right at any cost, one that had marred his record at Berkeley, and probably stemmed from the dogged arguments he used to have with his father over everything he did. He didn't mind being wrong—but when he knew he was right, he was inflexible. And he hated to be pushed around, especially by a guy like Westerfield, who held all the cards. When he was pushed, he had to push back. He wouldn't have made a good officer.

"Let's get down to the important stuff. How far did you go with María? I could tell that she thought you were the bee's knees."

Bandfield grinned. He hadn't gotten very far with María, and it had pushed him damned close to marrying her, despite the fact that she was Mexican, Catholic, and only eighteen. One night he had brought her back from a long, tender, and chaste walk to find her father and three brothers waiting on the tumbledown porch of their frame shack. He'd been glad to get away with only her tears to worry about. He should have realized that the old man would have considered Captain Westerfield to be a real catch, not to be compared with some raggedy-ass cadet.

"We were pretty well chaperoned most of the time, and María was a good girl."

"What happened after that?"

Bandfield felt his good humor gradually being restored. As bad as he'd felt after washing out, things were working out for the best.

"I was really lucky, Slim. I got a job flying Douglas M-2s for Western Air Express when it was starting up. Ever flown one?"

"Yeah, I got to fly most all the different air-mail planes after

I went back to civilian life. The M-2 is just a bigger, better DH-4. Of course, most anything's better than a DH-4. I've bailed out of two of them and crash-landed another.''

Bandfield was silent, remembering the terror of his own parachute jump, wondering if he'd have the nerve to throw himself into the black void of a Midwestern night as Lindbergh had done. Slim had been lucky: his chute had worked each time. He had only to gather up the mail from the crashed airplane and catch the next train to his destination. It was only a little more than par for the air-mail course, flying rebuilt de Havillands at night, in weather, without instruments.

''Where did you get that airplane, Bandy? It makes my poor old Ryan look like a tin lizzie.''

Bandfield flushed with pleasure. ''Hadley Roget's a building fool, I tell you. A little stubborn maybe, but he can make airplanes.''

''I heard about him when I was out on the Coast, working on the *Spirit*. He's supposed to have built some radical airplanes over the years.''

''That's the guy. We designed it and worked on the drawings and the engineering for almost a year. We started cutting wood in March. It still needs some fine-tuning, but I think it's ready.''

''Man, I know what you mean. We really threw the Ryan together in San Diego. The Ryan company was great; they did everything I wanted, if it could be done. If it couldn't, they would figure out something just as good.''

Talking amiably, they walked over to where the *Spirit of St. Louis* was sitting, its tail on a trolley, waiting to have the compass swung.

Bandfield immediately liked the Ryan. The finish was superb, with the cowling and spinner sparkling with machine-turned knurling. The intersections of the struts were all taped and streamlined, and the forest of fuel lines was neatly laid out. ''How come you forgot the windscreen, Slim? It must be tough to land this thing and not see out the front.''

Lindbergh stretched, accustomed to being asked about the Ryan's unusual cockpit arrangement. There was no windscreen, no forward visibility at all, the pilot's usual position being replaced by a huge gas tank. ''We did that on purpose, believe it or not. I don't want to be between the engine and the gas tank if I crash. The visibility's not so bad. You can't see out of the front of most airplanes on takeoff anyway, and on landings, I just make sort of a curving approach, and sideslip it in. When you're airborne, it doesn't matter much.''

He paused, grinned, and said, ''Out over the Atlantic I don't expect to meet anybody coming in the opposite direction, anyway. Let me show you something.''

He opened the door and pointed. ''I've even got a periscope, just like a U-boat.''

''That's the berries!'' Bandfield was impressed. The Ryan would be difficult to beat.

Lindbergh asked, ''How does your ship fly?''

''It's a little goosey. We didn't have time to build a trimmable stabilizer, so I have to fly it with pressure on the stick most of the time.''

''Just like the *Spirit*. That long wing and short fuselage make it unstable. Take your hand off the stick for even ten seconds, and the plane slips off into a spiral.''

''That's bad. If you fall asleep, you'll be in trouble.''

''No, that's good; I won't dare fall asleep.''

Bandfield laughed and then said, ''You know, it's funny, I like everything about the *Rocket*, but it still makes me nervous to fly. I don't know what it is. It gives me the heebie-jeebies.''

Lindbergh picked up a rock and tossed it. ''Closed cockpit.''

''What?''

''Closed cockpit. You're used to having the wind and the rain blowing in on you. In a cabin plane all those signals are missing, and it makes you uneasy. It took me twenty hours before I got used to the *Spirit*.''

They walked down the field talking, running through the litany of people they'd lost track of, their muddy shoes squishing through the thin mat of matted grass.

Lindbergh's look was somber. ''You've really screwed up the odds here. Byrd and Balchen both had pretty long faces after they looked in your hangar this morning.''

Bandfield tugged at his arm, and they stopped to watch a crew pull Byrd's big trimotor backward up a high earthen ramp.

''What are they doing, Slim?''

''Fokker figures that a rolling start is equivalent to adding five hundred feet to the length of the field. They're going to tie the tail wheel to a post with ropes. Acosta is supposed to be the pilot for the takeoff, and when he gets all the engines revved up to max power, he'll signal Byrd, Byrd will signal the ground crew, and they'll cut the ropes with an ax.''

Bandfield shook his head wordlessly. It seemed very complex.

"In theory, the airplane will pick up speed down the ramp and be airborne before using half the field. After Fonck's crash, everybody wants as much runway as he can get, any way he can get it."

"I don't know, Slim. It looks like they're making a tough job tougher. How do you feel about going solo?"

"I wouldn't have it any other way. Jesus, Byrd's taking a crew of four in the *America* with him. Hafner's got Rhoades for his Bellanca."

He was silent for a moment, reluctant to say ill of anyone. "The problem is, nobody gets along with anybody. It's going to be tough enough flying for thirty or forty hours without fighting all the way."

"I agree. Besides, all the big planes are crashing. Fonck smashed up, and Fokker turned the *America* over on its back landing earlier in the year."

Bandfield couldn't tell whether they were just trying to pump each other up, rationalizing decisions they had already made, or whether they believed it.

"Did you hear about poor old Noel Davis?"

"No. He's the guy flying the converted Keystone bomber?"

"Yeah. He and his copilot, Wooster, went in at Langley. Killed them both."

"Jeez, maybe solo is better."

Neither man said what he really thought, that while two men might be all right in the cockpit, two men were one too many when it came to sharing the glory.

"Bandy, great talking to you. I've got to go fiddle with my prop pitch setting—I change it every day whether it needs it or not."

"What are you going to do tonight, Slim?" It was Bandfield's first trip East, and he wanted to see New York.

Lindbergh's face crinkled into a grin. "How about coming to town with Mother and me? We could have some fun. We're driving in at about six."

Lindbergh saw Bandfield hesitate and thought that it was because he was short of money. Actually, Bandfield had met Lindbergh's mother, and had found her overpowering, too domineering to spend an evening with. Her arrival had spurred the attention of the reporters, and Lindbergh spent a great deal of time with her. Yet the field was boring and he might never get to New York again. Lindbergh pressed him.

"Look, Jack Winter's invited us out to dinner. He's a stock-broker, a friend of my backers in St. Louis. He told me to bring along anybody I wanted, especially if he's crazy enough to fly. He buys airplanes like Heinz buys pickles, and I'm sure he'd like to find out about yours. How about it?"

"You're on—is what I'm wearing okay?"

It wasn't even close, but Lindbergh said, "Sure. I'll pick you up at eighteen hundred—six o'clock, to civilians like you."

Even the tabloids could get only so much mileage out of Peaches Browning, gangland slayings, and mysterious women in black who claimed to be married to Rudolph Valentino, so the little band of airmen clustered on Long Island turned into a journal-istic mother lode. The newspapers seized upon aviation every-where as grist for their mills; a safe arrival was noticed, but an accident got two-column headlines. If a really lucky reporter could find a wife who had witnessed her husband's fatal crash, there were lead stories for two days.

As a result, Roosevelt and the adjacent Curtiss Field became magnets for tourists. Where before no one but pilots or me-chanics could be found there now surged hundreds of onlookers during the week, thousands on the weekends. Security became a problem for the flyers as well as the crowd. One man, intently peering into his camera, unable to hear the warning yells of the crowd, had backed comically step by step into the idling pro-peller of an Eaglerock biplane. The shattered propeller sliced off the tail of his coat and his pants, sending his wallet in an arc to land on the wing of a Jenny. One more step and he'd have been a true half-ass for life, a candidate for the Keystone Kom-edy hall of fame.

The crowds were generally well-mannered and benign, but their curiosity and their numbers caused damage. Fingers some-how poked their way into the fabric of the ordinary transient planes staked out on the flight line, and finally, to keep the strangers out, guards had to be posted around the hangars where the various race planes were housed.

The guard at Bandfield's little hangar nodded as Murray Roehlk laid his enormous shoulder to ease the door open. Mur-ray was shaped like a Packard radiator: square, sharp, and sloped-shouldered. He was five and a half feet tall, and almost that wide, his bulk emphasized by a suit cut to hide shoulder holsters and conceal his disproportionately long arms. They hung gorillalike yet ended in delicate, tapered hands that could fix anything from carburetors to altimeters. Hafner was a demanding employer who kept most people at their distance, but had gradually gained an equally high regard for both Murray's ruthlessness and his intelligence. Rhoades handled the airplane mechanics, the engine, and the controls, but Murray did all the instrument work.

As Hafner focused more on building airplanes, Roehlk had begun to take over the arms sales. Murray didn't like dealing with foreigners too much, but he got a kick out of dealing with the gangsters. Hafner had always provided the best guns at the lowest prices, earning a reputation in the underworld that served him well. Murray knew he was good with the mob, selling them all the tools of the booming bootleg trade, from Thompson submachine guns to hand grenades. He liked the responsibility and the associations, though they left him little free time for his hobby, building his own radio sets.

Inside the hangar, Murray fumbled until he found the switch. A dozen goosenecked lamps hanging from the rafters blinked on, illuminating the gleaming blue *Rocket*. Hafner and Fokker followed Roehlk inside.

"*Lieb Gott*—what a ship!" Fokker was a tough competitor; he pursed his lips in envy, seeking as he always did something to complain about. "Look, they're using a plywood monocoque body, like on the old Albatros."

Hafner ran his hand over the fuselage, a smooth plywood oval streamlined from nose to tail. The high cantilever wing, also covered in plywood, was melded to the fuselage with a deep, sinuous fillet. On his Bellanca, the landing gear was fastened to the wing and fuselage by a wild interconnecting jumble of struts. A single streamlined surface connected the landing gear to the *Rocket*'s fuselage. The windscreen faired the fuselage contours into the leading edge of the wing in a smoothly flowing curve.

"What do you think, Herr Fokker?" The two always reverted to their correct wartime relationship, as if to reject the informal American style.

"This must be twenty-five miles an hour faster than any other plane on the field. The wing is just like mine, looks like the same airfoil even. He can make it to Paris in thirty hours or less."

Hafner said nothing, but knocked his fist against the smooth metal cowling. "It might overheat. I'd rather leave the cylinders uncovered."

Fokker shook his head. "No, they've done this right. He'll win if he gets off when the others do."

Hafner's eyes met Murray's as they walked out the door, and he whispered an aside: "I still think it will overheat."

Later on the afternoon of the sixteenth, Bandfield stood in the foul-smelling latrine using a rough red shop rag as a towel. He shrugged with disapproval at the image peering out of the cracked sepia-toned mirror, edged at the top with a "Chew Red Man Tobacco" sign. He was tired after too many days of eating in airfield cafés, too many nights without sleep, too many times without a chance for a decent bath or even a wash. He walked into the operations lounge and flowed onto a battered couch, letting his wiry frame spread out.

He ran his fingers through hair weeks overdue for cutting, realizing that his clothes were wrinkled and he didn't have a tie. His regret that he'd accepted Lindbergh's invitation faded as he automatically listened critically to the sound of an engine being tested outside. Bandfield had earned his college expenses by knowing what engine noises meant. Hadley had helped him fix up a repair truck that carried all his tools and parts, and taught him to be an intuitive mechanic, one to whom the engines spoke their own language. He'd worked his way through Berkeley fixing cars, mostly Model Ts but sometimes more sophisticated foreign cars, and he found himself making more money on the Cal campus than his dad did back home. His dad had been his hero, a romantic figure crusading for just causes, like the plight of the farmers and lumbermen. His dad was always for the laboring man—as long as he didn't have to put in ten hours a day laboring. On the campus, Bandy's native politics were viewed as radical and inconsistent with the good living he was making with his repair truck.

A horn sounded outside the operations shack, and Lindbergh bounded in the door, carrying a gray tweed coat and a green-striped tie. "I thought you might want to borrow these—Jack Winter said he'd take us somewhere fancy."

Manhattan/May 16, 1927

Fancy in Salinas had been the Country Club Inn; Bandy had never dared set foot inside. His heart tumbled when he found out that fancy to Jack Winter was the Waldorf Astoria. He'd been quite comfortable on the ride in, listening to Lindbergh's serious discussions with his mother on how he was to behave in Paris. He'd gawked at the tall buildings on their walk from the garage up 34th Street to the rambling twin buildings that formed a hotel so fabled that they'd heard about it in Salinas.

The gorgeously decorated Peacock Alley, the Waldorf's multicolored showcase for the celebrating rich, more than lived up to its name, and his eyes fastened on a glittering passage of laughing, confident young women borne on the arms of equally happy young men in evening clothes. He felt a constriction in his loins when he saw, in the window of a diamond-bright jewelry shop, the collar of his borrowed tweed coat riding up around his plaid flannel shirt, pushing his tie askew. He was glad it wasn't a full-length mirror, for he knew that the bottoms of his wrinkled black pants were riding an inch above his high-top brown shoes.

It was like a movie trip down death row, a brilliantly lit struggle to get to the point of execution. The noise was deafening, a constant ripple of laughter and chatter, of fleeting names he'd never heard, places he'd never been. He had to steel himself not to turn around and catch the ritzy-looking couples pointing at him and grinning.

The walk became a jelly-legged nightmare as he straggled beside Mrs. Lindbergh and Slim, his feet, suddenly feed buckets, flopping in wide arcs to left and right. He was an ambulatory contradiction, the clownish focus of attention of a crowd of rich bastards, not one of whom would look at him. He hated them all, began to hate the Lindberghs, who didn't seem to see them, and most of all he thought he hated Jack Winter, the man waiting at the entrance to the restaurant, standing at the top of the little flight of stairs carpeted inches deep in luxury.

Winter and his wife were both smiling broadly. As the three of them approached, the pair seemed to grow in size, Winter's faultlessly cut evening clothes blossoming to block out the light behind them, his patent-leather hair glistening as brightly as his patent-leather shoes. His wife, dressed in a low-cut orange silk dress and a matching turban, was simply, starkly, beautiful. An orange-tipped white fringe, a feathery python, curled around her neck and down her arms, seeming to caress her with a life of its own.

Bandfield glanced from one to the other, speechless, wondering what on earth they were making of him, this country bumpkin from the West. Winter, his diamond studs holding their own in a fierce competition with the chandelier, pumped Lindbergh's hand while his wife and Mrs. Lindbergh exchanged near-miss kisses. Winter's dazzling grin plainly said that Bandfield was dressed well enough for him. Mrs. Winter, straight out of a Woodbury's soap advertisement, pressed his hand, murmuring her name, Frances, which he promptly forgot.

And with her name went all of his concerns about clothes, place, and time, for from behind Winter emerged a shy young woman, looking as desperately anxious as Bandfield felt. He had had many girlfriends, had made love to many women, and had almost been engaged once. But he had never been prepared to be poleaxed, to feel himself fall irrevocably in love with any girl before he had even learned her name.

"Millie, I believe you know Mrs. Lindbergh. May I present Charles Lindbergh and Frank Bandfield? Gentlemen, this is our niece, Mildred Duncan."

She held out her hand, and Bandy said, "I'm really glad to meet you," in a tone that made everybody believe him.

Winter's laugh was joyous and genuine. "Frank, Millie is gaga about flying, and I wanted her to meet you both."

As the Lindberghs and the Winters watched, Millie flowed naturally toward Bandfield amid the crackle of ice breaking, hesitantly offering her arm for him to take. Their mutual embarrassment slipped from them like the red slips from the sky after sunset, and they became instantly at ease with each other even as they forgot the others. Winter winked at Lindbergh and took his mother by the arm, and they went to eat, shepherded to their table by a headwaiter whose fawning would have sickened Bandfield had he noticed.

Bandfield stepped back before they sat down to really look at Millie. She was molded into a blue chiffon dress, its soft flowing lines broken at top and sides by knotted white scarfs. He had never seen anyone more lovely. The room became multidimensional. The one that counted was the hot, earnest level where he learned all about Millie. On the next level were the Lindberghs and the Winters, who tried in vain for a while to include them in their general conversation. Winter wanted to find out about Bandfield's airplane, but after getting a few short yeses and nos, gave up. The third level was the room, filled now with friends, including the snooty waiter who was asking him what he wanted to eat.

He hadn't looked at the menu.

"What are you having, Jack?" he asked, anxious for a clue so that he wouldn't order something too expensive.

"Oscar does the best steak tartare in the world."

He turned to the waiter. "Oscar, I'll have the same. And make mine well-done."

The waiter paused and looked at Winter.

"Make mine well-done too, please, filet mignon style."

Bandfield turned back to Millie. She was smiling fondly at him, as if he'd just done something clever. He felt it must have been the adroit way he handled Oscar.

"What did you order?"

"Lobster. We never get it in Green Bay."

He exulted in the animation of her face; every word seemed to have a counterpart expression in her eyes and on her lips.

She went on, "What do you eat in California besides oranges?"

"Abalone, the best seafood in the world, better than lobster even." It was a guess—he'd never tasted lobster, and had had abalone only once. "You dive down in the water, and use a tire iron to pull the abalone off the rocks. Then you pound it thin and fry it."

"Do you fry the rocks or the tire iron? Sounds just like our snipe hunts." She looked at him to see if he had taken the bait. "If you come out to Wisconsin, we'll get you on one. You can be the bag man—he's the most important." They laughed, not certain who was kidding whom.

"Sure, sounds great. And if you come to California, I'll introduce you to all the movie stars." He wondered at what he was saying; her humor had elevated his own, got him joking as he rarely was able to do with a stranger.

The thought of Hollywood obviously appealed to her. "I really want to go there. I'd love to see a movie star." She hesitated, not sure if she should confide in him. "Did you see *Son of the Sheik*? I couldn't believe it when Valentino died." She caught herself, shifting to less revealing ground.

"Do you like baseball?"

They were running the conversation together, each eager for the other to talk, each with too much to say. He felt at ease, expansive, and didn't worry much about which fork to use.

"It was the only sport I played in college. I lettered in my junior and senior years."

Mrs. Lindbergh watched with approval as Bandy and Millie submerged themselves in animated conversation, oblivious to the others. She was content to have Charles talking to the safely married Frances while she chatted with Jack.

Bandfield was bragging about his airplane when she asked, "Did you know Uncle Jack is giving me flying lessons?"

Unbelievably, her stock soared. A woman pilot!

"How do you like it?"

"It's fine, except I get sick all the time."

"You'll get over it. It's just nerves."

They went on at machine-gun pace until the shrimp cocktails arrived. They fell into a rhythm, eating the shrimp alternately, one talking while the other chewed.

He found himself telling her about his repair truck and the college guys. "They thought I was some sort of ragged gypsy, coming around with a truck with the sides rolled up. But I'd soup up their Model Ts, hang a Miller downdraft carburetor on one, an Iverson head on another, and they'd get a little speed out of it. Pretty soon I had to put them on a list. It got so busy I was even getting bribes to give people priority."

"Bribes!" she said in mock horror. "And what did your parents think of your taking bribes?"

He turned serious—it was a sore point. "Dad didn't take it so well. He was sort of a rebel, always reading Marxist literature. He even joined the Communist Party, honest! Every year he'd go off somewhere, up in the Northwest, in the woods, rabble-rousing. Somehow my making money rubbed him the wrong way. One day he just up and left, no word to anybody. I couldn't figure it out."

He was silent, and she reached over and squeezed his arm, sending his pulse soaring. Her own life was so protected; she couldn't imagine her father leaving the family.

The floodgates were open. "It killed my mom. She loved him so, even if he was hard to live with. She never admitted that he was gone for good, but she was never again the same. When she got sick, she was glad, glad to die and stop missing him."

The plates were cleared, and Bandy stared in amazement as the waiter ran a little silver roller brush across the white-on-white linen tablecloth, gobbling up the crumbs. He slid his butter plate over the stain from the French dressing he'd spilled.

By the time the steaks were served, he thought he was in love.

He knew it when she leaned over and asked, "Can I tell you something personal?"

He nodded, anxious, and she said, "Don't look now, but your fly is open. I noticed when you came in."

From anybody else, the comment would have generated a lifetime impotence. Instead, it cemented their relationship, bringing them closer as he fumbled with the buttons underneath the table.

There wasn't even a dip in the conversation.

"I knew Slim in flying school, you know. We crashed, had a midair, and they threw me out. I used to think it was terrible, but now I know it was the best thing that ever happened to me."

She took his lead eagerly. "Why?"

"Because if I hadn't, I wouldn't be here, and I wouldn't have met you."

The food was wonderful. Bandy glanced around the room and realized theirs was the only table that was dry. Everywhere else people were busily engaged in beating Prohibition's dry laws by pouring drinks out of bottles wrapped in brown paper bags.

Refusing coffee, the Lindberghs excused themselves. Winter took Millie and Frank's combined distress at parting in a glance and said, "Slim, I want to show Frances and Millie some of the nightlife, and we need Bandy along for protection. I'll see that he gets back to the field."

Lindbergh walked with Bandfield out to the lobby. "Be careful, Bandy—this isn't María." He winked and poked him in the arm. "See you tomorrow."

Jack had asked to have his car brought around; when it pulled up at the curb, Bandfield for the first time had his eyes forcibly torn from Millie.

He'd seen the car advertised in the *Times*. It was a Rolls-Royce Silver Ghost, a convertible with a rumble seat the size of a swimming pool.

"Hop in. We're off to Harlem."

He helped Millie climb up the little step at the side of the rumble seat, steadying her as she struggled to get her skirt-encumbered leg over the coaming, stealing a glance at her ankle and calf. He put one hand on the edge of the rumble seat and bounded in, striking his shin smartly on the edge of the retracted convertible top but masking the pain.

"You like English cars, Jack?"

"Yeah, they're swell, but this one is manufactured up in

Springfield, Massachusetts, and Brewster, over on Long Island, made the body."

The trip through the streets dazzled Millie, and Bandfield lapsed into silence, entranced that her hand had found its way over to his, enjoying the velvety ride of the Rolls as it headed north past Central Park. He could tell the neighborhood changes by the head-turning the car caused. All the way up Fifth Avenue it went unnoticed. They turned down Lenox and Jack leaned back to shout, "Spanish Harlem," and point to the melange of signs in Spanish.

Interest switched abruptly as they drove up St. Nicholas to Seventh; dark eyes sparkled and glossy-haired heads swiveled to watch the Rolls go by, and he could see admiring gestures from the men on the street.

Past West 132nd it changed. Nobody looked at the car anymore; the streets were filled with flashy cars, horns blowing, filled with white people, scarfs streaming out of windows; some of the vehicles had their tops down, the couples sitting up on the back of the seats, talking and laughing. They ignored the background of littered sidewalks and decaying brownstones that sprawled people of all ages into the steps and streets. There was something wrong about them that Bandfield couldn't identify, a strange and hostile quality. He'd not been around Negroes very much, but these all looked different from the few families he'd seen in Berkeley. Then he realized it was the clothing, so ill-assorted, young girls wearing long drab clothes, heavy older women swathed in layers, the men all in strange combinations of coats and pants. He turned to see Millie's expressive face appalled, registering sympathy.

They pulled up to the curb, where a tall coffee-colored man in a tan uniform ablaze with brass buttons opened the door for Jack as he said, "Here we are, Connie's Inn. Everybody always talks about the Cotton Club, but this is where you see the real talent."

The vibrations hit them as they walked down a flight of stairs past a sign advertising "Hot Feet," a revue with 30 Beautiful Brownskins 30. It was a strange riffing jazz that Bandfield had never heard before. Millie had her arm through his, and he could feel her bobbing to the music.

A table was found for them near the line of miniature churches, houses, streets, and tiny stores that served as barrier to the stage. Someone, probably for a theater production, had created a good flat facsimile of a town, with lights winking from different windows, and it served here to conceal the footlights.

The waiter brought setups automatically, and whispered to Bandfield to "put his bottle in his pocket, not on the floor." Above them were the "beautiful brownskins," and beautiful they were. Bandfield became so raptly involved that Millie kicked him sharply in the same shin he'd barked getting in the car.

She watched intently, moving to the sound of the music for almost half an hour before leaning over to yell in his ear, "The performers sure look different from the people in the street."

He studied them and saw instantly what Millie meant. They were young, confident, uncompromising. There was no servility in their glances, no sense of inferiority, and they seemed to share a common contempt for the people watching.

Millie was upset. She liked the music, but the contrast with the streets outside was just too great.

"It's just not fair. Let's get out of here—I feel like a creepy peeping Tom."

Bandfield shrugged—he was along for the ride. Frances sensed something, and glanced at Jack, tapping her watch. He signaled the waiter, and whispered briefly to his wife on the way out to the car. Yelling as if he were still inside, he told Bandy: "One more stop—French onion soup at the Brevoort."

The prospect of soup made out of onions didn't excite Bandfield, but the way Millie sidled across the soft leather to sit close to him did. As they rode through the streets, she'd point to people on the sidewalk, unaware of their own poverty, indifferent to the passage of yet another Rolls.

She leaned forward and shouted to Jack, "It's so terrible that most of the colored live like this. I never knew it. We don't have many colored families in Green Bay."

Winter yelled back, "You're right, but that's not the half of it. I'll show you something else you won't find in Green Bay."

He threaded the Rolls through the traffic, turning right on 59th. They went south on Broadway into the glitter of Times Square, then turned right again on 43rd to take them through Hell's Kitchen. It was an industrial slum, a turgid mixing of factories, freight yards, and warehouses that forced the laborers to live nearby in roughly angled, crowded tenements ready to slide into the street.

"Tumbledown town! Twenty years ago, we wouldn't have

gotten through here unharmed. I still wouldn't want to walk here.''

He didn't stop until they had made a loop back to Broadway. ''It's not only the colored who are poor, honey. I don't understand how the country can have so much wealth and so much poverty all at the same time.''

Her mood changed, somehow reassured by the egalitarianism of the poor. They rode in a tired, happy, excited silence the rest of the way to the tree-studded streets and squares of Greenwich Village.

Everyone knew Winter; the doorman at the Brevoort greeted him by name, and they were ushered into the restaurant although it was just after closing time and the chef was gone. There would be no onion soup. Bandfield was inwardly relieved.

''Come on, Bandy, I want you to meet Raymond Orteig, the man who owns this hotel, someone I hope you get to meet again soon. You too, Millie.''

The obviously disgruntled waiter sat them down; he left, and there was a strained silence until the passageway to the kitchen erupted in a flurry of waving arms and flying towels.

A short bald man, his smile twice as broad as his pencil-thin mustache, rushed toward them.

''Jack, where have you been? I've thought about sending a search party out for you.''

Winter embraced Orteig, his long arms reaching down to enfold him.

''Raymond, you are as charming as always. I have a young friend here who is trying for your prize. Raymond, please meet Frank Bandfield.''

Orteig stepped back and gravely looked Bandfield over, then extended his hand.

''Young man, I wish you the very best. I hope that you'll be very careful.''

Bandfield felt Millie squeeze his hand.

''It's an honor to meet you, Mr. Orteig. Don't worry about me; I've got a fine airplane.''

Orteig's irrepressible smile broke out again as steaming bowls of cheese-encrusted onion soup were brought in, followed by a tray of coffee cups.

''Jack, my thanks for bringing in Mr. Bandfield.'' He picked up a cup and said, ''Let's have a toast to a successful flight.''

Bandfield picked up a cup and sniffed it—it was champagne, the first he'd ever seen.

They toasted, his eyes meeting Millie's over the cup's rim. It was a good beginning.

Mineola, Long Island/May 17, 1927

WEAF had played "Blue Skies" three times that morning, the radio waves somehow washing through the pouring rain. She stared resentfully at the stack of magazines that Bruno gave her instead of companionship. Every advertisement was alike, and every one was wrong. *McCall's*, *Woman's Home Companion*, no matter, they were all run by men to intimidate women. If you used Hinds lotion, brushed with Kolynos, smeared on Odoro-no, and swabbed out with Lysol, you might just be worthy to cook a man's supper for him. It was baloney.

Yet Charlotte Morgan Hafner complied. She washed, combed, purified, and sanctified herself to be ready for Bruno and for the lovers he tolerated but would not acknowledge. Bruno's earthy European attitude toward bathing had taken her aback initially, but he had conditioned her, made her accept the fact that pilots were all healthy animals, usually hot and sweaty, their nails smeared with flying's trademark, ground-in grease.

Donald Morgan's long, slender fingers came back to her, always clean, always beautifully manicured, but now just small scattered bones somewhere in France. Her first husband had been an eighteen-year-old sophomore at Princeton and a virgin when they met. She was a dancer of seventeen and was not. She seduced him, and he insisted on marrying her, over her family's violent objections.

Life with Donald Morgan had been far from perfect, but he had valued her, staying with her and their daughter, Patty, even when he was desperately concerned about the rift within his family the marriage had caused. He went to fly with the French to gain enough glory that his mother and father would have to welcome him—and his own family—back. He gained glory enough, but he didn't return, leaving her wealthy but more terribly alone than she had ever been.

There was more than irony in the fact that when she married again, it was to a German flyer, an ace who had actually fought opposite Donald on the Western Front. She had married Bruno Hafner in large part to outrage Donald's parents. Despite the difference in their backgrounds, she and Donald Morgan had seemed to be a genuine pairing, liking the same things, being sufficient for each other. Their sex life, after its tempestuous illicit beginnings, had become routine.

With Hafner, everything had changed. They had few interests in common except their joint business ventures and a driving, almost obsessive sexual communion that seemed to flare end-lessly. It was a passion for which she was both grateful and ashamed. She and Bruno had a basic rutting appeal for each other that had dominated their early relationship, a mindless need for endless coupling that left them thirsty and exhausted but rarely satisfied. They could go from a bitter argument over finances to a tousled tumble on the office floor in an instant. A simple touch was enough to set them off; Bruno laughingly com-pared them to mating mooses.

The heat of their loving didn't impair their enjoyment of oth-ers, and they had soon reached an unspoken tolerance. Yet they returned to each other, time and again, their mutual sexual needs providing a basis for their continued business success.

But now she was lusting for another man, pressing her pubis against the dresser's edge in rhythm with the fast-stroked brush-ing of her shingle-bobbed hair, concentrating on the coming pleasure. In a box on the dresser were yesterday's purchases from Bonwit Teller. She'd bought a $24 corset for half price and picked up six pairs of chiffon stockings for under $4. She had a dozen corsets and plenty of stockings, but the lean days when she was a chorus girl were still with her, and she hated to pass up a bargain.

"God, I'm hot. I wish to hell he would call." She tried to remember whether Bruno had said whether he'd be back for supper. The tickets on the dresser were for tonight's perfor-mance of *Hit the Deck*; he would probably want her to meet him in New York. It was one of their few points of difference. They had already seen the show, but he enjoyed the inevitable visit to the young show girls backstage. She'd have preferred to see Harry Langdon at the Roxy. It didn't matter. Tonight she'd watch whatever it was in a warm, satisfied glow.

Tossing the brush aside, she examined herself critically in the mirror. A bulge around the middle reminded her of her third obsession: chocolate. Well, she couldn't stop eating chocolates, so she would just cut down on her drinking.

It was difficult being older than everyone she ran with. Bruno never let her forget the difference in their ages. In return, she never let him forget the difference in their bank balances.

He was making plenty of money, but spending it wildly; when he needed capital, he always turned to her.

She whirled away from the mirror, vowing to lose a few pounds this summer; until then the bulge could be suppressed by a corset. She ran her fingers over her firm, large breasts, grateful for the abundant pleasure they provided. She was damned if she would strap them down. There was no way she could have a boyish look, and when it got down to basics, men preferred a woman with curves, no matter what the fashion magazines said. She peered into a hand mirror, patting makeup to cover the small lines around her eyes.

I'm wasting time, she thought. Charlotte dressed quickly, trying to forget how bored she was with practically everything but sex and flying. Six years ago, her marriage had been a lifebelt; it was turning into a penance. Hafner's appeal was eroding into a solely sexual one, helped only by his letting her take a decisive role in the business. The problem was that she didn't like dealing in surplus armaments, working with sleazy characters from around the world. It was particularly bad because poor old Murray, the chauffeur, was always slavering after her, like a hound dog in heat. Bruno trusted him completely, and insisted that he be in on everything.

Roosevelt Field, with its ever-changing mix of strange airplanes and strange men, was a godsend. She got to fly three or four times a week, and viewed the various pilots as a Whitman's Sampler of sex. A few, like Lindbergh and Byrd, were aloof, but most of the pilots played the game very well. Some, like Acosta, were almost too aggressive. She actually liked them to be a little standoffish, to let her seduce them. God knew she didn't need much seducing herself.

She grabbed her helmet and a leather jacket. "An hour of flying and an hour of loving—that ought to do it."

Roosevelt Field, Long Island/May 17, 1927

Bandfield was amazed at how much he liked rich people when he got to know them. In California, he'd donned a defensive armor of derision about wealthy people, contending always that he didn't need money to be happy, while they, of course, did.

Jack Winter had changed all that. He was only forty, many times a millionaire, and obviously capable of a good time under any circumstances. He had inherited money from his father, who had made a fortune in timber, first in Wisconsin and then in Washington, before coming back to live the good life on Long Island. Bandfield laughed when he realized that Jack Winter's father was exactly the kind his own father had hated and had organized labor unions against.

Winter's father had inspired in Jack a tremendous admiration for Teddy Roosevelt, and Winter talked admiringly to Bandy of the need to embrace the vigorous, sporting life as every man's goal. It was implicit that he really meant every *rich* man's goal, but Bandy didn't comment.

Winter had volunteered for the Air Service in mid-1918, lying about his age, but had been rejected when he failed to pass the eye exam. Frustrated, he returned to business, and by following his dad's advice to always go opposite to what the mugs were doing, made a continuous fortune in the stock market, in good times or bad.

Jack and Frances were obviously genuinely fond of Millie; no one had said anything, but Bandy guessed they couldn't have children of their own by the way they doted on her, treating her more as a daughter than a niece. Surprisingly, they extended the same care to Bandfield as well, either because they liked him or because they liked Millie liking him.

Back in California, Bandfield had never had any personal knowledge of anyone who lived as well as Jack Winter. The morning after they had met, Winter had taken Bandy and Millie down to his marble-columned brokerage, complete with murals of the colonists buying Manhattan from the Indians. He explained the operation of the market, and it didn't surprise Bandfield when Millie seemed to know all about it; she was one smart cookie. It all made sense to Bandfield, except that he couldn't understand why anyone would spend his life doing it.

He understood everything that afternoon when the Rolls carried them to Winter's house on Long Island, a long rolling gray fieldstone with a private airstrip, a dock, and a ten-car garage tucked discreetly back behind the tennis courts and swimming pools.

Frances had dragged Millie off to gossip about the family, and Winter brought him into the library. Bandfield was amazed to see the walls lined with a complete series of *Jane's All the World's Aircraft*, as well as hundreds of books on flying. Winter wouldn't let him browse, however, and instead pumped him for all the aeronautical engineering knowledge he could. He was particularly interested in the streamlined cowling and wheel covers on the *Rocket*.

Winter wasn't an engineer, but the conversation confirmed his first impression that Bandfield knew what he was talking about. The two of them hit it off, and within two hours were planning to form a company to build the *Roget Rocket* in volume as soon as he got back from Paris. Lindbergh had said earlier that Winter was a good amateur pilot who had made enough money in the stock market to risk it in aviation.

The fact that Winter was buying the first Lockheed Vega showed his good judgment. It was being finished for him on the Coast. In the meantime, he wanted to buy a Loening amphibian to round out his private fleet of aircraft, and he asked Bandfield to help him learn to fly it.

"I'll put you on the payroll today, a hundred dollars a week, plus twenty dollars an hour for every hour we fly together."

Bandfield could only nod in agreement; most doctors didn't make a hundred a week. He was afraid that if he spoke he would break the magic spell.

Two days before, Bandfield wouldn't have accepted a free cigar, but that was before he realized that Millie was the most important thing in his life. He realized that he was going to need clothes and money to be with her, and Winter was the only source for either. Despite Winter's wealth—or, Bandfield grudgingly conceded, perhaps because of it—he was extremely easy to talk to, and very anxious to learn.

The plaid shirt and black pants were long gone. Jack had set up an appointment with Grover Loening to talk about buying an airplane, and without any embarrassment at all told Bandy, "You're going to need some new clothes."

They were almost the same size, and Bandy had been taken by Winter's valet to a dressing room the size of his house back in Salinas. George, the genial English valet, kept calling Bandfield "sir" as he laid out suits, shoes, sweaters, and all the accessories from the inexhaustible closets.

George was carefully folding the clothes into a trunk when Winter interrupted them. He led Bandfield out the French doors of the house and down a flagstone walk bordered by beds of roses picked out in early-blooming alyssum and pansies, until they reached the garage, a converted carriage house that sparkled like a hospital. They walked past the convertible Rolls, a Duesenberg, a Cadillac phaeton that Bandy would have killed for, and a series of stiffly formal older foreign cars. Winter was impressed that Bandy could identify the Minerva, and promised to let him drive the Isotta-Fraschini and the Hispano-Suiza.

Bandy's voice was tinged with lust. "Do you drive all these?"

"Once in a while. Mostly I use the new Buick to go back and forth to town. It's a darb, got a radio, you can listen to music all the way into town, can you beat that? I'm having them put in all the cars. Bruno Hafner is letting his man Murray do the work."

He stopped and rubbed his hands together. "This is what I wanted to show you. It's my favorite. Grab that side of the cover, and lift it off carefully, so we don't scratch the finish."

They uncovered a glittering 1926 Stutz Vertical Eight, a five-passenger speedster that gave Bandfield an auto-erection. The bright yellow body had horizontal stripes along the cowl that made it look as if it were going ninety sitting still.

"It's my favorite, but I can't drive it anymore—I kept speeding in it, and a motorcycle cop used to lay for me. You and Millie can use it while you're here. Go out on some country road and drive it fast enough to blow the carbon out of it."

The next afternoon Bandfield didn't blow much carbon out, for the twisting Long Island back roads didn't lend themselves to high speeds. Putting along at thirty miles an hour was better suited to the quiet contemplative mood in which Bandy and Millie found themselves. Murray had been there in the morning, and a radio was slung under the dashboard. As they idled along the roads, the trees still in leafy prepubescent spring green, they listened to the speaker putting out "Old Man River." When the song was over, Bandfield snapped the radio off. He drove carefully, reining in the gutty power of the Stutz so he could hear Millie.

"You should join the Book-of-the-Month Club. It's great—makes you read the books everybody is talking about."

He nodded assent. Back in Salinas, people didn't talk too much about books, but he'd join anything she wanted him to, the Elks, the Masons, anything.

"Did you read *The Sun Also Rises*? Hemingway is so powerful. I'd love to meet him. Maybe you'll meet him in Paris."

Bandy doubted it. "If—when—I get to Paris, I'd rather meet some French flyers than some fat old American writer. And I want to go see the battlefields."

Seeing her disappointment, he countered, "I read *Beau Geste*, though. Did you? It's about the French Foreign Legion. P. C. Wren wrote it. A grand story—it would be a great movie."

Literature was important to Millie; in the past a reply like Bandy's would have turned her away from one of her suitors in college. But somehow this handsome aviator, rough-hewn though he was, had an appeal that extended beyond books.

"This is the farthest I've ever been from home. How about you?"

"That's the best thing about flying—always on the go."

"We go to St. Louis a lot to see my cousins and watch the Cardinals. And we went to New Orleans once."

He took the lead, and told her about San Antonio, and Mexican food, and the chill high beauty of the Rockies. "I used to have to fly to Albuquerque once in a while—no passengers, just some mail or special freight. I'd fly along just above the mountaintops, and there would be herds of antelope, bounding along the valleys. There are pretty lakes up there, too, probably full of fish. It was gorgeous. And the Midwest is beautiful too, miles and miles of farmland."

She seemed to draw a little closer.

"It's really the only way you can see America. You know, flying is just like a lens. It's a big telescope that you can focus on the countryside."

When she nodded, the curls bounced on her forehead. He'd never seen anything so devastating.

"You know, when you see hills on a map, it's just squiggly little lines, and even when you see them from the ground, they're just flat bumps on the horizon. But from the air, you see how they're laid out. You see any lakes or dams, and how the valleys run, and if there are any passes."

She said, excited, "Just imagine if they'd had a plane when people were going west, a plane to go ahead and scout the passes."

"Yeah, and the Indians and the buffalo, too."

They were silent, happy to have found each other, unaware that each was playing the other masterfully, content to chatter and content to be still.

She liked the fact that he took her seriously, that he didn't patronize her the way the boys back home did. She took a chance.

"Do you know why I want to fly?"

He shook his head.

"Two reasons: fairy tales and Jules Verne."

"Jules Verne?"

"You know, *Around the World in Eighty Days*, the one about

the balloon flight. Every time I read it, I wanted to fly, to get away from Green Bay, and just see the world.''

He liked talking to her better than to anyone, better than to Lindbergh, better than to Hadley. And unlike most smart people he'd met, she listened well, asking intelligent questions.

"I love listening to you. You always know what to say, and I don't have to pry things out of you."

"Like you have to pry the abalone out of their shells?"

She meant it only as a wry comment, but it was wildly funny to him. He liked her sense of humor, brisk and allusive, even if he had to listen closely to tell when she was kidding and when she wasn't.

"You must be a good teacher. Do you like it?"

"I like it, but it's not enough. It won't take me anywhere. I'm dying to see the mountains the way you've seen them, to fly the oceans. Life is so short, and there's so much to do."

He squeezed her hand.

"Anyway, teachers are so underpaid, it makes me mad. Half the women who teach with me are dried-up little Min Gumps who never had a boyfriend, never had a vacation, never laugh. I'm not going to wind up like that."

He shrugged and laughed. "You don't think there's any money in flying, do you?"

"No, but there's a thrill in it. I don't care if it pays anything, just enough to live on, but I want to get on that old magic carpet and fly everywhere. That's why people love movies. They take them everywhere, even if they know it's just an illusion. Besides, as soon as I stop getting sick, I know I'm going to enjoy it, and I'll do the flying myself. I want to go solo, to fly along the beach, just above the waves, to fly through the clouds."

"That can be dangerous—you don't know which way is up in the clouds."

"Good! That's what I want to get away from, a world where everybody knows what's up and down, good and bad. I want to get into the air where there's only me and God and the wind."

He agreed fervently. He would have agreed with her if she'd just recited the alphabet.

"Besides, if I stay a teacher, I'll work for some smelly pot-bellied old principal till I die a dried-up virgin in Green Bay."

The word *virgin* was hot stuff, the first overtly sexual signal she had sent. He tried to think of some clever way to capitalize on the opening.

She was quiet for a moment, and then said with a diamond

intensity, "I'll make Uncle Jack proud of me." She waited half a beat and whispered, "I'll make you proud of me."

With a muted roar, the Stutz's ninety-two-horsepower Vertical Eight engine carried them from Hempstead to Hampton Bays, then over to Orient Point, where they parked the car on the beach to picnic out of the hamper the valet had provided.

Bandfield was amazed at her appetite. She matched him sandwich for sandwich, pickle for pickle, cup for cup of milk. They sat holding hands at the end of a derelict pier, feeding gulls that curled in a tight clockwise traffic pattern around them. Bandy tried to stall the gulls out, tossing pressed chunks of bread in high arcs that had them skidding in, wings flapping, calling in exasperation.

They drifted back to where he'd spread a lap robe on the sand. She sat primly in her lacy white dress, legs daintily crossed. He stretched on his side, occasionally glancing down to admire his new clothes, the first plus fours he'd ever worn, but most often staring up at her.

Across the road was a tumbledown building, an abandoned toolshed. Someone had written in broad red brushstrokes the word "Repent," as if to forestall the lovers naturally seeking the beach.

He pointed and said, "We don't have anything to repent—yet," trying to steer conversation back to the subject of virginity.

"Probably a Baptist out here, worrying about people necking on the beach."

"What religion are you?"

"Episcopalian."

Feeling too good, he got too smart. "Isn't an Episcopalian just sort of a cut-rate Catholic?"

She stiffened and drew back. "What kind of a crack is that? What religion are you? Or are you an atheist?"

He felt all the progress he'd made sliding away. "I'm sorry, I was just kidding, no offense. No, I'm not an atheist, but we didn't get any formal religious training. My dad was against it, and I don't think my mom cared."

She smiled, no longer angry. "What would a cake-eater like you know about religion anyway? You're just like the college girl who was an artist, but would never draw the line."

Corny jokes were more his style, and he countered with doggerel he remembered from Cal:

"And you're like the girl in the poem that goes 'She doesn't drink, she doesn't pet, she hasn't been to college yet.' "

She groaned, and he felt as if he'd lost ground again. In many ways, it wasn't fair; she was far better read than he and interested in many more subjects. He realized how narrow his life had become, how totally involved in flying and engineering he was. He tried desperately to recover.

"It was wonderful the other night at the Waldorf, wasn't it? I still feel a little bad about Slim and his mother—we managed to ignore them all night."

"They understood. He and Uncle Jack were busy drawing airplanes all over the napkins. I thought the waiter was going to make them pay extra."

They were still for a moment, and then she leaned over him, took his face in her hands, and said, "Bandy, you are being a gentleman, but I can't stand that sad look any longer."

Her lips were soft and full, and he pulled her over him so that she lay across his chest, her heavy breasts pressing into him. They kissed for long minutes, and he felt their passion growing when she rolled away.

"Whew, hot stuff, eh? We'd better get started back."

Flustered, he helped her fold the blanket. "I'm sorry if I was too forward, Millie."

"You? It was me. I kissed you. But we've got to be careful. I think we like each other enough to get into trouble if we don't watch out. A little more of that and I'd have you out of Uncle Jack's knickers and into mine."

He reached for her, and she laughed, pushing him away. "We've hardly met, and I've been brought up with some pretty conventional ideas about sex."

He was content to have been so close so soon. Her exquisite naturalness pleased and excited him, making him feel that he was something special to her. On the way out, they had stopped at a two-pump Sinclair station to find a bathroom for her. Returning, there were no gas stations, no restaurants, and she made him stop the car and bounded into the shrubbery, yelling, "No peeking!" Later he slid his arm around her shoulders. She fed him the line "Don't you think you'd better use two hands?" and he responded, as they both knew he would, with "No, I've got to use one to drive."

They were entering the muddy back road to Roosevelt Field when she pointed up to the sky. The underbelly of the low-lying clouds was crimson. "Something is on fire."

Bandfield floored the accelerator, and the Stutz leaped ahead.

As they turned into the field, he yelled, "Jesus, that's my hangar!"

He jumped from the car, the muddy ground sucking at his shoes. Out of the corner of his eye, he saw Lindbergh racing toward him, trying to cut him off from the hangar. He slowed abruptly as fuel tanks of the *Rocket* exploded in an incandescent black mushroom that carried the roof with it, collapsing the four walls of the frame hangar outward. Bandy saw the shattered *Rocket* airborne for the last time, rising twenty feet straight up before flopping down, the wings bent in a ragged V. The flames blossomed again and then died. There wasn't much to burn besides the airplane. Bandy stood transfixed with fury and frustration as people materialized on all sides.

The fire truck from Curtiss Field pulled up. The firemen unlimbered hoses, not to save anything, but to keep the flames from spreading to the next hangar.

Lindbergh pulled him aside. "My God, Bandy, this is awful. We'll get you another airplane."

Bandfield looked at him numbly, then stood raging by the embers for an hour, Millie brimming with silent sympathy. Finally, he asked Lindbergh to drive her home, determined to spend the night in the operations shack so he could go through the ashes in the morning. Something was wrong. He knew the hangar had not ignited spontaneously; he'd cleaned it up well.

He was up at dawn to poke through the still-hot ruins to see if there was anything worth salvaging. There was nothing, only the scrap metal of the wonderful J5 engine he and Hadley had scraped and saved for. Cliff Langworthy, the volunteer fire captain from Curtiss Field, came over to see him as he poked through the ashes.

"Sorry about this, Mr. Bandfield. We got here as soon as we could. There's not much you can do with an airplane when it's burning."

"Could it have been the wiring for the hangar lights?"

"Could be, but I don't think so. That's one of the few things we can check on and control. We can't control somebody leaving some greasy rags around, or spilling a can of gasoline."

Bandfield exploded. "There was no goddam gasoline or dirty rags in that hangar! I cleaned the goddam place up myself. And I topped off the tanks and secured the caps myself. The fire must have started in the airplane itself. If the fucking building had caught fire, someone would have seen it."

"No need to swear, Mr. Bandfield. I know you're upset, but hangars catch on fire all the time."

Bandfield slumped on the running board of the Stutz, head in hands, trying to compose a telegram to his partner, an anvil of guilt compressing his lungs into a tight dry ball. He'd been messing around with a girl when the airplane burned. He had been totally irresponsible, driving a fancy car, picnicking, doing everything but attending to business. The airplane, the flight, his career, all had gone up in smoke.

He walked over to the operations shack, one knee torn out of his borrowed plus fours by a sharp shred of the cowling he'd been so proud of, his hands and face filthy from the greasy soot. When he got to the door, he heard Hafner laughing inside, and a jolt went through him. The dirty German bastard had set his airplane on fire! He knew it, just as he knew he couldn't prove it.

The little group of pilots turned when he came in, each trying to convey sympathy. Lindbergh again murmured something about finding another airplane, and Byrd suggested he might have a spot for Bandy on his crew. Rhoades simply shook his head and punched him lightly on his arm.

But Hafner said, "To be honest with you, Mr. Bandfield, I'm very sorry about your accident. You would have been a great competitor, I'm sure."

The alarm bells, already quivering, went to full blast. Bandfield's dad had always told him to distrust anyone who started a conversation with "To be honest." An unreasoning fury drove the words from his throat.

"That's hard to believe, Hafner, since you probably set the son of a bitch on fire in the first place."

There was a dead silence, and the other pilots seemed to back away. Hafner looked at him, eyes wide, then turned to Byrd. "He's upset."

Lindbergh took Bandfield by the arm, whispering, "You're way out of line, Bandy. Bruno wouldn't do anything like that."

Bandy shook his arm free. "I'm going to ask for a police investigation, Hafner. You know goddam well that airplane didn't just catch on fire by itself."

"That's enough from you, Mr. Bandfield. You can do what you like, but take your dirty mouth and your dirty hands and face out of here before I forget myself."

Turning to look at Byrd again, he didn't see Bandfield's right hand coming up from the floor. It caught him on the side of the jaw, sending him sprawling back to bounce against the wall and slide to the floor. The impact knocked a framed picture of Clara Bow from the wall, its metal corner gouging a strip of flesh from Hafner's forehead. He lay glassy-eyed, as much from surprise as the blow, blood spouting like a fountain down his face and chest.

Rhoades dropped to attend to him while Byrd and Lindbergh hustled Bandfield out.

"You'd better get out of here, Bandy. When he gets up, he'll break you in half. What the hell got into you?"

Bandfield broke and ran for the Stutz, still convinced that Hafner had sabotaged his airplane, but embarrassed at his loss of control and miserable that he'd made such an ass of himself in front of the others.

Pau, France/May 18, 1927

Stephan Dompnier swallowed hard as his stomach pressed downward against his throat. Too much cognac, he tried to tell himself; he knew it was the prolonged inverted glide. It annoyed him to be made ill by a girl pilot, even one he loved.

He focused his attention on her intense beauty, biting down on her breasts in his imagination as he'd inadvertently found himself doing early that morning. She was concentrating, checking the bit of string that stretched back from the engine, making sure they weren't slipping as they S-turned upside down. The vision of her sweet body came to him strongly; it pleased him to know that at this moment it carried his seed, and indeed she might be pregnant by him. He had a quick visual image of a tiny embryo in goggles and scarf, staring upward at the sky.

"Landing?" he pleaded.

She nodded, pointing straight over her head, down into the ancient city of Pau, crisscrossed by the rail lines running west to Toulouse and east to Biarritz. Stephan had made his first flight here in 1917, in a Bleriot. Then the greatest hazard had been a midair collision, for the skies were filled with trainers, the ground a daily target for crashing airplanes. Now Pau was once again just a minor resort commune, its casino lofted above the gorge-bound Garonne River, the hotels perched upon the hills in red-tiled disarray.

It seemed impossible that this cool, precise pilot could be the same woman who had driven him crazy night and day for the last six weeks. In bed, she was totally abandoned, substituting imagination and enthusiasm for the experience he deeply hoped she lacked.

They glided on, upside down, and he laughed to think that was how they had started the day, coupling fiercely upside down, hanging off the end of the bed, her little body pumping ferociously at his, her eyes wild with excitement. They had awakened at four, and came together quickly. She would not let him rest; when his energy flagged, she summoned his excitement with her mouth in an eager frenzy. Heat roared over him as he remembered how they had giggled as she wrestled with him, somehow working her way under him, trying to reverse their positions without him withdrawing, finally failing in a roar of laughter. She had given up, and walked over to get her robe. He saw that her firm bottom was ripped, not by his nails, but by hers, long red streaks dividing her sweet rump into broad bands of white, creating a luscious flag of self-inflicted passionate pain.

It was a puzzle. She had said she was a virgin when he first took her, and she had seemed to be. He couldn't believe that she could have been so extraordinarily deceitful as to fake it, to carry pigeon's blood in a wax capsule as errant Roman women were supposed to have done on their wedding nights. It wouldn't have made sense. He had told her he didn't care, and was actually concerned that he was despoiling a virgin. And she swore that what she did was all new to her, all natural. He wanted to believe it, did believe it, gloried in believing it.

Now that he was so hopelessly in love, so utterly beside himself, it wouldn't matter if he found out that she had come from some whorehouse in Marseilles. Nothing she or anyone might do would change his feelings, charged with so much besides sex, for her.

Patty snapped the little Farman Sport upright with a flourish, glanced south to the Pyrenees for orientation, then cut the fuel and switched off the magneto.

"Dead-stick landing," she yelled.

He nodded; she was showing off, and why not? She was good. His thoughts ran back to when Patty had first asked him to teach her to fly. He'd never had a woman student before, and was inclined to refuse. But he had served with her father and could not deny her.

He leaned over. "You're too close in and too high."

Patty shook her head. "Ah, we'll see." If she landed long,

ran off the end of the field, turned over, so what? The war put things in perspective. There was little genuine risk.

Her glance caught him studying her. She sent a smile that burned down to his belly, and then returned to her absorption in the approach.

He told himself that she looked like her father, not really sure this was the case. He'd known Donald Morgan for only four weeks before his death. But a month was more than a lifetime at the front, and aces were heroes to the new pilots. Morgan was credited with five official kills, and his comrades said there were a dozen more. It was all the more amazing because he was an old man for combat flying, thirty. Dompnier was then twenty-two, the same age as Patty now.

He checked the smoke from the factories. The wind had switched and was stronger. She wasn't too close in at all; what must she think of his judgment! The huge field, still cluttered with dozens of hangars and hundreds of smaller buildings, was devoid of traffic. A Nieuport 29 fighter was being rolled into the hangar of the unit he commanded. For the thousandth time, he asked himself why he stayed on, an aging captain going no-where, and for the thousandth time he answered himself—for the flying. He could find other, better-paying jobs, but he couldn't live without flying.

God, he loved her; teaching her had been torture. When he let her solo, he had sweated as never before, almost collapsing in relief when she landed. That night, filled with champagne and passion, they had made love the first time. Now she had fifty hours of flying time, her license, and his heart. She knew she was good, and it worried him; overconfidence came easily to young pilots, especially the talented ones, and it was the greatest hazard.

They were too close to the hangar line.

"*À droit,*" he commanded, pointing to the north.

Patty shook her head and laughed, concentrating. She trod on the rudder pedals and fishtailed the tiny biplane, slowing its powerless glide, stirring his stomach.

"I give up." Dompnier put his hands at his sides and waited for the broad green flying field to reach up and meet them.

The trainer touched down simultaneously on its two wheels and tail skid, and Patty jammed in full left rudder. Two-thirds through the turn, she countered with full right, and the tiny airplane rolled forward to stop precisely on the spot from which they had started.

In the always-deadening silence after a flight, he yelled, "Ah, you are incorrigible and I love you." He would have kissed her if the mechanics, a covey of raucous enlisted men still glowing from the noon wine, Gauloise cigarettes drooping from the corners of their lips, had not been slouching forward to trundle the airplane into the hangar. In war there was never enough manpower for anything; in peace there was always too much.

Plainly pleased with herself, Patty climbed out of the cockpit, pulling off her helmet to shake out a silken avalanche of glistening blond hair. She pinched her nose, forcing back pressure to clear her ears.

Dompnier melted when he looked into her amethyst eyes. They were large, one just slightly oval, one slightly round, the piquant mismatch adding interest to beauty.

"How was that?" she asked.

"You've gone far enough. What more can I teach you?"

His flesh tingled as she reached up and caressed his face.

He went on hurriedly, "No more about flying, but tonight I'll teach you something else."

"My French Valentino, you are greedy, not needy! If you are going to teach me anything, you're going to have to go to America with me. My stepfather doesn't know it, but he's going to have a new copilot—me!"

Her words startled him.

"Never. Too dangerous, Patty, even for you."

She looked at him quizzically. "I thought we were never going to tell each other what to do."

He smiled, backpedaled. "Your mother would not permit it."

"No, she would not, but I'm over twenty-one, and I can wrap my stepfather around my finger. He'd see that a father—sort of—daughter team would make headlines." She blew a kiss at him and walked off in the air force flying suit she had wheedled from him, and had altered to fit.

Stephan watched her glide over to her car, a huge slope-nosed Renault, enjoying the movement of her hips beneath the taut fabric. It tantalized him until he realized that half the enlisted men were watching her, half watching him watch her.

He snarled at a sergeant for smoking near the aircraft, and busied himself with the log. Surely her mother would never let her try to fly the Atlantic! He would follow her to New York, and they'd have to marry. They had traveled throughout France together, stopping at inns he knew to be tolerant, where the proprietors were too sophisticated to ask embarrassing questions. She told him that it was different in America, that people were, as she put it, "nosy."

Stephan wanted to marry her, to take her off the market, to make her his own while she still was captivated by him. It did not matter that his parents would not be happy. For years it had been assumed that he would marry Angélique, the daughter of a family friend whose father happened to own a few thousand acres in the Loire Valley. It would have been a good match.

2

Bruno Hafner was angrier with the doctor attending him than with Bandfield. The young physician, just out of school, was worried about the effect the wound might have on Hafner's ability to undertake a long flight, and insisted on keeping him under observation. When Hafner protested too loudly, the doctor resorted to sedatives.

Hafner's enforced "vacation" was viewed by Dusty Rhoades with mixed emotions. It left him with little to do—and that always led to trouble, to the futile fight against his habit. He spent the morning trying to distract himself, elbowing his way through the good-humored, excited airport crowd that was only lightly sprinkled with pickpockets and con men. One enterprising salesman had a folding stand from which he sold "autographs of all the flyers" on regular penny postcards. You could buy a Richard Byrd for a dollar, a Hafner for seventy-five cents, a Lindbergh for fifty cents, or a Rhoades for a quarter, reflecting the flyers' fame and an assessment of their chances. Since the fire, Bandfield's cards had been marked down to a dime. Rhoades toyed with the idea of telling the police the truth, that none of the signatures were genuine, but decided to live and let live.

His charitable feelings stemmed in part from his own guilty feelings about his increasingly forced relationship with Hafner. He wanted to make the flight; he didn't want to make it with the

63

German. He recognized that it was his own fault that there were so few alternatives, yet he entertained the wistful fantasy that Hafner would develop both a complication and a conscience and tell him to go on alone.

He saw Lindbergh walk toward him, then suddenly duck in the hangar. Slim was apparently trying to keep his distance from everyone to avoid taking sides in the argument. Relentless, Rhoades followed him inside and caught him at the door.

"Got a second, Slim?"

Lindbergh's thin voice was stern, like that of an aging high school teacher whose patience has been exhausted. "Not really, Dusty. After what's been going on, I need all the time I can get just to do some thinking."

"Yeah, me too. That's what I wanted to talk to you about. You know Bandfield. Do you think he's all wrong about Hafner?"

The tall pilot stood, arching his back to stretch, eyes surveying the end of the field. Rhoades was Hafner's copilot, and Lindbergh didn't know the motive for the question. He decided to play it safe. "I was in flying school with Bandfield. He was first-rate, and would have made a good officer. I can't believe he's simply going off half-cocked. Nor can I believe Hafner is an arsonist."

"Me either."

"Both men have behaved pretty well since. Bandfield wouldn't apologize, but he dropped the idea of an investigation. And I understand Hafner just wants to forget the whole thing and get back to the field."

"Yes, that's what Charlotte tells me."

Lindbergh's expression didn't change. "Look, I've got to run. I think Hafner's right—everyone should let the matter drop. I'll just be glad when I get off from here, and get away from the crowds and the intrigues."

Rhoades watched him walk off, feeling pangs of envy that Lindbergh had a plane of his own, and gentlemen backers. As he watched, the jealousy turned, as modest as an early-morning bird song, into the first quiet signals of his driving need, a delicate early-warning message sent along the nerve endings of his extremities. For the thousandth time, Dusty told himself that he would not give in, that he would change the downward spiral of his life.

Almost immediately he felt the hunger settling in, bird song turning to a claxon. The quiet quiver escalated, as if its thermostat had been turned up, turning into a burning at his finger-tips and at the base of his skull, an implacable warning flush that said "Feed me!" even as it drenched his psyche in a repellent combination of need, greed, sin, and self-disgust.

He fought it as he always did, trying to think of other things. Gentlemen backers, he thought. My backer is no gentleman, but he is a source. Rhoades felt the fabric of his willpower shredding even as he tried to turn his attention away from the thought of the kit he kept in his car.

"Holy Mary, Mother of God, help me." In the last four years he'd repeated those words a thousand times, and poor Mary had never been able to help, nor had anyone else.

Lots of people had supplied answers to the wrong problems. He'd been told that he ought to get married, have a family, get out of flying into something steady. He knew he never would. The anonymous drifting from one job to another, the total freedom from responsibility except when actually working on a plane or flying it, and the easy comradeship were accessories to the addiction. The idea of going back to St. Louis to work in the Bemis Brother Bag factory, supervising young hillbilly girls fresh from the Ozarks, sickened him. He had seen what happened to his dad, working for Anheuser-Busch, drunk on his gallon of beer every day, until Prohibition drove him into amateur boot-legging. He was away from all that, and lucky to be flying at all.

And yet he knew it wasn't luck at all, but Hafner's calculation. Hafner needed him to do things that were not ordinarily done for hire, and would have him only on the terms of a dependency. Hafner had introduced him to cocaine first, and later heroin, all the while supplying him with money, responsibility, and guilt. Now he was hooked—on all three.

The whole sorry process had been fostered by his asocial existence. Until a few months ago, the free-and-easy women he bumped into in blind tigers around the country got about as close as he wanted women to come. He preferred purely physical relationships, just two bodies, two sets of organs working each other over, to climax not as lovers but as strangers. The thought of marrying someone, being responsible for her well-being and maybe even having children, had been frightening to him. Now that was changing, and he wasn't sure he could handle the new requirements.

Rhoades upended a wooden Coca-Cola crate, trying to stave off the moment when he would give in, and rethinking Lindbergh's guarded answers. He felt guilty around Lindbergh, knowing how much he would disapprove of Rhoades's habit if he knew of it. And then too, Lindbergh was not easy to like, too reserved and somewhat pompous. Yet Rhoades admired him. For a young guy without any previous experience, he did a great job with the reporters and with the public, who'd gone absolutely crazy about him.

That's what made the brush-off hurt. In the past Lindbergh had been equally courteous to everyone, generously sharing the information on prop settings that the Standard Propeller Company had sent him, or telling what he'd learned about flying the great-circle route over the ocean. Lindbergh had known that Hafner had hired an ex-Navy man to teach him navigation, but he had wanted to share the new information with Rhoades anyway.

Then he felt his resolution bursting into desire like a match thrown into a fire. Dusty went to his Model A and drove to a rural lane not far from where a farmer's stand was waiting for the first of the spring's produce. He pulled the front seat out and extracted the leather kit Hafner had provided him, just as he provided the supplies for it.

The fever was coming fast. While he did not yet *have* to have a fix, he didn't want to delay. He was worried about timing. If Hafner came back tomorrow, he'd expect him to be ready to fly. There was a note in his own handwriting in the kit, placed there during some earlier futile fit of conscience. It said: "A shot in the head is worth two in the arm." He grimaced. Maybe it would come to that someday, but now the shot in the arm was sufficient.

He spent the afternoon in pleasant aimless puttering. Balchen invited him to town for dinner, but he declined; he wouldn't need Balchen or anyone for a while. He ate a beefsteak covered with greasy onions and edged with watery mashed potatoes at the local café, drinking a bottle of Moxie with it. He went back to the hangar to wait. Around nine, he stretched out on the cot. He had barely closed his eyes when Murray shook him.

"Whatsa matter?"

"It's three-thirty, and they just brought Lindbergh's plane over from Curtiss Field. I thought you'd want to know."

Rhoades was instantly awake, thanked him. "Any word from the hospital?"

"No. I talked to the nurse and she wouldn't let me talk to Captain Hafner without the doctor's permission."

Dusty ran to the operations shack, raised a sleepy operator on the phone, and called Hafner's house. No answer. Rhoades slammed the receiver down, then called the hospital. The nurse gave him the same answer she had given Murray, but he wheedled the number of Hafner's doctor from her.

The phone rang for a long time before a woman's voice answered sleepily.

"Is Dr. Poole there? This is an emergency."

"Dr. Poole is on a train to a medical convention in Chicago. Have you called the hospital?"

Rhoades groaned, then called the nurse again. This time she put him through to the doctor who was on duty. "This is an emergency, Doctor. Captain Hafner is needed at the airport. We're about to make our flight to Paris."

He could tell that the doctor was young—the answer confirmed the impression of his voice.

"Look, Mr. Rhoades, I understand what you are saying. But this is Dr. Poole's patient, and the chart indicates that Captain Hafner had a sedative about nine o'clock. I'm not going to release him, especially not to go flying. You can talk to the hospital administrator in the morning."

Rhoades gave in. It was always possible that Lindbergh would turn back. He might have a fuel problem, or the weather might be worse. He decided he'd be prepared in case Hafner suddenly showed up.

He sprinted back to the hangar and yelled, "Murray, let's roll that fucking airplane out and get it ready!"

Murray bristled at the orders Rhoades was flinging about, but grudgingly admitted to himself that it was probably what Hafner would want.

After doing everything that could be done, Rhoades slumped on the wheel of the *Miss Charlotte*, looping his arm around the broad flat strut for support. That goddam Bruno. That goddam Bandfield. And that goddam Lindbergh. Dusty felt envious for a moment, then switched gears. Slim was just smarter, with better backers. He thought about going over and wishing him good luck, but decided against it. Lindbergh would be totally preoccupied with getting ready, and there would be enough people hanging on, shrieking for attention.

He was dozing, sitting on the ground, when the noise of the engine of the *Spirit of St. Louis* running up broke the morning calm. Dusty stood up and wet his finger, instinctively checking the breeze. It was downwind, maybe three to five miles per hour. He wondered about the adjustment Slim had made in his prop setting. He'd altered it to permit a better cruise speed at the expense of a longer takeoff run. Now, with an adverse wind, that was a mistake.

The minutes dragged by, double-laden with Lindbergh's preparations and the frustration of Bruno's absence. With a flurry of activity, the *Spirit* began to roll forward between two columns of well-wishers, mostly men and a few women who had been waiting for the last three days for something to happen. Like a second-rate opera company, the men on each side of the fifty-yard-wide takeoff path turned and took a few steps with the airplane, bringing their hats and caps up stiffly in a stage salute. Then the *Spirit* accelerated, the rough ground jolting it so that the wings shook in short jabbing movements, like those of a boxer warming up during the jog into the ring. Rhoades, fingers crossed, called on the Virgin Mary again in a quick prayer as the silver monoplane moved sluggishly down the damp field, corkscrew shrouds of moisture pearling back from the propeller blast. He knew precisely how Lindbergh was feeling—tense, waiting to see if the speed built swiftly enough, keeping the stick back in his belly and tromping on the rudder pedals to hold the airplane straight so the enormous overload wouldn't strain the gear. He could tell that the airplane felt logy, unresponsive, a groundling creature unable to fly.

It trundled on, accelerating slowly, leaving behind the statues waving their hats, watching to see if this airplane, like Fonck's, would fold up into a flash of flame and fire.

Rhoades yelled, "Keep it on the ground, Slim—you've got another six hundred yards!" His voice was lost in the swelling roar of the Wright engine.

As if in a negative response, Lindbergh lifted the *Spirit* off the grass. It lumbered along, then touched down again, but faster, at last more a creature of the air than the ground. It bounced once again and then pulled slowly away like adhesive tape from an old dressing, struggling, swimming as much as flying in the swirling mists. It seemed to falter, to sink as it approached the telephone wires at the end of the field, then cleared them as a cheer broke out.

Dusty cheered too, approving the crisper response that speed now gave to Lindbergh's touch on the controls. The *Spirit* disappeared, heading east by northeast.

He checked his watch—eight o'clock. He did some fast figuring, comparing the Bellanca's speed and fuel load with that of the *Spirit*. If Hafner showed up by eleven o'clock, they could still get off and maybe beat Lindbergh across. He couldn't average more than 100 mph. They could move up the *Miss Charlotte*'s cruise speed to 110 or 115, even if it burned more fuel. They'd get substantially the same winds as Lindbergh did. And there was always the chance that he would make a navigational error, costing himself some time. It wasn't likely, but anything was possible, if only the doctors would let Bruno out of the hospital.

At eleven, Rhoades gave up. He and the guards had long since eaten the sandwiches and drunk the coffee. They rolled the Bellanca back into the hangar, anger heating Rhoades like high current through a small cable. Here was one of the best goddam airplanes in the world, full of fuel, ready to go, and it was sitting on the ground because Bandfield had slugged Hafner. They'd just missed the opportunity of the century. He wished Lindbergh well, but he would have given his soul to beat him across. Maybe he wouldn't make . . . He drove the thought from his mind.

He joined the others in the operations shack to wait for reports on Lindbergh. There was no news yet, of course, but it was comforting just to be in the company of others who had been caught napping. It was midafternoon when Hafner rolled up in his Marmon, head bandaged, obviously furious, his dachshund, Nellie, hanging out the window, barking.

"Dusty, I would have been here earlier, but the bastards had me sedated. I'm not really awake yet. What's happening?"

Rhoades bit his lip. He wanted to yell at Hafner, but caught himself. "Looks like we missed it, Bruno. Too bad."

Passaic, New Jersey/May 20, 1927.

The room looked as if it had been ordered from a Sears catalogue: heavy yellow desks, green-shaded lamps, and paintings on the wall showing Indians in various states of melancholy. The leitmotiv was drinking. Charlotte Hafner glanced at the debris: there was a miscellany of liquor bottles and empty, half-full, and full glasses everywhere, with overflowing ashtrays in between. Some of the glasses neatly combined both functions, cigars floating in warm, stale bourbon and water like fetuses in a biology lab. An assortment of tools—wrenches, pulleys, and jacks—completed the decor.

She was boiling with frustration. Two days ago she had been

trembling with desire, drenched in the hot fever of anticipation of thoroughly satisfying sex. The rendezvous had gone suddenly and irrevocably sour when her lover showed up with a girlfriend. Charlotte felt that she was liberal, but she wasn't yet ready to go to bed with her boyfriend *and* his girlfriend. She had had no relief since then.

Bruno Hafner sat brooding, a two-inch-wide gauze-and-adhesive bandage on his forehead. Charlotte's frustration mixed with a natural sympathy for him. The flight had meant so much to him. Sighing morosely, he picked up a glass and wiped it with his handkerchief. He passed it in front of a desk lamp as if to count the remaining germs, then filled it halfway with scotch.

She took the glass from him and carried it to the sink. She washed two glasses, filled them one-quarter of the way with water, and brought them back. He filled the glasses with scotch.

"Ach, Charlotte, what really bothers me is that we had the better airplane! If that little bastard Bandfield had just not shown up!" He downed half his drink in a gulp.

"Don't worry about it, Bruno. There'll be other flights. No one has flown the Pacific, and there are lots of records to set."

He acted as if he hadn't heard her.

"One thing sure I've learned. Lindbergh was smart to go alone. The press loved it. From the day he arrived, he got twice as much coverage as the rest of us put together. I'll never make a record attempt with a copilot again."

She tried to change the subject.

"Ready for some good news?"

He nodded, plainly in need of some.

"Patty writes that she's coming home." His expression didn't change.

"It gets better. She wants to fly to Europe with you."

Hafner shook his head. "This is good news?"

"And she's in love. With a French air force pilot, an ace."

Hafner put his head down on the desk. "*Mein Gott*, Charlotte, don't cheer me up anymore, I can't take it."

She breathed easier; he was laughing and he could have been shouting mad. Compared to missing the flight across the Atlantic, Patty's news was small potatoes. "Would you fly with her?"

"Never, not with her, not with anyone. A French ace, eh? Just like her dad. Well, she could do worse."

Relieved, Charlotte wanted to end the discussion on Patty before he thought about it. Patty's marriage would complicate their estate problems, already difficult. She rushed on. "This place looks like a Mexican whorehouse, Bruno. Why don't you let me fix it up for you?''

"Don't change a thing." Bruno knew the fusty office looked just as it should for his customers, desperadoes from all over the world who would have tried to chisel his prices down if they thought he was living too well. It was better to have it rough and ready, with raw scotch to pour into glasses after the handshakes. Very little paperwork was involved in most of his business. "When we build our aircraft factory, we'll put in a decent office. We'll be dealing with a different sort of customer then.''

As Charlotte went back to put more water in her glass, Hafner glanced out the window with pride and pleasure at the huge yard that generated the bulk of his fortune. After the motion pictures and the barnstorming, he'd come to New Jersey in 1923, without any money, but with introductions to two of the largest scrap dealers in the east, Moe Bischoff and Salvatore Maniglia.

These weren't ordinary introductions, nice little letters beginning with "To Whom It May Concern." Instead they were brief, straightforward instructions from Polack Joe Lutz, a Chicago mobster. Lutz had been visiting the Coast and had hired Hafner to fly a few special missions to Mexico for him. Hafner had handled an awkward situation with the Mexican police very well, and Lutz had taken a fancy to him.

People paid attention to Polack Joe. Neither Bischoff nor Maniglia would have bothered to speak to him without the letter; with it they had let him enter their private preserves, and had grudgingly shown him the ropes. By 1925, Bruno had had a modest share of the surplus arms and mob supply racket. Then two things had happened. He had finally agreed to use Charlotte's money to expand his business, and Moe and Salvatore had erased each other in a shootout on the docks, leaving the field clear for him.

Bruno swirled the scotch in his glass, admiring as always the symmetry of the rows of artillery shells, stacked in neat little cones like the cannonballs in a Mathew Brady photograph, each stack covered with a doily of a tarpaulin. There were shells to fit any one of the acres of guns that surrounded them. Hafner stocked everything from *Minenwerfer* mortars to French 75s, and had heavier ordnance, up to 155mm, available. The yard was surrounded on four sides by perfectly aligned blocks of narrow two-story rough-pine World War emergency buildings. They were filled with small arms, rifles, bayonets, ponchos, hand grenades, mess kits, flame throwers, gas dispensers, gas masks, prophylactics, Sam Browne belts, anything needed to start or finish a war. In a garage set off to one side he was reconditioning some tanks, Renaults for Chile, and two Christies for AMTORG, the Soviet trading company. In another building were thirty Sopwith Snipe fighters, picked up for a song from the British, and for which he had an offer from Siam. He had respect for the Snipe—one had shot him down in late October 1918.

Lots of money was to be made selling arms, and the first thing he had learned was that a little grease on the palm was more important than any on the gun barrel. Hardly a war went on anywhere, from Africa to Central America to the Far East, that hadn't helped and been helped by Hafner Enterprises.

The irony was that as his fortunes went up, so did those of Germany. The inflation that had wiped out his family's fortune seemed contained, and he had heard that industry was picking up. It had long been his dream to go back, a wealthy man, and restore his family properties. In a few years, if things continued to go well, it just might be possible.

Still he knew, as Charlotte did, that it was time to move out of the surplus-arms business, much as he had enjoyed its rough-and-tumble drama. The spillover into dealings with the gangs added spice to the venture, for they had high regard for the quality of his submachine guns and shotguns. But lately, the ordinary customers had become too demanding, and some ordinary business hazards—late deliveries, mismatched ammunition and weapons—had brought threats of bodily harm.

"Damn," Charlotte yelled.

"What's the matter?"

She walked across the room, sucking her finger.

"I stuck myself with the ice pick."

She brought some pieces of ice for his glass. He glanced at her appreciatively. She was mothering him, trying to ease his disappointment.

She dropped the ice into his glass as if she were a bombardier, splashing the scotch, and asked, "Are you feeling better? There's a party at the country club tonight. Do you want to go?"

"I'm feeling better. We'll see about the party." His arm slid a wave of heat around her as he pointed down into the yard, where Murray was working on his car, a two-tone blue Rickenbacker speedster. "Did you ever notice his hands?"

"How could I help it? He follows me around like a cocker spaniel."

Hafner said, "Murray's got hands like a surgeon. I've seen him fix a little lady's watch, no bigger than a dime. He sticks that little glass in his eye and his fingers fly."

"Well, he's getting on my nerves. Every time I look around, he's staring at me."

He turned her to him, pressed his body against her. "He's bothering you, eh? Well, you're bothering me." He took her hand, kissed the little wound from the ice pick, slid her finger into his mouth, and sucked on it.

The foreplay was as choreographed as her old dance routines, and the results were as predictable. Her attention slammed tight as a camera's shutter to concentrate on his scent, his bulky presence, and he seemed to spread around her, surrounding her with his will and his need. He slipped his right hand inside her blouse, cupping her breast, then squeezing it, gently at first, then harder.

The effect was immediate, the same as it had been those long years ago when they had first met, when she was just intrigued with finding yet another flyer, even a German one. As Hafner's hand closed tighter, she felt the wonderful mindless drift to sensual surrender; she shuddered and pressed her pelvis to him, raising her face to be kissed. The familiar hot electric current surged through her, a great molten gush that rushed like a torrent from her nipples to the glowing volcano between her legs, a hard yearning that had to be fulfilled.

They kissed and he eased her backward, ruffling her dress up, pulling her underclothes down. She fumbled with his pants, ripping the belt open and tugging at the buttons, and they stumbled eagerly to the couch, undressed only enough to come together in a blinding surge of passion.

Climaxing almost instantly, they lay together gasping, then laughing.

"Are you all right? Is your head bothering you?"

"No, it's not my head that's bothering me."

They undressed slowly and matter-of-factly; he never took his eyes off her as she carefully folded her clothes and laid them on the desk, appreciating how little her body had changed since they had met. He had taken a particular pleasure in seducing the widow of a French ace; now he realized that she had seduced him as she had so many others.

He did not mind. He was not a constant lover, and saw no reason why she should be. Life was too short to worry about such things. In other matters—business, raising her child—she was superb.

He disrobed as he watched her, carelessly tossing his clothes to the floor; the mess would ordinarily have bothered her, but she liked it as part of the loving ritual. He extended his hands to her, and they lay together on their sides on the couch. She slipped her hand down between them to caress him.

"Are you up to a little more?" she whispered.

"Not yet—but help me along."

She rolled off the couch and knelt beside him, earnestly applying herself and bringing him quickly erect. Then she said, "You take it easy, just lie on your back—I'll do the work."

She rose over him, awkwardly clinging to the top of the couch until she caught her balance, then rocking back and forth on the springs until she mounted him. She positioned herself in a crouch, her feet flat on the leather cushions of the couch, moving with a steady beat, her eyes closed, head tossing from side to side. He reached up and held her jiggling breasts in his hands, and she responded, as she always did, by reaching back to cup his scrotum in her hand.

Hafner watched her. She was good, but she needed his sex more than he needed hers. Charlotte moved steadily faster, breathing harder, chest heaving. He knew that he would not have another orgasm, but enjoyed watching her, lost in that deep absorbing pursuit of endless sex that kept them together. In many ways, he enjoyed the comparatively placid second lovemaking better than the first. Always on their first time he was in a blinding fury, wanting to crawl up inside her, wishing his penis had a mouth on it, the better to ravage her, trying to grind himself into a melting, melding union with her. The second time he could enjoy her more fully; it was afterplay that was better than the foreplay, an afterplay that could lead to yet another round.

With a wild convulsive heave, muttering little cries, she climaxed, collapsing in a heap on his chest.

"They call that 'riding to St. Ives.' Did you like it?"

He wondered who "they" were. "I like it as long as it took you where you needed to go."

She rested for a while with her head on his shoulder, as they joked back and forth. "What would Elsie say if she came in?"

Elsie was Bruno's young secretary, no more than eighteen. She was sure he was sleeping with her.

"Ach, she'd be jealous, seeing me with such a fine-figured woman. She's just a stick, that Elsie."

A stick, but a young stick. It didn't matter. There was plenty for them both. She fixed him another drink, poured a short one for herself, then pulled out the gray journals that detailed the operations for the last month.

"As long as we're here, we might as well go over the books."

Hafner smiled at her, appreciating the quick transition from heated, almost violent sex to cool and calculating business. She sat naked at the table, pencil in hand, already absorbed in the figures. They were a strange combination; no one else would understand them. He didn't understand them himself, but he knew that they were a good mix. At least for the time being. He had found that certain people were necessary at certain times— his parents, early on, then his squadron mates, Goering and Loerzer during the war, Nungesser after, now Charlotte. Each person in his or her own time.

Manhattan/May 21, 1927

No one would believe it. He didn't believe it himself. While Slim Lindbergh was flying across the ocean, battling weather and fatigue on his way to fame and fortune, he'd spent two days and nights in a six-dollar room at the Hotel Montclair with Millie. He knew she was protecting him, first from his reaction to the fire, then to the depressing news of Lindbergh's departure. Millie had insisted on being with him, afraid that he'd do something rash. She had called Frances Winter to explain that she would be gone for a while, somehow disarming her objections by telling her the exact truth, that she would be with Bandy. What was unbelievable was that they had stumbled through his depression, her consolation, and their passion—and still hadn't made love.

But they had come so very close. At first Millie had been unrealistic, arranging the blankets in an S shape that let them hold each other tightly, yet be insulated from flesh-to-flesh contact. "They used to call it bundling in the colonial days. It was the only way people could court and keep warm."

"It's keeping me warm, all right, Millie. I'm hot as a pistol. I don't think I can take much of this."

"Just you wait and see. Love doesn't have to be all sex—we can be in love and just be tender."

There was no blanket between their faces, and the deep kisses soon overtook the tenderness. He hooked his finger around the blanket and edged it down. She closed her eyes and moved away, to give him room. Each time he moved the blanket an inch he would lean down and kiss the newly exposed flesh.

Millie shuddered with excitement. Her eyes were closed, her right hand clenched so tight that the nails dug into her palm. Her left hand patted the back of his neck, giving him assurance she could not put in words.

He had kissed her belly and moved the blanket down past her thighs in a single motion. He buried his lips in the edge of the sweet brown triangle of hair, and she spoke.

"I'm really sorry, but I promised my mother I'd be a virgin when I got married. It is very difficult for me to change my way of thinking, no matter how I feel, how excited you make me."

He put his finger to her lips. "Don't say any more. This is wonderful. How could I ever have been so lucky as to be here?"

They pressed together tightly, nude. She raised herself and said, "I think I know how I can help." She tenderly took him in her hand, moving him gently, then more rapidly.

When he came they were both embarrassed.

She giggled. "I didn't realize sex was so messy. In the books, it's all just sighs and asterisks."

They played some more, and a little later, her own excitement undiminished, she asked hurriedly, running the words together, "Do you have anything the menuse?"

He sat on his elbow, staring at her. "What on earth are you talking about? Asterisks? Menus? I don't know what you mean."

She blushed. "You know, the things the men use, safes, French letters, I don't know what you call them."

Bandfield laughed and put his head between her breasts, letting the passion mount again.

"Millie, you don't know how embarrassing it is to get those things. I don't even know where to go. Besides, you really want to wait until we're married, and I'm glad to wait."

As if to reassure herself, she martialed her arguments for technical virginity again. He agreed with her philosophically, at least from the waist up. From the waist down it was torture. Yet it was worth it; he felt he was building up a bank account of passion, one that would stand them both in good stead when they finally got married.

"Do you want me to go to Green Bay and get your father's permission?"

"Sure. Just tell him we spent two days together in a hotel in New York, and you'll get the full Wisconsin white shotgun wedding treatment." She took his hand. "Don't rush things. You're upset because of the fire, and because of Lindbergh. Let's see how things are in a few months."

He shook his head yes, told himself no.

His attitude swung with his hormone levels, which ranged from high to stratospheric. Intellectually, he knew she was wrong, that they couldn't be more intimate if they actually made love than they were now, yet he understood what she was trying to do and was proud of her for it. She became adept at manipulating him, but he was unable to satisfy her with his hands, was unsure if he could kiss her to a climax, and didn't dare suggest it anyway.

"Don't worry about it—women are different than men. Or so they tell me. It takes longer to get adjusted."

"But it's not fair."

"No, and it's not fair for me to be here with you like this and not make love. So let me worry about me, and you worry about you."

Eventually he accommodated himself to it, so much so that the relief she gave him was soon supplanted by a deadening depression when he thought about not making the flight. When he saw the headlines about Lindbergh's arrival in Paris, he was engulfed in a missed-coital tristfulness. One hundred million other Americans went mad for joy with Slim's success, but Bandfield burned with personal disappointment. He wondered how Hafner and Byrd were taking it. There might be faster New York–Paris flights—it had taken Lindbergh more than thirty-three hours—but there would never be another first flight.

Determined to get his mind off Lindbergh's triumph, Millie, starving as usual, finally dragged him out of the hotel. Winter had given him a two-week advance, and Millie insisted going dutch on everything, so there was plenty of money.

"We might as well see New York City! Who knows when we'll be back?"

They mixed education, eating, and sightseeing in equal measure as Bandfield tried to get life after Lindbergh back into perspective. She seemed to know everything without ever looking at a pamphlet or guidebook and worked hard to draw his attention away from his troubles. They went to the Aquarium by subway. The fleet was in and sailors crowded the streets like seabirds on a rock, eyeing Millie, whistling. She ignored them, concentrating on teaching Bandy. It was an old fort, she said, converted first to an immigration center, then to an aquarium. In his mind he immediately transposed the fish swimming forlornly in the cool green aquarium cells of water to the ocean, where, if things had gone differently, other fish might have been staring at him.

They grabbed a bus to Greenwich Village. His appetite, always hearty no matter what his mood, was returning, signaling imperatively that he wanted a regular meal. Millie was sampling the pushcarts, snacking as they walked, obviously searching for something.

"Funny-looking trees. I'll take you out and show you the redwoods and sequoias someday."

"These are ailanthus—supposed to be good for purifying the air."

He stopped, dumbfounded. The woman knew everything!

"Aha! Patchin Place! I've found this for you."

He looked bemused.

"Didn't you tell me your dad was a Wobbly?"

"What's a Wobbly?"

"You know, a socialist, a communist, one of those 'ist' words, people throwing bombs, wearing beards, you know."

He couldn't believe it. He'd told her once about his father, and she'd stored it away.

He nodded, and she went on, "Well, John Reed lived here."

Bandfield smiled. "He was Dad's hero!"

"Well, a lot of people think he was a communist. He's buried in Moscow, you know. If you haven't read his book, *Ten Days That Shook the World*, I'll get you a copy."

A huge Irish policeman loomed up, a comic-strip figure with his giant fists and huge billy club.

"Excuse me, officer, do you know which is John Reed's house?"

The cop smiled benignly at Millie, answering in a deep brogue, "Sure an' I don't, my darling, but you can ask the postman."

Stifling their laughter, happy with another secret joke, they walked on, hand in hand, Bandfield wondering if a person as sensitive as Millie could be a pilot, or even a pilot's wife. Flyers were a rough lot. Would she fit in?

Bandfield was starving, and as they walked, the restaurants looked successively better. They passed Bertolotti's, and the sharp scent of oregano almost buckled his knees; finally he dragged her into Fortuno's on Bleecker Street, telling the owner, "Bring us food, lots of food." They started with a plate of thinly sliced tongue, slathered in oil and vinegar. Soup, spaghetti, and a broiled chicken followed, and despite all she'd eaten, she stayed even with him. He wondered if he could afford to marry her.

They went back to the hotel and napped for two hours, cuddlingly with their clothes on. He stared at the ceiling, wondering what Lindbergh was doing. Gradually the realization came that whatever it was, it wasn't as good as being there with Millie. Even with clothes on.

He thought she was sleeping, and he slipped out of bed.

"Where are you going?"

"To get the papers and see how Slim is doing."

She was primped and ready to go when he came back an hour later. "I thought you were like the man who went out for a jar of olives and didn't come back for twenty years."

He grinned, washed hurriedly, and took her downstairs. The light was bright in the street. At the curb was a horse and carriage. He put her inside, enjoying her squeals of pleasure. He wouldn't let her look in the big paper bag. In Central Park he kissed her and brought a bottle of champagne out of the bag, along with two of the thick glass tumblers from the room.

"This is supposed to be good, aged champagne. The bellboy said he made it last week." He popped the champagne and poured. Then he produced two smaller boxes. From one he took a ring; from the other a magnifying glass. He handed them to her and said, "If you look close, you'll see a diamond. Will you marry me?"

Roosevelt Field, Long Island/June 24, 1927

Bandfield slowly folded the newspaper on its original creases and laid it back on the floor of the Stutz, where he had tossed it the week before. He slumped back in the seat, twisting his cap in his hands, trying to erase the front-page picture of two people he knew. Short, lean-faced Raymond Orteig was handing a check for $25,000 to Bandfield's old flying-school buddy, *Colonel* Charles A. Lindbergh. Even the check was an affront, an ornate oversize vellum sheet decorated with an American flag and a drawing of the *Spirit of St. Louis*. Lindbergh had gotten a check from Orteig; Bandfield himself had gotten onion soup!

It was depressing. No pilot, not Icarus, not Orville, no one, had ever been so honored. The President had sent the cruiser *Memphis* to bring him home, and there had been tumultuous ceremonies in Washington at which Slim was promoted from

captain to colonel and got the Distinguished Flying Cross. He'd
flown to New York in an Army pursuit plane and been brought
to the parade on Mayor Jimmy Walker's official yacht, escorted
by everything that could float, from fireboats to destroyers. Millions of people had lined the parade route, spraying a confetti
welcome from every window. The papers had said that eighteen
hundred tons of ticker tape and shredded phonebooks had showered down on Lindbergh's parade.

A glutton for punishment, Bandy had brought Millie to watch.
He had muscled his way to the front of the crowd, leaving Millie
pinned against a shop window, as Lindbergh's car edged by,
flanked by grinning mounted police. The tall pilot was standing
in the back, Mayor Walker on his left, Grover Whalen in front
of him, smiling from behind a walrus mustache. Bandfield had
yelled "Slim!" at the top of his lungs, but just as the big open
Packard touring car rolled by, Lindbergh had turned to wave at
a man who had shinnied up a lightpole, his child clinging pre-
cariously to his neck.

The gap between them, the planeless, out-of-work Bandfield
and Colonel Lindbergh, the new emperor of aviation, again
drove home just how much he had lost.

His hard conscience chewed on the injustice of it all. Yet in
a way it was perfect, Lindbergh's turning his back on him just
as fate had. If he had done as he should have done, stuck by his
airplane every minute, it wouldn't have burned. If it had been
an accident, some freak wiring problem in the hangar, he would
have been able to save it. And his presence would have pre-
vented sabotage. In either case, he could have been the man in
the Packard, waving to the crowd.

It only bothered him when he was alone. When he was with
Millie, whether pushing through the milling crowds of straw-
hatted men that jammed the streets of the garment district or
doing her familiar walking-cafeteria routine through the pushcarts on Hester Street, absolutely nothing else mattered. She
was a joy, a know-it-all he didn't mind knowing it all. She loved
the roiling crowds of foreigners, many still dressed in native
clothes she could identify at a glance—Russian, Armenian,
Hungarian. One day she insisted that they bring a box Brownie
so he could take pictures of her with women in their ethnic
costumes to show her schoolchildren in Green Bay. She took a
special pleasure in using sign language and smiles to cajole the
women into posing.

They walked the streets with arms entwined, oblivious to

both approving and disapproving stares, squeezing each other, prodding, poking, sometimes stopping to kiss. They played a "goofus" game, trying to be first to spot interesting, ridiculous, or frightening characters. She invariably won because he spent half his time watching the intense play of emotion on her face. She could change at a glance from a concerned moue about a shoeless child to a raucous laugh at a burly Armenian lady dressing down her tiny husband, then to tears of compassion for the often frightened, bewildered look of a new immigrant family. They had reached a point where they no longer had to talk at length; a word or a wink was enough to communicate. Like yesterday at the ball game—the Yankees had beaten the Red Sox 11 to 4, but the high point of the game was Lou Gehrig's record-breaking third homer. She had simply looked up at him, and he knew how truly happy and excited she was.

The big difference now was in their planning. She had happily agreed to marry him, asking only that they keep it secret until she had talked to her mother. They planned to return to California; she would teach while he and Hadley built and sold another plane like the *Rocket*.

He laid his arm lovingly on the Stutz, wondering how much longer he'd have it to drive, and when or if he'd ever have another car to match it. Glancing at his watch, he realized that Winter was due back from his hop in the Waco with Millie. Jack was determined to teach Millie if not to fly at least not to be airsick, and he had been giving her an early-morning flight almost every day. For the first time in his life, Bandfield worried whether flying was really safe; he'd far rather have flown with Millie himself, but Winter was adamant.

In his pocket was the latest letter from Hadley Roget, more irascible than usual, still furious about the hangar fire, complaining bitterly about Bandfield's dilly-dallying in New York while he was building another airplane. Inspired by the Lindbergh mania, a rich businessman had announced the Pineapple Derby, with a $25,000 first prize and $10,000 second prize for a race from the West Coast to Hawaii. The race date was August 6, and Hadley was scrambling to rebuild a wreck to enter. He'd enclosed a photo—hardly encouraging, for the battered Breese monoplane was in rough shape. He promised to have the engine overhauled by the end of June, pleading with Bandy to return and help.

Bandfield thought about it. Hawaii wasn't Paris, and the winning pilot wouldn't be Lindbergh. But it was something.

The familiar sound of a Wright-Hispano engine broke into his thoughts. It was a symbol of another era, one that Lindbergh had left behind in a single flight behind his Wright Whirlwind. He watched Winter whip across the field at twenty feet before pulling up in a chandelle. If Millie could take that, she could take most anything.

When Winter taxied in, he could see from the vomit smeared along the side of the fuselage and across the tail that she couldn't take it. She was resting, her face pale, with her head against the side of the cockpit coaming. Winter shut down the engine and leaped out, obviously angry with himself for having made her airsick.

Millie gingerly climbed out when Bandfield walked up with a bucket and pulled it out of his hands. "I threw it up, I'll clean it up." It was traditional, but Bandfield wouldn't permit it.

"No, my fierce little rasper, you sit over there, and I'll do it." He tenderly sat her on the Stutz's running board, taking the bucket back. As he worked, Winter apologized. "Millie, I'm sorry. You were doing fine till I pulled that stupid approach. I was just feeling my oats because I got news this morning that my Vega would be ready in time for the Pineapple Derby. I was going to ask you to go with me."

They spoke simultaneously. Millie said, "I'm going!" as Bandfield said, "She's not going!"

It was their first argument. Millie blamed being sick on not having breakfast. "We're going to Hawaii, Bandy, like it or not. You aren't going to be the only one to see the ocean at sunrise, and all the other pretty things you tell me about!" Her voice softened, and she touched his arm. "Bandy, you want to be a flyer, I want to be a teacher and a writer. I need this as much as you do. Is that so wrong?"

The answer was easy. "Us pilots are all replaceable. If Lindbergh hadn't made it to Paris, I would have, or Bruno would have. You are irreplaceable, and you might not make it."

" 'We pilots,' you should have said. And no one is irreplaceable, least of all me. If you are talking about me being irreplaceable for you, what about the other side of it? Aren't you irreplaceable to me?"

"You know what I mean. It's going to be a lot tougher than Lindbergh's flight. He could have missed France, but he'd have hit Spain or Norway, somewhere. If you're off four degrees going to Hawaii, it's curtains. There's nothing out there but a lot of deep blue ocean!"

She hesitated for a moment and asked, "Are you going to fly in the race?"

He nodded.

"If you are, I am." And he knew she meant it.

Roosevelt Field, Long Island/June 28, 1927

Every trip back to Roosevelt Field was agony for Bandfield; he could never avoid looking at the scar where the hangar housing the *Rocket* had been. This time he was on a mission of mercy. Richard Byrd had been very good to him when he came, an unknown pilot in an unknown airplane. Byrd probably needed a little morale boost, but was too proud to ask for it.

Bandfield knew how Byrd was suffering. He was the proudest by far of the lot that had assembled that rainy May, and Lindbergh's success must have been a bitter pill.

The rumors were rife that Byrd's crew was ready to abandon him, and that Fokker was trying to buy the aircraft back. The papers said he was receiving hate mail accusing him of fraud and cowardice. His replies had been weak; in the only statement he made to the press, he said simply that he "didn't wish to undermine the scientific character of the flight by hasty preparations." Bandfield didn't know why the explorer hadn't taken off, but he was sure that the reasons were sound.

The imposing name "America Transoceanic Company" was spelled out with unconscious irony over the hangar doors. The airplane was locked inside, a bad sign. If they were getting ready to go, the doors should have been open and people should have been swarming over the aircraft.

There was no answer to his knock. He walked around to the side entrance, peering into the gloom of the hangar. A guard, obviously just awakened, ran over to the door.

"Sorry, sir, no one is here. They are all due out here at the field tonight at midnight for an early-morning takeoff."

Bandfield shrugged and walked away, annoyed again at his timing. As he turned the corner toward the parking lot he ran into Charlotte Hafner.

She was standing with her hands on her hips, her head cast down, watching him from beneath lowered eyelids, every bit the wholesome hooker.

"Hello, stranger. I've seen you here many times, but we've never had a chance to meet."

Bandy had been only too aware of her presence on the field; wherever she walked she was preceded by a bow wave of admiration that alerted people she was coming. Usually when he saw her she was getting into an airplane with Dusty Rhoades for flight instruction.

"How do you do, Mrs. Hafner? I'm pleased to meet you at last."

"You and Bruno are old friends, I know." She laughed and shrugged, saying in effect, "It's not my fault."

He didn't reply. She was the most beautiful, mature woman he had ever seen—nothing to compare to Millie's fresh beauty, of course, but startling in her own way. She was dressed like Hollywood's conception of the lady flyer, in a fashion-plate leather coat, jodhpurs, and high laced boots, her large, firm breasts bulging animatedly under a filmy white blouse. She was carrying a helmet and scarf in her hands.

He had assumed she was a bleached blonde; now he could see that her hair was truly golden, with perhaps some slight streaks of silver. "Peaches and cream" was the perfect description of her complexion. The least suggestion of lines at the corners of her eyes and mouth made her seem to be smiling all the time.

He could not help himself. He let his eyes run down her body, appreciating the fullness of her figure. At last she put her hands out and turned around. "Inspection over?" she asked, loving it.

Bandfield blushed and apologized. "I'm sorry. The truth is you are absolutely beautiful, but I was rude to stare."

She reached over and touched his shoulder, running her hand down his arm almost as if she were checking the conformation of a horse she wished to buy.

"Don't apologize. All women love to be admired, especially when they get to be my age."

He moved away slightly. She followed him.

"Have you seen Dusty? He was supposed to meet me here, and we were going to take a hop in my plane." She pointed to the Waco 10 tethered a hundred yards down the field, canvas covers over its cockpits and the engine.

"No, nobody's here. The guard says they're coming in at midnight. Must be going to make the try in the morning. I hope they do, and I hope they make it."

"Me too. The papers are beginning to say ugly things about Byrd. Dusty says it's all nonsense, that he'll go when he's ready."

Her mention of Dusty was matter-of-fact, but then a look of irritation crossed her face.

"Sure Dusty's not here?" Her voice was a mixture of wistfulness and hope.

"No, I haven't seen him."

Her expression softened as she darted a glance at him. "What are you doing this morning?"

Bandfield thought fast. He didn't want to give this woman any instruction in Hafner's airplane. If something happened, a simple ground loop, anything, there would be hell to pay.

"I've got to get back to Manhattan."

"Couldn't you give me some breakfast? I know a little place not far from here where we could have bacon and eggs, maybe, or whatever you wanted."

She placed her hand on his forearm and squeezed. She had moved closer, and he caught her exciting scent.

"I'm sorry." He wrenched away, and said, "You'll have to excuse me, I've got to go."

She smiled wryly and said, "When you've gotta go, you've gotta go."

He dove in the Stutz and pulled away, a mixture of regret and relief pouring over him. He thought of her breasts and her obvious availability and toyed with the idea of turning around. Then he thought of Millie and mashed the accelerator down.

Salinas, California/July 15, 1927

The sun-dusted hillsides were resting, waiting for the next seasonal splash of rain to paint them green again. The few cows that Clarice Roget insisted on maintaining cut shallow paths up the hills, edging around the scrub oak and manzanita, coming home at night to the sprawling wooden structure that had begun as barn and then been turned into a combination garage/hangar.

She watched Hadley strut up the path with his cocky walk, arms flailing, legs swinging wide, knowing that he had forgotten the bitter disappointment of the *Rocket*, and was already spending the money Bandy was supposed to win in the next race. There was always a next race, always something just around the corner. Usually a bill collector.

She stood on the wooden porch of their unpainted house, washing out his underwear, the suds on her arm giving her deep leathery tan a glistening cordovan hue.

Hadley's assurance amid poverty galled, and she flushed red, the veins of her neck extending like rhubarb stalks. She smacked the scrubbing board into the tub in exasperation. "I tell you, Hadley, you'd be better off to burn that garage—"

"Hangar," he interrupted.

"Hangar, garage, it's a junk breeding ground. We ought to start farming, get some acreage where we can plant some beans and sugar beets, and start living a little normal."

It was such an old argument that she understood when Hadley simply turned away to walk back down the gravel path to where the new apprentice was helping him work on the old truck. He hadn't even bothered to repeat that lettuce was the coming cash crop, as he usually did.

Clarice glared out the window at her husband. Theirs was a comfortable marriage of total misunderstanding, one that only strong personalities could survive. They were so completely devoid of common interests that each remained an intriguing mystery to the other. She was flint-hard, farm born and bred, glorying in the rituals of planting and harvest, breeding and birthing. He was steel-sharp and devoted to machines, seeing in them an uplifting, challenging sculptural beauty that was usually lost on others, always on her. She liked to go to church services, he liked to tell naughty jokes. They repeatedly struck sparks, their differences both the root of their difficulties and the source of their strength. Physically they looked remarkably alike, both tall and lean, with straw-colored hair that their hard life was sure to turn white early.

The weathered sign over the hangar door said "Roget Aircraft," but the yard was filled with the pick-up automobile work Hadley did to make a living. Clarice's gnarled hands drummed on the table. Her eyes were troubled. Her husband had built a few good airplanes, she guessed, but none had made any money. She ran the books and knew that fixing cars was their bread and butter. The problem, of course, was that to Hadley and Bandy, cars were mere commodities, something they could fix and forget, while airplanes were utterly absorbing works of art in which they lost themselves. She knew, too, that they took half the normal time to repair an American car and twice as much as was necessary to repair an airplane. But in the past few years, word of Hadley's mechanical ability—and his set of metric tools—had spread and rich people were bringing exotic foreign cars, Lanchesters, Isotta-Fraschinis, Hispano-Suizas, from as far away as San Francisco. Clarice didn't want to see anything but forgettable Fords and Chevies in the yard; when they bent over a Rolls, they fell in love with it and lost money.

She turned and put a blue enameled coffeepot, as chipped by life as herself, on the stove to perk. Eight thick pepper-dusted slices of sidemeat sizzled in a black griddle, ready for the second breakfast. Hadley took most of his meals and gallons of coffee out in the garage. She figured he'd swallowed as much crankcase oil from his fingers as mayonnaise from the bread over the years, for he rarely bothered to stop to wash his hands. He would never grow up, never get the grease from under his nails or his back off a creeper. Hadley always talked about striking it rich some-day, creating an airplane that they could build in quantity, moving to Los Angeles and building a factory. The truth was that he thought he'd already struck it rich, getting to work on such nice machinery every day.

She'd been glad when Bandy left to fly to Paris, happier still that he had stayed away even after the disaster of the fire. It was good for Bandy to be away from her husband for a while, to avoid being pressed utterly into Hadley's mold, and she was solaced by the emerging independence she sensed in him. Perhaps it was inevitable; his father had been a rebel, a huge, lovable man who embraced every cause except earning a steady living for his family. George Bandfield had a wild red streak in him, a joyous brawling love for the underdog that took him into the Oregon forests to help the woodcutters and to the San Francisco docks to rally the longshoremen. He had dominated his wife completely, just as he'd tried to do with Bandy. But his son had reacted differently, tempering under the treatment until he was steel-hard and resilient, as conservative as his father was radical, as bullheaded as Hadley when he was right, but quick to admit it when he realized he was wrong.

Yet they all missed George Bandfield. His wife, Emily, had loved him unflaggingly even though she had seen her ranch eaten up acre by acre, to fuel his follies, adoring him with the mindless, assertive passion peculiar to women whose marriages are considered mistakes by everyone else. When George Bandfield left she stopped living in all but the literal sense. Always fragile and withdrawn, she had become just a paper image of an old woman, in bed for most of the day, barely able to let a hired woman feed and take care of her. Clarice knew that his mother's death had added to Bandy's sense of guilt. He once told her he felt his dad had left because his own success in school had been too much of a contrast.

Clarice felt that Bandy had two legacies from his father. The first was his profound love for the underdog, and the second was his mechanical aptitude. To be Hadley Roget's partner, he'd need them both.

She sighed and turned away from the window when Hadley rolled the truck to the side and began to work on one of his latest acquisitions, a blood-red Standard biplane he'd picked up from a wrecking yard, gear crumpled around its cowling like seaweed on a boulder. She knew he planned to use parts from it in fixing up the shattered hulk he was rebuilding for Bandy to fly to Hawaii.

Down in the yard, Hadley wrenched the rudder from the Standard's fuselage; an argument with Clarice always put a fine edge on Hadley's always volatile temper. "Goddammit, Howard, let's get busy. I ain't paying you to stand around and spit."

"You're not paying me anything, Hadley, I'm paying you, remember?"

Hadley glowered as the youth went on, "And to you, and everybody here, I'm Charles Howard, not Howard Hughes. I want to be able to move around without a lot of lawyers following me."

"Charles Howard" was tall and lean, with a broad face and a quick smile. His eyes were dark and darting, moving always as if something he could learn had just eluded him. A year ago, Hadley had taught him to fly. Now he was teaching him to be a mechanic.

"What's with this Charles Howard crap anyway, Howard? I know you have pots of money, but why do you need an alias?"

Howard put down a wrench. "Look, I'll tell you again. I want to be something in this industry, but I want to do it on merit. I could walk into any airline in the country and get a job as Howard Hughes because they'd all want to skin a dumb kid out of his money. They'd let me fly and tell me I was doing well no matter how badly I did."

Hadley was nodding. He had indeed been told before, but he wanted to hear it again, to see if this hardworking, no-nonsense young millionaire was sincere. He grumbled some more, trying to find an argument he could win. He stood glaring at the younger man like an ancient British gladiator thrown into the ring with some up-and-coming young Celt. Roget was tall, and his thin blond hair was sunbaked to silver. His spare frame was covered with a well-defined musculature looking like braided steel wire under his skin. Hughes was as tall as Roget and his negative image in coloration, with a deeply tanned skin and dark black hair. He didn't seem to be heavily muscled but had proved already that he was just as strong as the older man.

Hughes shot Hadley a grin and broke into his thoughts. "I don't know why you worry what my name is. You rarely call me anything but smart-ass. But I keep remembering that it takes a crusty old bastard like you to tell me the truth. Besides that, I like the way you work."

He turned to the Standard, then looked back.

"Charles Howard. Don't you forget, because that's the way the checks will be signed, too."

Oakland, California/August 6, 1927

Lindbergh had lit the torch; James Dole had thrown a bucket of gasoline on it. Pineapple Derby madness was already overshadowing the covey of proposed transatlantic flights, and pilots and airplanes from every corner of the country were converging on Oakland.

The flexible contest rules—the race had already been postponed twice—were bent to accommodate crazy contestants. Airplanes that had been intended to do no more than carry two passengers in and out of cow pastures were being filled with homemade gas tanks for the 2,400-mile flight across total emptiness. In backyards and barns, welding torches glowed, fabricating monstrosities that could barely get off the ground, much less across an ocean.

There was a fever, a contagion, and it was simply Lindbergh-itis. The slim, soft-spoken airman had given more than stature to an industry; he had given hope. Pilots who had starved for years were willing to risk anything for a chance at glory.

It had never been tougher for Bandfield; the prize money dictated that he compete, even though it meant compromising everything he believed in, everything for which he'd tried to stand for. Instead of flying a well-engineered, well-proven plane in which safety was an uppermost consideration, he was back working with Roget, trying to pull rabbit performance out of a tired old hat of an airplane. Hadley had persuaded Vance Breese to sell them an ancient beat-up crate that had been used on the Varney Air Lines Elko, Nevada, to Pasco, Washington, route. It was an open-cockpit four-placer that had crashed twice, the scars of its rebuilds evident in the cut-and-dry welding of its fuselage and the splices in its wing. Yet it had one great virtue: it was available. Now they were working night and day to install the tanks where wet mail sacks had lain and scared passengers had thrown up as it threaded through the passes in the Rockies.

Roget passed the time by riding Charles Howard unmercifully while the three of them spent twenty hours a day trying to stretch and strengthen the mail plane.

Howard was eager enough, but Roget was a constant critic. "Godammit, Charlie, I said to be here at seven o'clock. I'm busier than a one-armed paperhanger with the crabs, and you come sauntering in at nine. Where the hell were you?"

"Sorry, Hadley—I had a date, went to see *Wings*, then for a drive in the country."

"That's a pretty good movie, Charlie. I really liked the flying scenes." Bandfield felt obliged to make amends for Hadley's continual hard-timing of the boy.

"The movie stinks. I've seen it five times, and it gets worse every time."

Hadley snorted. "Well, smart-ass, why don't you make a better one?"

Howard looked at him. "I just might, Hadley, and I'll get you to fix up the airplanes for me. That was one of the problems—the airplanes didn't look like real World War airplanes. My date said so too, and she doesn't know anything about it."

"Well, your ass has a date with my foot if you're late again. Now get your kiester over to Manly's supply shack and get me some gasket material, and try to get back here before winter." Howard shot off on the double.

"How come you're so hard on that guy, Hadley? I know you're a mean old geezer, but he's not used to it."

"Look, Bandy, Charles Howard is just the name he works under. His real name is Howard Hughes, and he's the richest kid in town, the guy who put up the money for this airplane. I taught him to fly, and now I'm teaching him to build airplanes."

"Holy shit, Hadley. Then how come you're so mean-ass to him?"

"He told me to treat him just like I'd treat anybody else. He doesn't want any publicity. And he figures somebody would find out who he is if I was nice to him."

"Yeah, that'd be a tip-off. What kind of a pilot is he?"

"He's a fucking natural. He says after this, he's going to get a job as a copilot on an airline, then go into aviation in a big way. I want you to be nice to him, though—we may want to tap his bankroll again someday.''

Bandfield shook his head. Winter had taught him rich people could be nice; maybe Charlie Howard, whatever his name was, would be okay.

In the meantime, he had to figure some way to cram enough fuel tanks in the airplane to get him to Hawaii. Normally the Breese had a range of six hundred miles at the outside. Bandfield winced at the overload he knew it had to carry to get him 2,400 miles to Hawaii. They were going to have to beef up the landing gear, run another strut to the wing, and reinforce the fuselage to take the weight of the tanks and gasoline. It was baling-wire-and-bolt-on mechanics, the very thing he hated, and had sworn he'd never do again.

He kept a running tab on the weight not only because he had to for the judges but also to keep track of the center of gravity. If it hadn't been for the rules, he would have thrown the records away, because they provided nothing but bad news.

The Oakland flight line was like old home week, and he was pleased when Jack Winter walked in, immaculate in gray plus fours, maroon sweater, and white cap. He'd invited Bandy to make a thorough inspection of his gorgeously finished Vega himself. It was the first plane of the new Lockheed line, and no effort had been spared on it. It reassured him about Millie; if any plane could make it, the Vega could.

"Did you hear about Art Rogers?"

Bandy shook his head no.

"He went in yesterday on a test flight."

Bandfield rubbed his hands on some cotton wool. "Can't say it surprises me. The plane was too radical."

A special plane had been built for Rogers, the twin-engine, twin-tail *Angel of Los Angeles*. He had read about it and seen some photos. The *Angel* was an absurd conception powered by two tiny three-cylinder British Lucifer engines, notoriously un-reliable, mounted front and back on the little egg-shaped fuse-lage. Thin booms carried the twin-ruddered tail surfaces. Like most of the planes entered in the race, it was a half-baked design scratched out on butcher paper by a nonengineer.

Roget stuck his head in the hangar. "Come on out—here comes the Hoot Gibson special! It's crazier-looking than a bag full of assholes!" They strolled out to watch the big twin-engine Fisk triplane, financed by the cowboy star and carrying his portrait on the nose, ease around the pattern looking more like a three-masted clipper ship than an airplane.

"Christ, that crate is all drag and a yard wide."

Bandfield shook his head. "He's overshooting final. He ought to go around."

The Fisk, close enough now so that they could see its orange wings and black fuselage, moved slowly in a turn back toward the edge of the field.

Winter broke in, "Hey, he's trying to sideslip it back on course."

They watched in amazement as the Fisk slid like a lopsided stack of pancakes toward the bay. The engines roared as the pilot poured the power to it, but the triplane just edged wingtips first into the water, dissolving like a graham cracker in a glass of milk. As soon as they saw the crew swim free, they rolled on the ground, laughing.

That night Bandfield walked past the crumpled remains of the Fisk, a battered, ruptured duck with only Hoot Gibson's face still identifiable. The face was a reproach; the more Bandy flew, the more conservative he became, the more concerned about improving the slapdash engineering of most civilian planes. Even a professional firm like Lockheed could no longer afford to rush an airplane from the production line to a major race.

The accident jolted him into really taking a close look at his own plane. He walked around the Breese, sitting with its fabric peeled back, a drip pan full of oil under the engine, one tire slightly bald, the Varney Air Lines logo still visible under the hastily applied coat of paint. It was marginal, but he and Hadley would have it in shape for the race. They had solved the problem with strap iron and savvy, not with engineering elegance. Even if they won the race, it wouldn't mean anything for aviation, nothing like if Jack Winter's Lockheed did.

Suddenly missing Millie, he walked down to Winter's immaculate Vega, where a mechanic was painting its name, *Miss Duncan's Golden Eagle*, on the highly polished yellow-painted skin.

Millie was there, excitedly studying a clipping from the *Oakland Tribune* showing a cutaway diagram of the plane with its life rafts, drift meter, fuel tanks, emergency rations, radios, just about every modern convenience. Jack Winter was taking no chances.

Their wedding date was set for December. He had the feeling that all the details—or even the awareness—had not been assimilated in Green Bay, where a winter wonderland ceremony was supposed to take place. Jack, true to form, immediately told them that his wedding present would be the prize money for winning the Pineapple Derby. This immediately changed their honeymoon plans from Philadelphia to Havana.

It also changed their thinking. Bandy had planned on winning the $10,000 second prize, and spending it all on the honeymoon and building a house back in Salinas. Now, with the prospect of an additional $25,000—Winter was sure to win—they were talking about forming a partnership with Hadley and setting up a first-rate aircraft factory.

There was one fly in the ointment of love. In spite of the fact that their friendship and frustrated passion gave them a happiness usually found only in the last reels of a Mary Pickford film, he was jealous of the coverage the press was providing her. Petty as he knew it was, it was undeniable. It was bad enough that Lindbergh, his old flying-school chum, was world-famous. But his girlfriend, not even a pilot? The injustice rankled even though he knew it shouldn't.

"Great shot. You look like you're ready to fly without an airplane." She didn't notice the sarcasm, exhibiting an ingenuous delight in her photo with Jack standing by the propeller and looking mystically skyward.

And there was another element, more serious than jealousy or a lover's pique. Bandy didn't know how to tell her that the endless round of publicity was also affecting her judgment. He felt she was being drawn irrevocably into the flight, and wouldn't be able to withdraw even if she wanted to at the last moment. He wanted her to be very sure of what she was doing, aware of the risks involved before it was too late. But nothing he said seemed to matter. Jack had fitted her out in a cute military costume, an officer's tunic with Sam Browne belt, jodhpurs, and cute knee socks with clocks around the top. She looked absolutely darling, and couldn't walk two steps without having a reporter asking a question or a photographer firing a flash of powder at her.

The press treated Jack Winter well, but Millie was the real celebrity. And even worse than Bandy admitting his jealousy to himself was that she knew it, and kidded him unmercifully about it.

California was like old home week for Bruno. Women with whom he'd slept in his early-twenties barnstorming tours but whose names he'd forgotten began descending on Oakland as soon as they saw the headline "Famous German Ace Arrives." Hafner smiled as he wondered if Nungesser was looking down from some pilot's heaven, checking to see if any of *his* old girl-friends showed up.

Bruno's bulk filled a chair to overflowing in the little office overlooking the field. He scratched Nellie's head as he read Cy Bidwell's column in *Aviation Age*, for once agreeing with him. Bidwell argued that the Pineapple Derby was twice as important as the Lindbergh flight, because it was more than twice as difficult. The route was shorter, but Hawaii was just a dot in the middle of a vast ocean. A minor navigation error would send a plane off into a vast, empty Pacific.

Hafner put down the magazine and assessed the problem. If he had agreed to bring Dusty along, one man could have used the sextant while the other flew. But the furor over Lindbergh clearly showed that the press was for the solo pilot, and he was still glad that he had left Dusty on Long Island. Navigation wasn't his long suit, even though he had practiced in New York, while preparing for the Atlantic race. The problem was that he hadn't really been serious, for he hadn't worried about it, knowing that if he missed France he had an entire continent to aim for. The fact that two planes had already flown the route didn't change anything. The Army plane, *Bird of Paradise*, had special radio equipment and three engines. Then some dumb civilians, indifferent to the prize money, had taken off in mid-July in a Travelair monoplane and wound up in a treetop on some little island next to Oahu. It proved his point about flying solo. The press commented briefly on the flights, then turned its attention back to Lindbergh. The two flights didn't seem to affect interest in the Pineapple Derby, either.

Right now, though, he had other things on his mind. Winning didn't mean much in the way of dollars to him, but the prestige was critical for building airplanes and selling them. The option he had on a factory at Roosevelt Field had fallen through; the company was tied up in litigation, and he couldn't take possession. Charlotte was working on another deal; maybe she could pull it off.

God, they had a strange relationship. He wondered what his mother and father, both stiffly formal, would have made of it. If Germany had won the war, where would he be? Commanding a squadron in an African colony somewhere, with a proper wife back home in Germany and a sleep-in native girl. He laughed— Charlotte *was* his sleep-in native.

But she was good. They generated a magic that was hard to duplicate. Other women were fun, but none provided the obsessive intensity of Charlotte's lovemaking. And he needed her. She not only carried the business in her head, she knew where to go for money when they needed it, and brought the right people into the factory. Charlotte had made friends with Igor Sikorsky out on Long Island—he wondered just how good their friendship really was—and Sikorsky had provided leads on some magnificent engineers. And when Sikorsky's business fell off, as it did after the Fonck crash, Charlotte had even leased the ramshackle facility they were using and hired many of his junior engineers and mechanics, just so they'd have paychecks.

He rolled an ashtray shaped like an automobile tire back and forth on the desk, feeling edgy. The business with Bandfield had been unsettling. He was glad it was behind him. It was curious, but Charlotte had never inquired about the fire, never asked what he thought about it.

The magazines and newspapers were filled with talk about the "modern woman." Hell, he'd married one. It was a good arrangement, one that suited them both. But he didn't know how long it would last. One or the other would tire of it, unless the business expanded and served as a safety valve. They could stay together for as long as they were wealthy, busy—and frequently apart.

He knew that one of the saving graces would be her enjoyment of being a businesswoman, of having a say in matters normally reserved for men. Charlotte was as totally dependable as a business partner as she was unreliable as a spouse. He needed her for the day-to-day work; he could do the long-range planning. More important, their tumultuous relationship embraced a particular level in which he valued her respect, and she in turn demanded his. As earthy as their partnership was, he could never comprehend it in any but the most abstract engineering terms. It was as if they were two essential gears in the clockwork of life, each gear fitted with teeth of totally different sizes and shapes, yet somehow still meshing at certain speeds and certain times.

It was strange, after all their intimacies—and they had been intense beyond telling—and all their fights, he had never told her how he felt. It was something he would like to have done, if he could have known the response in advance, if he could be assured that she would not ridicule him.

The nasal-toned Oakland operator had been promising to put the call through all afternoon, but he still jumped when the phone rang.

"Hello, Charlotte? How are things in Long Island? What time is it there?"

Charlotte cradled the French-style phone between her head and neck.

"Don't yell, Bruno, I can hear you fine. It's seven here. I'm calling from the New Jersey office."

She reached down and ruffled Dusty's reddish hair. He kissed her bellybutton with sucking sounds that caused her to clasp her hand over the mouthpiece.

"What's going on at the plant?"

"Plenty. That's why I called. I need a decision from you right now. A special situation has developed with the Aircraft Corporation. I can get controlling interest for us for almost nothing. Curtiss is trying to buy it and Ned Dorfman doesn't want to sell it to them. You remember how Curtiss cheated him on that bomber contract. He hates them."

Rhoades looked up at her and grinned, mouthing the words "Say hi to him for me."

Hafner snorted. "Who doesn't hate Curtiss? They've screwed everybody in the business. What does Dorfman want for it?"

"He'll swap stock with Hafner Aircraft on a one-for-one basis, and one million cash on the side. He really just wants out. Says he's going down to Florida to waterfront property. We can swing it, but we'll be short of cash for a while." Rhoades ran his tongue up and down her thigh.

Bruno was enthused, shouting into the mouthpiece, "Wonderful! We won't have to build a new building. And he's got some great engineers there, more of the Russians Sikorsky brought over and couldn't find work for. We need the factory space." Hafner gazed out at the flight line, his mind racing ahead. "And we can use most of his working people. They're the best in the business with aluminum construction. We'd have to let most of the management go, all except the guy running contracts—his name is Ferguson, I think. He knows how to soft-talk the brass at Wright Field."

Charlotte fluttered her eyes at Rhoades, put her finger to her lips. "So you think it's okay to go ahead?"

"*Ja*, go ahead. I'll be back as soon as I can to help work out the details."

Rhoades moved between her legs, slid up to her.

"What's that? I can't hear you, Charlotte. Speak up—this is a bad connection."

Charlotte shifted to ease Rhoades's access. "It must be the line, Bruno. I don't hear anything."

Her hips began to move. Rhoades moaned. Charlotte put her hand over the mouthpiece.

"Hang up, dammit," he gasped.

"Just keep moving," she whispered back.

"Charlotte, are you there? I can barely hear you."

"I can hear you fine. The real beauty of acquiring them is that they control both the Mead & Wilgoos Engine and the Premium Propeller companies, and have a big chunk of Federated Airlines. We can build a plane, put our own engines and props on it, and fly it on our own airline."

"Go ahead and give him a handshake, Charlotte. Have the lawyers draw up some papers and we'll settle it when I get back."

He carefully replaced the earpiece into the hook, pleased once again at how well Charlotte served him.

The same was true for Dusty. As the line went dead, Charlotte wrapped her legs tightly around him, ratcheting him to her with convulsive undulations.

"I'm sorry about that, but it took him a long time to get a call through, and I had to talk to him."

Rhoades laid his head by her cheek, moving, oblivious to everything. She stared at the ceiling. The airplane business was so risky; you went from one design to the next, with everything riding on how well it did. You could never be safe, never take it easy. Maybe that was why she liked it.

Elated by the conversation, sexually stirred by Charlotte's voice, compressed and distorted as it was by the phone, Bruno Hafner flexed his arms, trying to work out the recurring ache laid across his shoulders ten years before by a British bullet. He'd spent only four days in the hospital before going back to his unit. Now, after long flights, the pain returned.

He glanced out the window to where Murray was fussing around the *Miss Charlotte*, supervising the installation of the radio. The question of radios had come up on Long Island; he'd decided against it because of the weight involved. There was no question about making landfall across the Atlantic. In the Pacific he'd need all the help he could get to reach Oahu. He glanced down at the U.S. Hydrographic chart spread out on his desk. There was nothing between San Francisco and the little arc of islands that was Hawaii, and damn little beyond. Except for a lot of water.

Murray had really done a good job investigating what Hegenberger and Maitland, the two Army pilots of the *Bird of Paradise*, had done, and scouted the market, finally coming to him as eager as a puppy with diagrams for both a transmitter/receiver set and a direction finder. He had agreed to the direction finder, but said no to the transmitter/receiver. He wasn't very good at Morse code—taking it in English rather than German somehow intensified the difficulty—and would be busy enough with the sextant. Murray tried to tell him that it was the wrong choice, that the Army plane hadn't been able to use the direction finder very much, but Bruno was adamant. There was no sense carrying something he couldn't use.

It was, after all, only a matter of risk, something he'd grown used to flying on the Western Front. There the degree of risk had been constant, even though the kinds of risk had changed. At first, flying against the French in a quiet sector, the danger was mostly the risk of crashing from inexperience. Then as he gained flying skill, that risk declined, but his unit was transferred to where the British were operating, and combat risk went up.

Even as he gained experience and victories, the risk stayed very small. He would go into battle eagerly, pursuing his lust for killing with confidence in himself, but concerned about the quality of his airplanes. Late in the war, even the good designs like the Fokker were flawed by bad materials and sloppy workmanship. He remembered when they finally got the D VII fighters. Wonderful machines, barely fast enough, but very strong and able to hang on their props and fire straight up. Things still would happen. He closed his eyes and it was like yesterday, flying with Fritz Frederichs on a test hop. They had played around in mock combat, and were coming back to land when the ammunition cans in Fritz's Fokker exploded, turning him into a burning cinder in seconds. A stupid design error had placed the ammunition boxes where the heat of the engine had ignited them and blown up the fuel tank, snuffing out the life of his best friend.

The risks were different here. He knew his plane and engine

could make the flight; the only imponderable was his navigation skills. He thought they were sufficient; if they weren't, so be it.

He yawned and stretched pleasurably. That's what the weaklings couldn't understand, the necessity of having your senses heightened, to take valid risks to make life worth living. He didn't mean stupid things like racing a car across a train crossing, but something worth doing. He could have let Murray put the little time bomb in Bandfield's plane back in Long Island, but he'd done it himself, partly because he wanted to be sure it was done right, and partly because he enjoyed the danger involved.

There wouldn't be any need to bother with Bandfield. That loudmouth Roget had selected an ancient crock for him to race this time. Hafner could see the tail of the Breese, set up on a tripod and sticking out of Roget's canvas hangar. It was a piece of shit, just right for Bandfield to fly.

Oakland Municipal Airport/August 16, 1927

Tension draped across the field like the tendrils of a Portuguese man-of-war, the sudden bark of an engine running up breaking the thick silence like an exploding paper bag. The airplanes were marshaled in a semicircle less than two hundred feet from the field's edge. To get as nearly a racehorse start as the field would permit, the first plane was to taxi to the start line, and the second into the waiting circle, both marked in lime on the sand. The entrants would then sequence from the marshaling position in the order in which Millie Duncan, the uncontested queen of the contest, had drawn them from an old felt hat.

Precisely at twelve noon, with a wave of his checkered flag, the starter shattered the tension like a crystal vase hitting the floor. A Travelair monoplane, the bright-blue-and-orange *Oklahoma*, was first off, to the spontaneous cheers of the crowd.

Bandfield sat in the cockpit of his battered Breese, for most of the week the only airplane in the contest not to have some brave name lettered on its side. Earlier in the week, he and Hadley had talked about a comic name—*Miss Blivet*, *Miss Hap*, *Hawaii or Bust*—but finally settled on *Salinas Made*, too unhappy with the plane to make more than a gentle joke about it. Vance Breese had dropped by and with Roget had spent the last two evenings trying to talk him out of the flight, telling him the airplane wasn't sound and the margin for error was too small.

Roget, always cranky, had gotten almost belligerent, yelling, "This time *I'll* burn the goddam airplane."

Bandfield listened to them respectfully; Breese was a famous name, and Hadley was in many ways a genius. Finally, he broke in. "Gents, I appreciate what you're saying, and I know what I'm risking. The problem is, we need the money to stay in business. If things go right, I plan to land in Hawaii within two hours of Jack Winter's arrival. If things go wrong, then I won't have to listen to any more of Hadley's rotten jokes."

Bandy hadn't told Hadley about Jack's generous offer to invest the prize winnings in a plant. Long ago, he'd learned the hard way not to believe anything until he had it in hand; when he and Millie had the checks, they'd tell Hadley.

Deep down, he knew the prize money was secondary to getting another shot at the big time, a second chance he'd never thought he'd have when the *Rocket* had gone up in smoke at Roosevelt Field. Hadley and Breese had been right about the airplane—it was a fucking dog, apt to come apart in flight. But more than anything else he wanted to be in Hawaii while Millie was enjoying the celebrations. He feared what success might do to her if he were not there, and the thought of seeing her go by in a parade, as he had seen Lindbergh, was too much to bear.

Hadley, his usual foul mood drowned in tight-lipped apprehension, was just finishing testing the radio. Totally self-trained, Hadley had an indomitable approach to life. When they couldn't find a transmitter/receiver set on the West Coast that they could use, he'd worked out a deal to "borrow" one from the Army. It amused Bandfield to see the usually grouchy Roget turn on the charm when he wanted something. By the time he'd finished telling a few jokes—the one about "three pieces of strange pussy a day is no record, but it ain't a bad average" getting the biggest laugh—the Army master sergeant from Crissey Field who'd worked with the *Bird of Paradise* crew practically insisted they take the radios. It was another reason he had to make it. There was no way the sergeant could explain the shortage if he went down at sea.

The *Dallas Spirit* taxied to the line. Bandy waved at Captain Bill Erwin; in the back, strapping himself in was Al Eichwaldt. Bandy had been upset at first with Erwin. The older man had practically adopted Millie when she arrived. If he hadn't been an eight-victory ace from the war—and on Spad XVIs, the worst plane at the front—Bandy would have been angry. But Erwin was so good-natured, so fatherly, and so friendly to Bandy that they finally got along well. They were in a Swallow, and Erwin had complained more than once about the way it flew. It had been a rush job, and just didn't seem to be put together correctly.

Erwin saluted again as he applied power, and the *Dallas Spirit* hustled down the runway, lifting off from almost exactly the spot where the *Oklahoma* had broken ground. Bandy wished them good luck.

Roget nudged him as the roughly finished *El Encanto* lined up. Norm Goddard had modified a surplus Navy two-seater Vought observation plane into a crude cabin monoplane, stuffing it with fuel everywhere, including a big bulging tank strapped to its belly like a suitcase on a luggage rack. The *El Encanto* had barely reached a grudging fifty miles an hour when it veered into a wild ground loop, scattering dust in a circle that drifted toward the bay. The landing gear folded as the airplane slid off the field toward the spectators, tumbling until it came to rest. The crowd hung back, expecting a fire, but Goddard had cut the switches, and the *El Encanto* lay there, its wing thrust like Ahab's arm toward the sky. Bandy's heart went out to him.

Hafner grimaced; one less to worry about. He was sweating from the heat of the sun filtered through his Pyralin windows, and glanced nervously back at Nellie. Long used to engine noise and vibration, she was sleeping quietly in her special case. Murray had fashioned it out of thick cork sheets for both insulation and flotation purposes.

Livingstone Irving was next off in a later-model sister ship to Bandy's airplane, the Breese *Pacific Pabco Flyer*. More experienced and more cautious than Goddard, he sensed that the airplane was not accelerating properly, and cut the switch to coast to a stop. A tractor towed him back to the starting gate.

Bandfield was worried. Two of the first three airplanes had been too heavily loaded to get off. Where did that leave him?

His stomach constricted as Millie's airplane, the Lockheed Vega *Miss Duncan's Golden Eagle*, entered the starting gate. He wondered what she was thinking; they'd had time only for the briefest good-bye, kissing more for the benefit of the photographers than for themselves. At precisely twelve-thirty the Vega started its roll.

Bandfield watched, praying as it swiftly gathered speed, sending a drifting spray of dust over the crowd. He tried to see Millie in the back as it went by, but the tiny square window where she sat was just a blur. Winter pulled it off the ground, and the Lockheed climbed strongly, the high-pitched resonance of its engine bidding a plaintive farewell. Bandy remembered one of Tony Fokker's aphorisms: if an airplane looks right it would fly right. The Vega certainly looked right. Millie would be safe in it.

He watched with a mixture of hatred and respect as Hafner taxied his Bellanca *Miss Charlotte* to the line, his arrogant winged-sword insignia emblazoned on its side. Bandfield's emotions had become mixed. The man was daring, no question about it, and a master pilot. And if he had set the *Rocket* on fire, he had also inadvertently set up Bandfield's romance with Millie. Who knew what would have happened if he'd gone on to Paris, to do as Lindbergh was—flying all over the country? Somebody else surely would have scooped Millie up.

Hafner was delayed when the *Dallas Spirit* reappeared, a huge section of fabric flowing behind it. Erwin made a beautiful wheel-on landing. As the plane passed Bandfield he could see that the stitching must have come loose just behind the cockpit; the fuselage fabric was peeled back like the skin of a banana. It was a miracle that it hadn't fouled the tail and sent the plane crashing into the ocean.

Bandy could see Hafner's arm sticking out the side of his cabin window, pounding the fuselage side, and knew how he must be boiling with rage at the delay. When the flag went down, he got away quickly, climbing out as swiftly as had the Vega.

Bandy was surprised to see that the *Miss Duncan*, fast disappearing, had climbed to at least six thousand feet and was on a course that would carry it to the north of the Farallons. Winter had been diligent about attending the weather briefings; he must have seen something about the wind that others missed.

Martin Goebel was right behind Hafner in the Buhl biplane *Sunrise Special*. Both planes stayed low over the bay until they disappeared, one dot extinguished after the other, beyond the Golden Gate.

Roget slapped Bandfield on the back and climbed down. Bandy guided the Breese carefully to the start line, making cautious wide turns to avoid straining the landing gear. An old habit, intended to relieve nervousness, caused him to count the airplanes on the field. On the right were almost twenty civil types ranging from a Jenny to a Travelair. On the left were six military DH-4s and a Martin bomber. The starter, all duded up in plus fours and boots, stood with the checkered flag. Sweat glistening in his palms, throat dry, he glanced over at Roget, who was waving the oil-stained "good luck" straw hat he always wore at big events.

The flag went down, and Bandy stood on the brakes, pushing the throttle to its limits. When he felt the brakes about to slip, he released them and the *Salinas Made* lurched forward. It rolled straight ahead, so slowly that he could look to the side and identify the cars where the crowd stood cheering—an Essex, a Studebaker, a Chandler. Reacting sullenly to the torque, the Breese started to turn to the left, and he fed in right rudder, keeping it straight.

It pounded down the sandy runway, gaining some speed, fifty, fifty-five miles per hour. The furrows of all the other aircraft were in the sand ahead of him, all showing the three marks of the wheels and tail skid, then two, as flying speed lifted the tail. His own tail skid was still down, firmly planted. He pressed forward on the stick, and the nose came down. Out of the telltale trails ahead of him, he saw two of the wheel marks stop, showing him where the Vega had broken ground. On the right was the twisted, broken *El Encanto*. He passed it, his plane beginning to feel light for the first time. Ahead was the bay. He pressed on, feeling the wheels leave the ground, bounce, leave again; he was airborne but didn't dare climb, letting the Breese wallow along in ground effect, just a few feet high. If his engine coughed, he would get wet for sure.

3

It was a pig, a stinking, wallowing pig. Bandfield swore at the ill-mannered Breese monoplane, hoping to shame it into becoming more manageable as the fuel burned off. In exasperation, he stopped trying to fly it, letting it go on its own like a huge, fuel-burdened model airplane. He sat with his legs spread, feet on the floor, hands off the stick. With 450 gallons of fuel sloshing back and forth, the airplane bobbed and weaved, nosing around like a drunken bear, never quite falling off on a wing, never quite stalling, simply lumbering through the air, wobbling from side to side like the cheeks of a fat lady's ass going upstairs. The extra surface area it presented added induced drag that kept the airspeed oscillating between 75 and 85 mph.

At that rate, he'd finish a laughable dead last. He glanced at Hadley Roget's innovation tucked into a panel on the floor. It was a simple T-handle, painted red and safety-wired, connected to four bolts that held the landing gear on. If he removed the safety pin and pulled the handle, the landing gear would fall into the sea—or so Hadley predicted. It meant he'd have to land on the belly when he got to Hawaii, but it might mean that he'd *get* to Hawaii, and faster at that.

Bandy had protested the installation. It added weight and it hadn't been tested. Worse, if only one side released, the gear would bounce in the slipstream until it beat the plane to death.

"Fuck it." He reached down and pulled the T-handle. The left bolts slipped out, then the right followed. The gear gyrated back up to rip along the fuselage side and lodge on the horizontal stabilizer, the wheel gouged into the fuselage fabric. The airplane, now unbalanced and configured not for flight but for death, bucked desperately upward like a harpooned whale.

"Goddammit, Hadley, you and your goddam cockeyed ideas."

Bandfield was pushing forward on the stick, trying to keep the nose from climbing further to a stall and spin that would sling him like trash into the Pacific.

"Think, goddammit, think!" He tried to shield the grossly overweight airplane from further stress. Any maneuver that would shake the gear loose would tear the airplane apart. Sweat popped out on his forehead as he leaned into the stick, managing to hold the nose below the point of stall. He had full power on, and the airplane was trembling, rattling, threatening to go into a head-snapping dive. It quivered, and he brought the throttle back; he felt the landing gear move again, and the nose came down, enough to break the stall and let him advance the throttle again. He had stabilized the stricken airplane in a mushing knife-edge between flying and falling.

He considered turning back, trying to minimize the distance between himself and the shore, but each time he entered a bank the airplane shuddered as if it would destroy itself.

There was another jarring clatter. The nose came down and the gyrations stopped. He watched in gratitude as the airspeed picked up first to 100, then to 105 mph. The gear must finally have broken loose from its near-fatal embrace.

The sequence of events puzzled him until he thought it through. The gear could have weighed only about one hundred pounds, but it represented a lot of drag and surface area. When it lodged in the back, it had upset the center of gravity and added an enormous amount of drag. It was a wonder he hadn't crashed. Once the gear was gone, though, the airplane was cleaner than it had ever been. No wonder it flew better. Right after he throttled Hadley, he'd pat him on the back and tell him what a good job he had done!

Aboard the *Miss Charlotte*
1:30 P.M. PST, August 16, 1927

Bruno Hafner was sweating, moving the controls around the cockpit as if he were stirring a giant bowl of cake batter. Nellie was whining and coughing; she was probably airsick. The fuel-laden *Miss Charlotte*, normally so sweet to handle, was flying nose high at 80 mph, right on the ragged edge of a stall.

He looked down in disgust at Bandfield's Breese monoplane plodding along below, a bright silver cross against the deck of clouds that hid the surface of the sea. "If that *Schweinerei* doesn't start moving, I'm going to leave him."

Hafner was already impatient; he'd flown a great wide circle to bring him back to cruise in Bandfield's blind spot. He knew how to navigate and had a direction finder, but he didn't want to miss the dot that was Hawaii. Murray had told him about Hadley's coup with the Army radios; he planned to take advantage of it and fly above and behind the Breese for most of the trip, cross-checking his own computations with the route of Bandfield's flight. When Hawaii was in sight, he'd simply pour on the gas and pass him, for the Bellanca was at least fifteen miles per hour faster than the Breese.

Something fell away from the tail of Bandfield's airplane, a twisted cross that disappeared into the clouds. The Breese leaped ahead.

Puzzled but grateful, Hafner pushed his throttle forward to maintain station, high and to the rear, letting the airspeed build. The *Miss Charlotte* became docile once again, and Hafner reached back to scratch Nellie's ears through the wire of her cage. He thought briefly that he probably should have left Nellie home with Murray. He was *almost* sure that Murray took good care of her; it was too bad dogs couldn't talk.

Aboard *Miss Duncan's Golden Eagle*
5:30 P.M. PST, August 16, 1927

Millie awoke for the fourth time since they'd left. The trip out to the Coast had been exhausting, and she had gone to parties almost every night. It was incredible now to be on her way, actually en route to Hawaii and to "being someone." Flying wasn't yet the poetry she'd imagined it would be, but at least she wasn't feeling sick.

Scottie Gordon, the navigator, smiled at her, showed her the chart. The Vega was clipping along at 123 mph on a true course of 252 degrees. He leaned over and yelled in her ear: "You slept right through the only ship sighting we've had. About half an hour ago the clouds opened up and there was a Japanese ship down below. I used the binos and it was something like the *Tachibana Maru*."

She glanced at the red X plot marks. "Aren't we a little north of course?"

"We're creeping along the edge of a high-pressure zone; we'll cut back south later."

"How's Jack doing?"

"Happy as a clam. He's already eaten two sandwiches and drunk a cup of coffee."

She sat back in her chair, trying to figure where Bandy was. The Vega was twenty miles an hour faster than the open-cockpit Breese; they'd been gone five hours, so he was about a hundred miles behind them. She tried to imagine how he looked, goggles down, wind blowing his hair wildly as it had on the double-decker buses in New York.

By bending down, she could see forward to the back of Uncle Jack's head. He was so generous. This morning he'd said that he would come in on the factory with Bandy and Roget; with the prize money, it meant that they'd have enough capital to get started.

Aboard the *Miss Charlotte*
7:00 P.M. PST, August 16, 1927

The spectacular setting sun had turned the *Salinas Made* briefly into a brilliant orange ball. Then the plane had lumbered on below, shedding its colors until it disappeared against the flat gray of the undercast. Hafner sighed in relief when the navigation lights of the Breese winked on, two dots, one red, one green, above the endless gray clouds that hid the ocean.

He had sat high above other airplanes on other days. In 1918, Bandfield would have been cold meat, perfectly positioned for a diving attack. Hafner reached forward and cocked imaginary machine guns, waggling his wings. How sweet it would be to drop down and send two lines of bullets through the common little upstart! With all the gas he was carrying, he'd burn like the flaming coffins the Americans called observation planes late in the war. One squirt and they were alight, the flames fanned to white heat by the rush of wind.

It was ironic. During the war he had routinely killed young men he didn't know, with whom he had no quarrel save that they were flying planes marked with roundels instead of crosses. The chaps in the Bristol, for example—he probably had had much in common with them. Below was a vicious little man who had cheated him out of the Orteig Prize. It would be amusing to dive down and frighten Bandfield, but the *Miss Charlotte* was still far too heavy to do anything but fly straight and level. A sudden movement, and the extra Gs would pull the fuel tanks right out through the belly, like an elephant dropping a calf.

He wondered where the others were. He'd seen the *Oklahoma* limping back to the field with black smoke trailing from its engine, obviously out of the race. Winter's Vega was far ahead. He checked his watch.

An hour later, sleep began to steal up on him. He bit his lips and pounded his fist against his thighs, then strained to reach back and pour Nellie a drink of water. He glanced at the diagrams Murray had drawn for him. The Signal Corps had installed a transmitter at Fort Windfield Scott at the Golden Gate, and another on the island of Maui. Each transmitter put out two lobes of signals, a dash-dot for *N* on the right and a dot-dash for *A* on the left. The course line lay where the two signals overlapped to form a continuous tone. It had worked well just out of San Francisco. He turned it on again. There was nothing, total silence. That goddam Murray had warned him that the system wasn't reliable; he was right again.

Edging the window open, he leaned forward to let the rush of air awaken him. The draft blew his charts back over his shoulder, past the tanks to lodge in the rear of the airplane, far out of reach.

"*Donnerwetter!* Now I *have* to stick to Bandfield!" Hafner was suddenly awake and a little ill at ease.

Aboard the *Salinas Made*
9:00 P.M. PST, August 16, 1927

Jesus, how did Slim do it? Bandfield asked himself. He groggily poured himself a cup of coffee. Lindbergh had flown for thirty-three hours and landed at night. He was only a little over eight hours into the flight and was already almost passing out.

Part of it was the night before, of course. He had slept very little, going over every element of the flight, wondering if Hadley was right about the risks. He'd been working long hours, trying to get the airplane ready; now it was catching up with him.

He nodded, sleep dimming his reflexes, requiring a gathering of will for any act. He leaned his head to the edge of the windscreen, letting the rush of air tug at his goggles. He opened his mouth and the rushing wind blew his cheeks wide, drying the saliva so that his lips stuck to his teeth.

His exasperation with Hafner's following him had long since worn off. Hours ago he had been stretching, twisting his neck to get some circulation going, when he saw the unmistakable angular outline of the Bellanca silhouetted against the lighter evening sky. His first reaction was elation at having the loneliness of the Pacific broken; then he realized Hafner was coming along for the ride, letting him do the navigation.

Just like that square-headed prick, he thought. It puzzled him until he sorted out the strategy. Hafner would figure he could loaf along until he got in sight of Hawaii, or until his direction finder picked up the Maui beacon. Then he'd put his nose down, pour the coal to it, and land first.

But Hafner didn't know Bandy had dropped the gear. Now he was at least as fast as the Bellanca, maybe faster. It was still a horserace, and this time Hafner would be the horse's ass.

Aboard *Miss Duncan's Golden Eagle*
10:00 P.M. PST, August 16, 1927

The airplane was incomparably better than anything Jack Winter had ever flown, a real thoroughbred. Gordon had sent a note forward, giving their position and their fuel consumption; they were flying eight miles an hour faster and burning three gallons an hour less fuel than he had planned. He thought about advancing the power a little, to get even more speed, but decided against it. Things were going so well he wouldn't change anything.

The moon had risen twenty minutes earlier, and now the band of low clouds below, soft hillocks of moisture, were bathed in a gorgeous yellow light. He scribbled a note and sent it back to Millie on the little string pulley they'd rigged up.

She read: "In ten years, passengers will be paying $500 to do this, and you are doing it first, free!"

She creased the note and put it in her bag. There was a book in this flight, and she was going to need all the material she could get. She could get ideas from Bandy, too, loafing behind them somewhere—she hoped.

Millie reached over and pulled on the canvas curtain Jack had rigged for her privacy until it closed. It was dark and the engine drowned out any noise, but she still felt uncomfortable using the little hospital bedpan that she had brought on board to relieve herself. She struggled out of her clothes, wondering how she was going to write about this part of the flight in her book.

Aboard the *Salinas Made*
10:03 P.M. PST, August 16, 1927

Bandfield roused himself with a shudder; he'd drifted off to sleep, and wakened to a searing sense of desperation and fear. He moved his flashlight around the cockpit, checking the instruments. Ahead, the exhaust-collector ring glowed cherry red, the staccato flash of the exhaust stacks winking continuously around like a demented sign in Times Square, the mellow blue-and-yellow flames telling him that the engine's fuel/air mixture was correct.

He had drifted up to about 5,500 feet; now he let the airplane glide down toward 5,000, where he leveled off and allowed the airspeed to build to 120 before throttling back. The *Salinas Made* settled down to cruise at 5,000 feet and 108 mph. The airplane was on "the step," flying at an attitude where drag was minimized. He brought the mixture lever back, slowly, listening to the beat of the engine. There was a sudden pop, and he pushed the mixture lever forward slightly until the engine smoothed out.

He was wide-awake and totally depressed. He glanced back to see Hafner's plane still in position above and behind him. He ran another check on the radios, tapping out a request for a position. In quick succession, he got replies from the USS *McDonough* and the S.S. *Manulani*. His Morse-taking capability was rusty, and the *Manulani* had to transmit three times. The last time the radio operator, either careful or sarcastic, transmitted so slowly that it was almost a dot or a dash at a time. Then a third call came from the S.S. *W. S. Miller*, giving him a line that intersected the other two in a tiny triangle, right on course. With a sigh of relief, he put the sextant back in its case; no sense in even bothering with it.

The leaden weight of depression tugged at his eyelids. He yawned constantly, as his psychology went through a demanding game with his physiology. When he grew irrepressibly sleepy, he would take his hands off the controls. The plane would drift off course and a jolt of adrenaline would trigger him awake. But it was a process of diminishing returns. He had no idea what his adrenaline reserves were, but they were much reduced, and the flight was only half finished. He toyed with the idea of dropping down below the cloud deck to fly along the surface of the sea, to try to get some exhilaration from chasing waves. He didn't know the height of the cloud base, and decided against it.

The hours passed into an opaque tunnel of boredom. The instrument panel did tricks, growing larger and larger in his vision until his eyes seemed to be resting on the altimeter, then growing smaller and smaller until he felt he needed a telescope to see it. Pain didn't help. He slapped his face and bit his lips, chewed the inside of his mouth. The pain registered at a very low level, not intruding on the overpowering desire to sleep.

He made hourly course corrections, tracing that invisible great-circle line over the globe that was the shortest distance to Hawaii. He was only five thousand feet up in the ocean of air; beneath, the ocean of water went down what—ten thousand feet, twenty thousand? He wished Millie were with him; she'd know. He'd ask her when they got to Hawaii.

He ran a routine fuel check and snapped fully awake, terror gouging his adrenal glands. He had not yet transferred any from the rear main tank, but the gauge read half-empty. The gear must have punched a hole in it when it pulled free. The big question was where the hole was. If it was in the bottom of the tank, he was lost. He'd never make it to Hawaii or back to California. Even if the leak was halfway up and he didn't lose any more, all his reserves were gone. He picked up the charts and rechecked his navigation. There was no margin to spare.

In the past, he had always grown more awake flying when night fell, the sense of quiet beauty summoning concentration for the task. Now, with the fuel worries, the old habit was re-inforced, and he felt as if he'd never sleep again. Yet there was nothing to do except plod ahead, and as usual with long flights, he drifted into erotic daydreams, aroused by his thoughts of Millie. He was glad they were waiting until they were married to make love. It was old-fashioned, but proper, and his love for her was truly proper. He wondered what kind of a guy the navigator, Gordon, was, if he would try to flirt with her. It wouldn't do him any good, and Millie would never tell even if he did, because she wouldn't want to create a problem. He'd already gotten a reputation as a hothead by hitting Hafner.

Bandfield's chemistry stabilized, and he began to analyze his fuel situation. He drank some of the tepid water in the other flask. It tasted brackishly of coffee. Hadley must not have rinsed it well when he filled it. He took out one of the drying ham-and-cheese sandwiches. When he'd finished, he reached into his pocket for a Hershey bar.

The chocolate reinforced his irrational contentment. Alone, over a truly trackless ocean, with fuel and position indeterminate, he nonetheless felt like a king, for he was flying, and that itself was enough. The higher, the farther, the faster you went always made it better, for there was the supreme sense that you were alone in a place no other man could be. He checked the rear tank fuel again; it seemed to have stabilized. Maybe things were going to be all right. Even Hafner's tailing along behind him was no longer an affront.

Bandy was surprised at the charity of his thoughts, guessing it was the intoxicating euphoria of flight, the relief that the leak was apparently stopped. The layer of clouds below now seemed higher. An idea began to form. He'd just play a little joke on Hafner, to see how he liked it.

He reached down and felt along the instrument panel till he found the switch for the navigation lights. He turned them off, then pulled the throttle back, letting the Breese nose down toward the clouds. He'd drop through to five hundred feet; if he wasn't in the clear, he'd climb back up. If he was, he'd scoot along beneath the clouds, leaving Hafner on his own. It would do him good, make a navigator of him.

The clouds enveloped him like a wet gray sweatsock. He wondered what the base was and whether he'd break out at all. Hadley had told him a long shaggy-dog story about a girl whose legs had run all the way to the ground—maybe the clouds were like that, running all the way to the water.

Aboard the *Miss Charlotte*
2:30 A.M. PST, August 17, 1927

Hafner checked his watch again, and scanned the horizon ahead. When he glanced down, the Breese was gone.

Anxiety clutched him, and he rocked the Bellanca into a 360-degree turn, thinking he might have overflown Bandfield. There was nothing, just the pale yellow moonlit surfaces of the clouds.

He resumed his course of 240 degrees magnetic, fiddled with the direction finder. It was dead.

Ach, well, he thought. I've done dead reckoning before. I'll just fly out the time and the distance and let down. If I can't find the islands, I'll find a ship. If I can't find a ship, I'll land this bloody bastard and sail it to Hawaii.

Hafner knew that he had courage to spare when it came to things he could control. The problem was that he wasn't sure he could control the navigation problem, and a faint rinse of sour-tasting fear touched the back of his throat. Now he wished he hadn't brought Nellie along.

Aboard the *Salinas Made*
4:30 A.M. PST, August 17, 1927

The cloud cover combined with the night to turn the five hundred feet of clear air over the sea into a gelid black mass, a palpable solid through which he passed without disturbance. Bandfield had tried to let down to wave-chase the surface of the sea, but there was no light at all, no way to avoid simply flying into the ocean. He climbed to four hundred feet, flying on instruments.

It was enjoyable at first, the challenge of glancing quickly from the altimeter to the airspeed indicator to the compass to the turn-and-bank needle and then back again, keeping him awake. He soon tired of it, and climbed back up to two thousand feet, well within the clouds. Without any turbulence, without any icing, it was as easy to fly in the clouds as below them; he wanted to wait a bit, to get a little farther from Hafner before he popped up again.

Sleep nibbled again at his consciousness the way coffee spreads through a sugar cube, seeping up by capillary action, soaking, softening, until the entire cube crumbles. He began to doze, fighting it by closing first one eye then the other, then closing them both and counting to ten, before opening them wide. Once, at the count of eight, the cube crumbled and he fell asleep.

The whistle awakened him. He started, shedding sleep like confetti. The plane was spinning nose-down into the clouds. The instruments were in wild disarray, the turn needle tucked to the right, the ball skidding to the left. Desperately off balance, the bitter coffee bile rising in his mouth, he tried to make sense of the maverick instrument pointers. The airspeed was constant at seventy miles per hour, the unwinding altimeter screaming his spin toward the sea.

His throat muscles contracted in fear; altimeters lagged, so he didn't know how high he was above the beckoning Pacific. In a single motion, he brought the throttle back to idle, booted left rudder, and pushed the stick forward slightly. The ball and needle came together and he felt the controls bite the air. He shoved the throttle forward, hoping that the carburetor had not iced up, and pulled back strongly on the stick.

The murky gray parted and he was peering down into a polished black saucer that reached up to merge on all sides with the clouds. He tugged harder on the stick, the G forces pushing him to his seat; he could feel the seat braces bend, hoped that he had welded them of strong enough material. He knew he couldn't believe his senses, but the black mass seemed to be shifting bit by bit from straight below to straight ahead and the *Salinas Made* bottomed out, its belly just above the slashing waves, the priceless Whirlwind engine surging with power as if nothing had happened.

A black web of fear set him shivering, teeth chattering uncontrollably, hands thrumming on the controls. The airplane quivered in concert as the instruments came back into range and the sloshing fuel began to quiet.

He settled down, checking the airplane over very carefully, then began a long instrument climb back to altitude. He tried to compute how far he'd been from death. One hundredth of a second, no more. If he hadn't dropped the gear early in the flight, it would have caught the wave tops and slammed him into the sea. As it was, a single instant more and there would have been nothing left but debris and an oil slick on the surface of the Pacific.

He climbed slowly until he broke through the cloud layer, now down to five thousand feet. The moon beamed like a Hollywood searchlight, and he flipped on his navigation lights, searching the sky for Hafner's Bellanca. Having even an enemy in view would be comforting after the sickening spin. Hafner was nowhere in sight.

As his nerves steadied, Bandfield tried the radio again for another position fix, squinting to get the tiny white lines and numbers of the frequency dials properly aligned. It was dead, probably displaced and wires disconnected during the wild spin. He wondered if the compass was still working right. It had been spinning like a top, and had just settled down when he'd turned to a 235-degree heading. He'd have to go the rest of the way on dead reckoning, a term too appropriate for the task, given that he was lost, short on fuel, and totally without communications.

The blessed sun rose right on time, 6:34 A.M., spreading the clouds first with a shimmering pink, then orange, then bursting through to turn the sky bright blue. He ate another sandwich and drank some water, waiting for the clock to run out, for Mauna Loa to poke its sweet smoking head up through the clouds.

A sense of utter loneliness came over him. Hafner had not reappeared, and he had seen no other living thing, ship, plane, or bird. Maybe he was dead, down in the sea, and this was all some sort of dream. He'd long since let the noise of the engine and propeller grind into an anonymous white silence. He brought his hand to his mouth and bit down hard, letting the pain and the tooth marks prove him to be alive.

Aboard the *Miss Charlotte*
8:00 A.M. PST, August 17, 1927

The dawn had been welcome for Hafner, too. He took a carefully measured sip of cognac from the flask he kept in his navigation case, then washed it down with a pint of water. He picked through the food Murray had prepared, settled on a waxed-paper-wrapped piece of chicken.

He passed half back to Nellie and sat munching, aware of how much better the sunlight made it. Last night he'd gone through tremendous strain, fighting back the fears of a lifetime that had somehow squeezed into the cramped cockpit of the Bellanca. He had never once been sleepy; instead, his strength was drained by the constant dry aching fatigue of fear, the numbing realization that Bandfield had deserted him in the twin oceans of air and sea, and that there was no recourse, no alternative available to him. The course he'd chosen was purely guesswork, a process of elimination that factored in all the information he had, most of which was many hours old.

Periodically, he would rack the Bellanca, lighter and more spirited now that fuel had burned off, into a tight turn, and he'd scan both the sea and the sky, hoping to see an airplane or to find a break in the undercast that would reveal a ship or even a flock of birds, anything to give him a hint of his direction. Each time there was nothing, and each time the clutching spasm of fear would draw him a little more tightly together, his scrotum contracting, his stomach twisting.

It bothered him most because the danger was not proximate; it would be hours before the real life-or-death choices would be put to him. Often in the past, in combat, in acrobatics, he had been only seconds from death, not caring because he held the answer in his hands and feet, able to move the controls, fire the guns, exert control over the situation. Now the only control he had was negative; he could end it all in a plunging dive to the sea, something he knew he'd never do. Or he could wait, and hope that his course was correct, that a ship would appear.

He vacillated between hoping that Bandfield had crashed and that he would suddenly pop up somewhere, on course to Hawaii. When—if—they met again, Hafner swore to kill him, face to face, man to man.

Aboard the *Salinas Made*
1:30 P.M. PST, August 17, 1927

The strain of *needing* to see the islands had wakened him thoroughly. Millie and Jack would be on the ground in Hawaii by now, surrounded by hula girls and reporters, accepting the first-prize money. A pang of conscience went through him as he wondered if he had left Hafner to die; he dismissed it. The fuel check was easy now that he was down to the main tanks. Either he found land in the next two and a half hours, or he would be sailing the worst yacht in the Pacific.

There was something on the horizon—two gentle smudges, pressing through the clouds as a young girl's breasts bud through a summer frock. He sighed in relief at the anticlimax. All he had to do was steer to them, Mauna Loa and Mauna Kea, then turn north and west again past the shores of Maui and Molokai and on into Oahu. He pulled a map from the satchel on the floor, and located the Army base at Wheeler Field. It was almost at the center of the western end of the island.

He ran a fuel check. It would be close, but he'd make it. The Wright Whirlwind and the ancient Breese airframe suddenly seemed to glow with charm; they were bringing him to Oahu, to Millie, and to $10,000. Not bad for a lash-up that Hadley had advised him not to fly. He was going to beat the navigation problem *and* the fuel problem. He was going to live!

The clouds were breaking up, and he could see the surf curling on the shores of Molokai, the island of lepers and Father Damien, as he went by. He turned in toward Oahu and Wheeler Field at one thousand feet, letting down slowly, looking for other airplanes. When he crossed over the coastline the airplane seemed to take on a palpable solidity, as if the ground below had stiffened it in all the right places. Except for an Army training plane, wings bright yellow, off to his left, he had the sky to himself. Below, the green beauty of Oahu spilled out before him, ten times as attractive as he had imagined, more inviting than any land he'd ever seen.

He picked up the Waianae mountains that backed Wheeler Field, then saw the typical Army layout of hangars and post. He advanced the mixture and dropped down, determined to buzz the field and see Millie wave to him before he tried the wheelless belly landing. The Army would see what he was going to do and have the meat wagons ready.

He checked the field. A flight of three Curtiss Falcons was taxiing out, and two Boeing PW-9 fighters had appeared from nowhere, bobbing up alongside. The pilot in the closest Boeing pulled in, grinning and holding up a single finger. He was first! Where was Millie? My God, where was Millie?

Breathing hard, heart pounding, Bandfield's hands trembled as he entered the pattern, slowing the Breese down to 95 mph, then 80, searching the flight line all the while. The yellow Vega would have stuck out; it wasn't there. Maybe they had landed on another island.

He forgot about the jettisoned landing gear, coming down to level off as if the wheels were below him. He stalled and dropped with a shudder to the green grass surface. The impact forced the struts up through the wings, and the Breese slithered around in a circle as he cut the switches. He pulled himself up from the cockpit, feeling totally foolish, trying to get away from it before it exploded. Then the cheering crowds arrived in trucks, cars, and buses.

A group of pilots grabbed him and carried him to a beautiful young Hawaiian girl who heaped a garland of leis around his neck and almost kissed him on each cheek. "Where's the Vega? Have you heard anything from Winter?"

A big major introduced himself. "I'm Major Bill Grant. Congratulations—you're the first one we've seen. The last report we had on anyone was the message you got from the *W. S. Miller*. How much time should we give them before we put out a search?"

The pilots crowded around, staring at him, wondering if he was too tired to realize he'd won, that the $25,000 was his.

Bandfield yelled, "Start now, goddammit! The Vega was much faster than my airplane. They're either down, or they've missed the island. Get out every goddam thing you've got and get it in the air."

The major walked away, irritated with this smart-ass civilian who'd humiliated him in front of his men. James Dole, short, self-important, wearing a white snap-brim hat, came smiling up with the check in his hand.

"Mr. Bandfield, it's my honor . . ."

Bandfield ignored him, turning to run and grab the major by the arm.

"Listen, I'm sorry, I'm crazy with fear. My girl's on that airplane. Please don't get mad. Just get me an airplane to go after her."

Grant looked at him. "Take it easy, Mr. Bandfield. I'll go in and notify the Navy. We'll put up a full sea and air search. You'd better get some rest."

Bandfield staggered back with the group of pilots, subdued now. Hawaii revolved around him, new odors, bird calls, flowers, and he was unaware of it all. He had only one thought, that of a yellow Vega, circling, looking for those gray dots that he had found. It must still be flying.

Wheeler Field, Hawaii
4:00 P.M., August 17, 1927

Bandfield was stretched out in the flight surgeon's office, the painfully austere white walls and cane furniture somehow offset by some plants with absolutely obscene waxy red flowers. He was totally bushed, the hard work and twenty-six-hour flight providing an easy target for the two ounces of Old Grand-dad, its label clearly marked "For Medicinal Purposes Only."

Major Grant came into the room.

"We've had a radio report from Oakland, Mr. Bandfield. Three of the airplanes returned to Oakland. Three did not, including yours. They have no word on either Winter's Vega or Hafner's Bellanca."

Bandfield followed his characteristic practice of embracing guilt, telling himself that if he hadn't abandoned Hafner, Millie would have been all right. He went through the whole routine, blaming himself, then telling himself that he wasn't so important that God would hurt Millie to punish him, then retreating into the wallow of guilt again.

A crackling roar sounded over the flight line. Tired as he was, he recognized it as a Liberty engine, instead of the Wright Whirlwind he was praying for. He got up and walked to the window as the phone rang.

A yellow-winged Loening amphibian, wheels extended, made a precise pattern and landed into the wind. He saw it turn around at the far end of the field, to taxi back to the Wheeler operations building.

Grant hung up the phone and turned to him, smiling. "It's one of the rescue ships, Bandy. Looks like they've got somebody."

They raced out to the ambulance and sped, siren roaring, down streets bordered by flowering trees and redolent with plumeria perfume. Bandfield sat with his eyes closed, praying that it was Millie. The Loening was big enough to carry Winter and Gordon too.

They pulled up at the operations building just as the Loening taxied in and shut down. The pilot clambered out of the front cockpit and slid back along the wing as Bandfield ran up and grabbed a strut. He thrust his foot on the little steel steps and leaped up to peer in the cockpit—at Bruno Hafner, wet and very angry, a bedraggled Nellie clutched in his lap.

Oakland Municipal Airport
10:00 A.M. PST, August 18, 1927

The atmosphere in the *Post Enquirer* radio shack was funereal, the silence broken only when the radio crackled to life, people drifting in and out, talking in whispers. The tiny room was fouled in a distinctive fog of stale smoke, spilled coffee, and unwashed bodies. Hadley Roget recoiled when he stuck his head in the door.

"Dolan, I'm surprised the air in here doesn't short the radio gear out. You can cut the smoke with a knife."

Ray Dolan, obviously under severe strain, nodded abruptly and looked away. After Bandfield had landed and Hafner had been rescued, there had been absolute silence.

By midafternoon, the crowds had increased until a respiratory rotation system started, people outside rushing in to fill the place of those who staggered out to breathe.

The jubilation that had followed Bandy's landing had changed into a morbid gloom. Dolan, chairman of the race committee, was white, his hands shaking, leaping at every vagrant buzz of the radio. He had told Hadley earlier that he felt like a murderer, that Dole was a murderer. The relatives, ground crews, and hangers-on of the missing aviators forged into the radio shack, enduring the foul air and eventually displacing almost everyone else as the minutes lengthened into hours.

A monumental rescue effort was underway. The *Golden Eagle* was out of fuel, down somewhere in the endless Pacific. Search missions were to be flown from both California and Hawaii. The Navy was already searching, diverting the destroyers that had been stationed en route and deploying every available patrol plane.

The field pulsed with the false reassurances that attend futile efforts. As at the election-night headquarters of a losing politician, every morsel of positive news was greeted with enthusiasm, while reality was shrugged off. A wild surge of elation greeted the news that red flares had been seen streaking from Mauna Loa, but nothing developed from the rumor.

The hugeness of the task was not discussed. All the airplanes in the world searching would not have been enough, for there was no way of knowing if the Vega had crashed just beyond the Farallons, just before Hawaii, or anywhere in the Pacific between or beyond. Yet the search had to be made for the sake of the searchers, if not for the lost. A glimmer of hope was held out that the Vega would be able to float indefinitely, with its empty tanks and flotation bags. There were continual mutual assurances that Winter had carried a rubber life raft. Millie Duncan could be sitting in a raft; they must search for her.

* * *

Every plane on the field was made available for the rescue effort. Dolan became the organizer, allocating areas to search and times to fly. Bill Erwin and Al Eichwaldt, the fabric of the *Dallas Spirit* repaired, were off at 2:15 P.M. The two were old professionals, and Jimmie Irving had donated the two-way radio set from his wrecked aircraft. It somehow made everything seem safer. Eichwaldt began sending reports one after another. The first came only five minutes after takeoff: "2:20. Going strong. We are passing the docks and will see the lightship soon. We are carrying the tail high at 1,700 feet and making close to 100 speed. Will call again passing the lightship."

There were a spate of trivial messages as Eichwaldt familiarized himself with the equipment, making the typical amateur's mistake of sending unnecessary words. Hadley ached to go outside and draw a breath, but was riveted to the spot, watching the operator record the messages.

Later the room rippled with a brief flurry of excitement when a message came in from Wheeler Field. The crowd waited breathlessly as the Morse code was copied, then groaned in resentment. The message read simply: "Race committee in Hawaii advises Hafner to receive second prize."

Messages from the *Dallas Spirit* crackled through the gloom. "2:40. From now on I will double up on my messages so you can copy me better as I know my sending is none too good. Tell Jimmie the radio set is working fine. Send my love to Ma."

"2:50. We are flying at 300 feet and under the fog with a visibility of 30 miles and are passing the Farallons now."

The crowd in the radio shack looked concerned; the classic way to an accident was to attempt to fly under the weather.

Hadley asked, "What kind of an instrument pilot is Erwin?"

"He's okay. He passed the flight check, didn't he?"

Dolan's voice was high, strained, ready to crack. "We didn't check them for instrument flying."

Hadley commented, "He might be a little rusty, but he'll be fine. He shot down eight Germans; a little fog isn't going to bother him."

More messages came through, none vital.

"3:49. The ceiling is now 700 feet. We are flying at 500. We have not seen anything at all of other planes or anything since the Farallons and all is okay except Bill just sneezed. We are keeping a sharp lookout for the *Golden Eagle*."

Hadley could visualize the tension on board Erwin's airplane. Eichwaldt was covering his own fear with rough humor. When it grew darker, their danger would become as great as that which had claimed the others. Whenever there was a silence, the crowd in the radio shack tensed. Roget felt the whole effort was pointless, that there wasn't a chance in a billion of finding the *Golden Eagle* in the present weather conditions.

"4:20. We just passed close to a rain squall. The air was very bumpy. Visibility is clear ahead."

Other messages indicated ships they had sighted. The weather had apparently improved. People passed in and out of the radio shack as tension curled the air, palpable with blue-gray smoke. The messages became increasingly grim as time passed.

"8:00. It is beginning to get dark."

At 8:20 P.M. the radio operator whistled. Erwin's radio was powered by a wind-driven generator, and the cycles of the transmissions varied with the airspeed. The radio operator could tell from the rise and fall of the cycles on his meter that the *Dallas Spirit* had stalled and spun. The white needle on the gauge was a mute mechanical witness to the emotional drama in the Swallow.

"8:51. Belay that. We were in a spin but came out of it okay. We sure were scared. It sure was a close call. The lights on the instrument panel went out and it was so dark Bill could not see the wings."

The pilots in the room shot worried glances at each other. A spin in the dark over the ocean was usually fatal. The crew of the *Dallas Spirit* had been lucky.

Roget closed his eyes and imagined himself in the cockpit, feeling what Erwin was going through as his senses told him one thing and his instruments another. Even an experienced instrument pilot was vulnerable to the sensations of vertigo, to believe what one's ears and eyes reported instead of the random pointing of the tiny dials on the instrument panel. There was no such thing as seat-of-the-pants flying. If you didn't have instruments, or didn't know how to use them, and got in clouds, you would inevitably stall and spin.

Roget wondered if they had working flashlights. Despite all the Eveready ads, flashlights were something you carried around until the battery went dead and you needed it. Two people's lives ultimately depended upon the dim glimmer of the instrument lights. Erwin and Eichwaldt were both probably shivering with fear. It would be worse for Erwin, for he would know precisely the danger, while Eichwaldt would die still in the hope that Erwin would master the situation. Hadley writhed in sympathy.

The subdued murmur within the shack ceased when the radio clattered. There was another transmission.

"9:02. We are in a . . . SOS."

Then there was silence; the frequency meter showed a peak, and then fell to nothing as the *Dallas Spirit* finally crashed into the sea, the lapsed pointer a final malevolent confirmation of two deaths.

There was a total silence in the room. Then Roget said, "Now we've got two more to look for. And maybe nobody to find."

PART TWO

THE STAKES GO UP

4

The thin heat of the early-morning sun began to battle with the crisp white frost feathering the red-tile roof of the mission-style terminal. Bandfield buttoned his old leather jacket, grown tighter in the last two years, and slumped against the wall of an arch of the covered walkway. As always, he was quite early for the meeting. He spent his time admiring the new airport.

Aviation had come a long way in the last decade, from flying out of cow pastures to this beautiful airfield, with its concrete runway and long line of Maddux Airlines hangars filled with Ford Tri-motors. Across the runway were the curious half-dome hangars where they were building the crazy-looking Slate all-metal dirigible. He had seen it once, an enormous tin ship that looked like an accordion-pleated egg, with some nutty turbine system for power. Good luck, he thought. It was tough enough to get a normal-looking aircraft to fly, much less a "revolutionary" one.

God knew Roget Aircraft could use some luck after struggling almost through another year. No one yet knew what the stock-market crash the month before meant, but it had been a fantastic year for aviation. Some weird-looking Russian bomber had flown from Moscow to New York. Two Brits had flown nonstop from England to India. Jimmy Doolittle flew a complete flight, takeoff to landing, on instruments. The *Graf Zeppelin*, the good old-fashioned kind of quick-burning dirigible, built of aluminum and fabric and filled with hydrogen, had flown around the world.

Even poor old maligned Richard Byrd had redeemed himself for his humiliating flight in the *America* by being the first to fly over the South Pole. Bandfield had ached for him in 1927, when Byrd had finally flown the Atlantic, only to crash in the sea off the coast of France. At least he had broken with Tony Fokker, and flown a Ford Tri-motor over the South Pole. Balchen, who could get along with anybody, even Byrd, had been his pilot.

Earlier, Bandy had parked his waxed and gleaming Roget Rocket, the fifth—and last—to be built, next to a line of open-cockpit biplanes. The first *Roget Rocket* had burned, but three of its namesakes were earning their keep flying from New Orleans to Atlanta for Southern Airlines. It wasn't much to show for almost three years of sweat and strain. Yet tight as things were, he was still sometimes glad that Roget Aircraft had stayed small, and hadn't yet made it into the big time. Lockheed had sold one Vega after another, but was then absorbed by Detroit Aircraft, which intended to become the General Motors of the air. The stock-market crash had ended those dreams, and now Lockheed was in trouble, like everybody else.

Ten thousand dollars. I won't take a cent less than ten thousand for it, he thought. He knew that he would, though, that he would grab $5,000 if it was offered, anything to keep Roget Aircraft alive for another few months.

That's what the meeting was about. By pure chance, two of the men he admired most in aviation, Wiley Post and Slim Lindbergh, were together in California, attending a meeting on some new Civil Aeronautics Association rulings. He had asked them to look at the latest version of the Rocket, and they had agreed to meet him in Glendale. Lindbergh was of course by far the most famous, but Bandfield thought that the one-eyed Wiley Post was going to be one of the truly great pilots of the next decade. Both men needed new airplanes, and he had been told that Post needed a fast cabin monoplane with a good range, and was leaning toward the Vega. Lindbergh had said only that he wanted something in which he could fly with his new wife as copilot.

Bandfield thought he could meet Post's needs easily. The Rocket was a better airplane than the Vega, although it didn't have its reputation. It might boil down to price, and he wasn't sure what the Lockheed people would do. They might be as desperate as he was.

And it depended a lot on what Post wanted to use the airplane for. Aviation was still cursed with people wanting to set meaningless records, dropping like rocks into the Atlantic or the Pacific, causing expensive searches, but rarely being found. The whole business grated on him. Each time he read of an attempt, he thought of Millie. Since she had gone, more than a dozen had followed her into the oceanic void. They were lost without hope or purpose, and far from helping aviation, they harmed it.

Lindbergh's requirement would be different. He was working with Pan American, testing flying boats. He had already set the most important record ever made, the Paris flight. And now he was aviation's statesman-engineer, always seeking progress, but never at the expense of safety.

The only problem was that Lindbergh might want more than Roget Aircraft could deliver. Bandfield wondered how much of Lindy's interest stemmed from their old friendship. They had not met since the days on Long Island, but they had corresponded every few months, and Lindbergh was always supportive.

The rest of the field was still deserted, quiet in the sun, when a deep-blue Franklin Airman convertible sedan rolled up; Lindbergh was alone in a car the company had named for him.

"Hello, Bandy. Burned up any more airplanes?"

His eyes twinkled and he grinned the shy, lopsided grin of old, but he was different. There was a wary presence in his manner, and he repeatedly looked over his shoulder, as if he were being followed—or hunted.

"Wiley Post isn't coming. He sends his regrets."

Lindbergh checked the terminal and the parking lot, scanning for reporters or just fans.

"His backers heard you were against selling airplanes for record flights, and that's what he wants it for, a trip around the world. Is he right?"

"Yeah, Slim. After the fiasco in Oakland, when all the airplanes were lost, I made up my mind we wouldn't sell airplanes just for setting records. We want to sell airplanes that make money doing a job, carrying passengers or freight, not just jumping from A to B. That doesn't prove anything, and it costs too many lives."

Lindbergh's eyes were serious. "You may be right, Bandy, but you're premature. I don't know any airplane, including yours, that can make money flying people around. Southern Airlines is going bust, even though your Rockets are doing a good job. I think it will be a few years before it can happen.''

Bandfield's heart sank. ''Maybe not on airlines, but they pay their way hauling executives and troubleshooters around. I was hoping Post wanted the airplane for the oil company he works for.''

''Yeah, but what's the market for that? In the United States, maybe twenty or thirty airplanes, worldwide another ten or so. If that's all there is, if that's all there's going to be, you and I are in the wrong business.''

Bandfield shrugged. He was beginning to think that himself.

''Could we go out to your airplane to talk? I don't want anybody to see us, or I'll spend the rest of the day shaking hands and signing autographs.''

Walking quickly to the Rocket, Bandfield asked, ''How's the old married man, Slim?''

''Great, Bandy, I want you to meet Mrs. Lindbergh first chance we get. How about yourself?''

The words ''Mrs. Lindbergh'' puzzled Bandy for a moment; he thought Slim was talking about his mother. Lindbergh interpreted his expression incorrectly, and thought he'd made a gaffe. He remembered when Bandfield had met Millie Duncan, and had heard that he was still carrying a torch for her.

''No, I guess I'm a born bachelor, Slim. Or should I call you Colonel now?''

''Slim's just fine. I sure never thought I'd make colonel, though. Neither did anybody else.''

Lindbergh walked around the Rocket, then climbed inside.

''Just like old times at Roosevelt Field, eh?''

Bandfield let Lindbergh get his long legs sorted out behind the control column and settled himself in the left seat.

''Sure, but we've improved the airplane a lot—a four-hundred-and-fifty-horsepower Wasp, wheel brakes, radios, the works.''

Lindbergh pulled a map torn from a Rand McNally atlas out of his pocket and spread it on the throttle quadrant between them. ''Bandy, I want a special kind of airplane, one in which Mrs. Lindbergh and I can fly some long-distance survey flights. It's got to be able to use wheels and floats interchangeably, and be simple enough to fly for her to feel comfortable in it. Should have a cruise speed of about one-fifty and a range close to a thousand miles.''

''We could put floats on the Rocket easy enough, Slim.''

"I'm sure you could, but that's not what I want. I need a new airplane, something that breaks new ground. A low-wing monoplane, if possible, one that looks modern." He paused. "One thing I've learned from these darn reporters is that looks are important. I've got to have an airplane that looks new and fast. Of course, it has to be fast too, but a fast new airplane is even better than a faster old one. Get me?"

Bandfield nodded his head in understanding.

"And I want it soon. I'm talking to Lockheed, and they've shown me some preliminary drawings of a low-wing Vega. It looks pretty good, but I wanted to talk to you, too."

"Let me think about it, Slim. I'll be honest with you—we're strapped for money. We couldn't do anything on spec. We'd have to have cash in advance, and I'm not sure how you feel about that."

Lindbergh bobbed his head in an authoritative manner. It was a new gesture, reflecting his new status in life.

"Believe it or not, Bandy, for the first time in my life, money is no problem. But time is. I need to know in the next two weeks what you can do, earlier if possible."

"I'll let you know in a week."

They walked back to the car. "Great news about Byrd and the South Pole, isn't it?"

"Yeah. And how is my old buddy Hafner doing?"

Lindbergh laughed. "He's doing all right, Bandy. You know he made a lot of money in the stock market. I hear he's going to Europe pretty soon to try to sell airplanes over there. And his stepdaughter's getting married to a French war ace. I met her once. She looks just like her mother."

"Well, if she does, that's pretty good. So long, Slim."

Bandfield watched the Franklin depart, its air-cooled engine rumbling as smoothly as Lindbergh's own life. What a difference that thirty-three hours to Paris had made for him—from buck-ass mail pilot to international hero in a little over a day.

He knew that wasn't fair, that the flight had been the easiest part. Getting the backing, building the airplane, having the brains to take off at the right time—that's what had made Lindbergh. But to the public, the thirty-three hours was what counted.

It had taken less than twenty minutes for the sun to burn away the frost on the tiled roof, and for two possible sales to dwindle into nothing. There was no way he and Hadley could come up with an airplane with the performance Lindbergh wanted and test it adequately in the time frame Slim was talking about.

He could see the headline that would finish them off once and for all—"Lucky Lindbergh Crashes in Roget Airplane." Shrugging, he walked toward the Rocket for the trip back to Salinas.

Enroute to Orleans, France/December 15, 1930

Patty edged her way back out of her mother's first-class compartment, a smile fixed on her face. She steadied her hand on the well-worn brass rail in the corridor and tried to calm her stomach. She must be pregnant! Her period was a month overdue, and for the last three mornings she had been nauseated.

She managed to get back to her compartment and sat down, closing her eyes to the beautiful French countryside flashing past, a confection of villages, canals, fields, and herds.

On the other hand, a week in Paris with her mother and Bruno was surely enough to make anyone ill. She shuddered at the thought of the week to come. She knew that the two were hot-blooded, but wasn't prepared for the aphrodiasiac effect that Paris had on them. She'd scarcely been able to get her mother out to go shopping. The woman was over forty years old and apparently had the instincts of a feral rabbit. And she wasn't at all sure that there wasn't something going on with her stepfather's colleague, Dusty Rhoades, as well. Just what a girl needs for her wedding, she thought, a nymphomaniacal mother.

Still, she smiled to herself as she closed her eyes. Perhaps it explained her own hot blood. Stephan's ardor was already waning compared to hers; he joked about it, but it wasn't really funny to him. She was sure that was why they were here at all, why there was going to be a marriage at Stephan's benign insistence. He wanted to pin her down, secure her in marriage before someone else came along.

The train curved around a bend and went dark as it flashed through a tunnel. The rhythm of the rails changed as they passed over a trestle, and the new meter caused her stomach to leap in time. She put her handkerchief to her mouth and looked around for some sort of receptacle. The moment passed and she sank back.

She loved Stephan, and loved making love to him, but didn't feel that marriage was essential, not yet. At least not until she thought she was pregnant. Now it might be necessary after all. If there was some strange little lump inside her, cells multiplying like a machine gun, it was time to get married.

The ordeal of Paris was behind her. At least she hadn't gone with them when Bruno insisted on driving up to Douai, where he'd fought a good portion of his war with the Richthofen circus. From what Charlotte had said, the Frenchman whose chateau they'd occupied had been anything but pleased when Hafner bounded up the steps and knocked on the door to "present his compliments."

The ordeal of Orléans was ahead. Stephan had been there a week already, trying to smooth his mother's feathers, ruffled at the suddenness of the wedding. The Dompniers had always hoped that Stephan's "infatuation"—as they inevitably termed it—would pass, and he'd marry someone sensible whom they had selected for him. They were appalled that he was marrying an American, and scarcely mollified because she had taken religious instruction. Madame Dompnier had insisted on a wedding at home, in their own chapel. On the surface it sounded tender and familial; Stephan's halting explanations inadvertently revealed that it was instead intended to limit the number of people attending and thus the shame. Ordinarily a Dompnier wedding took place in the Cathedral of Sainte-Croix.

It bothered Patty only to the degree that it bothered Stephan. Anyway, by Friday night it would be over, and they would be off on a legitimate honeymoon. And if there was a baby nestled in her belly, he or she would be legitimate too.

Stephan had been ecstatic when she dropped the hint about the baby, much to her relief. Apparently he regarded it as his hole card for his family; once a grandchild was on the way, all the reservations would tumble. She wondered if Stephan was sincere about his desire for a child, how confirmation of the news would affect him. She would tell him as soon as she arrived, so that there would be time to call the whole thing off if he felt differently. If he did, she'd go to Sweden and get an abortion.

Out of the question, she thought. She'd just hole up with Charlotte and Bruno on Long Island, have the baby, and raise it. There'd be no finger-pointing from Charlotte.

She fell asleep, her stomach somewhat settled, her emotions not at all.

Orléans, France/December 15, 1930

Stephan lay in the enormous bed in the room of his childhood, the windows open to the courtyard below. How quickly everyone cast off his adult life and resumed his place in the family hierarchy! He had been home for no more than twenty minutes when his sister Monique had started the usual argument, and, as she always had done, flown to her room in tears.

Poor Monique. No matter how she blamed him for her unmarried state, he knew different. Monique was now, this very month, thirty-two. She had been sixteen in 1914, in a fervor of blooming adolescence and patriotism, when she had given herself to an endless series of soldier lovers. By the time the war was over, she was a legend of the camps, a true angel of mercy, and her chances of marrying anyone but a foreigner were gone forever. He knew that she had not changed her ways materially, that she was always going away to "visit friends." He felt sorry for her, not for reasons of morality, but because she was so desperately unhappy with herself. She was still beautiful, but what would she do when she was not?

On this visit, as always, she had upbraided him for leaving home, deserting her, running off to enjoy himself flying while she had to care for their parents.

Monique was as slender as Stephan but slightly taller, an unfair distribution of family traits that had once disturbed him. He had looked at her closely. She seemed destined to fade into the same worn veil of the past as had their mother. He noted with a brotherly tenderness that her breasts, once so pert, now drooped in resignation, as if they sensed they had more than fulfilled one part of their function, enticement, but were condemned never to fulfill the more important task of providing nourishment.

Her voice was indeed their mother's, sharp as a flint. "We need a man to run this place. Look at your father—he is dying on his feet. And Maman has simply given up. And because of you, I can never marry, never leave this filthy hole."

Nothing she said made sense to Stephan, but it never did. The place was no longer maintained as it had been when he was a child, when there was still money flowing in from the vineyards and the rents, but it was more than presentable for a wedding. And his father was as placid as he had always been, dourly argumentative about religion and politics, but otherwise seemingly willing to live and let live. In many ways, he was easier to get along with now than he had ever been.

Poor Monique, and poor Maman. She was more religious than ever, praying every day in the chapel for her live children as well as her dead. He wished he could tell her about the baby—it would give her a happy heart attack. She had not yet accepted that he was marrying a non-Catholic, and all but ignored the fact that Patty had taken instructions, been baptized, and genuinely intended to raise their children as Catholics. Perhaps his mother sensed that the whole process was done not for Stephan, nor for principle, but simply as a means of getting along, of being accepted.

But his mother was strong-willed and capable. He knew that when the wedding had been announced, she had managed a frenzy of activity, keeping Pierre and Monique hopping with the arrangements.

Stephan rose and stood by the window. Was it all the war? Would their lives have been so turbulent if his brothers were still alive, still working the estate? He saw his father enter the courtyard, then go to the arched doorway that led down to his cellar, walking with the rolling gait his war wounds had imparted. He had gone into the war with the face and chest of a bulldog; he had emerged with a walk to match. What a drinker he was! Never drunk, never sober, he maintained an alcoholic equilibrium so exact that he might have had some sort of brandy thermostat inside him. He made no secret of his drinking, and brooked no criticism of it either.

Appearances were deceiving. Stephan's father for once was definitely not taking everything with equanimity, nor tempering his usual carefully monitored intake. Now he ran his hands along the top shelf, searching not for a bottle but for a book. He did not find it at once, and he panicked, afraid that his wife had somehow located it.

The book was his own shorthand accounting of their finances. The wedding was going to be the last straw. When it was over, he would have to sell everything, and move into a smaller place in town. Monique would have to find quarters of her own.

He opened the book. It had its formal counterpart in Paris, where Henri Troyse-Rozier, the senior partner of the bank the family once had had an interest in, tried his best to help them. Everything that could be sold had been sold. Henri had gone past both the bounds of friendship and the rules of his firm to provide the bulk of the money to prepare the house for the wedding. Now the villa was mortgaged beyond redemption, as was the country house at Saint-Jean-le-Thomas. The only unencumbered property was the warehouse and wharf tucked away in the corner of the harbor at Marseilles. Vacant now, it had once been the heart of his father's business, bringing in dirt-cheap wine from Italy and Spain to blend with the worst pressings of his own vineyard. He sold the resulting mixture at cut-rate prices to the bureaucrats of the French army around the world. It had been a totally secret process, for the idea of French soldiers drinking *pinard* of foreign origin would have been intolerable to the press and to Frenchmen alike.

The Hafners' generosity in providing such a bounty of funds for the wedding had only underlined how far the estate had fallen into disrepair. In the six weeks since Stephan had said he was going to be married, all the mortgage money had gone for roof repairs and plumbing and for gardeners to cut back the overgrown grounds. He had opened rooms long closed, the ballroom, the library, the large dining room, and the money had poured away in an endless stream to make them usable. The chapel had been the most expensive. He looked in the book and winced: more than 14,000 francs, just to make it suitable for a wedding that would take no more than an hour, be celebrated for a day, and last perhaps what—five years? These American girls put husbands on and off as a French girl did hats.

Except poor Monique. She did with lovers what French girls did with hats—or perhaps, more appropriately, with loaves of bread, consuming them.

He put the book back, and drew down a bottle so old that the encrusted dust was as hard as the handblown glass itself. It was an Armagnac from 1813. There was no label. It came from their own family distillery, and to him and the fortunate few he had shared a few scarce bottles with, it was the best in the world. There were five bottles left. Three of them had been intended for his sons, one for his daughter, one for the first grandchild. Now he had two spares.

He sat down and poured a splash of the golden, syrupy brandy into the thin-walled bulbous glass he had carefully washed and brought with him. He sat, warming the amber liquor with his hands, thinking that in the end it didn't matter. One had to keep everything relative to the events of the war. He had been a reservist in 1914, one of the thousands who had actually ridden to the battle of the Marne in taxis, a distinction millions now seemed to claim. He'd ridden back in a creaking hospital cart, unsprung and horse-drawn, with shrapnel in his back and legs.

There was no Edith Cavell or Florence Nightingale in the miserable little hovel where he was operated on, nor any anesthetic either. When the butchers they'd recruited for doctors were finished, his legs were permanently damaged, great collops of flesh cut away with the metal shards of shrapnel. He had recovered to serve the rest of the war in the gigantic Schneider munitions plant in Paris, a reserve major pushing papers. He reached up and touched the scar concealed beneath his still-dark mat of hair. A German trenching tool had put it there, a slash with a spade that had almost scalped him. Somehow the doctors had left that wound alone, and it had healed very well.

After the war there had still been very little money, and the land had gone, properties and acreage, year by year. Now they were down to the house and the land immediately around it. The family distillery, which had been only a diversion for his grandfather when the family owned thousands of hectares of rich farmland, was now the principal source of income, selling sound workingman's marc, and running a few bottles of Special Reserve which he kept for trading. He had only one acknowledged hobby, collecting fine cognac, Armagnac, calvados, and marc. He was widely recognized as a connoisseur, but in recent years could only trade to get the particular bottles he wanted.

His other, but unacknowledged, hobby managed the best local *auberge*, Le Montespan, with her husband. In his youth, Elisabeth and he had been tempestuous lovers; now they were very good friends who sometimes still managed a loving hour together.

He rubbed the back of his legs. The wounds that truly pained him were not from German shrapnel, but from the German machine guns that had killed his oldest son, Alexandre. The second son, Robert, had died in a stupid accident, crushed when a farm wagon turned over on him. It had nothing to do with the Germans, except that if there had been no war, no invasion, Robert would have been away at school and not working in the fields like a navvy, available for the accident, and things would be different now.

There was a knock at the door. He quickly checked to make sure the book was back in its hiding place, then let Stephan in.

He poured his son a drink from a less precious bottle. Stephan didn't want it, but knew better than to refuse.

"Papa, we have rooms for everyone, except the one American, Mr. Roehlk. Can we put him up at the inn?"

"But of course. But why not the same with this Rhoades fellow? Is he a member of the family?"

"No, but he is apparently Captain Hafner's confidant; Mrs. Hafner requested that he stay with us if at all possible."

"Let's put the Boche in the inn as well. He can stink up their bedrooms instead of ours. I never believed I would see the day when a live German would be in my house." He paused for a moment, nose deep in the glass, pulling the soul of the Armagnac deep into his lungs. You could get drunk just smelling this, he thought. He looked up in horror. "I never believed that I would be related to one, even by marriage."

"Papa!" Stephan's tone was sharp. "You only have to put up with him for a few days. Do it for my sake, for Patty's sake."

Pierre Dompnier drank the Armagnac, and poured himself another from the lesser bottle. He offered the bottle to Stephan, who shook his head.

"And what dowry does the Boche bring? Has he any money?"

Stephan laughed. "He has plenty of money, but no one has ever discussed a dowry. I think they feel Patty and I must marry, as we have . . ." He paused, trying to soften the idea. "As we have spent so much time together."

"Probably linens and some furniture. The rich don't get rich by giving it away." He looked sharply at Stephan. "And how do you feel about this man? He may have killed your comrades!"

Stephan shrugged. "Yes, he may even have killed Patty's father. But he was just doing a job, as I was. Somewhere in Germany there are eight families whose sons I killed. I'm not proud of it, I would not want to see them, but I would not wish them to hate me, either."

They walked together down the cool hallways, so familiar to him, unchanged since his youth. Papa was the easy one, going off to lie down and burn away the Armagnac. Now he had to talk to his mother.

She was sitting in her bedroom, the wooden shutters closed, a shawl over her head, crying softly. He looked at her before he spoke. She was totally in black, her dress relieved not even by a nun's white collar. Her face seemed to sink within the folds of her shawl, from which, like a child in a Munch painting, some terrible silent cry of pain, inaudible but palpable, eternally screamed.

"Maman, you must pull yourself together. You must be able to greet Patty and her family, and be gracious to her. If not, I'll leave tonight, and we'll have only a civil ceremony in Paris."

It was necessarily cruel. The thought of marriage outside the church—marriage in which they might lose control of any grandchildren—was unthinkable.

"They'll be here this afternoon. No more of this nonsense. Get yourself dressed, get out of those mourning clothes, have your hair fixed, do whatever you have to do. But be gracious!"

She sobbed and nodded, her hands flying around the rosary.

When Stephan left, Antoinette Dompnier pulled a tablet out from the drawer in her table. On the top page was a numbered list, in her precise handwriting, of all that had to be done, running from "(1) Contact Father Closterman" to "(27) Arrange with Sassard for the cake." On the following pages, in the same sequence, she had listed the status of each project. Most had check marks on the front page, signifying that they were completed. The only major things that remained were the final fittings of the dresses for Monique and herself and confirming the entertainment. Stephan had said something about this Hafner fellow, this German, helping with the entertainment. She muttered to herself, "Perhaps his wife will dance."

She was glad that Stephan had been completely open. The bride's mother had been married to an American flyer, apparently, and before that had been a chorus girl! And the stepfather, a Boche flyer himself! A fine combination for in-laws, wealthy or not.

She returned to the list, pleased that enough was finished that she would have time to pray, to strengthen herself to endure what must be done.

They had so little money, and so much to do. She had driven Monique unmercifully, somehow forced Pierre to help, and then enlisted the aid of old Debre in the distillery to do the rest.

Now she was content. It would be a perfect wedding, befitting their family and the house. And then, she knew, it would be time to move. That old rogue Pierre thought he had fooled her all these years with his fumbling with Elisabeth down at the inn, with his mortgages, with his drinking. They were now hopelessly in debt, but their son would have married. Poor Monique; she was unmarriageable, and she would have to survive on her own.

Back in his room, Stephan took a tumbler of cognac and two tablets, and threw himself on his bed. It was stupid to have returned, to think that he could add anything to their lives. They should have had a civil marriage in Paris, and let it go at that. Now they had to endure God knew what. Patty was worth it all, he told himself. She was worth it all. And perhaps she was pregnant!

The last thirty minutes of the train ride had not been pleasant for anyone. Patty had asked all four of them—Bruno, Charlotte, Dusty, and Murray—to sit in her compartment while she lectured them.

"Bruno, the French are not like the Americans. They will not be delighted that you dined with the Kaisers and were an ace. So don't talk about that. And don't talk about how smart you were about the stock market. Just say pleasant things about the house and the weather."

Bruno shifted his bulk and looked at her in pained surprise.

"As you wish, Patty. I'm sorry that you have such a poor opinion of me."

"And your mother," Charlotte bristled.

Patty ignored her, saying, "Please don't make any risqué jokes, even in English. They understand more than they speak. Please, please, watch your language. Madame Dompnier is very religious."

Charlotte's color went from vermilion to umber, and her lips worked.

Bruno smiled, and Charlotte snapped at him, "Stop smiling, Bruno. You're the one who is a problem."

To Dusty and Murray, Patty said simply, "Help me."

Stephan met the train with a Renault seven-passenger sedan, so ancient its blue-black paint was crackled like dried mud. But it had acres of running board and a huge platform in the rear for the baggage. He embraced Patty and shook hands with the others.

"Mr. Roehlk, I'm sorry, but my father's place is small, and I have made arrangements for you at the inn."

"Suits me, Stephan." Murray used the term "Mister" only with Bruno. He preferred the inn—he could do what he wished, and perhaps find some mademoiselles.

Apprehension mounting, Stephan managed to hold Patty's hand and still point out the sights in Orléans as he drove out the road to the Dompnier estate. When he had left, his mother had still been sitting in her room, and his father had been stumbling toward his liquor cabinet.

Stephan whispered to Patty, "I'm not sure how this is going to go. If there is a problem, we'll go back to Paris tonight."

She nodded, concerned with her own family and their friends. She couldn't imagine why Charlotte had insisted on Dusty's staying at the house with them—or rather she could, but then she couldn't understand why Bruno would put up with it.

Bruno was quiet, and Charlotte was clearly impressed by the countryside. Rhoades slept in the corner of the car, and Murray drummed his hands nervously, anxious to get to the inn and have a drink.

Stephan wheeled the big Renault into the road leading to the house, Murray eagerly leaping out to open and close the gate in the stone fence. Stephan drove up the curved drive, flanked on both sides by an enormous double row of trees, the inner the poplars that march across France, the outer the inevitable chestnuts. When they reached the covered porte cochere, the family was assembled like servants greeting a returning master. In the front, smiling and waving handkerchiefs, were Monique and their mother. Behind them, in his major's uniform, was their father, smiling from ear to ear.

Stephan jammed on the brakes. He couldn't believe it, not the uniform, bulging as it was from the accumulated cognac of the years. Patty's eyebrows rolled up like burst window shades, and Charlotte sucked in her breath and reached for Bruno's hand as he leaped from the car in an apparent fury.

At the edge of the stairs, Hafner stopped and drew himself up to his full height, looking squarely at Pierre Dompnier. Then he saluted. Pierre returned the salute, and the two stood for a moment eyeing each other. Stephan was going to begin the introductions when the two groups coalesced into a series of laughing embraces.

Monique, as demure as a nun, had settled Patty in the end room, buffered from Stephan's room by her own and the larger suite she had given Charlotte and Bruno. She put Rhoades at the other end of the hall. He tripped twice going up the winding set of uneven stairs to a room in the tower, its ceiling plaster just redone, moisture already showing from the leaking cistern above.

Charlotte was busy unpacking.

"Bruno, I'm proud of you. The salute was a masterstroke!"

"You always underestimate me, Charlotte—in business, in bed, everywhere."

The old liquid stirrings coursed and she said, "Never in bed."

Monique carried a glass in her apron, just as her father did in his jacket. His was for Armagnac, hers was for listening, and she pressed it against the wall and smiled. This wedding might not be so dull after all.

Madame and Monique had outdone themselves with dinner. It had started with oysters, served with a cold dry Sancerre that even Murray liked. Foie gras followed, glistening on a bed of truffles. Debre, the sole remaining workman of the distillery, had shot the deer and hung it, and the haunch of venison was perfect, accompanied as it was by a ruby Château Margaux.

After coffee, Pierre insisted on taking Bruno down into his cellar to show off his collection of brandies. Charlotte, Patty, and Madame Dompnier sat in the formal living room, while Dusty and Monique drove Murray back to the inn.

Hafner and Pierre, with the Dompnier hound, Edouard, at their feet, sat down at the table, a round of wood placed on the barrel. Bruno scratched Edouard behind the ears, and soon had his head on his lap, eyes closed in contentment.

"I think you will like this."

He pulled the half-emptied 1813 Armagnac out and poured two crystal balloon glasses one-quarter full. Then he took a second bottle of the same and sat it meaningfully in the middle of the table.

"À votre santé."

"Prosit!"

Bruno almost bolted the liquor down, Prussian-fashion. He caught himself, and took a long time savoring the aroma, before taking a tiny sip to roll around his mouth.

"This is superb, the best I've ever tasted."

They drank in appreciative silence for a while until, beaming, Dompnier poured again, precisely one quarter of the glass.

"It must warm and breathe—it lives."

They talked first of the weather, then of their families and of the lost sons. Bruno's brother had been killed, and he could say in truth he knew what Stephan and his father had suffered.

Dompnier apologized for what he called "this sad remnant of a great estate."

He filled the glasses and moaned, "We were not aristocrats, but we had the wherewithal of aristocrats. We had vineyards, and an import-export firm, and even part of a bank in Paris. Now . . .'' He put his hands palms up at his side.

"Ach, the war cost both of our families then! My brother was killed in Italy, of all places, helping out the Austrians at Caporetto. And after the war—*zut*, we lost it all, house, factory, hunting lodge, everything.''

Pierre, his alcohol thermostat undone by the champagne before dinner, the wines during, and now the Armgnac after, felt his eyes tear. This man was a brother, a German brother!

They talked of the stupidity of war.

"And the stupidest of all was the Versailles Treaty!''

Hafner looked up, amazed.

"We should never have done that to Germany. What happened to us after 1873, the crazy need for revenge, will happen to you. It's already happening. The Nazis won more than a hundred seats in the last election!''

Hafner watched him closely. This man was no fool.

They were drinking seriously now, no longer extending the pleasure of the Armagnac with the customary care. Dompnier briefly considered switching to another year; he was sure that Hafner could not tell the difference. He decided against it; the dowry was surely going to be discussed.

The first bottle was gone, and Dompnier opened the second, the wax protecting the cork as hard and brittle as ice. He tossed the cork in the corner, and said, "Please call me Pierre. And may I call you Bruno?''

They embraced, and filled the glasses. Bruno asked about the abandoned warehouse in the south.

"It is in good condition, but there is no use for it. It has about ten thousand square meters under roof, and there is a railway spur and a *quai*. But there is nothing to buy or to sell. Nor will anybody make an offer on it. But the taxes are low, and I will keep it as long as I can.''

Even with his brain laden with the very best brandy he had ever drunk, Hafner realized that he could do good business with this man. He had a sense of family—and he needed money.

"Pierre, is it a French custom for the two fathers to discuss the dowry in private?''

The word poured into Dompnier's ears as melodiously as the Armagnac cascaded into his glass.

"I believe so, Bruno. It is not an issue, of course. We are so delighted that Stephan has found someone he loves, someone so beautiful.''

"Yes, of course. But I am concerned that they have a good start in life. I don't want them to have to work as hard as you and I have had to do since the war."

They drank in respect to their work and their worth.

"My wife cautioned me about a subject, but I feel I must mention it to you. May we talk frankly?"

Pierre nodded, not daring to speak.

"Unlike most others, we were helped rather than hurt by the stock-market disaster. We wish to be generous."

"I'm glad I discussed my own situation before this. We may not be able to match your generosity. Madame Dompnier—Antoinette—will be very sensitive about this. She would not wish to have our misfortune underlined for the world to see."

Charlotte lay in her bed, wondering if Bruno was all right. The talks with Madame Dompnier had gone wonderfully well, the wedding plans were perfect. The house showed that they had refinished it just for the wedding. She wondered how they could afford it. Patty had apologized for not knowing what entertainment Bruno planned, and Madame had gone along with it. Charlotte shifted uneasily. She hoped it was not a German military band.

There was a shuffling at the door. She opened it a crack and found Bruno slumped against it, dead drunk. As she had many times before, she let him put his arm around her and began to carry him in. Out of the corner of her eye, at the end of the hallway, she saw Monique scurrying up the stairs to Dusty's room.

Antoinette and Pierre had long had their own rooms, separated by a huge bathroom installed just before the war. She heard him there, being violently ill.

Serves him right, she thought.

The retching sounds continued, then subsided. She didn't hear him leave. Perhaps the old fool had choked to death. He would, to ruin the wedding if nothing else.

As she rose to check on him, the door opened and Pierre came in, dark face a roasted-pepper red from his exertions, his legs unsteady, but smiling.

"My dear. Everything is going to be all right. A miracle has happened." He explained nothing, but turned and lurched back down the hall to his own room, weaving from side to side.

As she crawled back into bed, she muttered, "The miracle was that he didn't choke."

Orléans, France/December 18, 1930

Charlotte and Madame Dompnier had made the joint discovery on the morning of the sixteenth. Their husbands were gone. A note on the kitchen table said they would return late the following day.

No one had any idea what it meant, but all were comfortable with the breathing space, particularly Charlotte and Dusty, after he had undergone some pretty close questioning about Monique. In the end Charlotte pretended to believe that Monique had gone to his room only to be sure that he was comfortable.

Murray Roehlk was totally disconsolate. Bruno had gone with the senior Dompnier in the big Renault, and had not said a word to him. There had been no mademoiselles worth looking at in the inn, or in any place he had walked to in the town. He stayed away from the Dompniers, for fear of Monique. She had propositioned him yesterday morning, and been quite piqued when he had backed away.

It was not that she was unattractive. It was because she would be related to the Hafners by marriage, and he could not be disrespectful to Charlotte. So he sat on his bed, as short and square as himself, staring into the flames of the little fireplace, drinking cognac, and wishing that he were back home in the States, where his tightly controlled fantasies of Charlotte could be acted out in the Jersey brothels he patronized. Yet even in his adoration of her, he was realistic. He knew that she was a wild-ass, screwing half the guys at Roosevelt Field, and maybe taking care of a few others on the side that he didn't know about. He'd been relieved when she had settled down with Dusty. Murray somehow didn't mind that he didn't exist for her except as Hafner's errand boy, for she, the most beautiful woman in the world, had always been pleasant to him. He was in love with her, and would always be, and if he would never kiss her in real life, he had made love to her every time he screwed another woman. He was inured to the jokes made by the practiced whores he bedded; they kidded him about his intensity, his insistence that they say nothing. He kept his eyes closed and his imagination open, and it was always Charlotte in bed with him. In its own way it was a perfect relationship, for he could never tire of her, nor she of him.

Monique had her hands full, regrettably with the business of the wedding. Big, bluff Father Closterman had refused to conduct the ceremony, declining to be in the same house with a former German officer. As a young priest, just ordained, he had served for three years at the front, and he had seen too many dead and wounded Frenchmen, and he carried a sin within him. During the retreat of March 1918, he had manned an abandoned machine gun, mowing down rows of the oncoming Germans. That was not his sin. When the flow of battle suddenly ebbed, a wounded German officer had asked for absolution in weak but fluent French. Father Closterman had walked away, leaving the German to die unshriven. That was not his sin. His sin was that he still enjoyed the thought. When Monique appealed to his Christian charity, he had appalled her with the bitterness of his reply. "Christ didn't serve at the front, Monique, even though we pretended that he did. I cannot conduct a service for your family, a sacred marriage, with a German there. For me if a German comes in, Christ leaves."

In the end, old Father Rignot, semiretired for years and virtually senile, was pressed into service. Madame Dompnier retired to her room for the day when she found out.

"What does it matter?" she muttered. "It is a mockery in any event. The girl is no more Catholic than Hafner."

Hafner and Dompnier had returned, exuberant and delighted with their mysteries, refusing to tell anyone where they had been or what they had done. Madame had savaged Pierre in the quiet of his bedroom.

"Where have you been? Your place was here, not drifting off on some drunken binge with that Boche! What have you done? That German has bewitched you."

From somewhere within Dompnier's beaten psyche, a lion roared, "Be silent, woman, or I will cuff you! And be pleasant to Bruno, or else!"

He had immediately dragged Bruno to see the Dompnier lawyer, Jacques Petit, an old friend of the family, who greeted them with measured enthusiasm. Normally, when Dompnier came to see him, it was for some legal magic, some method of stretching his frail resources even thinner. This time it was different. As Hafner spoke, Petit became very attentive, his tiny physique, so appropriate for his name, seeming to swell with enthusiasm. At the end of the two-hour session, he said, "Let me summarize the agreements. First, I believe that you are being very generous, Monsieur Hafner, perhaps unreasonably so. Will Madame Hafner agree to this?''

Bruno spread his hands on the table, fingers down and flexing as if he were going to play a piano.

''Monsieur Petit, Patty is her daughter, not mine. She will of course be delighted. But the assets we are talking about are my own, and her agreement would not be necessary. I have many reasons to be grateful to her, and this is the best way I can show it.''

''Then let me state things as I understand them. You wish to provide a dowry of twenty-five thousand dollars for Stephan and Patty. And you wish to enter into a partnership with Pierre for the renovation and use of the facilities in Marseilles. As consideration for this, you are willing to pay a sum equivalent to the existing mortgage on the estate, and a rental of two thousand francs per month.''

Pierre actively salivated, choked, and had to have a glass of water.

''And Pierre, for your part, you will provide as a gift to the young couple your interest in the country house in Saint-Jean-le-Thomas. Correct?''

Pierre nodded.

''And what about the mortgage on that property?''

''I thought that with the estate clear, and the rental money coming in, I could borrow enough money at the bank to pay it off.''

Petit agreed.

''And what will Antoinette say?''

Pierre looked worried. ''I'm not sure. She should be grateful, but she will worry about the appearances.''

''And how will she feel about your entering into a partnership?''

''She will applaud it, I am sure.''

Bruno spoke very earnestly. ''The facility is perfect for my needs, Monsieur Petit, but I cannot operate it without Pierre's active participation. I will hire people to do all of the physical work, the bookkeeping, everything, but I must have a family member who can visit and make sure that things are well.''

At the end of the session, Petit had insisted on taking them both to the inn, where he ordered a magnum of champagne, and agreed to keep silent on everything until the next day, during the wedding luncheon. Pierre was so exalted that he managed a tryst with Elisabeth.

Orléans, France/December 19, 1930

The next morning the civil wedding had gone with a brisk efficiency Patty had not seen elsewhere in France. Only Rhoades and Petit were present, as witnesses, everyone else being deep in preparation for the religious wedding and the reception to follow.

Murray drove them back to the Dompniers' in the old Renault, Stephan and Patty sitting quietly hand in hand, Dusty riding in the jump seat facing them.

Stephan said, "I'm worried. Things have gone too well so far."

"Can you believe that Bruno and Pierre would get along so well? I've never seen Bruno like this."

Murray called back, "Bruno likes Monsieur Dompnier, and he is always generous with people he likes. Most of all, though, he wants to do business with him. He thinks there are some real possibilities for the warehouse in the south."

Stephan laughed. "It will be a miracle if he can figure out something that works. My poor father has nothing to give in return, save his stock of brandies."

Patty shook her head. Bruno could be generous—but never without reason.

The house had become beautiful overnight, alive with guests and so filled with presents that they overflowed the endless tables and had to be stacked along the hallway walls. Monique had searched the private and public hothouses for miles around, and the house was bursting with everything from blooming roses to orange trees.

From somewhere, Father Rignot summoned what remained of his senses and conducted a brisk and meaningful mass, speaking in a low, frail, but perfectly understandable voice, just audible over the joint sobs of Charlotte and Antoinette.

When the wedding was over, they adjourned to the massive ballroom, where linen cloths concealed every kind of table from antiques to boards on sawhorses. A huge grand piano had been pulled from beneath its white duster and tuned, and a miniature Oliver Hardy sat at the keyboard, playing continuously and beautifully. He was so short that he had to lean off the edge of the piano bench to reach the pedals, yet his up-tilted rump was so large that it overhung the bench's rear. In the center was a massive tiered and becolumned wedding cake, attended as anxiously by the local baker Sassard, the very best in the area, as if it had been a patient in a hospital ward.

"Patty, may I suggest that you powder your nose? This is going to be a long afternoon."

Stephan was right. The food was marvelous, served with good humor by ranks of young girls, family friends. But the business of the afternoon was entertainment and speeches, and the bride had to be present for it all.

"Don't worry about the comments, Patty—there will be nothing risqué, none of the honeymoon jokes so popular in America. The aim is to express lofty sentiments in a friendly and a familiar style."

First came the local talent. Monique sang, quite well for an amateur. Monsieur Petit declaimed a long romantic poem of his own composition, the nuances of which were lost upon most.

The blockbuster was Madame's special treat, two young singers from the Comédie Française with an inexhaustible repertoire.

Hafner kept looking at his watch. Finally a note was handed to him. He excused himself and bustled from the room. The two singers were leaving to thunderous applause when he returned. He conferred briefly with Oliver Hardy, who drew himself up as far as his five feet and two hundred pounds would permit before departing in a huff.

Hafner weaved to the center of the room and rang the chimes of the dinner bell.

"*Messieurs et mesdames.* Thank you for coming. Thank you for sharing our joy. And now, a special American treat. I have the honor to present to you *le jazz hot.*"

A brass band broke into a roar, and a beautiful black woman, clad only in loosely slung fringes of bananas, leaped into the room and began gyrating to the insistent percussion of a gleaming-toothed drum player and long tortuous riffs from the brass.

Madame Dompnier watched transfixed. The bobbing bananas revealed high, pointed, cream-colored breasts surmounted by large brown nipples, an interesting array of dark curly hair, and an extraordinary flexibility that seemed to make the deeply intrigued Father Rignot wish he had done more missionary work. Madame had fainted earlier, her head falling smartly to the table between her plate and her napkin. This time she had a firm grip on the table and as consciousness passed, simply slid limply beneath it.

Patty missed Madame Dompnier's unscheduled departure, enraptured with the athletic dancing and the throbbing brass accompaniment.

"Stephan, is that really Josephine Baker?"

"No, but it looks like her."

The stunned silence of the crowd broke into a hum of excitement and then a roar. Bruno leaned back and yelled into Charlotte's ear.

"I tried to get the real Josephine Baker, but she wouldn't come because I was German. This little colored girl is in her troupe. And I think she's just as good as Josephine."

Charlotte got up to be with Madame Dompnier after she had been discovered and was being led from the room. Pierre had not noticed the commotion, riveted as he was on the tantalizing bananas in the middle, which seemed to be leading lives of their own.

Le jazz hot grew considerably hotter, going on for almost as long as the Comédie Française singers, although it hadn't seemed that way. At the end, "Josephine Baker" made a spectacular running-somersault of an exit, and the guests gave her a standing ovation. Madame had returned, and when she saw Father Rignot leading the applause she recovered slightly.

Coffee was being served, and it was nearly time to cut and eat the cake, a tradition reserved by the Dompniers for the last event, the signal to leave.

Pierre Dompnier stood up and tapped the side of his glass. The crowd grew silent as he began a long song of praise of Stephan and Patty, of his wife, Antoinette, of Monique, of Charlotte and Bruno, and of most of the guests. Eyes were glazing and heads nodding when he finally finished. Then Bruno lurched to his feet.

He acknowledged all of Pierre's compliments and added a few of his own. Charlotte tugged at his suit jacket, trying to get him to sit down. He smiled down at her and put his finger to his lips.

"My new friends, we came here to celebrate a marriage. Let me tell you now that there are two marriages to be happy about. The first, and most important, of course, is Patty and Stephan's. May they always be happy." There were cheers, a general ringing of glasses.

"The second marriage is one of our two families in business. Pierre and I are partners in a new venture, one that will be of interest to you all."

A ripple of excitement mixed with embarrassment waved through the crowd. It was no subject for a wedding! The man was drunk, but Pierre was nodding enthusiastically. Charlotte looked at him, stricken. Madame Dompnier was breathing fast.

"And I want you to know how we are celebrating this new partnership, by celebrating our children. Pierre, stand with me."

Pierre, his beam fueled equally by brandy and greed, stood up and grasped Bruno's hand.

"We each bring different things for Patty and Stephan. Charlotte, my lovely wife, and I will give them twenty-five thousand dollars in cash, to do with what they will. Pierre and Antoinette are making them a gift of their lovely country home in Saint-Jean-le-Thomas. And . . ."

The rest of his words were drowned out in Monique's cry of pain and Madame's head hitting the table again.

Patty cut the cake with her new father-in-law's sword, and the crowd gratefully withdrew. Less than an hour after she had begun the destruction of Sassard's masterpiece, everyone was gone, and the postmortems were going on.

In Madame Dompnier's bedroom, Monique's hysterics had come under control when she realized that the gift of the country house was really a small matter. She finally comprehended that the main house was saved, and that this would be her inheritance.

"Wait, there's more."

Madame leaned forward, her equilibrium distressed by the hard full circle of her emotions from unending hatred of the Hafners to what was going to have to amount to love.

"Bruno gave me the cash for the country house's mortgage. It is free and clear, just as this house is. We are free at last, able to live a little." His mind leaped forward to the cognacs he would cellar, the Armagnacs he would drink.

Madame's voice was dry and brittle. It was too good to be true. "And what do we have to do? What is this about that wretched warehouse in Marseilles?"

Pierre raised his eyes heavenward. This woman would have thrown Jesus's wine away because she hadn't tested the water.

"He has an import-export business of some sort. I will help him with it. It will be like old times."

Monique spoke up. "I will help too. I like Marseilles."

* * *

Downstairs in the library, Bruno was excited.

"Charlotte, this is the best deal we've ever worked. We have a legitimate business in France, just when there are wars starting in Spain and in Africa."

"You don't know anything about French law or French customs. Why do you think you can do business here?"

"That's the beauty of it. Don't underestimate old Pierre—he's very shrewd. And that midget lawyer of his, Petit, he knows his way around as well."

"Does he know the kind of business you are in?"

"Of course! I told him right off, and he approved. He even made a suggestion. There are nationalists in Libya who want the Italians out. He knows how to reach them. The man is a gem."

"And Monique?"

Bruno was momentarily confused, thinking Charlotte had learned about Monique's romps with Dusty. Then he realized she was talking about Monique's role in the project.

"Pierre says that she's dependable. Look what she did organizing this wedding! It was perfect. I'm going to put her on the payroll, too."

Charlotte was silent. "Well, I can't fault you on a thing, although I damn near dropped my drawers when that jungle bunny jumped in the door."

"She was good—she livened things up after all the poetry and singing."

The only dissonant note of the evening was when he announced that Dusty and Murray were staying behind to set things up in Marseilles.

En route to Paris/December 19, 1930

Stephan was having trouble with the Voison that Charlotte had given them as a wedding present from her own funds. It was new, and try as he would to keep the speed down during the break-in period, it would leap ahead, reflecting his own anxious desire to put Orléans behind them and to get started on their married life.

He glanced over at Patty, and she was crying.

"Why are you unhappy?"

"This is supposed to be my only wedding, and Bruno Hafner insisted on being the bride."

Stephan laughed. "Cheer up. If you have a funeral, he'll insist on being the corpse, as well."

She turned on him, furious. "I'm serious, Stephan. I doubt if your mother and father even remember that I was there. They fell in love with Bruno, probably the only two people in the world, counting my mother, who ever did."

Stephan shifted down to thread his way around the war memorial in the village square, then accelerated.

"Nonsense. They know Bruno bought his way in. You are their daughter now, the mother of their grandchildren."

Patty burst into tears.

"It's not going to be much of a honeymoon. My period just started."

Stephan looked at her in dismay, not because of the honeymoon. He had wanted the baby. They had been on a honeymoon for three years—and no pregnancy. Was there something wrong with her?

Or perhaps with him?

5

Winter played its usual final dirty trick on Ohio, sweeping frigid wind across Lake Erie to change a well-intentioned warm-air mass into a glistening sheet of ice. The ethereal beauty of budding leaves nestled in crystal ice jackets like green flies in clear amber was lost on drivers whose cars had careened into ditches.

Shedding water like a seal, Major Henry Caldwell sprang upstairs two steps at a time to the new offices of the Design Branch. His thin-soled brown shoes were caked with mud, victims of the endless construction and reconstruction going on at the new base. He winced when he pulled off his trench coat. "I fell on my ass out there; it's solid ice from Cleveland to St. Louis."

"Just be glad you're not flying, chief. Anyway, don't worry about it. Hoover is going to straighten the weather out right after he fixes the economy."

Hadley Roget sat imperturbably in the Sears herringbone suit he had bought two years ago and faithfully worn to work every day since. The clothes fitted his slender frame no better than the bureaucracy suited his taste.

He tossed a standard Army manila folder to Caldwell and stretched back in his swivel chair, cradling his unruly white hair in lean fingers, blanched clean of grease and oil by the months of paperwork. The folder carried a green coordination sheet on

154

its cover, a penciled stepladder of recommendations for rejection.

"Here it is again, Henry, all signed, sealed, and disapproved."

Caldwell, slender and hard-muscled, a tightly wound bundle of energy, hefted the folder. Inside were Roget's carefully drawn plans and calculations for his radical "fifty-five-foot wing," named for its proposed length. Two years ago, knowing that Roget Aircraft was skating along the familiar narrow line demarcating starvation and oblivion, Caldwell had hired him for $250 a month—big money at Wright Field—on the basis of a sketch and a letter describing an idea.

Roget and Bandfield had devised a lightweight steel-tube framework stiffened with corrugated aluminum skinning and streamlined with a smooth, stressed-metal covering. It was lighter, stronger, and easier to fabricate than older designs, and while it would be especially good for larger aircraft, it could be adapted to fighters as well. Their problem, the same one facing almost every company in the industry, was a total lack of capital to build an airplane using the new method. Caldwell had agreed that it would revolutionize construction techniques, and he wanted the Air Corps to benefit. However, in its customary infinite wisdom, headquarters had turned it down a second time.

"I don't know what to tell you, Hadley. I went to bat for you. They even told me I was out of line!" He paused to control himself, his anger evident. "I think the fuckers believe I have an interest in your company!"

He let his fury simmer. "There must be political pressure to stay with conventional construction. Keystone has powerful Congressmen in their corner, and all they can build is fabric-covered biplanes."

Hadley knew the big lumbering Keystones well. They staggered along at eighty miles an hour with crew members sticking out in the wind as in a World War Gotha. When they crashed—which was often, given that they couldn't fly on one engine—they turned from airplanes into grinding masses of splinters and wires that chopped their crews into hamburger.

Roget's voice was raw. "Yeah, and with 1917 performance. Even the Hafner A-11 is sixty miles an hour faster than the Keystones, and carries almost as many bombs."

The A-11 had been a bitter pill for him to swallow, for it had beaten the first Roget aircraft ever entered in a military competition. He and Bandy had put their heads together to build a militarized metal version of the Rocket they named the Rapier, and they thought they had a winner. Instead, for reasons he knew Caldwell would inevitably tell again, the A-11 won. It was a good-looking single-engine attack plane, with a ring cowling and huge spatted fairings over the landing gear, the first military product from Hafner's booming Long Island factory. Its performance was no better than the Rapier's, but its steak had more sizzle.

Caldwell realized he'd stumbled onto treacherous ground. When the A-11 had beaten entries from Curtiss, Douglas, and Roget Aircraft, there had been hell to pay in all the aviation journals. He covered his dismay with a chortle that was half lust, half glee. "Just like Charlotte Hafner is sixty miles an hour faster than the competition. You should have been here the first time she showed up."

Roget had heard the story three or four times, twice from Caldwell. He didn't interrupt, knowing that the major was trying desperately to steer the conversation to neutral territory. They both knew that what had to come later was going to be painful.

"Hafner Aircraft had submitted an unsolicited bid for an attack bomber. We gave them the usual stiff arm—Christ, you know how we get crazy bids three or four times a week from oddball outfits."

It was a second gaffe; Roget Aircraft had clearly been an oddball outfit in the eyes of Wright Field's brass before they got to know Hadley.

"We knew who Hafner was, but the company had no military track record. Then one day we get a call that the Hafner airplane will be in at ten o'clock on June 1. Nobody thought anything about it."

Caldwell loosened his tie. Roget liked him for many reasons, not least of which was that he wasn't spit-and-polish. A green patina shrouded the brass on his uniform, his shoes weren't shined, and he needed a shave. Usually he had his ancient terrier, Bosco, with him; the two looked remarkably alike, except that Bosco was rarely hungover and usually had a better haircut.

"Exactly at ten o'clock, this black bullet roars across the field at nought feet, I mean *nought* feet. I was in operations, looking right out at the field, and there was no daylight between that ship and the ground."

Caldwell's voice had gone higher still, and his arms and hands were cranked showing the maneuvers the A-11 had been going through.

"For twenty minutes it plays a tune on the goddam tarmac. At the end, the airplane pulls straight up, the engine is shut off, and the pilot makes a dead-stick landing out of a half loop, rolling right up on the apron to stop."

Roget could see the next scene.

"We all run out there, ready to tear a strip off the pilot, and who pops out? Charlotte Hafner, hair streaming back, tits bulging out of a half-buttoned blouse, looking better than Jean Harlow. Christ, she had that airplane sold before we even knew the price. What a saleswoman, what a pilot."

Roget articulated what everyone had been quick to suppose. "Did you sample that, Henry?"

Caldwell's voice dropped an honest octave. "Me? Hell no! It was there, you know that, we all knew it, but I'm not so crazy as to screw somebody I'm buying from. If I ever have to pay for it, it will be straight over the counter. But I wouldn't have minded. She's a great-looking woman."

Roget believed him; people like Caldwell were the real blood and guts of the Air Corps, working for peanuts, doing what they thought was right regardless of the effects on their careers. Charlotte could have taken her blouse completely off and it wouldn't have influenced Caldwell.

"She's the brains of the outfit. Bruno Hafner is the muscle, but he spends his time running guns."

Roget lapsed into silence. He'd gotten to know Charlotte pretty well over the last year, over Bandfield's violent objections. Bandy didn't want to have anything to do with Hafner Aircraft, never having gotten over the miserable chain of events of 1927. Hadley could never bring himself to believe that Hafner had started the fire that destroyed the original *Roget Rocket*. He felt that Bandy's unreasoning hatred stemmed from the fact that Bruno Hafner had been rescued while poor Millie Duncan had disappeared, drowned somewhere in the Pacific.

Bandy was never the same after the search was finally called off, his depression finally generating an almost eccentric insistence on safety in airplanes. The obsession, if that was what it was, had good and bad effects; without it, they never would have come up with the new wing design.

The bad side was that Bandy flatly refused to engage in any more races like the Pineapple Derby, nor would he permit aircraft to be sold for risky long-distance flights. Lockheed and Bellanca had no such compunctions, and as a result, they were sewing up the market. Wiley Post's backers had wanted to buy a Rocket, but they knew Bandy wouldn't sell it because he thought the round-the-world flight they proposed was too risky, so they had turned to Lockheed, and Post had made history with the Vega.

And only in the last two years, when things had grown desperate at Roget Aircraft, with no orders, no money, and few prospects, had Bandy been willing to fly in military competitions. Even so, the only reason he'd made the last-ditch swing through South America was that it was Roget Aircraft's only chance to survive. Flying against competent pilots—many of them old friends—in well-engineered aircraft didn't bother him as much, because he felt the risks were known by the people involved.

The rationale was inconsistent with his personal behavior. Bandfield was taking greater and greater risks, and doing it with increasing frequency. He wouldn't let anyone else do any of the dangerous tests, the nine-G dives, the spin tests, the things that test pilots like Bill McAvoy, Jimmy Collins, and others charged thousands of dollars to do. Sometimes, Hadley thought, Bandy wanted to die, to force an airplane beyond its limits and his, to be able to rejoin Millie, or to be beyond thinking about her.

The South American trip hadn't helped business much. They'd lost to Curtiss in Chile and to Boeing in Bolivia, and were bucking Hafner in Peru. It was their last shot; if they didn't win there, Roget Aircraft would probably close its doors.

Caldwell was looking at him, wondering where Roget's mind was. When Roget resumed he said, "Anyway, I got to know her in the last year. I think the only thing that keeps her and Bruno together is the way he lets her run the business and do the demonstration flying."

Caldwell said, "Yeah, I hear that if you can get her into the club after a show and slip a few bourbons and branch waters into her, she lets her hair down about Hafner. He's a strange bird. Never stopped being a German ace, if you know what I mean."

Hadley nodded. "The Hafners and Grover Loening are the only people I know who made money in the stock-market crash. They sold out in August 1929, then bought back gradually after the market had gone to pot."

They were quiet, smiling comfortably at each other, knowing that at last it was time to get down to cases. Hadley spoke. "How many A-11s has the Air Corps bought now?"

"Forty-six, and maybe we'll buy another twelve in the next year's appropriation, for attrition."

Roget pursed his lips and whistled, thinking what even twelve, let alone fifty-eight, airplanes would have meant to Roget Aircraft. He thought about teaching Clarice to fly, had an image of her with an unbuttoned blouse, and laughed to himself. She'd scare more people off than she'd attract, God bless her.

"The A-11 was designed by Armand Bineau. The smartest thing Charlotte's done is to hire Bineau as chief engineer."

"You know, I always thought he was a Frenchman! But he was one of the raft of Russkies that Sikorsky brought over after the revolution."

Caldwell nodded. "French name, of course, but he's a Russian through and through, a courtly old bastard, always dressed up as if he were expecting the Czar to drop in for tea."

"Yeah, I've heard Charlotte say that's one reason he gets along with Hafner, who's a bit of a snob. He got used to bumping around with royalty when he was an ace during the war."

A demonic siren sounded outside, a rising oh-my-God shriek that made the end of the world seem an anticlimax. Both men ran to the window. They could see a fire truck and an ambulance racing toward a towering column of smoke from the fire area where old cars and airplanes were kept for the firemen to practice on.

"I wish they wouldn't blow that goddam thing; it always makes me think somebody's gone in, even when I know it's just a drill," Caldwell said. "Anyway, Bineau could go anywhere in the industry, or he could set up his own factory, so Hafner treats him with kid gloves."

They were avoiding the issue. With the wing rejected, there was no reason for Roget to stay at Wright Field. He could never stagnate in the bureaucracy, designing by committee. Caldwell knew he would leave, and decided to face the issue squarely.

"What are you going to do, Hadley? You own the rights to the wing. The Army turned it down, so it's yours to use. That was the deal."

"Charlotte Hafner made an offer for it when they rejected it last year. She'll give me fifty thousand dollars for the design rights, and six grand a year for my services. Not bad for a shade-tree mechanic."

"Some mechanic. You going to take it?"

"Not if Bandy sells a few airplanes. If he doesn't, then I'll have to. Simple as that."

He and Bandy had only a handshake agreement, more than satisfactory to both men. Bandfield had taken over the factory—it wasn't much more than a converted garage—and Roget got full rights to the wing design. Now they would just mix everything back up again. Bandfield always knew Roget would be coming back—he had just never expected him to be bringing fifty grand with him.

"What's he doing now?"

"He's down in South America, trying to sell a few Rapiers."

Roget knew what a bitter-thin hope this was, more of the self-delusion that had nursed an industry since the war. After the Armistice, everyone expected airplanes to flood the skies the way Ford had flooded the countryside with Model Ts. But the demand, civil or military, had never materialized. Lindbergh's flight had touched off an aberrational boom of optimism that had launched dozens of companies like Roget's. Most were already gone, victims of poor sales and undercapitalization, the promising prototypes crashed or scrapped. And even many of the well-financed, well-managed larger firms had gone under. Dayton-Wright, besides having the services of Orville Wright himself, had built four thousand airplanes during the war—and probably less than a hundred afterward before it folded.

But a brave front was the industry keynote. "Everything's shut down while Bandy's in South America. We've got a racer about half finished, and a little trainer, just something to knock around in. We call it the Kitten."

There was a wistful pause. "There might be some money in one or the other."

Caldwell reflected on his own situation. An Army major's pay was not much compared to that of an engineer working for a prosperous aircraft company. With the budget cuts, the promotion picture had just about dried up—demotions were in fact more of a general promise, despite the fact that ranks had been stagnant for years. But at least in the Air Corps the work and the pay were a lot steadier, for few of the companies made money consistently.

His real inducement was that he could be of genuine service at Wright Field, trying to make sure that the small amounts of money available went to the best companies for the best airplanes. It was nerve-racking, though; business was so bad that any company that lost a contract went right to its Congressman. Caldwell spent a good 20 percent of his time justifying his decisions on an engineering basis, when all any Congressman wanted to talk was home-district economics. In a way, the Depression made it easier—people were out of work everywhere, so they couldn't say he was discriminating against any one district.

"Being here will help you, Hadley. There's a lot of precedent. Most of the big names in the industry got started here—Donald Douglas, Reuben Fleet, Virginius Clark, Don Berlin. Next time I see you, you'll be flying in something you want to sell me and I'll probably buy it."

Roget's tone was rueful. "Sometimes I think that's the only way to do it—to get on the inside. Did I get on the inside?"

Caldwell laughed. "Yeah, you're on the inside, Hadley, with your crummy jokes and your sour puss! Sometimes we get complaints about 'insiders,' but the fact is, unless you've spent some time here, it's hard to know what the Air Corps needs."

He picked up a straightedge and balanced it on a fingertip, trying to frame the words so that they wouldn't be defensive. "I've never seen anybody take any kickbacks, or anything like that. The contracting system is pretty straight."

"Well, I think we'll stick to the civilian market—what there is of it—for a while, anyway. We sure as hell haven't made any money with the military."

"No money on the civil side, Hadley, you know that. How many companies have gone in and out of business in the last five years? A hundred? Two hundred? Some of them made some pretty good airplanes, too."

He was echoing Hadley's own sentiments.

Caldwell got excited, his arms swinging, words rushing. "Why not try a military trainer? You could come up with something modern, a low-wing monoplane maybe."

Suddenly embarrassed, as if he'd said too much, the major straightened his tie, picking at the yellow sheen of egg yolk from yesterday's breakfast.

"Maybe, but I want to talk to Bandy first."

"Well, I feel I've failed you and the Army, Hadley. There should have been some way for me to sell your idea, and keep you working here." He hesitated and then said, "You aren't going to peddle it abroad, are you?"

There was real concern in his voice. U.S. airpower was falling behind Europe's, particularly France's and Italy's. Even Germany was secretly rearming, building "civil" airplanes that could easily be converted to wartime use.

"Nah, I couldn't do that. And it's not your fault, Henry. The

Army's still spending more on fodder for cavalry horses than it is on airplanes. You are working wonders with the money you get, given the crazy procurement system. Someday it will be appreciated.''

They chatted for a while, and Caldwell left, now obviously depressed.

Most of the other desks in the spartan bay of offices were new, their varnished oak finish gleaming bright yellow under the suspended incandescent lights. Always different, Hadley had scrounged a battered rolltop from the supply office. He rustled through the pigeonholes, looking for letters he had to answer before he went back to California. He didn't have much of a filing system, but he knew where everything was. At the bottom of the stack was the year-old unanswered letter from Charlotte, God bless her. Next to it was one from Bandy telling about his troubles trying to sell the Rapier in South America. The damn airplane would hardly get off the ground at La Paz—too little wing area, too much weight. He'd write them both, to see if Charlotte was still interested, and to tell Bandy to come back and get started on a new project.

Ancón, Peru/March 14, 1932

The dingy beige stucco walls swallowed the hundred-degree temperature in order to feed it back slowly later. There was no breeze from the beach, and the corrosive March heat ladled broad brush-strokes of sweat under the arms and down the backs of the brown Peruvian uniforms.

''Don't drink that, Bandy—Hafner's pouring his drinks out the window, I saw him.'' The bad water, poor food, and endless wenching of the trip had thinned ''Charles Howard's'' lanky frame out even further. Bandfield had finally gained some understanding on this South American tour of Howard Hughes's insistence on going incognito. If he had gone under his own name, he would have been met by newspaper men and women trying to get into films at every stop. As Charles Howard, an unknown mechanic, Hughes got to pursue the local belles at every stop. With his dark good looks and the tremendous sense of humor his anonymity fostered, he cut a swath with everyone from serving girls to officers' wives, enjoying a freedom that was becoming increasingly impossible for him in the States.

Bandfield was always pleased and surprised at the way Hughes threw himself into his role; he was Charles Howard, day and night, and no matter what had to be done, from carrying bags to repairing the airplane, he would do it. They had had a bit of trouble with the names on the way down; Hughes, preoccupied with the scenery and the women, wasn't responding when Bandfield called him Charles. They arrived at a compromise on the name business—Bandfield would address him as Howard, as if he were using his last name only. The passport and the introductions were always in the name Charles Howard, but they both felt comfortable with the mild subterfuge.

But now his mobile face was taut with apprehension.

"Bandy, I know this guy. He worked for me on *Hell's Angels* as a stunt pilot. He's a real prick."

Hughes was worried. The final flight was tomorrow afternoon, and Bandfield was boozing. Howard Hughes liked getting his hands dirty, the flying and the señoritas. But he didn't like to lose, especially this time, when they had their first real shot at winning. Worse, the dismal tour was turning him into a combination father confessor, psychiatrist, and cheerleader.

Bandy grimaced as he sipped the tepid Pisco punch. After half a dozen bouts with dysentery in South America, he usually drank only beer or boiled water. But he found himself in a situation he couldn't avoid, a social evening with the Peruvian military—his would-be customer—and Bruno Hafner, his rival and enemy. Hafner had handled it perfectly, acting as if they were long-lost friends, enjoying the fact that Bandfield had to be civil to avoid a scene.

"I know him too. He burned my airplane. And now he wants to drink with me."

A drinking bout with Bruno was the last thing he could afford. They hadn't sold a plane on the South American tour, and he was overdrawn on his letter of credit. Even with the money Roget made at Wright Field, they couldn't go on much longer. Hughes had offered to help out with the finances, but Bandfield had long since decided that he wouldn't take any money from anyone unless they had some genuine prospects of sales.

He had been pretty successful in avoiding Hafner until this evening. They had been competing twice a day, in the early morning and late afternoon, and their chance meetings were always marred by Hafner's bragging. He was politely correct until some of the Peruvian military came around, when he always managed to refer to his victories on the Western Front in a way that made Bandfield look like a Boy Scout.

It was psychologically compelling. Nearly all of the South American military looked to Germany for training and equipment, and they put an extraordinary premium on Hafner's ace status. The aircraft competitions were run on a dual track. At the top level were a series of contractual requirements that made sense and gave a cloak of legitimacy to the offer to purchase. The requirements had some combination of specifications for speed, bomb load, range, etc., plus the usual details on delivery and method of payment.

At the next level, the judges who had the final say were almost always fighter pilots, and the competition was usually evaluated almost solely on the dogfighting capability of the airplanes, without regard to their ultimate use.

Bandfield knew there was a third level too, one he refused to use—simple bribery. At every airfield hints had been dropped about certain requirements "at the Air Ministry," which had been clear indications that graft was expected. He couldn't bring himself to address the problem. Even if Roget Aircraft had the money to give away, he wouldn't have done it.

But so far he thought things had been going well. Today the contest had been a race in time to climb to altitude—five thousand, ten thousand, and twenty thousand feet. The Peruvians had to have high-altitude capability to cross the mountains that filled the country from border to border. The Pratt & Whitney engine of Bandy's Rapier had been fitted with a supercharger to get more performance, and although Hafner's export version of the A-11 had beaten him to five thousand feet, he had easily won the other two contests. It made them even for the competition.

Colonel Jorge Santos came over. A little over five feet tall, lath-lean from too much smoking, he wore his hair oil-slicked back in a wide pompadour. The only bulk he had was provided by a resplendent Sam Browne belt and a holster carrying a gun as big as a French 75. As head of the Peruvian air corps, he would make the final decision on which airplane to buy. The APRA communists were near revolt at Trujillo, and both the army and the navy wanted bombers in a hurry.

"Capitán Hafner has proposed another contest, Mr. Bandfield. He wants to race to see who can drain a bottle of beer in the fastest time."

Bandy had not spent all his time at Berkeley working—he could chug-a-lug with the best of them, and the Pisco had raised his ordinarily high level of combativeness.

Before Bandfield could reply, Santos went on, "He wants me

to caution you that German university students have a great deal of practice in drinking beer, and that it might be an unfair competition.''

"He's on, Colonel. How many bottles?''

"Just one, but perhaps I neglected to say while doing a handstand.''

Bandy's Pisco shifted in anticipation.

"Okay.''

"Ah, yes, and I'm sorry, I also neglected to say, on the windowsill.''

Hughes grabbed Bandy's arm. "Let's get out of here, Bandy. They're setting you up. That window is on the second floor. You'll kill yourself.''

Hafner had pulled his mess jacket off and handed Santos the soiled ribbon of the Pour le Mérite he had earned in the *Jagdgeschwader* Richthofen. Tugging his suspenders into place, he jumped up on the window ledge and did a handstand. His hands were huge, spanning the dark wooden sill. Santos placed the bottle of beer in front of him.

"Now," he said, grabbing the top of the bottle between his teeth and arching his neck to the side. Santos counted *"Uno, dos, tres, quatro . . ."* as the beer spewed out of the corner of Hafner's mouth. He gulped a few swallows down—up, really— and swung his head to sling the bottle between his arms out the French windows.

Hafner flipped forward, landing on his feet.

"Your turn, Mr. Bandfield.''

"Don't be a sucker, Bandy. This guy must be a professional acrobat.''

Bandy moved to the window. He positioned himself, gripping the sill.

The dream was the same. He was flying Winter's Vega, the engine had quit, and Millie was in the back, calling to him. For five years now he'd made that last endless glide to the sea two or three times a week. He was somehow flying the airplane, somehow sitting outside, admiring the Vega's yellow finish, unable to aid Winter's desperate efforts. It was always the same, the switch from the controls to helplessly watching from the outside until the Vega hit. There was never a splash, it simply disappeared, blotted up by the sea. Then, below the surface, covering an area as large as the Vega, was Millie's sweet sad face.

The dream ended as it always did, with him suddenly sitting bolt upright, silently calling out Millie's name.

Hughes was sitting by the bed, watching him intently. Finally he said, "Well, good morning there, chief! How are you feeling?"

"Okay."

Hughes broke into laughter. "It's a goddam good thing you landed on your feet and not your head. I'd be taking you home in a box."

Bandfield struggled to adjust the pillows, groaning. "That bastard Hafner slopped beer all over the damn windowsill. It was slick as ice."

"Yeah, the whole thing reminded me of one of the early chapters of *War and Peace*, except the Russian guy pulled it off. They sure suckered you."

"I'm glad you enjoyed it, Howard. Excuse me for not laughing. Between the pain and thinking what Hadley Roget is going to say, and the worst hangover of my life, there's something wrong with my sense of humor."

Hughes's expression changed. "Yeah, Roget is going to be furious. He didn't really expect us to beat Jimmy Doolittle flying for Curtiss. But here in Peru, with just Hafner and the A-11, we really had a chance."

Bandy nodded. "Well, we'd better win this one, or we're out of business. If we could get an order for even a dozen airplanes, it would get us by until the end of the year."

The hospital was set under a stunted line of trees on the edge of the beach, and the sharp reflected light from the yellow sand thrust into his eyes like a hollow white needle. He moved his legs. The casts clicked together, and pain lashed him. Christ, both ankles must be broken.

Bandy turned to sit on the edge of the narrow camp bed, torn mosquito netting draped around his head like a nun's hood. "I'd have felt better about the Peruvian army doctor if he hadn't kept mooching cigarettes."

"What the hell were you thinking about, letting that goddam German con you like that? You must have had eight drinks."

A convulsive wave of bile-laden nausea shuddered through him, and he felt his liver part its moorings. Eight drinks. No wonder he felt like dying.

"What time is it?"

"Ten o'clock. I asked them to postpone the demonstration for a day, but Hafner refused. Don't blame him. He'll be taking off about four. Jesus, Roget will nail your ass to the hangar wall. This was the only contract we had a shot at, and now we're scratched."

"Scratched, hell. Just get me in the airplane and strap the casts to the rudder pedals. You may not be the greatest pilot in the world, Howard, but you are a damn good mechanic. Let's rig up some sort of clamp. I think you can reach the pedals if you pull the access plates away on the side of the cockpit."

"Look, I'm not wiring you in any airplane in your condition. How would you bail out if something went wrong?"

"Nothing is going to go wrong. Besides, we'll never be much over five hundred feet off the ground anyway. I'm not even going to wear a chute."

"You should have been wearing one last night," Hughes roared. Bandfield threw the limp pillow at him. He missed, knocking over the plain white water jug he'd drained during the night without thinking about germs. Between the Pisco and the bad water, he'd probably be better off if he crashed.

Hughes put the water bottle back. "You can't fly like this. It would be better not to fly at all than have Hafner show you up. He's been a fighter pilot all his life. No offense, but I'm not sure you could take him even if everything were even. And he's a mean guy, a killer. When we were making *Hell's Angels* I could tell he enjoyed it when there was a crash."

Bandfield realized that Hughes was right. He just did not understand how desperate the situation was. It wasn't only that they were out of money; they'd been out of money before. The real problem was that they were at the end of the line with the company. He'd been putting together some magnificent ideas for a new transport and a new bomber, planes that could use the wing structure he and Hadley had invented, planes that would not only be good, but be safe. If he didn't come up with a few sales, the whole business went bankrupt, and he'd have to go to work for some other firm either as a test pilot or a buck-ass engineer, riffling a slide rule in a drafting bullpen.

"Well, we've been competitive in all the tests so far. It's going to boil down to who is the better pilot, and that's going to be me. He really doesn't need the order the way we do, so he won't be trying as hard as I will."

Hughes had a flexible tape out and was measuring the casts, laughing to himself. "Goddam, Bandy, I've seen five-hundred-pound bombs that dropped slower than you did."

"Howard, I thought I'd never stop falling. It was worse than bailing out. Get me another Sal Hepatica and a fistful of aspirin, and let's go out to the field.''

Hughes paused at the door. "Look, Bandy, this isn't the end of the world, although this town could be the world's asshole. Why not forget the military stuff? We could go to the National Air Races in Cleveland, maybe win some prize money.''

Despite the pain and the boredom and the overpowering concern about the company's finances, Bandy instinctively rebelled. Racing was the worst form of competition for aviation, no more than a carnival bloodletting. Everyone said it improved the airplanes, but it didn't. They just put bigger and bigger engines on smaller and smaller airframes, and more people were killed. If there wasn't a crash, the crowds felt cheated. Still, it might be the only option.

"Yeah? What would we fly in the races, a Jenny?''

"Well, if you'd stop being stupid, I could lend you the money to finish the racer you and Hadley have been struggling with so long. You could pay me back out of the winnings. If you don't want a loan, I know Jimmy Haizlip. He could maybe get us a job flying for Wedell-Williams. They've got three or four airplanes, and they're always looking for fearless pilots like us.''

Bandfield thought about it. He and Hadley had stopped work on their own racer when they ran out of cash. They had only done the basic airframe; it could be modified into something competitive, maybe, with a little money.

"What about the Granvilles? Do you know anybody there?''

The Granvilles had built the Gee Bee Model Z that had won the Thompson Trophy last year. It had crashed on a world-record speed run, but they would surely have some more airplanes to fly.

"Maybe, but not without a lot of practice. The Gee Bees are almost too hot, even for me.''

Bandfield sighed with resignation. "Well, if you'll take a promissory note, we might borrow enough to fix up the racer. If not, I'll just rob a bank and get some dough.''

The afternoon rain that presaged the fogs of April seemed to help; by four o'clock Bandy's head had stopped pounding. Hughes had lowered him into the cockpit, then fashioned a steel-tube cage that fastened his legs in, plaster casts from the knees down, to the rudder pedals. He was literally a part of the airplane, bolted to it as firmly as the wings or engine.

When they rolled the Rapier out, Hafner was obviously surprised to find that Bandy was flying. He had been expecting a walk-on-walk-off win.

Grinning, he came over with Colonel Santos to stand looking up into the Rapier's cockpit. "How are you feeling, Mr. Bandfield?"

"Wonderful, Captain Hafner. These Peruvian doctors are miracle men!"

Santos beamed at them. "You gentlemen understand the rules? You are to meet over the field at one thousand feet at ten minutes past four. Captain Hafner will come from the north, heading due south; Mr. Bandfield will do just the opposite. Then a regular dogfight, over the sea, due west of the airfield. Keep in sight so I can judge. Agreed?"

The dull-copper sun glittered low on the horizon, in Incan appreciation of the brilliant blue-green sea's contrast with the austere sands of the Peruvian coastline. To the east the Andes saw-toothed to the sky. Bandy knew he had to win quickly, or his ankles would give out from the strain of booting the rudder back and forth.

Dogfighting was very different from aerobatics. In aerobatics you had to be smooth and coordinated, so the control movements were relatively easy, going through programmed maneuvers that flowed readily from one to the next, with all the G forces on the airplane manageable and well defined. In dogfighting, all the maneuvers were vicious, sharp, with stick and rudder used against each other as much as together. The idea was to present a difficult target, and to force, rather than maneuver, the airplane to where you wanted it.

Neither airplane carried a military load or an observer. Today was a dogfight, pure and simple, and Santos would be determining the winner of the one-on-one duel. It didn't make sense, because the rebels didn't have any fighters and the Peruvian bombers would probably never have to engage in air-to-air combat. But it fit the pattern of bonehead pursuit pilots buying the airplanes, and the only thing that really registered with them—besides the silver that crossed their palms—was winning the dogfight.

As Bandy leveled off, trimming the airplane and pushing the mixture and propeller settings forward, he saw the bright red A-11 streaking south. It looked like a dropping hawk, its talons the huge fairings over the landing gear, its beak the big round Mead & Wilgoos 650-horsepower radial engine. Hafner had done a good job of streamlining, with the engine cowled so tightly that there were bumps to accommodate the rocker arms.

Suddenly it was time. Hafner bored in, a thin blue-black stream from the exhausts showing that he was using maximum power. Bandy pulled back in a climb, cutting the supercharger in early at the risk of blowing the engine. Hafner followed, but Bandy let his Rapier hammerhead to drop straight down on the A-11. Hafner turned and climbed almost vertically, the two planes passing belly to belly in opposite directions. Both went into steep turns, in which the A-11's speed permitted Hafner to gain the advantage slowly.

Bandfield quickly realized how good Hafner was, and that the Rapier's better maneuverability was the only thing saving him. With a fierce concentration, he was just able to flick out of Hafner's line of flight, to stay out of the putative path of mythical bullets. He realized escapes wouldn't win in Santos's scorebook.

They dueled for another twenty minutes in a spiraling series of corkscrew turns that left Hafner always slightly higher, but just out of ''shooting'' position. In desperation, his ankles beginning to ache under the strain, Bandfield rolled from a full vertical turn to the right into one to the left. As he rolled through a level attitude, a shadow blocked out his view of the sun, and Hafner's A-11 eased in directly above him, canopy to canopy, the German grinning down beneath his goggles, his big wings overlapping the Rapier's. Bandfield could see only the long nose of the A-11, the three-bladed propeller spinning in an arc ahead of his own. He unconsciously pushed forward on his stick to avoid a collision, and Hafner followed, mirroring each control movement.

Bandfield twisted in the cockpit, sweating to find a way out from the murderous embrace of the A-11. All the while, Hafner smiled, at ease, enjoying the advantage of position his superior skill had provided.

Keeping the pressure on, Hafner squeezed closer to the Rapier, his fingers on the stick sensing the changes in airflow between them. At a distance of three feet, the air tended to push them apart. At less than that it tried to suck them together, and he rode the invisible knife-edge margin between.

It had been easier than Hafner had thought it would be; Bandfield's legs were obviously bothering him. He looked down, enjoying the sweat pouring down Bandfield's face, relishing the obvious desperation in his movements. He felt the old bloodlust stir within him, and mentally went through the ritual motions that would have armed and cocked the empty machine guns. It would be so fulfilling to just drop back, press the triggers, watch Bandfield spin endlessly to the ground.

Bandfield could only keep pushing over, lowering his nose in the hope that Hafner would elect to break off. The German pilot followed easily, the maneuver no more difficult than the last part of a loop. A stream of oil crept back from under Bandy's cowling, spreading over his windscreen.

Hafner shaved the distance between them just a hair, keeping the margin so tight that Bandfield couldn't begin a turn without causing a collision. He drove Bandfield steadily toward the sea.

At the Ancón airbase, crowds of Peruvian officers and enlisted men stood in separate groups, watching the two airplanes stream toward the coast in their inverted embrace. Santos stood next to Hughes.

"Señor Bandfield is in trouble, my friend."

"No, Colonel, he's got Hafner just where he wants him."

Santos shot him a black-eyed glance and laughed.

The Rapier looked like a dump truck carrying a crashed airplane on its back. Bandfield found himself caught a mile from the runway, five hundred feet from the sea, his visibility cut to a small gap that the oil had not covered.

Hafner maintained position, herding him toward the airfield, pushing him down. At the edge of the field, there was no choice—if he went on, the rising hills at the end of the field would claim them both. The sale was not worth dying for. Bandfield cut his throttle, surrendering with his touchdown, while Hafner pushed the nose up, rolling the A-11 across the field and then giving a first-class aerobatic show.

There was another big party in the Peruvian officers' mess that night. Bandfield didn't attend.

Issy-les-Moulineaux, France/March 16, 1932

She tried to concentrate on the beauty of the night, the Venetian-blue sky reminiscent of the name of a perfume she had worn the first time she and Stephan had made love—Guerlain's L'Heure Bleu. There was still sufficient light to pick out the naked arms of obsidian black chestnut trees growing on both sides of the narrow street, somehow surviving in the small round circles of ground picked out of the cobblestones. Stephan was driving maniacally, sounding his horn and flicking his lights, the yellow reflection bouncing off the stone walls of the houses built square with the twisting roads. Patty closed her eyes and gasped as an ancient Frenchman, clad in a blue cloak and beret, clutching two long loaves of bread, leaped aside to flatten himself against the wall. She grasped the strap on the door of their Bugatti 50 and looked at her husband closely: Stephan rarely drank, and the champagne must have made him tipsy.

It had been quite a day. Stephan had left the air force in a glorious ceremony at Le Bourget, where the 1st Pursuit Squadron had honored him with a flyover, nine parasol-wing Dewoitine D-27s in tight formation.

At the officers' mess, the champagne-laden toasts had unsettled Stephan to the point that she had been afraid he was going to back out of his decision to enter civilian life. The way he was driving now, he might never have a civilian life.

"Slow down, Stephan—you don't know who is coming!"

"That's why I flash my lights, darling Patty, so that they know I'm coming. I wish I'd known that Angélique was coming! I'd have kept you home."

The good-natured courtier of the past was now the typical French husband, demanding and with a temper as short as his height. And she was failing him badly on two accounts: she had failed to conceive and she had failed to please his family. Their most recent visit to the country home near Saint-Jean-le-Thomas—she still considered it to be more the Dompniers' than her own house—had brought things to a head.

"Angélique shouldn't have been invited! I don't care if the two families are old friends. She shouldn't have come with all her brats!"

Stephan had laboriously arranged a week with his family in one more attempt to maintain the harmony the wedding had generated. After Orléans, his family had been enamored of Charlotte and Bruno, but had never really come to like Patty. Their emotions were mixed about Stephan's heirless state. On the one hand, they desperately wanted grandchildren from their only surviving son. On the other, they were not certain they wanted the Dompnier bloodline, impeccable for centuries, contaminated with Patty Morgan's.

The visit had started well. Their house was huge, with great French doors opening onto walled gardens. There was a walkway along the walls from which you could gaze on the tides racing to Mont-Saint-Michel. But inside there was an austere air of decay fostered by walls festooned with trophies of the hunt, ample evidence that the Dompniers had done their part in slaughtering fauna all over France. Patty vaguely remembered the den of her grandparents' house, where a friendly moose head, one antler slightly lower than the other, with layers of dust converting the glassy eyes into a leering wink, had decorated one wall. At the Dompniers', the trophies didn't stop with heads; hundreds of family photos, all in heavy frames that seemed to armor rather than present, competed for space with an army of tails and hides that showed the scars of pests and bullets. Every wall and doorway was a pincushion of horns and hooves of all sizes and descriptions, long, short, furry and cartilaginous, virtually every hard part of an animal that could be hung upon. An Indian fakir could have been uncomfortably thrust against any wall and never missed his bed of nails. In dusty counterpart, obviously discontented stuffed birds and beady-eyed squirrels sat, forever immobile, on any flat area, while no chair or couch went without its fox-fur throw.

Madame Dompnier had another little hobby—tortoiseshell baskets. Her vivid description of how she did it—from trapping the poor dumb beast to boiling the bones from the carcass to varnishing the shells—almost made Patty a nonstarter for breakfast and began the general declining trend of events.

After Sunday-morning mass, they had invited Angélique Giscard and her family for the afternoon. The daughter of old friends of the family, whose own country home bordered the Dompniers', she had once been Stephan's intended. Then Stephan's infatuation with Patty had changed everyone's plans. Angélique had married a wealthy manufacturer in Amboise, producing for him with bovine regularity children of alternate sexes, a boy, a girl, a boy, a girl. It was almost certain that her visit was a celebration of French family fecundity, an example to Patty.

Patty rarely drank, but the going was getting steadily rougher and she had fortified herself at lunch with extra wine and even accepted an Armagnac from her father-in-law's traveling collection. The spirited conversation turned on shared events of the two families from years ago, and she had time to think. Over a long series of suppressed giggles, it became manifest to her how impossibly funny it was that Angélique's first boy looked just like Stephan. Stephan's father pressed her to tell what she was laughing about, and Patty was amazed when her observation terminated the afternoon in a flurry of flouncing dresses, children pulled along by their arms, and a rising round of shouting in French too fast for her to understand. They might have forgiven her if she had not laughed again when Angélique's first-born, following her down the stone stairs, stepped on the hem of his mother's skirt and pulled it down.

In the words of P. G. Wodehouse, Patty had sunk to the rank of a fourth-class power—and she didn't care.

Even the pleasure she found in the flying lessons that Stephan continued to provide was diminishing. She was now an expert instrument pilot, as fully qualified as Stephan himself, but he would not permit her to engage in any record flying. As a result, the France she had loved so much now stultified her. Stephan wanted a conventional French wife, proper in bed, bountifully fertile, and oblivious to his *cinque à sept* requirements. She was unconventional, tired of being proper, not certain that she was the unfertile partner, and painfully aware that he was seeing a young widow each Tuesday and Thursday afternoon.

It was not working out.

She loved him still. Perhaps the new job would help them adjust. And she knew him well enough to know that he too was terribly worried that he might be at fault, that he might be the sterile partner. It was an inadmissible subject of discussion, but she was so familiar with his turn of phrase that his concern was evident.

He slid the Bugatti to a stop in a spray of gravel, the fast car's inadequate brakes just managing to dig in before the rough board fence was reached. He parked in the lot adjacent to the low-lying sawtooth-roofed buildings of the Caudron aircraft factory. Put up during the war next to the very field where flying had first been nurtured in Paris, it was now decaying, just as aviation itself was decaying in France. She thought that part of Stephan's irritation might be caused by the unending chaos of the French air force and its manufacturers.

The old Stephan showed through, and he smiled at her.

"Come, *chérie*, let me show you what I'm going to be doing. I made arrangements for a guard to let us in."

At the gate a one-armed, enormously fat Breton, obviously an ex-*poilu* eking out a disability pension, grunted at them as he turned massive keys in plated locks that would survive for years beyond the lifetime of the fragile wooden doors they protected. He led them down long narrow hallways, the unpainted framework dimly glowering in the lapped edges of the pools of light from widely separated forty-watt bulbs, to the experimental area. Without a word, he turned on the overhead lights and plopped down in a chair, his expression saying that they could do what they wished, he was going to rest.

Patty had visited her mother two years earlier, and been given a tour of the Hafner factory. It had been spic-and-span, and the experimental shop had glistened like an operating room. She was appalled at the Caudron plant, with its sawdust-littered floor, open cans of thinner, and ancient belt-driven machines granular with encrusted machine oil. But in the center of the room, its wings supported on ordinary wooden sawhorses, was a beautiful airplane.

"This is what I will test. If it does what they say it will, I'll fly it in the Coupe Deutsch races, and then perhaps we'll take it to America, to Cleveland."

"It's beautiful, Stephan."

They walked around it. A low-wing monoplane, with retractable landing gear and an enclosed cockpit, it was covered with mats to protect the glistening deep-blue finish.

"It looks very fast, Stephan. Will it be safe?"

He nervously pursed his thin lips. "*Oui*. A bit tricky perhaps, on the approach, but otherwise all right. I'm looking forward to it."

"Have you had any second thoughts about leaving the air force?"

"No, I should have gone years ago, but there was nothing I could do in flying that would have been as satisfying. This will be."

As they made the progress back toward the car, she slipped her arm in his.

"Stephan, I'm sorry about the business with Angélique. I meant no harm. I was just feeling sorry for myself, and drank too much."

He squeezed her arm against his side with his own.

"How can I be too unhappy about not having children? Who knows if it is my fault or yours? But you shouldn't have been unkind to Angélique; her husband will never let her forget. It may even affect his feelings for his son. And you know that I never touched her."

They walked in silence. He felt a little better for having raised the issue of America. There was a doctor there, he had been told, somewhere in Texas, who could do wonderful things for fertility with the glands of unborn animals. He could never admit it to Patty, to anyone else, of course, but he was going to go there and take a course of treatment.

Patty was pleased with the mention of America as well. To make up, she vowed to write Angélique's family and apologize.

Farmingdale, Long Island/May 9, 1932

Murray slowed the big Duesenberg down to avoid the group of workmen slouching along on their way to the plant, each man carrying his lunch in a string-tied, newspaper-wrapped package. He knew how glad they were to have the jobs the A-11 provided. Production had been winding down, and the orders Hafner had secured in South America would give them a few more months of work.

As he drove slowly up the Hafner Aircraft Company's circular drive, he noted with approval that mallards were mixing in with the domestic ducks. They swam in tight circles in the pond that reflected the new administrative section Charlotte had built in front of the old Aircraft Corporation plant. Bruno was asleep in the backseat, exhausted from a bad crossing on the *Mauritania*, his dachshund, Nellie, blissfully dozing at his side. He had gone straight from Peru to Buenos Aires and then to Germany for a six-week stay on "family business." When Murray had picked him up at the pier, Hafner had nonetheless been jubilant, in a better mood than Murray had ever seen him in, despite the fatigue.

As he parked the car, Murray reflected that life had worked out far better than an utter realist like himself could have expected. He had grown up in northern Queens at College Point, his dad a rough brawler who neatly combined working at a brewery and owning a beer garden, an economic combination that ultimately caught the eyes of the brewery accountants and earned him a six-year jail sentence. High school had never been Murray's real goal, and what he learned in the streets proved to be invaluable to Bruno, who had given him almost total authority to run the armament side of the business. It was a bonus he had never expected, but was glad to deal with. He knew that a lot of Hafner's faith in him came from his facility with instruments and other sophisticated devices. His specialty was what the mob euphemistically called "pineapples." As a hobby, he was enamored with radios of all sort. He had picked up his first radio knowledge from a correspondence course, finding that he read "radio" as some people did the comic pages, and that any small electrical or mechanical device was an open book to him. It had often puzzled Murray that he liked to use his hands for two totally different sorts of things. He used them as battering rams, to punch out positive responses from recalcitrant people who didn't wish to do what he or Bruno wanted, and he also used them as tweezers, to pick at some delicate thing and make it operate.

Fully awake by the time Murray had switched the Duesenberg's ignition off, Bruno Hafner bounded up the stairs two at a time, waving Charlotte's telegram and clutching the dog under his arm. He bowled past Dusty Rhoades without a word, burst into her office. She was standing at the window, behind a molded wood desk stained in a blond finish that matched her hair almost perfectly.

"What's this about Santos changing his mind?"

She put her arms around his neck and kissed him, then dropped her hands to rub his shoulders. "Relax, Bruno. Everything's okay. Glad to see you." Her words were soothing, and he responded to her gentle massaging touch across his shoulders.

In Peru, Santos had become greedy, and wanted a little more on his end. The deal before had been 10 percent of the gross for twenty-four aircraft. When he protested, Charlotte upped the ante to 15 percent of the gross for forty-eight. She knew he'd have to cut some more people in at the Peruvian War Minister's office, but was sure the sale was firm.

"Thank Christ! I risked my neck for that order, flying Bandfield into the ground." The remembrance of the flight still gave him pleasure; it could have been improved only if Bandfield had crashed.

Her expression didn't change. She watched him closely, in nervous anticipation, trying to guess how he felt. Before he left for South America, Bruno's moods had been swinging more wildly than ever before. He seemed to need a victory of some sort every day, a reaffirmation of his skills and intellect, or else he plunged into ugly depression and lashed out at everyone. Ominously, the duration of his moods was changing in inverse proportion to his successes. The more he achieved, the more Hafner Enterprises prospered, the more difficult he became. Good news lifted him higher for shorter periods; bad news cast him lower for longer times.

The variation in tempers was defined by what was left of their sex life. He wanted her now only occasionally, either when he was at a peak of euphoria and felt expansive, or when he was in a black pit of depression and sought to degrade her with a quick, brutal coupling. The old incandescent passion was long gone; now she provided him only indifferent conjugal service in either mood. Her own burning sex drive was diminishing, apparently assuaged by her business success.

And by Dusty. She would never have believed that he could come to mean so much to her. Somehow, over the last year, she had fallen in love with him, and was totally unable to explain why. She knew this had to do with his drug habit, something she was resolved to rid him of. Amazingly, given her experience and appetite, she even loved the fact that over time he had become a lousy lover who sometimes suffered from impotence, sometimes from premature ejaculation. It didn't matter. She loved the whole man for a change, not just the sports equipment. The drugs had made him passive, no longer especially eager to fly, apparently content to work at the plant just to be with her. He wasn't an engineer, but he had good instincts and knew the material suppliers so well that he always got good enough prices that Bruno never questioned his value.

Yet Bruno's presence had the same depressing effect on Dusty that it did on her. When he was away, Dusty became progressively more ardent; as soon as Hafner came back, Dusty began to withdraw guiltily into a shell. It was understandable, for just dealing with Bruno was a never-ending psychological battle. She kept control of him by playing constantly switching subjects, changing roles, sometimes contradicting, sometimes being silent. Charlotte based her tactics on his mental state, making positive suggestions for the business when he was up, slipping in negative thoughts about people and events she was against when he was down. Now she sensed it was time to divert his attention, to soften him up for the excellent briefing Bineau was about to give.

"Did you hear that they found Lindbergh's baby? He'd been dead for some time."

The press had treated the kidnapping in the most tasteless, sordid style, and Hafner had reveled in it. He'd always considered Lindbergh to be an intruder who had taken his prize, and the public never let him forget it. The year before, at a black-tie dinner honoring Orville Wright, the crowds had swarmed around Lindbergh, ignoring Hafner.

He snorted. "Too bad, but it serves the high and mighty bastard right."

Charlotte stared at him. It was an appalling attitude even for

Hafner, and with difficulty she pulled herself together, conscious that there was work to be done. She tried to shift his emotions with the same precise control that Murray used in changing gears in the Duesenberg. Her conversation was a matador's cape, switching his boiling anger from subject to subject until she could find safe ground, the narrow emotional zone where they could talk sensibly.

For the moment it seemed safe, his mercurial anger suppressed by the bad news about Lindbergh. She could sense almost to a degree how well he was containing the rage of his self-hate, storing it like steam within a boiler, sometimes releasing it in a tirade of anger, sometimes converting it to a synthetic friendliness that portended evil.

Charlotte had learned to use the blackness that consumed him, offering him alternative targets and stoking his ego with the safety valves of prospective new triumphs. She knew that he wanted to cloak himself with achievements that would match what he had done in combat. It was too bad there wasn't a Blue Max for business, some bauble of reassurance that would satisfy him. She wondered what it was that combat did for him that nothing else—not success, not drinking, not sex—could do.

In a normal voice, she said, "We've settled all the legal questions regarding licensing Hadley Roget's wing."

It was the wrong note. Hafner's face suffused with anger at the mention of the name.

"Those jake-leg engineers have never built anything worth flying. Why the hell you paid him good money for a metal-wing design, I'll never know. I'm a better engineer than either one of them, and Bineau is twice as good as both of them put together!"

She jumped on the opening. "Armand disagrees! He likes their wing concept. Let me show you what he's proposing."

Bruno tried to resume the offensive. "Did you do what I told you and tell Bineau about his raise, about getting a share of the profits? We have to keep him sweet—he's priceless."

She nodded. "Yes, and he's delighted. And as long as we let him build the airplanes he wants, he'd work for bacon and beans."

Charlotte pushed a button and two golden oak doors opened into a luxurious indirectly lit conference room paneled in the same light wood as her desk. There was a stage and podium, and a glass case along one wall. In it were jewellike scale models of the Hafner products, past, present, and future. The Mead &

Wilgoos engine line, the Premium propellers, a Hafner trimotor in Federated Airlines markings were all neatly modeled in the same scale. There was even a clever diorama of the harbor in Marseilles, a frowsy tramp freighter moored at a distance, a lighter with ominous-looking covered boxes en route to it.

"Jesus Christ, Charlotte, I wish you hadn't talked me into spending all the dough on this palace. We're getting overextended."

"Who taught me that it takes money to make money? You've outgrown the junkyard look. You deserve it."

She sensed her control over him return as he savored her compliment. He strode forward to loom over the display table, where two models were covered by green baize drapery.

Bineau and two other Russians walked in, followed by seven members of the senior engineering staff. Rhoades brought up the rear. After some small talk, Bineau went to the podium. As fluent in English as in French or Russian, Bineau cloaked his engineering in flowery language worthy of a poet.

Bineau ancestors had been brought from France to Russia by Peter the Great and there prospered immensely. The son of a brilliant engineer and courtier in St. Petersburg, Bineau had been educated at the Imperial Naval Academy before working with Igor Sikorsky at the Russian Baltic Car Factory. When the war came, he had flown with Alexander de Seversky in a Baltic Sea bombing squadron. A heart condition, probably brought on by the excessive zeal with which he combined his engineering and his combat flying, placed him in the hospital for six months. Then he was sent to France as a part of a Russian plane-buying commission. He stayed there after the 1917 revolution, eventually joining his colleagues in the fertile aviation fields on Long Island.

It was a universal mystery how he could not only stand working for Hafner, but actually seem to enjoy it. Bineau was shielded from Hafner's usual wrath by both his ability and his demeanor. The Russian never raised his voice or seemed anxious, no matter what the situation, and he gave Hafner the same elaborate but sincere courtesy that he extended to all.

The truth was that Hafner was in awe of the man, impressed with his brilliance and fascinated by his personality. Bineau's manner of speech was perhaps the key. His voice had the range of a Barrymore, and he modulated it constantly in perfect accord with his subject. Most ingratiating of all, he had a way of inviting agreement, his merry eyes beckoning you into a complicity in a delightful, well-intended secret.

Bineau's two principal colleagues, Barinov and Kalinin, were beside him. Barinov spoke English well enough, but Kalinin used a Russian-French-English patois that Charlotte termed Exasperanto. The two men always let Bineau do the talking, and so did Charlotte for an engineering briefing.

"Captain Hafner, I freely and gladly admit that the basis of what you are about to see derives from Hadley Roget's wing. We will be the first to use the structure, but you can expect, as night follows the day, that our competitors will adopt it."

Hadley's design had been as simple as Bineau was elegant, not only solving the problem of adequate strength, but giving space for fuel, equipment, and even retracting the landing gear.

With his customary flourish, he uncovered the first model, announcing with bravura, "The Hafner Skyshark."

Bruno was visibly moved. "Jesus, that's beautiful!"

Armand pointed to the model's nose. "Two guns, and a streamlined turret that protects the gunner from the slipstream." His voice was lilting; you could almost see the wind around the model.

Charlotte chimed in, "At two hundred and twenty miles an hour, he'll need it."

Bineau went on, "But, Captain Hafner, I want to tell you again that without Roget's wing it wouldn't be possible to get speed like that in an airplane this big—it has a seventy-foot span, and will weigh almost thirteen thousand pounds fully loaded."

While Bruno was leaning down, admiring the lines—he'd long since learned not to risk a knuckle rap by picking up one of Bineau's models—Armand pressed a switch, and the gears extended and then retracted.

Bineau continued, "I want to pay tribute to your staff for the concept and the hard engineering behind it. My colleague Alexander Kalinin did the stress work, making full use of the inherent strength of the design. Sergei Barinov is a genius at the drafting board and in the wind tunnel."

Kalinin stepped forward, clearing his throat. "You vill note de deep fillets on de ving, and de boot"—the word seemed to have ten o's—"on de horizontal stabilizer."

Bineau's enormous white eyebrows semaphored disapproval at Kalinin's intrusion, and he said, "Yes, certainly, and we believe these will both boost speed and eliminate flutter."

The small team of Russians had spent thousands of man-hours on the theoretical calculations, and were scheduled to have almost a thousand hours of wind-tunnel time at New York University and Langley Field. The only downside to Bineau's report was that the new 650-horsepower engines would not be ready until the following April.

Hafner nodded in eager agreement. "When the Skyshark flies for the first time a year from this June, we are totally confident of its success," Bineau concluded.

Hafner asked the usual questions on performance and costs, and was pleased by the answers. Bineau stressed that although the Air Corps had rejected the wing when Hadley offered it, the Corps recognized its mistake now, even after purchasing a service-test quantity of the Boeing B-9 bomber—thirteen, including the prototypes.

Bineau became absolutely evangelical. "This airplane will sweep the B-9 off the board. It is to laugh! The B-9 is no longer competitive."

Charlotte broke in. "I've saved the best for last. Major Caldwell says that if our projected performance figures are met, he will guarantee a production order for at least one hundred Skysharks."

Bruno slipped his arm around Charlotte, and even as she remembered the passionate night long ago in Passaic, when he had made exactly the same gesture, she had to steel herself not to cringe.

"Honey, let's send Caldwell a car, maybe a Model A convertible."

Rhoades spoke up for the first time. "Bruno, if you do that, he'd regard it as a bribe and you would never get another order from him or from the Air Corps. You don't need to bribe him— you've got the best airplane."

Hafner smiled. "You're right. I was thinking about the old days of the fighter competitions in Berlin, when Fokker would make sure that all the pilots were taken care of."

Bineau continued, "Bruno, we not only have the best airplane, we have the best airplanes. The next aircraft is without question the result of Charlotte's perseverance."

He bowed low to her, extending his arm in a graceful sweeping movement as if he were wearing a sword and a plumed hat. If anyone else had done it, it would have been impossibly phony. Bineau made it perfectly natural. "I said we were too overworked, that no one could do it, not even our staff. In her gentle way she insisted, and we hired a few more people."

Like a magician pulling a rabbit from a hat, he produced the second model.

"*Voilà*, again, the Hafner Skyangel," he said, unveiling a sleek passenger transport. Only the bomber's fuselage had been changed; everything else was the same. "A crew of three and ten passengers cruising comfortably at three miles a minute. It will drive the Fords and Fokkers and even our own trimotors from the sky, and all the single-engine transports with them."

Charlotte watched her husband's expression change from the embarrassment Rhoades's comment on bribery had caused to one of choirboy hopefulness. She felt she could risk reminding him of her role in the project.

"Bruno, do you remember the night you called me from Oakland, and said we could build transports with our own engines and props? This is it."

She let him absorb the idea. "We'll build the transports on the same line with the bombers, and won't take orders from anybody until we reequip the Federated fleet with maybe sixty or seventy airplanes. We'll have the industry tied up."

Hafner's entire physical demeanor changed, the years and inner anguish both slipping from him equally. Prospective success gave him a roaring rush of pleasure. For the moment, the entire world was golden, and the people in the room were the agents of his harmony. Only at times like this did he find in life the strength and pleasure that mortal combat had given him.

He grabbed Charlotte's arms and whirled her around. "What a doll baby you are!" He turned to the group, smiling broadly. "And Armand, you're the best thing to come from Russia since caviar."

He shook the hands of other engineers, and even slipped his arm around Rhoades's shoulders.

"Dusty, did you ever think you'd see anything like this?"

"Russia lost a great designer when we snared Bineau, and there's nothing that Charlotte can do that would surprise me. I've heard you call her 'champ,' and champ she is."

Bruno sustained his upbeat mood the rest of the morning while he went over their holdings with Charlotte. The engineers left, pleased that they had pleased Hafner, and the room which had seemed so wastefully opulent when he walked in now seemed just right. Charlotte had a stack of journals, gray-bound with green spines, each labeled in gold letters.

She handed him summary profit-and-loss statements and an interim balance sheet. "You can see this is a tough time. We need money for current operations, and I don't see it coming from anywhere but capital.''

He nodded.

"We're losing money every day on Federated with the trimotors. They're too slow and don't carry enough people.''

"What do you hear about their stopping the mail subsidy?''

"Nothing but rumors so far, but I believe it will happen. The government might start to fly the mail again.''

"Yeah, that's what I hear too. Say, I didn't want to mention it in front of Bineau, but why only ten passengers in the new transport?''

"It's the only way we could use the same wing as the bomber. If we wanted more passengers—sixteen or twenty—we'd have to build two completely different airplanes, and we just don't have the capital or the engineering capacity to do it.''

"The next one has to be bigger,'' he answered.

That afternoon, Charlotte took him out to the small hangar next to the main factory. Inside was a gleaming red-and-white Gee Bee Model Y Senior Sportster monoplane, a tiny open-cockpit two-seater whose big engine gave it a hydrocephalic look. Standing under a trimotor's wing it looked like a child's pedal toy.

"How do you like my baby? I'm going to fly it in the National Air Races at Cleveland.''

Bruno made a swift assessment of the gains versus the risks.

"No, *mein Gott*, that's too risky. I'd rather you just stuck to flying the company planes for publicity.''

"Dammit, Bruno, I'm bored. I need the challenge of the competition.''

"We can't afford to lose you—I couldn't stand it if something happened to you. Leave the races to people like Amelia Earhart.''

A sudden pleasure at Bruno's rare compliment was washed away immediately in resentment.

"Look, I'm tired of hearing about Amelia Earhart. She's just a beginner—I don't think she can fly worth a damn.''

"She must be doing something right.'' Bruno knew immediately it was the wrong tack.

"It's her husband, Putnam! He works it so that she can't cough without getting a headline.''

A wave of foreboding that he didn't understand passed over Bruno. "Every time I fly one of our planes the press just assumes that I'm along for the ride,'' she said. "They act as though some other pilot is doing the work. In a race, I'll be the only one in the airplane.''

"Charlotte, racing is a man's game. You don't need to take chances pushing an airplane around the pylons, fifty feet off the ground. Too many people get hurt that way.''

Even as he took her hand, he felt his mood changing. In the past Charlotte had been just a valuable business asset, someone to use to get where he wanted to go. Yet the more valuable she had become to him in business, the more he resented depending upon her.

He hadn't minded when she had played around sexually—he'd done plenty of that—although the business with Rhoades was becoming too long-term, and that bothered him. He understood too how she manipulated him; he permitted that. But this self-assertive independence was something else, something that might not be tolerable. And there was more. The realization that he needed her for comfort as well as for strength annoyed him. He didn't want to be dependent on anyone. Yet after fighting the world for years, he had isolated himself from it. Charlotte was his connection, and he didn't want her killed in some stupid race.

"Charlotte, I don't want you to do it. I forbid it.''

She was resolute. It was an issue that had to be faced.

"Bruno, I won't give in on this one, no matter how much you bluster. I'm going to race whether you like it or not. You're just worried that you won't have someone to run the plant if I kill myself.''

He was silent, uncertain of his own feelings. In a quiet voice, he said, "Be careful. That's a mean little bastard, and a Gee Bee killed Lowell Bayles last December. We can't have anything happen to you.''

"I'll watch it. You watch it too.''

She was content; she'd won all the meaningful points, and he was still not enraged. She let him slip his arm around her as they walked back to the factory. Rhoades watched from the window, shaking his head in a mixture of jealousy and amusement.

Sayville, Long Island/June 16, 1932

Patty and Stephan lived in a guest cottage near the enormous Tudor mansion Bruno had bought Charlotte after she had sold the Army the A-11. In the years that Patty had been away in

France, Bruno and Charlotte had somehow assumed totally new personalities. Her stepfather, formerly frivolous in his work habits, was obsessively preoccupied with the aircraft plant. In the past he'd been willing to delegate, to let Armand Bineau and his crew pretty well run things, with Charlotte there to protect his interest. He had to be at the center of every meeting, kibitzing, making notes, demanding more and more frequently that things be done his way.

Charlotte told him that he was driving everybody crazy, but the changes had some totally unexpected side benefits. He was much easier to live with; his hours were predictable, and at home he would work in his little office till late at night. He'd developed a new hobby, photography, and was buying camera equipment almost every week. Two rooms and a tiny bathroom in the basement had been converted to a professional darkroom, and he spent hours developing his own prints.

On balance, Charlotte seemed content. She and Bruno had separate bedrooms, and Patty no longer saw any indication of intimacy in their conduct. She remembered that earlier in their marriage, when she was just a child, their randy sexual activity had caused her more than one embarrassing moment, and she had learned to make plenty of noise before coming into a room she knew they occupied. Then there was the debacle in Orléans!

Yet with it all they seemed still to be friends, to enjoy the house, the business.

She stopped Charlotte on the veranda and said, "Stephan will be competing in the National Air Races this year. Will you be there?"

"There? I'm going to be competing too, in my Gee Bee."

She sighed, rolling her eyes, and it came to Patty what the real change in her mother was. She was no longer inveterately flirtatious; she had grown beyond the *femme fatale* manner of just a few years ago. It was a becoming difference, one more suitable for her age and work at the aircraft plant.

Charlotte's voice was pensive as she said, "It won't be easy to get away. The factory is running full-tilt, and Bruno is into everything. I have to follow him around, patching up the personnel problems he causes with his damn buttinsky attitude."

"You've changed, and so has he. Do you mind if I say you're both easier to live with?"

Charlotte laughed. "Not if you mind if I say you're not. You remind me of myself ten years ago, vaguely discontented and ready for adventure. Do you want to talk about it?"

Patty laughed. "Translated roughly from motherese, that comes out as 'Where the hell are my grandchildren?' "

"Right. It's one thing to be modern and control the size of your family—it's another not to have any kids at all."

"It's a bigger problem than being modern. We've tried for years. Stephan and I have both been to doctors. They say it's just fate, that it will happen in time. I'm ready to adopt a baby, but I know Stephan won't agree."

"It would be tough for his family to accept."

"That's not the trouble. It's his ego. What do you think we should do, Mother?"

Charlotte leaned over and took Patty's hand, just as she had when her daughter was a child.

"Patty, I'm going to ask you a favor. Don't call me Mother, call me Charlotte. It's not because I'm worried about growing old, but because I want to be able to treat you as a woman, not just as my daughter. I don't have many people I can really talk to."

"Sure, it's very modern. I'll slip, but sure."

"You have many more chances in life than I did, especially in flying. I never really mastered instrument flying, and Stephan says you're very good."

"What's come over you, Mother—I mean, Charlotte? You seem to be entirely composed, rested, content."

"I've grown up. Thank God." She looked a little embarrassed, and stared straight into Patty's eyes. "I don't need men or flying as I once did."

Patty glanced out over the lawn. The openness was even more startling than the change in demeanor.

Charlotte was arranging flowers in a vase, an activity so out of character that Patty couldn't comment on it.

Patty nodded approval of the flowers, and, pressing, asked, "Why are you so content?"

"Well, I have my daughter back with me for a while. The businesses are doing well, and damn few people in America can say that. Bruno's been on his best behavior around here; I can't remember the last time we had a fight. It's funny, because he was more nervous than I've ever seen him when he came back from Germany. I thought someone had threatened him."

She was quiet for a while, then went on, "Mainly, though, I think I'm happy because I've finally admitted to myself that I'm hurt because what I've done for flying hasn't been recognized.

I want to set some records, to win some races, to make my name known. In the past I wouldn't admit that to myself."

Patty shook her head. "You're being too hard on yourself. Everyone knows that your demonstration flights have been the main factor in Hafner Aircraft sales."

"That's part of the problem. The Army knows, sure, but not the public. Practically the only flying I've ever done was for the business."

Patty's eyes lit up. They were getting closer to the subject she wanted to broach when Charlotte sailed the conversation into totally uncharted waters.

"And, of course, there's the fact that I have a decent lover."

Patty struggled to keep her face composed, her voice even. They had never discussed any subject like this before.

"Should I ask who, or be politely silent?"

"You don't have to ask. I'll tell you, because I want you to know. It's Dusty Rhoades. Surprised?"

Appalled might be a better word, Patty thought. "No. Why not? You've been associated a long time, and propinquity is almost always a factor in things like this." She paused. "And you weren't exactly discreet, even in Orléans."

"This isn't a 'thing like this,' but propinquity is certainly part of the cause." She watched Patty, amused at her attempt at nonchalance. "Let me fill in the blanks I see on your face. Yes, he's still handsome but he's put on weight. Yes, he is kind. Yes, I'm going to marry him someday. No, I don't know when. I'd have to get a settlement from Bruno that protected you, and I don't see that happening. Any others?"

"No, and don't worry about protecting me. Stephan takes good care of me."

"Well, the question you should have asked, because I know you must have heard the rumors, is 'What about his drug problem?' Right?"

Patty nodded.

"That's part of it too. He *needs* me, and that's something new for me in a man. I'm going to help him beat his habit, rehabilitate him."

There was doubt and anguish in Patty's face.

"Why am I telling you all this? Because I don't want to bother to cover up with you. I have to with Bruno, of course, although I'm sure he knows. But it would be inconvenient to make up stories with you too. What difference does it make? It's my business, and you're a grown woman."

Patty stood up and paced the floor. Charlotte was right, but it was a lot to take in. "Maybe we ought to talk about something else. Like flying. When can I get checked out in the Hafner airplanes? And if I do, will I be a threat to you?"

"Not a threat, a blessing. I'm not crazy about your flying, but I know how you feel. I felt the same way at your age. I'll turn it all over to you as soon as you can handle it. I will have to do the demonstration flights for a while; Bruno thinks I have a special rapport with the Air Corps. But you'd fit right in." She paused. "I've got a tip for you. Do your record-setting flying from city to city. There are a million records out there that have never been set—Kokomo to Hoboken, Cucamonga to Mojave—and the first time you fly it, you set a record. The press eats it up, and it's easy. Stay away from the pylon racing; it's too dangerous."

Her expression changed from concern to anger as she continued, "I want it to be different for you! No matter what I do, the press doesn't care. That damn Amelia Earhart gets all the publicity."

It was as close as Patty had ever seen Charlotte come to crying. She knew what the problem was—Amelia Earhart had just returned from her solo flight across the Atlantic, and you couldn't pick up a magazine or go to the newsreels without seeing her.

"She's just an appealing figure, Charlotte. She looks like Lindbergh, and someone knows how to get publicity for her. Bruno is content as long as the Air Corps is pleased by your flying. Maybe you ought to get a press agent."

Charlotte had recovered. "Well, maybe. There's one thing more, though, a *quid pro quo* for flying. I want you to start assuming more responsibility in managing the business. You've avoided it long enough. I want you to start putting in a forty-hour week at the plant."

Patty jumped up and kissed her; she wanted the work more than the flying.

New York City/July 2, 1932

The French consul in New York had arranged for a reception for Stephan and Patty at the Wings Club, and most of the aviation notables in town attended, including Charlotte's *bête noire*, Amelia Earhart. When they met in the receiving line, Amelia was very gracious, and Charlotte almost snubbed her. Nevertheless, when the receiving line ended, Amelia came to Patty and gently tugged at her elbow.

"Can we go somewhere and talk for a moment?"

Flushed with pleasure, Patty walked with her down the hall to the library. Earhart closed the doors behind them, and they sat at a huge walnut table layered with aviation magazines from around the world.

They sat for a moment, each studying the other. Amelia's voice was low and vibrant, entirely different from the scratchy high-pitched tones of the newsreels. Not so tall as she appeared in her photos, she projected an aura of vulnerable authority, as if she were cast as the Saint Joan of flying for women, and was not comfortable in the role. Yet underneath her apparent fragility a resilient inner strength was apparent. A thousand questions occurred to Patty, but the first one came from Amelia.

"Would you like a cigarette?"

"No, but please have one if you wish."

"I'm glad you don't smoke. I don't either, despite the Lucky Strike ads. I take the money from them, but I never say I smoke. I hate it."

Amelia gave a little shudder, then moved her chair closer to Patty. The most famous woman aviator in the world kicked off her shoes and curled her feet up beneath her. "I understand that you learned to fly in France?"

"Yes, my instructor taught me to fly, then I persuaded him to marry me."

Earhart smiled, relaxing. As she let her guard down, her face softened, and the set smile that she provided photographers on cue turned into an intimate grin that said, "I like you, and I hope you like me."

"Your instructor was lucky. What made you want to fly?"

Patty realized that an interview was in process.

"It's in the family. My father was a pilot in France during the war. He was an ace, but he was killed in combat. My mother flies, and oddly enough, my stepfather is also a pilot from the war. The German side. I guess it was inevitable for me to want to follow in all those footsteps."

"My spies tell me that you are an expert instrument pilot."

"I'm not sure I would say that, but my husband has given me almost one hundred hours of instruction in a Caudron cabin plane. I hope I've learned a little."

Earhart pursed her lips, obviously hesitant.

"This is a little difficult for me. For one thing, I've heard that your mother doesn't like me—I don't know why. For another, we've just met. But I want to ask a favor of you."

"Don't worry about Mother; she's larger than life, and I'm sure if you got to know each other you'd be friends. And if I can help, I will."

Again, there was a moment of silence. "I've been asked to go to Detroit for the introduction of a new Hudson car. I'm to be 'mistress of ceremonies.' I hate that term; it sounds as if I were going to service the entire audience."

Patty smiled.

"The car is going to be called the Terraplane, so they've invited some aviation figures to be present. Believe it or not, Orville Wright will be there, and that's the main reason I'm going. How could I refuse if he is willing?"

Patty was still unable to see how she could help.

"I've borrowed a new airplane to make the trip, a four-place cabin Waco with a Continental engine. It's really quite beautiful."

She paused, and then blurted, "It also has a complete set of flight instruments. I'd like you to go with me and give me some instruction on instrument flying."

Patty sat up. What a compliment! Stephan would be pleased, and Charlotte absolutely furious!

"I'm honored, but aren't there many pilots who are better qualified than I am?"

"Not better, perhaps, but there are others, all men. I'm frightened of male instructors. I learned to fly from Neeta Snook, and even though I've flown with many men pilots, some of the best, it's hard for me to learn from them. That's why I do the cigarette advertisements—I use the money to train women instructors, and to teach other women to fly. I'm tired of flying being strictly a man's game."

Patty nodded vigorously. "I think men find sex in flying. I'm not talking about groping around in a cockpit. There's just some mixture of death and sex in flying that appeals to them."

"You're right. I know just what you mean. To men a plane is like a good bed partner. Women get a more spiritual lift from flying." She paused. "Not that there is anything wrong with a good bed partner."

Patty laughed, and Amelia went on. "You know, most instructors either try to make a girl student pilot sick or they pinch her bottom, or both."

"My mother pinches back; I think that's why she's been so successful."

"There's the same sort of difference with clothes. Why men pilots feel they have to dress up like businessmen, with coats and ties, I'll never know."

"You always look wonderful."

"No, it's your mother who looks wonderful. I'm scrawny and not very feminine-looking. She always looks like a movie star."

She patted Patty's hand. "How about it? Will you do me a favor?"

"You're on!"

Amelia, obviously delighted, leaned over and hugged her.

Detroit, Michigan/July 21, 1932

The breeze from Lake St. Clair was simply more heat-laden moisture and comforted no one. It was an hour until dinner, and Patty lay naked in bed, flapping a towel for comfort as the beaded moisture of her bath was slowly replaced by perspiration.

The trip up had been marvelous. The airplane was delightful, stable about all axes, and capable of an honest 100-mph cruise speed. Earhart deferred to Patty, letting her make most of the takeoffs and landings.

It took Amelia a little time to get used to the hood Stephan had made for Patty to use while learning to fly instruments. It was a simple strap-on device, looking much like an accountant's green visor, but it blocked out the view of everything but the instrument panel. It was the next best thing to actually flying in clouds.

Patty watched outside for other traffic, and gave Amelia course and altitude directions that let her practice turns, climbs, and descents. She particularly enjoyed dropping in on the airports at Pittsburgh and Cleveland, where Amelia caused an instant furor of activity. It was the first time Patty had been around a genuine celebrity, and she loved it.

At Detroit, they landed ironically enough at the Ford Airport at Dearborn. With one last apologetic look at Patty, Amelia took on a different persona. From the moment she swept from the biplane's tiny cabin door onto the lower wing, Amelia had been "on," plugging aviation, and introducing Patty as "the Lindbergh of the thirties."

Dinner at the Chapins' that evening made her think wistfully of France again: it was overdone roast beef, overcooked string beans, mashed potatoes, and overcooked gravy. There had been plenty of hard liquor available before the meal, but only iced tea with it. The coffee was wonderful.

Whatever Chapin's faults in the gastronomy department, Patty could only admire his public relations skills. The next day the Terraplane was presented to the world from a shipping terminal only four blocks north of the main Essex plant. While some dealers and salesmen were given tours in the two thousand identical demonstrators that Chapin had assembled for a parade, the rest ate a huge lunch in gigantic tents spotted around the square.

The high point was the christening. A champagne bottle had been carefully etched with acid so that it would break without putting a dent in the sweeping chromium grille of the new car. Amelia, in a high-necked dress that was drenched with sweat, gave the grille a gentle tap, and high-test aviation gasoline poured out over the Terraplane. Orville Wright, after hours of sitting anonymously with his fedora clamped sternly around his ears and eyebrows, stood up and clapped. Patty wished her mother had been there, to see if she would have tried to seduce him.

She and Earhart got up early the next morning, and repeated the exchange of lessons on the way back to Long Island. On the approach into Roosevelt Field, Amelia pulled back on the throttle and yelled, "Patty, thank you so much. I've learned a lot. Please, let's keep in touch. I'm sure we can help each other in the future."

Laredo, Texas/July 24, 1932

American food had always puzzled Stephan, but this was absurd. He had suffered some terrible food on duty in Algiers, but one expected it there. He pushed away the plate of beans and rice. For one solid week he'd eaten nothing but goat, in stews, steaks, and roasts, and with only beer to drink. His system was beginning to stage a revolution.

The only thing positive was that no one would know he had been to the sunbaked Texas town, as forsaken as a Foreign Legion outpost. Patty's trip with Amelia Earhart had been a godsend. He had told her that he had to go to San Antonio, on assignment from the French air force, to see the American training establishment. He had spent one day there, and then had taken the lurching, gritty train south to Laredo and the hardly antiseptic clinic of Dr. Ravenal Drinkley.

Accustomed to European hospitals and spas, he was dismayed by the rambling bunkhouse structure at the edge of the desert, broiling in the hundred-degree heat. Something had apparently been lost in the translation between what Drinkley was doing and what Stephan's own physician, Dr. Lissarague, had thought he was doing. Lissarague had heard that Drinkley was a specialist in fertility, when in fact most of the other patients were seeking potency.

But Drinkley, who inspired confidence despite his enormous bulk and the fact that his white medical coat tended to be a display of menus past, had assured Stephan that increased potency was just a fortunate—and sought-after—by-product of a vast increase in fertility. He quickly agreed to take the week-long regime.

He was the only European there; the clientele were from California for the most part, and he thought that two or three of the older men were incognito film stars. The rest were from South America, primarily Argentina, but a few from Brazil.

All were apparently wealthy; one had to be. The course of treatment cost $1,000, payable in advance, and including the monotonously goat-laden meals. Stephan had dipped into a private account, and the expenditure for the treatment was going to interfere substantially with future dalliances.

The ghastly meals were derived from the treatment. Drinkley had a secret process by which glands from goats were placed in a centrifuge; the resulting essence was then not only injected in the patients, but served in a revolting concoction that was taken four times a day. The unfortunate goats from which the glands had come appeared at every meal in some barely disguised state. Drinkley made a virtue of the fact, claiming that the cooked-goat diet helped the body adjust to the raw-goat injections.

Drinkley apparently dissolved his goat extract in some sort of beeswax emulsion; the twice-daily injections left large lumps that took time to absorb. On the day he left, Stephan's legs looked as if he were trying to smuggle marbles out beneath his skin.

Between the treatment, the food, and the heat, Stephan knew that he would deserve any babies he conceived. At the end, he was aware only of an increased sense of potency, but that could easily be attributable to abstinence. It had been easy to refuse to join the others, anxious to check their progress, on their clandestine trips across the border to Nuevo Laredo's red-light district. Lurking in the back of his mind was a hideous conjecture that some youthful indiscretion was responsible for his fertility problem.

Salinas, California/July 30, 1932

Clarice Roget mused at the tremendous change in Bandfield. Ordinarily brimming with energy, he had come back from Peru in a supercharged state as they worked desperately night and day to get the bomber proposal prepared. The shock he had felt over Hadley's accepting money from Hafner Aircraft for the fifty-five-foot wing disappeared as the engineering fever caught him. Never at rest, his fingers drumming the table, feet rocking back and forth, twirling from one spot to another like some sort of human milk-shake machine, he was exhausting just to watch.

Up at six and at the drafting table by seven, he would work all day on the bomber, running reams of figures through their pathetic old adding machine, making his slide rule hum as he checked and double-checked. Then he would bolt down an enormous supper, whatever Clarice put on the table, it didn't matter as long as there were two or three helpings and plenty of bread and butter. After the cake—she always had at least one kind of cake, maybe two—he'd race out to the barn to work on the racer, on cars, whatever Hadley wanted. Around midnight he and Hadley would hunker down over the kitchen table, under the glare of the bare bulb hanging down from the ceiling, to split half a pie and drink a pot of coffee, talking over the day and planning the next.

It was as if he worked to rid himself of the Pineapple Derby demons and the sadness that had stolen his youth. Clarice was always cataloguing the eligible girls that she knew, wondering who would take him from his memories. He missed that Duncan girl dreadfully, she knew, but it had been going on too long; it was time for him to find another woman.

He stood, fidgeting, as Hadley carefully threaded an eight-foot pipe onto the end of the two-foot-long monkey wrench. Grunting like a warthog, Howard Hughes—why Hadley bothered to call him Charles she never could figure out—took time to fit the carefully padded jaws around the battered Monocoupe's propeller hub nut. He laughed. "Always get a bigger hammer, Bandy," he said.

Roget pulled down on the levered wrench, and there was a satisfying pop as the nut broke loose.

"Those bastards are always devils—but at least they keep the prop on." Hadley wiped his hands and pulled Bandfield into the corner.

"I've got my eye on one hell of a plant in Downey, Bandy. Did you know Charlie Rocheville?"

"No, but I sure loved his airplanes, especially that little midwing two-seater. Called them Emscos, didn't they?"

"Yeah. They're having big tax troubles with the government, and I can pick up the plant for a song."

"Jeez, that would get us out of this garage and into a real factory."

"Yeah. We could build two or three prototypes at a time in that son of a bitch—a bomber, a fighter, maybe a trainer. And there are all kinds of tools for production." Roget bubbled on, telling him how the plant was worth over a million, but they could pick it up for $10,000 in back taxes and about $50,000 in cash. There was $30,000 left from the license deal, and he thought he could get a loan of $20,000 from the bank.

Bandfield knew what he had to do: pick up at least $10,000 or more in prizes in Cleveland.

That afternoon they flew over to Downey in their latest creation, the bright yellow Kitten light plane. They had worked on it off and on for years, and it was their hole card, their backup in case the bomber design was not accepted. After looking at the market pretty carefully, they thought they could sell as many as twenty to thirty Kittens a year, if they could get a good dealer network.

Downey's huge field, isolated way out in the country some twelve miles from Long Beach, was deserted. A modern factory building, assembly bay, machine shop, and administrative section were locked up like so many other plants in Depression-burdened America.

"Breaks your heart, don't it?"

Bandy nodded, pulling himself up on a dusty window ledge to peer inside the assembly bay. There were two long lonely production lines, empty of everything but fixtures and tools. At one end was a forlorn Emsco trimotor, heavy with dust and the inevitable pigeon droppings, tires going flat.

"Does the airplane go with the plant?"

"I think everything goes, just as you see it."

A hot lust for the property suffused Bandy. "Jesus Christ, let's buy it, no matter what it takes. We could do anything with a setup like this. How did they fail? Rocheville is a first-class designer."

"I don't know—the Depression, of course, but I think it was mainly because they were using this as a tax dodge for other businesses. They weren't serious about airplanes."

"We'll be serious."

With one stop for fuel, they flew back to the Roget airstrip, ignoring the gorgeous sere brown of the California landscape, each lost in his own thoughts. When they got down, Hadley said, "This is a whole new ball game, Bandy. You can be the chief test pilot and run the engineering department. I figure we can pick up a lot of skilled out-of-work people from Douglas and Northrop, easy."

"Workers won't be our problem."

An argument had long been brewing. Hadley had been sensitive to Bandfield's depression, and repressed his own naturally combative nature. To compensate, as a means of expression, he had been working furiously on a project of his own, one he intended as a surprise for Bandfield. He sensed the trouble in the air and decided to defuse the situation by showing Bandfield his proposal for a new airplane. Attempting to butter him up, he took Bandy by the elbow and steered him toward the secluded rear section of the hangar. The "back room" was always kept under lock and key, and Bandy had honored Hadley's request not to go in until Roget asked him to. He knew it was supposed to be a treat.

Hadley's grin grew as he led him back through the assorted Roget promises of the past. He threaded his way between the Rascal racer, still not complete but almost there, and the shattered remains of the flying wing that had promised so much. It was a long-range airplane Hadley had lovingly built, mostly wing with twin rudders set out on tail booms; he had bailed out of it when he encountered violent wing flutter on a test flight. The yellow ceiling lights cast dancing shadows on the bitter endings of so many promising starts. Only the familiar, intoxicating smell of oil, dope, and gasoline was comforting.

He followed Hadley into the darkened room.

"Okay," the older man said, and turned on the overhead lights.

In the center of the immaculate floor was a full-size drawing of a jet-black racer, a bigger edition of the Rascal. A mock-up of the right wing, supported by a sawhorse, extended from the drawing. The cowling was huge—Hadley intended it to enclose a Wasp Senior radial engine. The retractable landing gear was designed to pull up into the fuselage, just as on the Navy's Grumman fighters. The mocked-up wing was short and thick. The tiny cockpit was faired into the rudder coaming with a bulbous sliding canopy, just big enough for his head.

"Jesus, it looks like a cross between a Wedell-Williams and a Gee Bee, the best features of both."

"That's not all, Bandy. Watch."

Hadley ran power cables to a plug on the side of the cardboard fuselage.

"Look at this!" The older man threw a switch, and an electric motor moaned behind the fuselage drawing. The wing quivered, elongating, the black tip extending out for another six feet. At the point of farthest extension, there was a one-foot strip painted gleaming white for emphasis.

"Holy Christ, what is this? A variable wingspan?"

"Yeah, it gives you twelve feet more wingspan, and you'll have inboard flaps and outboard slots, too."

Roget extolled the plane's features. The landing gear and flaps were electrically driven, like the wing.

"This should give us maybe three-ten, three twenty-five miles an hour. You land with the wings extended too, of course. Keeps landing speeds down in the seventy-mile-an-hour range."

A transcendent tinkerer's joy suffused Hadley's face. "I'm— we're—calling this one the Roget Rambler, cause she's really going to ramble. Don't worry about the strength, either, Bandy. I've got this figured out so that it can't be overstressed, no matter what speed you're going when you retract or extend the wings, and they'll always work together."

Bandfield didn't say anything. He walked around the mock-up airplane, checking the extension mechanism. Hadley looked like a grandfather giving out Christmas toys to the family.

"What do you think? We could fly it with the wings extended in the Bendix, retracted in the Thompson. In the Bendix you could even pull the wings in bit by bit as you burned off fuel, and pick up your speed as you went."

Bandfield was silent. The airplane looked wonderful, and he was going to have to be negative about it. Hadley simply had to start being more businesslike.

"It looks great, but I've got to talk to you. Let's see if Clarice will give us some coffee."

Hadley was taken aback, puzzled and hurt. The Rambler was easily the best thing he'd ever done, and Bandy was reacting strangely.

In the kitchen, they sat around the oilcloth-covered table. On the side was a tablet on which Hadley did his sketches and Clarice tried to scratch out the numbers that would somehow stretch her budget. Bandy guessed that she hadn't seen a dime of the license fee; it wouldn't occur to Hadley to spend money on anything but airplanes. Even groceries came after parts at the Rogets'.

"What's the matter, Bandy, don't you like the airplane?"

The younger man spooned sugar into his coffee, turning the eddies of the condensed Pet Milk from rich cream to light brown. He stared at the trademark, wide-eyed concentric cows trailing off into some bovine infinity in the center of the can. He wished there were somewhere he could go to get away from the problem at hand.

"I'm not going to talk about the airplane, per se. But I don't know any way to say this except straight out. Times are changing. I'm not talking about the Depression, or Roosevelt, or maybe repealing Prohibition. I'm talking about aviation. And I've got to tell you something unpleasant. You're just not being serious enough about your airplanes."

Hadley snapped to a scorpion stance, back arched, ready to pounce, all the old aggressiveness at the ready. His voice raised in indignation.

"What do you mean? Just because you've got an engineering degree doesn't give you the right to talk like that. There's not another airplane in the United States that's more advanced."

"No, you're exactly right. And we haven't even flown the Rascal, and you're already dreaming about something else. And we've got the bomber to do!"

He stopped to take control of his voice. "Hadley, these aren't model airplanes, these are hot, untried, full-sized ships, and we've got to start spending the necessary time to develop them. You can't make them and then throw them away like a toothbrush."

"That's what everybody else is doing, Bandy. You don't see the same airplanes every year at Cleveland, do you?"

"Yeah, you do, the winners mostly. Jimmy Wedell started out with a tiny little airplane with a Chevrolet engine, and he's developed it into the hottest thing around. It's not a killer like the Gee Bees."

Unconsciously, they had squared off, moving so that the table was no longer between them, assuming a crouch, arms positioned for protection, hands beginning to curl into fists. Bandfield sensed it and blushed; he would rather put his arm in a prop than strike Hadley.

"And it takes time to work the bugs out. Airplanes are different now, more power, more stress. You can't just play with them anymore."

Hadley didn't say anything. Bandy was glad Clarice had left the room.

Bandfield's voice changed to a kindly, pleading tone. "Think about it. When you learned to fly, when you started building airplanes, everything was the same. Wood spars, wood ribs, wood-and-wire fuselages. No stress analysis. You'd just eyeball it, then maybe make a part a little bigger if you didn't think it was strong enough. Then they started using steel tubing, with maybe aluminum ribs if you were fancy. That's where you still are, and that's all over. Metal airplanes with retractable landing gear are going to be what everybody needs. And you can't build them the way you can wood-and-rag ships, with a handful of men in a tiny shop."

Hadley responded, "That's why I want the Emsco plant, dumb-ass!"

More confident, Bandy retorted sharply, "Yeah, and that's why I'm talking like this to you. You want the plant, but you're still wedded to your old ideas. The physical plant is only half of it, maybe less than that, only ten percent. The first thing you have to have is a philosophy about building quality. You've got that now, no question. The second thing is a concept. What kind of airplanes are you going to build, how many, and who are you going to sell them to? That's what you've never worried about in the past."

Hadley's jaw was twitching, a sure sign that an explosion was coming. He wanted to crush Bandy with a remark, but the best he could do was "Says you!"

Bandfield continued, "Nobody else has worried about it either, much, for some reason. We've been floundering around building airplanes for the fun of it, always assuming somebody would buy it if it was a good airplane. The fact that no market ever materialized didn't bother anyone."

Hadley sat, eyes cast down, his hands bending the blade of a table knife back and forth.

"Out of probably a thousand would-be plane builders, only four or five have succeeded—Douglas, Boeing, Curtiss, Martin, a few more. The rest folded, some of them famous names. The Wright brothers themselves couldn't make it. Look at the rest—Loening, Dayton-Wright, Travelair—all gone because they couldn't compete."

It was the right tack. As tough as times had been for Roget Aircraft, they had been bad elsewhere, too. Bandfield knew that failing never really bothered Hadley if he felt the cause was external events. If it was the fault of the airplane—as in the case of the flying wing—he was miserable.

"The reason the big guys succeeded was that they had an idea and followed it. Douglas built quality transports, big airplanes, around-the-world jobs. Boeing built fighters. Curtiss was a giant, did some of both, and Martin and Grumman tried to stick to the needs of the Navy. If we want to succeed in a big way, to really do something for aviation, then we've got to do the same thing. Target what we want to do, hire the right people, and then stick to it."

The knife blade snapped, and Roget threw the pieces against the wall.

"What the hell do you think I had in mind?"

Bandfield sensed he was near the point of no return, and let a friendlier tone enter his voice.

"You're one of the brightest engineers in the world—I'd never be able to hold a candle to you—but you're still playing around with airplanes as if they were model kits. I've got a race in Cleveland coming up, and you've forgotten about the Rascal. You've spent your time designing a brand-new airplane with brand-new bugs. You should have been thinking about how to improve the Rascal. Shit, I haven't had a chance to fly *it* yet."

The older man was obviously crushed, but Bandfield was relentless. "Airplanes need to be cultivated, to grow. You just want to build 'em, fly 'em, and forget 'em, just like your old joke about sorority girls. What we need to do is improve the Rascal, put a canopy and retractable gear on it maybe, bring it along. Then we can build the Rambler over the next year or two, get it running right. I've seen too many crashes from people rushing things."

They were silent. In the background, Bandy could hear the scratchy Atwater Kent radio pouring out "Night and Day." What he was talking about was as different from Roget's thinking as night was from day.

"Look, you know I think Bruno Hafner is the biggest prick in the business. But he's got enough sense to stay out of Bineau's way, and Charlotte does the same. They run a professional factory. I've got the greatest respect for Bineau, even though I don't think he's in your league as an engineer. But he does his development work systematically."

Hadley was sourly defensive. "Yeah, and he's got all of Bruno's dough behind him." He got up and rustled through the icebox, pulling out two Baby Ruth candy bars. He tossed one to Bandy and tore the wrapper off the other with his teeth. Bandfield peeled the wrapper back. The damp of the icebox had changed the chocolate to an unappetizing moldy white. He ate it anyway, afraid to give offense.

"Sure he does—he could afford to screw around the way you do, but he doesn't. He's got more sense," he went on. "Hadley, you know it's not the money. I'll fly the race, and if I win, I'll give you all the money, no strings attached. But if you want me to be a part of the plant, we've got to operate differently. If you want me in the new company, I'll put up the dough, but I'll be the test pilot and the *president*, and we'll do things my way."

He paused, realizing he had to sink the harpoon deeper if he was to keep Hadley's attention.

"On the way in I walked past your flying wing. That was a damn good airplane, radical, but with a lot of promise. You cracked it up by pushing it. You could have tested it for six months and solved the flutter problem. But you pushed ahead, and had to bail out when the tail came off. No more airplane! All the work down the drain. It could have been a winner, but the wreckage is gathering dust in the hangar."

He gulped and continued, "From now on you have to—we have to—stop acting like it's still 1920. There's no point in taking over a million-dollar factory and building the same kind of airplanes that you did here. And I hope you're thinking all-metal, because the time for tube and fabric is over. You know that, Hadley."

There was an edge to Roget's voice. "It's gone for fighters and bombers, but it'll be around a long time in light planes and trainers, and so will wood." He was silent for a moment, then tried to sound conciliatory. "Bandy, I hear you, but I'm not sure I agree entirely. I've spent twenty years doing things my way. It's tough to start new methods now."

"Let's get it all on the table. If you do get the new factory, and you really want me to work with you, there will have to be a lot of changes."

Roget nodded cautiously.

"You won't be doing many of the things you used to do. There will be almost no hands-on work for you at all. You are past that. You'll be supervising a team of engineers and a team of production people, making sure they draw what you invent. And you'll be seeing that they build it right."

Roget's expression was blank, and Bandy's voice took on a pleading note.

"Otherwise, there's no point in investing your time and effort. We've got to use your talent as a lever to move a dozen people to do what we can't do alone."

The older man looked sullenly at the table.

"Face up to it. Unless we get a work force, accountants, a material manager, a floor manager, specialists, what can we do with a big plant like Emsco?"

"Bandy, I want the plant to build a bomber with the fifty-five-foot wing. We could get some big contracts, if not from the Air Corps, maybe from South America or something."

"You are already thinking wrong. Unless you get it from the Air Corps, it's not worth doing. You set the highest standards in the world for craftsmanship, then turn around and lower your sights on sales. It's all wrong."

"Jesus, how come you got smart so soon and rich so slow? You sound like Bruno Hafner, but you ain't got a pot to piss in." Roget looked pugnacious, triumphant.

"Let's not argue. We've been together a long time, and you've treated me wonderfully well all my life. I'll do anything you want, but for once think about Clarice. Don't you think she's entitled to a little security, a little stability, a few luxuries?"

It was a chance but telling shot. Clarice had subordinated herself to Roget's mad infatuation with airplanes all their married life, complaining all the while, but getting only a grudging enjoyment from the tyranny she exercised over the kitchen and the account books.

"Well, think it over. If you want to get into building airplanes on a production-line basis, you need me. If you don't, you can take the money, dump it in the factory, and then watch some other guy take it over when you can't pay the overhead."

Before he left, wishing to make amends, he said, "Maybe we could put a canopy like that on the Rascal. It would give me maybe two or three more miles per hour anyway."

Bandy left, sick at heart. Their years of nonstop arguing had really been an engineering dialectic. This was the first real fight they'd ever had. It was more distressing because there was a role reversal; in the past, Hadley had done all the ranting and raving, keeping him on the defensive.

It didn't matter. Either Roget came around to agree with him and let the factory give him what he wanted—a chance to build better airplanes than Hafner, Boeing, or anybody else—or he would get out of flying. He wanted that factory. Badly.

6

Cleveland, Ohio/August 27, 1932

It was obvious that race organizer and aviation evangelist Cliff
Henderson had the antidote to the Depression. For eleven months
a year, Cleveland was submerged in the industrial malaise gripping the country, worse off than most cities because all the heavy
industry was shut down. But a month before the National Air
Races started in late August, the town came alive. Henderson's
magic way with press and personalities brought everyone on
board to share his conviction that racing was the salvation of
aviation, and that aviation was the salvation of the economy. It
was the only thing that would knock baseball out of the sports-
page headlines as the Giants and the Senators continued their
battle toward the World Series.

The half million people who would pay to see the races would
resent the extra million crowding the roads leading to the airport—Riverside Drive and Five Points Road especially—to catch
a free glimpse of the carnival that Henderson staged. He couldn't
put airplanes under a big tent, and there was a continuous stream
of visual excitement—parachutists, autogiros, aerobatics, and
military planes. Something was happening all day long, necessary distractions to keep people occupied during the long intervals between the races. The races themselves were hard to follow
unless you had grandstand seats, for the tiny airplanes, flying
not more than fifty feet off the ground, disappeared from sight

as they growled around a ten-mile triangular course with engines screaming, reappearing to flash by on the home stretch. The real thrill, the crowd-gripper, was the speculation about whether they'd all reappear. A crash in front of the grandstand was icing on the cake.

The audience had about the same economic profile as the participants—95 percent were broke or nearly so, and 5 percent were very well off. But there was plenty of cotton candy and millions of neon-pink hot dogs filled with grease from unmentionable parts of long-dead animals, and the kids could beg for toy helium-filled dirigibles and blimps. The spice that made it carnival for individuals in the crowd was their certain knowledge of surviving death while enjoying the vicarious thrill of watching others at risk. One could see the hopes of the audience bulging like a weight lifter's biceps, and sense the Roman-circus anticipation of a bloody crash.

Bandy scanned the front-page headlines of the *Cleveland Plain Dealer*. "Cleveland Socialites Start National Air Race Parties," "Doolittle Lands Wheels Up," "Cliff Henderson Tells Pilots: Put Up or Shut Up."

There was not a single mention of the arrival of the Roget Rascal, itself a miracle owed solely to the sale of rights to the wing to Hafner Aircraft. Charlotte had been a brick, speeding up the payments so they could pay off their debts and buy the rest of the material to finish the racer. He smiled wryly at the irony. Bruno Hafner had kept him out of the race to Paris, but Charlotte Hafner had helped him into the races here. Christ, it was a funny world!

Time, economics, and intuition had dictated that they build a virtually new airplane as a simple design with a tiny seventeen-foot-span slab wing and a long nose that Hadley had buttoned tightly around an Army-surplus Curtiss D-12 engine. Bandy had looked at the list of entrants, and he was the only pilot still behind a liquid-cooled power plant. There were a couple of in-line air-cooled Menascos, but the rest were flying air-cooled radials.

On the next page was a four-column photospread on Charlotte Hafner. The main picture showed her in her now-classic pose, standing half in, half out of her Gee Bee's cockpit, helmet in one hand, lips glistening, hair blowing back in the slipstream of the idling engine, the tugging of the white scarf revealing her rounded bosom.

A photo of any woman aviator brought back painful thoughts

of Millie. He always wondered what they would be doing now had she lived, and he castigated himself for the thousandth time for failing to keep her from going. As always, he suffered the last angry thoughts, the ones he had to shake away, thoughts of how she must have felt during the last few moments of her life, when she knew it was ending.

The story focused on the new Hafner Cup being awarded for a transcontinental derby for stock commercial aircraft. First prize was the cup—Bandy thought it looked like a floral wreath for a gangster's funeral—$5,000 and an Auburn roadster; second prize was $3,000 and a Pontiac coupe; third was $1,000 and a Model A sedan. It was a handicap race, with contestants taking off from their hometowns, sponsored by the local car dealers. The racers were rated on an elaborate system that considered distance, time en route, and horsepower. It was smart advertising for Hafner and the car companies, well worth the cost of the prizes. Charlotte naturally was not competing for the cup her company had sponsored, but announced that she hoped to win the Katherine Stinson Trophy race.

He folded the paper and looked off into the distance. Charlotte was apparently immune to aging; she was as beautiful as he remembered her. He wondered what she was really like. The stories about her sexual prowess and her flying skills were legion, but most of that was probably bullshit.

At the bottom of the page a squib said, "Foreign Pilots Arrive." Poland's George Kossowski had brought his gullwing fighter, a P.Z.L.6; the German ace Hans Westoff was demonstrating the Udet Flamingo sportplane; and Stephan Dompnier was going to fly a Caudron racer.

He passed his time in the maintenance pits with the various crews, trying to learn as much as he could. Bandy needed race experience. Flying a fighter was one thing, whipping a racer around a tight measured course was another. He had flown in pickup events around the country, pushing a Laird Speed Wing around the pylons, but Cleveland was distinctly a notch up. He planned to enter as many races as he could, but to fly in only one, the Standard Mystery Derby. The multiple entries meant he could do some practice flying every day during the time trials, trying to pick up all the racing savvy he could.

He had selected the Standard Mystery Derby because it carried a $15,000 first prize, and was generally considered to be the second-most-important event of the closed-course races. More important, the big guns like Roscoe Turner and Jimmy

Doolittle weren't going to enter it, preferring to save their engines for the Thompson Trophy race.

The racing crowd was a friendly fraternity off the course, sharing possessions and effort easily. Once the starting flag was dropped, however, it was every man for himself. The various race teams worked on the ramp in 102 bays arranged in sixteen rows. He wandered through them all, lending a hand here and there, using his back as a sawhorse while a wheel was changed, or holding down on the horizontal stabilizer while an engine was run up. In the process, he got to know everybody and examine everything from Benny Howard's sleek white Menasco-powered Pete to a workaday Monocoupe. The time he had free from tweaking his own racer he spent with Howard Hughes and the Gee Bee bunch.

Hughes, now as good a mechanic as he was a pilot, had taken a job with TWA as Charles Howard. He had then immediately asked for leave to work with the Granvilles. No one else could have gotten away with it, but Hughes did, for by now practically everyone in aviation knew about his ruse. Hughes was hoping to get a chance to fly one of the smaller Sportsters, and he brought Bandy up to speed on the behind-the-scenes activities.

"Are you going to Charlotte Hafner's big party at the country club tonight?"

"No, I didn't get an invitation."

"Man, there are no invitations. Everybody that's racing is going to be there. I wouldn't miss it for the world."

Reluctantly, Bandfield let himself be persuaded. He wanted to learn as much as he could, and the party was a good place. Besides, it might be interesting to talk to Charlotte again. It would be worthwhile to get some insight on Bruno's plans for Hafner Aircraft. He could never like the German ace, but it was impossible not to admire his success in a tough field. All over the country, aviation companies were folding, but Bruno managed to keep his firm profitable. Maybe he could learn the secret of his success from Charlotte.

Hughes always insisted on doing the driving. They were in the Chevrolet sedan he'd purchased on arrival. The experience had been worth the whole trip for Bandfield. They had walked into the showroom, and Hughes had pointed to the car and said, "I'll take that one." The bemused salesman almost seemed cheated when Hughes counted out the full price of $650 in cash, with no haggling. It was just another of Hughes's many contradictions.

Bandfield had long since learned about the source of Hughes's funds, the oil-well-drilling-tool companies, but he was always amazed that Howard, as rich as he was, was quite indifferent to money—as long as he had enough to do exactly what he wanted. It didn't bother Hughes to eat in the same rotten little airport restaurants that the rest of them did, and he wore the same sort of nondescript oil-stained clothes day in and day out. He took turns when it came to picking up the tab, but he was never flamboyant about his wealth. The car was a good example.

"This is a nice car, Howard, but with all your money, why don't you buy a Packard or a Cadillac? A Pierce-Arrow, maybe?"

"Too conspicuous. The last thing I need is anybody looking at me. And if you take a broad out in a Cadillac, a lot of them put on the dog, play hard to get. They act natural in a Chevy, and you can get right to them." It was a typically pragmatic Hughes viewpoint.

The drive to the country club took them along the edge of a run-down factory area. The plants, long idle, were odd geometries of corrugated sheet iron, broken by the sharp angles of elongated windows designed to admit light on hustling assembly lines. Some were coated in a red oxide that gave off a ruddy sunset glow, but the rest were slumped under coats of rust and grime. A few of the buildings were well maintained by firms that had some faint hope of resuming operation, hope that the Depression would end sometime, but most were coming apart, the windows broken, with weeds and even trees growing up between the ties of the railroad spurs that once had served them. For no reason that he could identify, the most poignant were the construction yards, where conveyor belts still stood extended above the piles of sand and gravel, like starving primitive cranes in the act of feeding their young.

In a neat arrangement, calculated long ago by the employers as a means to get people to work on time, the factories were bordered with houses as identical as checkers. Bandfield knew them well, having lived in one in Monterey the year his dad worked at a cannery. They were called straightbacks, with a fifteen-foot-wide living room running across the front which led straight back to a tiny bedroom and kitchen. He couldn't tell, but he thought most would have an indoor bathroom—toilet, claw-leg tub used regularly every Saturday, and a pedestal sink.

A tiny coal stove that would glow red-hot in the winter would be set just at the end of the living room, so that its warmth would drift into the bedroom. The kitchen and bathroom would make do with heat from the coal-fired range.

Judging by the number of people who sat slumped on the slanting steps of the wooden porches, most of the living rooms would have folding cots set up, to handle the children or adults who had moved in to share the tiny rent.

The one dominating feature was the lack of color. Everything was gray, houses, clothing, and faces. Even the leaves of the trees had grown gray with the tired dust of the Depression.

At a stop sign, a little boy and girl were standing, dressed in overalls of ragged gray ticking. The girl had a doll tucked under her arms, head in, legs flopping down. She lifted her hand and flexed her fingers in a little wave.

Hughes had missed it all, saying not a word until he turned a jog in the road and came on a brightly lighted little commercial center. A crowd had gathered in front of the doughnut shop to watch the cascade of dough rings splash into the hot grease, frizzle, then automatically be flipped to get a squirt of liquid sugar. The hot, greasy sweet smell mixed with the sudsy odor of a saloon. Next door to the tavern, convenient for dropping the kids off while Dad had a beer, the incandescent bulbs of the theater marquee chased themselves in sequential blackouts. Black letters on the back-lit marquee announced the film: *Sky Devils*, starring Spencer Tracy. Hughes punched him and said, "That's mine, Bandy. I made it with outtakes from *Hell's Angels*. Cost me less than half a million to put it in the can, and it's made that back already."

Bandfield noticed that there was a quiet, well-mannered line waiting for the box office to open. Maybe Hughes knew what he was doing. Maybe he'd find a way to make money with airplanes as well.

And maybe his father, old George Bandfield, knew what he was talking about too! What the hell was wrong with a country that would let buildings like this go idle and people starve? The odd thing was that he was part of the problem, building useless things like racing planes when there were hungry people around.

"Did you see those little kids back there, Howard?"

"No, I learned a long time ago never to look at anybody on the streets. First thing you know, they want a handout."

Bandfield shook his head as Cleveland fell away behind them into well-ordered fields. Something must be wrong with the system, and he wasn't helping. There should be something he could do. He was still musing three miles later when they turned into the country club's driveway. It was long and rolling, bordered by painted white stones and trees whitewashed a neat four feet up their trunks. Beyond the symmetry of the trees were the well-watered fairways and the pool-table greens.

"No gray allowed," he said out loud. Hughes looked at him, bushy eyebrows arched. Bandfield remembered that his father always used to complain about golfers wasting their time, turning good land idle.

"Golf's a stupid game, Howard. Did you ever play?"

"Christ, Bandy, I'm an expert. I'm going to win the Open someday—didn't you know that?"

Bandfield didn't reply. He might have known that Hughes would be as ambitious—and as capable—in golf as he was in flying, films, and girl chasing.

He wet his finger with saliva and scrubbed at a spot on his lapel. Since the palmy days on Long Island, when Jack Winter's valet had showered him with clothes, Bandfield had gradually reverted to the usual pilot's wardrobe of a scruffy suit, a few shirts, and a couple of pairs of pants. This morning he'd placed his suit pants under the mattress in his hotel room in the wan hope that some of the wrinkles would be pressed away.

As they got out he felt his usual remorse about any social function, wishing he were back in the hangar with the airplanes. Hadley had been smart, refusing to come along and commenting, "I'm not going to dress up and go in and stand around talking to a bunch of guys I was talking to all day."

At least Bruno wouldn't be there; he was supposed to be back East somewhere working yet another Hafner deal. Charlotte had planned far enough ahead to have the country club at her disposal, and taken the care to have half of Cleveland's best-looking debutantes on hand. There was plenty to drink, and the food was laid out in a lavish display that would have fed the American Expeditionary Force for a week.

Hughes disappeared as soon as they entered, and Bandfield went straight to the buffet, where a smiling Negro in a brilliant white jacket was dispensing platter-sized plates. Bandy moved through the line, concentrating on the peeled boiled shrimp and the thin slices of roast beef piled on miniature slices of bread. There was a big bowl of mixed olives, green and black. He put a dozen on his plate, and realized that it looked greedy. He picked up a slice of rye bread, covered the olives, then added six more to the top. Six was reasonable.

Submerging in the fronds of a potted palm, he devoted himself to eating and people-watching. Like any good instrument pilot, he kept a scan going across the three most important parts. First there were the good-looking girls, so plentiful that it was difficult to concentrate. Then the race pilots, constantly grouping and regrouping, getting louder as the party wore on, as the drinks went down. Finally, there was Charlotte, circling constantly, working the crowd, steering important people to each other, helping out when she saw someone cornered by a bore, making sure that the trays of drinks were circulating fast enough.

Bandy watched how the most famous names in racing kidded each other. There was a definite pecking order, with Turner and Doolittle at the top, and the others ranking themselves down almost as they had finished in last year's races.

Hughes came by, and Bandy tried to get him to talk about Hollywood. "I'm tired of talking shop, Howard. Tell me about making pictures and living high with the starlets. Did you ever date Jean Harlow?"

The veneer of Hughes's friendship went transparent and the real Howard Hughes loomed large behind the familiar figure of Charles Howard. Even his voice was different as he said, "Bandfield, the only thing I ever talk is shop, and only with the experts. That's why I've spent so much time with you and Roget."

Taken aback but trying to joke, Bandy said, "If we're so expert how come we're so broke?"

"Because you don't know how to make money. I do. But I don't know how to make airplanes, and I'm learning from you. When the time is right, I'm going to ask you to help me."

"Yeah, but how about the starlets? Come on."

A lid slammed down on Hughes. "Fuck the starlets, Bandy, let's talk airplanes."

"What were you all saying about fucking starlets?" Roscoe Turner, a man who had forced the world to pay attention first to his persona, then his skills, came over, smiling, resplendent in fawn trousers, sky-blue tunic, and diamond-encrusted wings the size of a Buick hubcap. His soft Mississippi drawl commanded attention. Still irritated with Bandfield, Hughes drifted away without apology.

Turner watched Hughes leave, smiled, and said, "You used

to work at Western, didn't you? I delivered an airplane there. I thought I remembered you."

The flamboyant Turner was obviously restless, the well-waxed point of his mustache twitching. Bandy sensed that he wanted to talk, to unburden himself.

"You know, when I think about these closed-course races my gut just crawls. You can't see anything, and the goddamn turbulence from the propwash is trying to turn you over all the time. Wait here a second."

Turner went over to a tray of drinks, brought four back.

"Let's move against the wall. That asshole Roy Dickens is here, and I just don't feel like arguing with him tonight." Turner watched in amusement as Bandfield carefully slid the two drinks onto his plate. "Hungry?" he asked as they stepped into a little alcove.

Bandfield didn't know who Dickens was, but was honored to be talking to Turner.

"Dickens just gets on my nerves," Turner continued. "He's always on his muscle, always complaining, never giving anybody a break." He pointed across the room to a tall Ichabod Crane type, a rawboned New England farmer with a hooked nose and buck teeth. Dickens, at least six-four, was a well muscled two-hundred-pounder who somehow still looked scrawny. His voice was loud and raucous. Bandfield watched and noticed that people backed away from Dickens as he moved.

"Still, Bandy, we're damn lucky to be here. These are the best pilots in the world, bar none. And most of them good guys. Just don't get in their way on the racecourse."

He sipped half his drink. "You could walk out there and ask anyone—except Dickens—for the shirt off his back, and you'd get it no questions asked. If your engine was acting up, they'd stay up all night to fix it. But God, don't expect any mercy on the course."

He finished one drink and started the other. "One of the guys brought his mother to the races last year—bad idea, I think—and she watched everybody for a few days. When it was over, she told him, 'I don't understand it. You men all work together all day long until the race, and then you try to murder each other.'" His voice had dropped.

Bandy nodded, waited.

Turner grabbed his arm and lowered his voice to a whisper. "She's right, Bandy. That's what we do, we try to murder each other."

Bandy didn't know what to say and was somewhat relieved when a reporter buttonholed Turner. Anxious to make up, even though he didn't know why his friend was angry, Bandy went over to Hughes.

"You should have hung around, Howard. Turner was just talking about how dangerous it was on the course, how pilots tried to murder each other."

Hughes grimaced, embarrassed at his earlier show of temper. "Sorry about popping off like that, Bandy. You know, Turner may be right. Everybody has every cent he owns tied up in the race. If he loses, he's out of business, might not even be able to come back and race next year. So when it gets down to the pylons, it's Katie-bar-the-door."

Hughes took a deep sip of his Coca-Cola. "Your drink as good as Pisco punch, Bandy?"

Bandfield nodded, strangely pleased that Hughes was so obviously trying to make up for being rude earlier.

"Heads up, Bandy! There's something coming our way!"

Charlotte had appeared from nowhere, dragging along a beautiful miniature edition of herself, and, limping behind her, a short, dark man.

"Bandy, Charles!" She said "Charles" as if it had quotation marks around it, letting him know she knew who he was. "So nice of you to come. I want you to meet my daughter and her husband."

Bandfield had a glass in one hand and a disaster area of a plate in another, all shrimp tails, olive pits, and horseradish sauce. He dumped them both in a palm-tree pot and wiped his hand on his suitcoat pocket.

"Patty, Stephan, may I present Frank Bandfield and Charles Howard. Gentlemen, my daughter, Patty, and her husband, Stephan Dompnier."

Bandfield said, "I've read a lot about you, Captain Dompnier. I understand your machine is very fast."

"Very fast when it runs well—but so far it is not running well; there are some difficulties with the engine."

Hughes asked Patty, "Are you entered in any of the events?"

Pleased to be treated as an equal, Patty said, "No, although I might try one of the aerobatic contests. I'm going to practice some more in the next few days, then see what happens."

They made the usual small talk, until Dompnier asked about the Roget Rascal. Bandy plunged into conversation, and didn't notice that Hughes had taken Charlotte into the ballroom.

Patty listened for a while without comment, then said, "You men are incorrigible! I've been listening to nothing but airplane talk all day. The band is playing and I want to dance."

Bandfield nodded and turned to leave. Stephan said, "Mr. Bandfield, I'm sorry, but for the past few weeks I've had a little problem with my legs. I was in your Southwest, and apparently contracted some sort of rash. I'm not dancing tonight. Will you do the honors for my wife?"

Bandfield put out his arm and led her into the ballroom where Buddy Baskette and his Shaker Heights Heroes were playing "How Deep Is the Ocean" underneath a revolving mirrored ball.

Patty was light enough on her feet to avoid Bandfield's. He was trying so hard to say something clever that his hands were wet with sweat.

She noticed. "Are you all right? Would you like to go back?"

"No, I'm fine, I'm just a little nervous. I haven't danced in a long while, as I'm sure you can tell."

She floated in his arms, easing the need for conversation by singing the words of the song softly. It was over too soon, and he took her back to Stephan, who looked like a Singer's midget standing between Roy Dickens and Roscoe Turner. Dickens was swaying as if he'd had too much to drink, and his voice, always loud, was slurred. Dompnier, looking uncomfortable, spoke.

"Thank you, Mr. Bandfield. Colonel Turner was just talking about some of his cross-country flights."

Dickens's booming voice sneered, "*Colonel* Turner? *Colonel?* He's no more a colonel than I am. A fancy uniform don't make you no colonel."

Dompnier looked appalled as Dickens, obviously thinking he was on to a good thing, went on, "Well, *Colonel*, you get rid of that goddam flea bag you used to haul around?"

Patty had heard Dickens's voice, and came over as he droned on, "Old *Colonel* Turner here, he used to carry this shitty-assed lion named Gilmore around with him, like it was a big deal."

Dompnier pulled himself to his full height and yelled into Dickens's chest pocket, "Be careful of your language, Mr. Dickens. My wife is present."

Dickens's hands shot out and caught Stephan by his shoulders, lifting him to his own eye level. "You watch what you say, Froggie, or I'll smash you."

Turner moved behind Dickens and grabbed his arms as Bandfield's fist slammed noiselessly just under the big man's rib cage.

Dickens's breath whooshed out, and he was doubled over, gasping, as they hurried him out, Turner murmuring something about "too much to drink."

When they returned, Dompnier was standing at the side, rigid with fury, embarrassed as much by being saved as by being assaulted. Bandfield said, very formally, "Captain Dompnier, on behalf of the other American pilots, I apologize. Dickens is always obnoxious, and there is nothing I can say to excuse it."

Turner said, "Well, let's get a little good out of a bad situation. Ah'll tell you fellows about a little trick our friend Mr. Dickens uses, to show you the sort of Yankee gentleman he really is."

Stephan feigned close attention, trying to find a way out of his physical humiliation. Vague, irrational thoughts of duels ran through his head. If only the man had not been so enormous, if his movement hadn't been so sudden. If only the other two had not intervened!

Bandfield sensed Dompnier's burning indignation, and understood it. Dickens was a slob. Taking advantage of the Frenchman's size and the element of surprise was nothing compared to his insensitivity in treating Dompnier like a rag doll in front of his wife.

Turner, hands up and flying, went on, "You know, you fly so close out there that you can't wait for the airplane ahead of you to actually move, you have to watch its control movement to see which way it's *going* to move. Everybody knows it, even a polecat like Dickens knows it. I've seen Dickens flick his controls to fake turning out when you try to pass him. It looks like he's moving right into your path."

He drained his drink and sucked an ice cube into his mouth, crunching it. A frazzled-looking Dompnier finished his own drink and started on another.

"Your natural reaction is to slam the stick to the side and kick rudder." Turner moved his hand and kicked his leg as if he were flying. "If you do, you go outside, and lose position and time, which is what he wants. What you've got to do is bore straight ahead and hope he's bluffing. And knowing Dickens, he is." He paused. "Of course, if he's not, you have a midair. So you've got to be careful."

They shifted the talk to the Depression and to France. Patty came back and took Stephan's hand. He shook his head at her, and she moved off. He had to be away from her, to talk to the other pilots until his anger cooled.

Cleveland, Ohio/August 28, 1932

Bandy had a lot to think about the next day. He had really enjoyed dancing with Patty Dompnier, and he still felt embarrassed for her husband. He couldn't imagine what had gotten
into Dickens, but he knew it wasn't over. He was so preoccupied
that he didn't do well in his time trials, flying wide, and averaging only 219 mph. Yet he was almost satisfied with the Rascal's performance, even if he wasn't with his own. Roget had
pared the frontal area down as much as possible, and the landing
gear was little more than a case-hardened automobile spring
with a tiny wheel attached—another Roget patent. He turned
230 mph in the straights, fast enough to win if he flew better
than he had today, and if he was lucky. And he had to be lucky.

He thought about the empty factories and the little girl, and
he wondered again what he was doing there. The whole racing
process was symbolic of the way competition for the few available dollars drove aviation into the murderous frenzy that Turner
had talked about. Flying at 250 mph, fifty feet off the ground,
and pulling into high-G turns every four or five miles, there was
no way to minimize the danger, no way to look out for the other
man.

The risks didn't make sense if you just looked at the prize
money, usually just enough to pay part of the expenses. The real
goal was the breakthrough from impoverished obscurity, scraping to get new spark plugs, to being on top of the world. You
could go from unknown backyard mechanic to national hero
overnight, just by winning a big race. And winning a race sometimes depended upon just putting in a little more effort, taking
a bigger chance. The Granvilles had failed in two aircraft businesses, and built their 1931 winner on borrowed money in an
abandoned dance hall. Now they were at the top of the heap.
That was where he wanted to take Roget Aircraft.

Bruno had insisted on getting corner suites in the Statler Hotel
for Patty and Stephan, but even with windows on both sides
open the late-evening summer heat raised the room to a warm-
taffy temperature. Patty sat in a high-backed wooden chair
watching while her husband stood, fists clenched, staring out
the window.

"Stephan, you've got to snap out of it. It was an unfortunate
encounter with a drunk, one person out of the three hundred at
the party. It could have happened in France, anywhere."

"No, it could only happen here, in this grubby country with its terrible food, dirty hotels, and stinking weather."

She walked over and put her arms around him; he was rigid, frozen in his indignation.

"My darling, Dickens is an ignorant man. All the other pilots detest him. Even before you were talking to him, didn't you see how people moved away from him? He was shunned."

She felt him give, just slightly.

"But for Bandfield and Turner to interfere! That was intolerable. And I had to accept it, like some helpless child."

"They responded in the American way, Stephan. You have to understand, this is not France, this is not the officers' corps. Bandfield is rough-hewn, and so is Turner, for all the genteel manners he affects. But they were sympathetic to you, they wanted to help."

Her hands began to rub his stomach, to sweep up over his chest. He turned quickly and kissed her.

"Were you embarrassed? Did I disgrace you?"

She would have laughed but knew that it was too serious.

"No, but come over to the bed and let me disgrace you a little."

Later he lay beside her, his hand on her belly, relaxed and smiling, "I'm sorry. I was being foolish. Nothing matters but right here, the center of my universe." He rose up and leaned over to kiss her navel.

It bothered her, and it shouldn't have. This was the first time they had made love spontaneously in months. Their love life, once so tempestuous, had become as regulated as a time clock, dedicated to procreation and not recreation. She still felt great passionate urges, but he had seemed to lose all interest in anything but his clinical determination to make her pregnant. For the last year, he'd been trying to engineer their lovemaking, always bringing in new theories. He wouldn't share them with her—he refused to discuss the possibility that he was sterile. Instead, she would notice that he would make love only during certain periods, or only after having a cold bath, or only with her astride him. She wasn't sure where he got his ideas, but there was a great deal of correspondence with some doctor in Texas.

"I guess we'd better get dressed and go upstairs. Bruno's back, and Mother wants us to have dinner with them."

Stephan sighed and traced his finger between her breasts and down to her little mound of hair. "I wonder if something's going on in there. I hope so.'' He laid his ear against her belly and stared wistfully at the wall, almost as if he were trying to listen to the click of cells dividing.

Six floors above, in an identical corner suite, Bruno and Charlotte were going through an increasingly familiar ritual, circling around an argument like Indians around a wagon train. Both had their agendas prepared, and were busily sorting through the delicate pre-argument formula that required polite entry. Either one could explode; the winner made the other go first.

''Are you all right, Bruno?''

''What's the matter, don't I look all right?''

''That's the problem. You look too good. You must have lost thirty pounds in the last six months, and you didn't get that tan in a bar.''

''I'm just trying to keep up with you.''

''Sure you're not trying to keep up with your secretary?''

He snorted. ''I'm not so hard up that I have to resort to screwing an eighteen-year-old girl.''

Bruno was lying about his secretary, and she knew it. If anything, his secretary was already too old for his taste; young girls seemed to be a particular passion of his. The really intriguing part of the puzzle was his old wartime uniform; he'd had it cleaned and pressed, and she'd seen him trying it on. That was no doubt why he'd lost the weight. Maybe there was going to be a reunion.

Charlotte picked up a Lockheed brochure, showing Lindbergh's new monoplane. Anne Lindbergh was standing by it, looking up adoringly at her husband. She was a tiny woman; Charlotte wondered what she was like. She was sure she enjoyed a totally different relationship with Lindbergh from her own with Bruno. She turned the page, and there was a full-length photo of Amelia Earhart standing by her latest Vega.

''That bitch Earhart is making headlines every day with that Vega. You can't pick up a paper without seeing her skinny face.''

The litany was so familiar Bruno groaned. ''Well, I tried to talk to you about a transcontinental flight. Next thing you know, she's going to make a hop from Hawaii. It's easy—no problems like those in the other direction. Maybe even I wouldn't get lost coming this way.'' He said it as a conciliatory joke, something to get her in a decent mood before Stephan and Patty arrived.

Charlotte walked over to the sideboard and poured a thimbleful of gin over the ice in the cocktail mixer. She shook it with silent fury and drank it straight from the shaker.

"Patty seems to think Earhart is wonderful. She knows I don't like her, but she acts like Earhart is God's gift to aviation." She took another thimbleful, hesitated, and poured it out.

"Her husband, George Putnam, is forcing her to fly."

"How do you know that? People probably are saying that about me, and I can't keep you out of a cockpit."

"It's true. I talk to the other women pilots. He even has her cut her hair and wear clothes so that she looks more like Lindbergh than Lindbergh. Makes everyone wonder if she's normal."

Bruno glared at her, wondering if Charlotte was a good judge of what was normal. Or if he was, for that matter.

"I'm not so sure about her myself. And I'm not so sure I like her being so friendly with Patty."

"Are you implying something? That's a hell of a thing to say about anybody. And what difference does it make about Patty? She might as well have a girlfriend. Stephan isn't doing her any good."

As he knew she would, Charlotte walked over and slapped him. He had won round one, had the high ground.

He smirked at her. "I wish I'd been there last night. I would have taken care of that lout Dickens."

"Yes, a brawl would have been wonderful. You could have completely destroyed Stephan by protecting him."

"Look," he said, retreating to a safer line of reasoning, "let's drop that, and get back to Earhart. It's just that Putnam's smart. He is in the publicity business, and he's made Earhart a celebrity by keeping her in the public eye."

Her hand stung, and she rubbed it on her hip.

"I'm trying to do the same thing with you, letting you fly in the military competitions. If you want me to get you a publicity agent, I will. You know, you could be the first woman to fly around the world. You and Patty could do it together, just like Post and Gatty."

Charlotte's anger evaporated in a chill of apprehension as the conversation turned in the wrong direction. "Wait a minute. I'm a realist even if Earhart is not. Flying is not worth dying for. I don't mind taking my chances, but I don't want to do any ocean flying, not in bad weather especially. I can fly in the clear, and I can fly instruments if someone will navigate. But I'm not exposing Patty to any dangerous flights, and I'm not going to do it alone.''

"You don't have to. Post took Gatty. Now I hear he's having an autopilot installed for a solo flight. We could get one for you, put it in one of the new transports. It would be good publicity. Believe me, *Liebchen*, if you don't, Earhart will.''

Charlotte realized this was doubly dangerous ground. If Bruno flared up now, he might force her to agree to do something she was afraid of doing. She shifted her attack back to Earhart. "She's always so fucking wholesome. Did you ever read her book? Sounds like it was written by some goddam twelve-year-old nun. But she's tough underneath—you try to upstage her when a reporter's around and she'll cut your armpits out.''

Bruno looked at his pocket watch, a gift from a grateful Pierre Dompnier. It was nearly seven. Patty and Stephan would be there shortly.

"Look, Charlotte, you can't have it both ways. You can't want the publicity and not make the flights, and you can't treat the press like you do, like one of the boys. Amelia gives them the pap they can print. They are not going to write about a woman who curses and pinches them on the arse. They may like you better than Amelia, and I think you probably like them better than Amelia does, but their editors are only going to print sugar-candy stuff.''

It was the winning point. More than once he'd found her crying, embarrassed that she had ruined an interview. Bruno was becoming increasingly bored with this familiar routine, and he wanted to end the conversation.

"If you don't want to fly around the world—and I think you should—let's figure out a string of record flights you do want to make. I think we could fix up one of the bombers with tanks in the bomb bay, and go for closed-course records for distance, speed, and maybe altitude, too.''

Charlotte found comfort in this.

"Maybe, Bruno. It sounds better than flying around the world. That scares me, no kidding. I don't want to be over some big goddam ocean and not know where I am, and maybe have an engine cut out.''

"Just wait till Amelia does it—then you'll do nothing but complain.''

"She'd never make it. Bruno, she's a lousy pilot, no matter what they say. I've watched her time and again, and it's all she can do to get an airplane on and off the ground.''

Hafner changed the subject. "What's your competition going to be like?"

She frowned. "Mostly Gee Bees like mine, and one clip-wing Laird biplane. I should be able to win, or at least take a second."

Bruno decided to make amends. He needed this woman for a while longer. In time, he would solve all the problems, her involvement in the business, for which she was getting disproportionate credit, and the stupid romance with Dusty, which had become embarrassing. In Germany, he would have had to call the man out, duel with him. Well, he would take care of them both. "I asked Armand Bineau to design a racer for you. It doesn't make sense for us to be advertising Gee Bee products."

"I've already got one hell of an airplane. It's all I can handle. Don't have Bineau do anything until I talk to him. I want something safe as well as fast."

Bruno's voice took on his Kaiser's officer quality, the set of his lips changing quickly from a tense line into a V-shaped smile. He barked out, "There is *no* airplane you cannot handle!" Having settled the question for all time, he changed the subject. "Are you serious about having Patty and the Frenchman come into the business?"

"Yes. I want Patty to stay in this country, and Stephan says aviation is dead in France."

"If he wants to come in with us, he can help his father and Monique running the Marseilles operation. Things are busier all the time there, and having a former French air officer would be good camouflage."

"He can't do that! He's embarrassed enough that his father is selling bootleg arms. Besides, he wants to fly."

"Yes, Charlotte, but we are living from contract to contract, just like everybody else."

Charlotte's voice took on the resolute tone that signaled she would not yield. "Stephan is my daughter's husband. We will make room for both of them in the company."

Hafner accepted her response. He could use Stephan in France; he didn't want him around the plant. A little time would have to pass, and the situation would take care of itself.

"We can if we get another contract," he said. "Just don't make any promises until we see what happens with the new airplanes."

Charlotte checked her appearance in the mirror. Looking

good for a daughter was different from looking good for a man, and her long hair was swept back into a bun. She applied a little lipstick just as the knock sounded. The door was a fragile partition between two fields of tension. Bruno stood very erect next to Charlotte, thumbs tucked by his trouser seams in a position of attention.

Charlotte opened the door, and kissed them both. Bruno said, "Come in, Patty, come in, champ. I heard about last night. I'll have to have Max Schmeling give you some lessons."

Time and motion froze as the other three turned to stare at him in horror.

Bruno went on, "Well, Patty, are you pregnant yet? I'll bet Stephan's father would agree with me, by God—we need some grandchildren in this family, we do, by God!"

Cleveland Airport/August 28, 1932

A mood as dark and gelatinous as sea-urchin soup hung over the Cleveland Institute of Aviation hangar that Stephan had rented. His mood had been foul for the last two days. The aircraft's engine was still acting up, and his ground crew was no help. The two surly Frenchmen spent their time yammering about the inexcusable quality of American food and the lack of drinkable wine. The magnificent cigarettes, smoked end to end, compensated somewhat, but both longed to go back to Paris.

They were the only two sent from France with Dompnier. Pierre Nicolau was from the Caudron factory, and he knew the racer inside out. He looked like Jean Gabin, knew it, and mimicked him as much as possible in word and gesture. René Coty was from the Renault engine works, but had not yet been able to get the engine working right. A brooding Parisian with curly blue-black hair separated from his eyebrows by a slim gash of pockmarked flesh, he kept a cigarette dangling from his lips at all times. Something in his manner suggested that taking advice was not his strong suit.

It was their glowering presence that had inhibited Stephan from asking for help earlier. Now he had no choice—he had to qualify tomorrow, and race the following day. He had asked Hadley Roget to drop by and look at the engine.

Promptly at nine, Roget walked in, followed by Bandfield. Both men walked around the racer, admiring it, oblivious to the obvious dislike of the two mechanics.

Hadley listened to Stephan describe the problem, and what they had done to correct it. The engine would run perfectly well on the ground; as soon as he was airborne it would backfire, sometimes so badly that he wasn't sure he'd get it around the pattern to land.

Roget nosed around. The engine was installed so that the crankshaft lay on top, with the cylinders pointing toward the ground.

"Inverted engine, huh? What attitude do you run it up in on the ground?"

Stephan was annoyed by Bandfield's presence and was trying not to show it. He said, "Ah, three-point, of course. Nicolau holds down the tail, and I check it at full power. On the ground it is fine—in the air, pouf!"

Roget had Dompnier go through the drill; the engine sounded perfect.

"Stephan, this time let's run it up in a level attitude. Put a sawhorse under the tail and we'll see what happens."

Bandy placed a canvas cover on the stabilizer, then piled sandbags on it, while Roget and the two mechanics tethered the Caudron to tie-downs set in the concrete.

Dompnier started the engine. The airplane twitched and trembled, straining at the ropes. In less than sixty seconds, the engine song changed from a fluid roar and began backfiring, belching smoke and flame from the exhausts, the vibration shaking it as a terrier shakes a rat. Dompnier shut it down.

A quiet look of triumph crossed Roget's face, and he began pulling the cowling off. An hour later, he turned to Dompnier.

"There's your trouble. The oil return line is too small. When the oil pressure goes up, it can't handle it, and back pressure from the pump dumps oil down the rocker arms. Did you notice a rise in oil pressure after you took off?"

"*Oui*—from about one hundred to one-eighty. It seemed to me that high oil pressure is good, not bad."

"Not this time, my friend. I think we can fix this, but it will be risky. We have to run a new oil line, and bore out the inlet. If we don't tap into anything we'll be okay. Will you risk it?"

Stephan shrugged. "I have no choice."

"Lemme take a look at the pistons, too. You might have scuffed them during the backfires."

In another thirty minutes they had the pistons laid out. Two were clearly marred, one so badly that it couldn't be used again. Dompnier had spares, and the five men fell to work. By mid-

night, the engine was back together and Dompnier had run it up
in a level position, the air-cooled Renault engine breaking the
night-dampened silence of the airport.

Dompnier jumped down from the wing and embraced Hadley.

"Thank you, and thank you, too, Bandy."

"You're welcome, Stephan. We'd all better get some sleep.
It's going to be an early morning."

Cleveland Airport/August 29, 1932

The slanting rays of the late-afternoon sun had turned the haze
into an incandescent ball. The crowds were streaming away in
long lines, and a weary Frank Bandfield sat with Roget, their
backs braced against the Chevy's bumper, watching a red-
and-white Gee Bee Sportster practicing aerobatics across the
northeast edge of the field.

"Whose airplane is that, Hadley?"

Roget, never idle, was cleaning spark plugs as they sat, pressing their ends into a cone-shaped tin and letting high-pressure
air sandblast them clean. Squinting, he said, "Looks like Charlotte Hafner's bird."

"She's damn good. I don't think she's moved a yard out of
the field boundaries, and she's done everything from snap rolls
to spins."

The tiny Gee Bee landed out of a loop, touching down just
inside the field boundary. It taxied to a stop inside the wire fence
surrounding the hangars Hafner had rented. The pilot got out
with the log book in her hand and ran inside, while mechanics
pushed the airplane into the hangar. Without apology, they
brushed past Bandfield and set up a protective restraining ring
of wire, threaded through steel stanchions, designed to keep
onlookers out. He was a little annoyed, but stood there, grasping
the wire with both hands and jingling the little red "Team Members Only" signs.

Bandfield was waiting outside for Charlotte to emerge, but it
was Patty who walked out, short hair glistening in the sun.

"Hello, Bandy. Thanks for helping Stephan with his engine
last night."

"Aw, you're welcome, we were glad to do it. But I have to
say you surprised me just now. I thought your mother was flying.
You were really great." He suddenly felt awkward, all hands

and feet, uncomfortable that she might think he was somehow following up on their dance of two nights before.

She turned and nodded in the direction of the hangar. Then she pivoted and said, "Don't go just yet."

The words "Well, how about a cup of coffee . . ." turned into an uncontrollable scream as pain coursed through his arms. Patty slumped to the ground laughing, and inside two mechanics fell into each other's arms, hysterical from the oldest joke in aviation—the electric fence hot-wired to a Model T magneto. Four turns sent a harmless jolt of electricity through anyone dumb enough to grab the wire.

"I'm sorry, Bandy, I couldn't resist. We don't often get people over here, and the guys get bored."

Feeling was returning to his arms, and he smiled weakly. "Yeah, that's a good joke. We used to pull it back in Salinas. Ha ha."

Concerned but still smiling, she took his arm and rubbed it, and he realized the electricity wasn't all in the wires.

"I have to act a little rowdy once in a while just to make sure they know I'm one of the guys."

"You sure don't look like one of the guys in that outfit."

She glanced down, and buttoned the upper button of her blouse.

"Bandy, maybe you can help me. Stephan has been in a blue funk ever since that ridiculous incident at the dance. I'm worried that Dickens—or Stephan, for that matter—will do something stupid during their race."

Bandfield nodded. She was smart. It was just something like the fight that might cause either one of them to try to do a little more than was safe during the race.

She continued, "I'd like to get them at least to be civil to each other. I talked to Dickens earlier, and he offered me a ride in a friend's airplane he's making a test flight on."

"He shouldn't take you on a test flight—might be risky."

"No, he says it's just routine. He was apologetic, and I don't want him to be angry with Stephan."

Bandfield shuffled, uneasy at the prospect. "He won't be too happy to see me."

"Well, I'm worried about you too. Why not apologize for slugging him? What will it cost you?"

"Seeing as your little trick with the wire keeps me from moving my arms, it might cost me a black eye."

"You can move them, all right. I've seen that hot-wire trick played often enough to know how much sympathy you deserve, and you've already had your quota.''

She kept her arm linked in his as they strolled across the dry grass, spotted here and there with empty Coca-Cola and Quaker State Oil bottles. He liked being close to her.

''When I talked to Dickens earlier, he apologized. He said he was just drunk. He promised to apologize to Stephan, too, if I'd take a hop with him. Just be nice and we'll get this all fixed up.''

They talked about the dance and the Caudron's engine, and her mother's chances in the women's unlimited race the following morning.

''Dickens said he was test-flying the airplane to pay back a favor to an old friend of his who has entered in the Cleveland-Dayton-Toledo round-robin race.''

''I didn't think Dickens had any friends,'' Bandfield scoffed.

As they approached the hangar Bandfield could see Dickens's head sticking up on the other side of an ancient Bach biplane. The patched and tattered airplane had obviously spent too many winters parked outside in the weather, and Dickens was checking everything with extra care. Bandy watched with distaste, unable to understand why Dickens would ask Patty to fly in such a wreck. When he glanced into the cabin, he saw that there was a bench fitted instead of the usual two separate seats. In the air, she'd have a hell of a time getting away from him if he decided to make a pass.

''Hello there, Bandfield. I guess I owe you one for that sucker punch the other night.''

''No hard feelings, Roy. Have one on me, as a gift.''

Dickens gave his usual nasty smile. ''No, I've got hard feelings all over my ribs. I'll pay you back someday, you can count on it.''

After the walk-around inspection, Dickens slid over to the left side, and Patty climbed up into the right. After propping the engine for them, Bandfield trotted alongside as they taxied slowly to the edge of the grassy field. The landing gear was splayed out like an old washerwoman's legs, the paint on the struts cracked like varicose veins.

Dickens leered at him as he went through the engine run-up, the tired engine coughing and backfiring. Bandfield could tell that the spark plugs were fouled with oil. Dickens stood on the brakes as he put the throttle forward to full power, deafening the onlookers with the sharp staccato exhaust noise. The plane strained forward like a sprinter against the chocks, slack fabric quivering, landing gear bending forward.

Bandfield made the classic "cut the engine" sign and bounded up on the wing. Dickens brought the power back and Patty opened her door.

With his left hand, Bandfield unbuckled her safety belt; he shot his right hand under her rump and scooped her out of the cabin, backing off the wing and falling with her on top of him.

Dickens sneered at them as he reached over and closed the door. Then he put on full power and the Bach began its takeoff roll.

Bandfield struggled to his feet, pulling Patty up with him. She was furious, but he held her to him and pointed at the airplane, now struggling a hundred yards down the runway.

Dickens had the power fully on, and as the Bach slowly accelerated, its landing gear began to spread, the wheels drifting farther and farther apart.

They stood stock still, his arms still around her, as with a mime's precision the airplane struggled toward its pratfall. There was a grinding roar as the gear snapped parallel to the wings and the Bach's propeller snubbed itself into a stub and the plane slammed on its belly.

Bandfield whispered, "Dear God, don't let it burn."

The airplane, wheels spread out as if it had stepped on a giant banana, slid to a stop, and Dickens sprang out the side like a runner stealing home, racing away from the inevitable explosion.

The Bach sat for a moment, white vapor showing where the fuel from the ruptured tanks was reaching the red-hot exhaust manifold. A hurricane of flame preceded the sound of the explosion that tossed the airframe fifty feet in the air. It hesitated at the top of the arc, then dove down to impact vertically, wings flying up parallel to the cabin, the tail driving down the collapsing fuselage like a retracting spring.

For a frozen moment, there was no sound anywhere, and Bandy could hear Patty's frantic breathing. Then the strident sirens of the emergency wagons wailed.

The comic crash had diverted his mind but not his body from the excitement of holding Patty Dompnier tightly. She had ceased to struggle, and he was now aware that he was pressing a giant erection against this lovely woman, the wife of a friend.

She had noticed, at first annoyed, then amused.

"Thank you for saving me." She looked back over her shoulder, hesitating for a moment. Then, Charlotte's daughter, she paraphrased Mae West's line from a New York play. "Is that a wrench in your pocket, or are you just glad to see me?"

Blushing, he let her go as Dickens wandered back in a state of shock.

Embarrassed by her own joke, but not wanting to leave, she asked, "How did you know it was going to happen?"

"I didn't. If I'd been sure it was, I wouldn't have let Dickens go either, I'd have kicked a hole in the rudder or something. But I knew I didn't want you to take the chance."

She nodded. "Thanks." Then, unable to resist, she added, "For everything."

An hour later, he was still trying to think of something clever to say as he polished the last of the Simoniz compound off the Rascal's fuselage. The line about the wrench had been funny; she must have inherited her mother's bawdy sense of humor. He wondered if she'd inherited her free and easy ways.

Cleveland and Patty inevitably reminded him of Oakland and Millie. Patty Dompnier was totally different in appearance and manner, but he felt the same stirrings of fundamental hunger for her. Might as well forget about it—she's married, he told himself.

Bandy knew there was a point in preparing an airplane when it was better just to button everything up and wait for the race. He tossed his polishing rag down and stretched out in the warm Ohio sun to watch the women's unlimited. Charlotte was competing against some of the best women flyers in the country, with the single exception of Amelia Earhart, who didn't fly closed-course races.

Most of the men pilots resented having women compete. The prizes were small enough without having to share them with women, many of whom were wealthy in their own right. Some rash talk about letting them race against the men had been buried in an avalanche of curses and catcalls.

The women's unlimited race results would depend almost entirely upon the pilots' skills, since two of the women were flying Gee Bee Sportsters identical to Charlotte's except for color. He could see them lined up for the racehorse start, quivering under power, dust swirling behind them.

All three bore the Granville Brothers trademark paint scheme of gleaming white fuselage and wings edged with a scallop of contrasting colors. Charlotte's plane was trimmed in red, with the racing number seventeen on the side and the wingtips. Gladys Traden was number nine, and her scallops were green. Gloria Engles bore a black eight-ball for a number, with matching black trim.

The fourth airplane, flown by young Nancy Alderman, was a taper-wing Laird biplane, clearly outclassed.

Roget joined him, leaning down to yell in his ear, "Hey, Bandy—do you know why women can't fly upside down?"

It was the tenth time he'd heard the joke in the last four days. "No idea. Why not?"

" 'Cause they would have a crack-up!"

Hadley had gotten a laugh with this one from everybody but the French mechanics.

The decibel level of the engines went up and the starter's flag went down. Gladys Traden got off first, forcing Charlotte to fly high and outside. All the airplanes disappeared momentarily around the far turn, then came back in a blur as they whipped in front of them, hungry hornets racing wide open.

He wondered about Charlotte's mental set. A closed-course race was the most dangerous flying short of actual combat, and apparently she loved it.

The three Gee Bees looked as if they were tied in formation as they bored around the course, never changing position as they whipped around the pylons. They lapped the Laird the fourth time around, and Nancy Alderman graciously pulled up high and wide, giving way. She continued to fly the course, waiting for someone to drop out.

Gloria Engles had attached herself to Traden's wing, flying in the number-two position all the way around, the turbulence from their prop wash combining to keep Charlotte well back and out of position. On the next lap Engles abruptly pulled deeply into the course in a tight turn that increased the force of gravity on her body four times, pressing her into her seat. She kept the elliptical wings of her racer hanging vertically as she rerounded the pylon.

Must have missed the turn, Bandfield thought.

He glanced at Charlotte, now flying number two to Traden, then back to Engles. She was gone. A billowing black cloud of smoke summoned the crash trucks, roaring out with sirens blaring.

"High-speed stall. I saw her snap. Goddam women shouldn't be racing anyway." Roget's expression was grim.

An involuntary response to the tragedy gripped the throttles of the two remaining Gee Bees, and their lap speeds slowed slightly. The Laird drifted down to reenter the pattern, lonely, watchful, waiting to finish third.

Charlotte had drifted a little farther back in her number-two spot, a thin stream of white smoke pouring from her exhausts staining the white fuselage sides with an oil smear. The two Gee Bees roared past on the final lap, dead level, thirty feet separating them. Traden's right wing's fabric suddenly bellowed out to burst like a balloon, sending her aircraft snap-rolling to the right before burying itself inverted in the ground.

"Holy Christ, that's two down."

Charlotte, in a nervous fog, blasted past the checkered flag, then pulled up and headed off the course, gaining altitude slowly, trying to compose herself. The Laird circled again, Alderman delighted to have an unexpected second place.

Bandy had a box lunch from the airfield café, but he couldn't touch a bite. The vision of the two women going in wouldn't leave him.

"You'd better eat, Bandy. Twenty laps is one hell of a race, especially around this itty-bitty course." Hughes pushed a waxed-paper-wrapped sandwich at him.

"At least the legs are all the same length. But at two hundred and forty miles an hour, you'll be turning every fifty seconds or so, pulling lots of Gs. Lemme in there."

Hughes had a roll of adhesive tape and a pair of scissors. He cut and pasted twenty small strips of tape along the bottom of the instrument panel.

"It's easy to lose track of where you are. Pull one piece of tape off after each lap, so you know how far you have to go."

A haunted-looking Stephan Dompnier limped by, glancing neither right nor left.

Eight airplanes were manhandled to the starting line. Hadley stood towering beside the little airplane, polishing the windscreen with a chamois for the hundredth time, ready for any last-minute emergency. Bandy sat in the Rascal, shivering in spite of the sultry Cleveland weather and the heat roaring back from the 485-horsepower Curtiss engine. He glanced at the panel; the oil and cylinder head temperature gauges were up, the coolant temperature was up, the oil pressure was down. Goddam, another five minutes on the ground and the damn thing would cook itself to death. He eased the throttle forward to clear the engine, burning the plugs clean and keeping air flowing through the radiator, and Hadley turned his back to the blast, squinting to keep the dust out of his eyes.

Bandfield's qualifying time had been good enough to get him the third position in the line. It was a good break, because of the hazards of the racehorse start. The planes were lined up wingtip to wingtip; when the flag came down, they would be off and heading for the first pylon like wasps flying down a funnel. Number-two spot had gone to Roy Dickens, sitting comfortably in the Cessna racer he had flown for years, an airplane as pretty as he was ugly. He stuck out of it like a witch on a broomstick. The Cessna looked nose-heavy because of the disproportionately large Wasp engine that powered it.

A universe of people milled in close proximity, pressing down upon the racers in an inverted pyramid of flesh. A quarter of a million watched from the bleachers, and as many more were spread out around the field. Another three or four thousand—insiders, the cognoscenti—were in the pit area, past the wire that restrained the crowds. A covey of ten or twelve people gathered around each airplane, and each racer had a senior mechanic stationed like Hadley just outside the cockpit.

But as the minutes ground down toward the starting time, each solitary figure of a pilot became the tip of the inverted pyramid, carrying on his back the weight of the watchers as well as the job at hand. As the seconds ticked off, the pilots' vision narrowed to a tunnel which saw part of the cockpit and a little section of the windscreen. At the start he would become absolutely alone, launched like an arrow into a winding roar of confusion, a freewheeling gear in a Chaplinesque clock speeding to oblivion.

Dickens reached down and bottomed out his seat, pulling his head within the confines of the windscreen and doubling his legs up so that they almost reached his face. He'd had to make special cutouts in the instrument panel just to be able to squeeze into the airplane. He glanced to his left at the little Frog in the blue airplane and shook his head. It wasn't fair. The French government subsidized their racing team, paid Caudron and Renault to do their best. He'd put the Cessna together with hard work and an engine salvaged from one of last year's crashes. The Frog was rich and didn't need the prize money. Every cent Dickens had and all he could borrow was invested in the Cessna. He wanted to win, needed to win.

Looking to the right, he sneered at Bandfield's airplane, crude in comparison to his or the Frenchman's. All he had to do was get off first and take the first pylon, then let the rest of them catch up with him. If he got ahead of the Frenchman, he'd never let him pass.

Dompnier had won the pole position, and his head was now twitching in the cockpit, glancing from his instruments to the starter's flag and back again. The racehorse start worried him; his retractable gear might not be strong enough to hold up on the rough field surface. But if he could get off first and be first around the pylon, the race was won.

Bandy stared at the Caudron with admiration. It was the fastest plane on the field by ten miles an hour or so, capable of 260-mph laps when it was running right. It should be running right now, he thought, after all the care Roget had given it. God, after all their efforts, working double shifts to keep the bomber project going while they built the racer, they might have given the prize away to Stephan by rebuilding his engine. Maybe they'd given the factory away! It had been crazy to help Dompnier.

On his right were five more airplanes—Roy Moore in a Keith Ryder Special, Bill Ong in Howard's Pete, and then a line of nondescript mechanic's specials, put together with cutting torch and spare parts.

Coveys of sweat-stained, grease-covered ground crews surrounded each airplane, blinking through the grit thrown back by the propellers, tugging on the wingtips and holding down on the tails to ease the strain on the brakes. The power would be full on when the starter's flag went down, and then they'd let go.

Bandy had finished a Thermos of ice water and gone to the bathroom twenty minutes before, but his throat was parched and he needed to urinate badly.

Roget leaned down and yelled in his ear, "Dompnier's going to be first off, Bandy. I got a look at his prop. They pump it up with compressed air to fine pitch. When he takes off, a bleed valve opens, and it moves the prop to coarse pitch for the race. It's a hell of a gadget. I wish we had one."

"What's second prize? Seventy-five hundred?"

"There ain't no second prize for us. You got to win the fifteen grand or we'll lose the option on the plant. Don't go thinking second place."

Bandy nodded agreement. He felt the nervous excitement building in his gut, a weird circular clawing that began in the pit of his stomach and forced bile up to his mouth like toothpaste squeezed from a tube. He spat into the slipstream, forgetting about the guys holding down the tail.

In the past, he'd trembled with the building tension until the starter's flag went down, and then everything was automatic. He hoped it would be the same today.

He tapped the clock. The second hand lurched toward start time, a long strand of temporal molasses that seemed never to disconnect. He brought the engine to full power just as the red-and-white-checkered flag came down. The outside world crystallized into silence as the rising pounding of his own engine totally deafened him. Bandy danced on the rudder to keep the Rascal straight in the wildly bouncing slipstream. One of the mechanic's specials veered left to run its prop right through its neighbor before they'd moved twenty feet.

Bandy saw the accident, knew no one was hurt. The goddam Caudron was already off the ground, gear coming up. He tugged at the stick and skidded toward the inside of the track behind Dickens, who was leading somehow, and Dompnier.

The Rascal was running perfectly, accelerating to top speed just before he reached the pylon marking the first turn. The racecourse was tricky, with farmers' water tanks scattered around the perimeter looking just like pylons. It would be easy to make a mistake and fly off the course. The straightaways went by in less than a minute, then it was rudder, aileron, left wing down, pulling back on the stick to bend the airplane around the turn. G forces squashed him down in the seat, multiplying his weight to over six hundred pounds. Back to the straight with aileron, rudder, right wing down to level, release back pressure. It was brutal flying, a blacksmith's formula of pound, bend, pound, bend.

The grandstand had been a riot of color before he took off. In his turns he saw it as a variegated blur binding together two checkerboards that he knew were the parking lots. Rudder, aileron, wing down, back pressure. It became a horizontal dance, a ritual coercion of a gravity steamroller. Sweat sluiced down his face and arms. Once his hand slipped off the throttle. Better the throttle than the stick.

The pilot animal took over, the element within him that tuned itself to the machine, to the concept of winning. The other personality, the human element, sat back and watched, dispassionate save for fear.

Dickens was in the lead, with Dompnier half a length behind, twenty feet ahead of Bandfield. The rest of the pack were stretching out, waiting to be lapped by the faster leading trio.

He looked down at the twenty strips of tape.

"Christ, what lap is this?" He had already lost track, and determined to fly till everybody stopped.

His engine was running strong, broiling the cockpit with solid hot fumes untainted by telltale burned oil. The wind picked up. Straight down the field on the first stretch, it blew inward on the second, outward on the third.

On the second turn, the wind forced him toward the pylon. The outside world telescoped down to a narrow band of vision, his brain barely recovering from the blood-draining pull of one high-G turn before he was in another. In his turns he caught sight of the ground from the corner of his eye, two or three people, a man holding a square board with a number on it, automobile tracks in the dying grass, then it was level again with nothing in view but Dickens and Dompnier. A pylon loomed too close and he pumped the stick forward in the vertical turn, bucking the G forces to jump outward and losing another hundred feet on Dompnier.

He had no awareness of the passage of time, no ordered sense of motion. The racers became centrifugal extrusions of metal and man, spun out at random distances. The ground fifty feet below was a peripheral green-brown ribbon. He stared only at the two racers shimmering with speed ahead of him, no time to glance at his instruments. The sound and the feel told him the airplane was okay. When it wasn't he'd know it all too well.

Dickens knew he was flying perfectly, shaving the pylons, keeping down low in the smooth air. He could see Dompnier's airplane in the little rearview mirror mounted on his windscreen.

In the Caudron, Stephan Dompnier moved the wings as extensions of his shoulders, the engine as part of his heart and lungs. He watched the red airplane ahead. The pig Dickens was flying beautifully, but his Cessna was slower than the Caudron, and he knew he could pass him on the next lap.

Behind him, Bandy wished he'd counted the laps. It had to be ten at least. His arm muscles ached, the left from bending the throttle forward, trying to push it in the firewall, the right from controlling the maverick stick dancing in the turbulence of Dompnier's prop wash. He was flying automatically now, grazing the pylon on each turn, pulling another half G to wrench the Rascal around a little quicker. He didn't hear the engine screaming, the wind whistling around the canopy, didn't feel the heat searing his shoes. He only saw Dompnier and Dickens, both now seeming to inch back, lap by lap, like heavy weights drawn on a string.

A juddering vibration forced Dompnier's eyes to the instrument panel. The tachometer was leaping in concert with the backfiring engine. Something was wrong, a valve going, a ring sticking. He saw the Cessna edge away, and then as he slowed, he watched Bandfield vault ahead of him.

Sweating, Dompnier played with the mixture control, easing it back and forth slightly to try to smooth his engine out. He racked the stick to his belly, squeezing speed from safety, clinging close to Bandfield by force of will and tighter turns. He clung to Bandfield's wing, matching gut-wrenching G for G.

A slight change in noise told Bandfield that he'd somehow picked up a few rpm. The engine was smoother, and he was gaining on Dickens foot by foot. The Cessna and the Rascal rocketed around the pylons, dumping the pilots into their seats with the G forces, airspeed reaching 250 mph on the straights with only a mile or two speed difference between them. He riveted his eyes on Dickens's airplane, watching the sharp movements of the controls as Dickens entered a turn—aileron in, wing up, aileron out, wing down—and on into the stretch. He was duplicating the movements exactly, unaware of it, unaware of anything except the blur of ground flashing by below, the jackhammer vibration that matched the airframe's groaning in the turns, and Dickens's red airplane creeping slowly back to him.

His thin body shuddering under the G forces, Dompnier forced his eyes down to the instrument panel. All the needles were off the scale, but the engine was running well again, no longer backfiring, and he began to gain on the leaders. Dickens was falling back, and he could see Bandfield ready to make his move, trying for the lead.

Bandfield's airplane had pulled just to the side of the little Cessna when Dickens rocked his ailerons and flicked a skidding turn out in front of him.

Dompnier watched, clinically detached. "*Merde*, he's bluffing, just as Turner said he would."

Bandfield saw the Cessna's control movements, ignored them. It was win or die, a high school game of chicken such as he'd once played in Model Ts on the country roads around Salinas.

Dickens flicked his controls again, saw the Rascal relentlessly boring in, the shimmering circle of its propeller aimed directly at his cockpit. Dickens wrenched his red racer down and outside as Bandfield slammed his plane over the top of the Cessna's cockpit with inches to spare, then dropped down to take advantage of the clear air of the lead.

Dompnier growled with delight. "He made it." The old 1918 ace's killer instinct stirred within him. Dickens's faked maneuver had cost him time, and he'd fallen a length behind Bandfield, and now was only half a length ahead. First Dickens, then Bandfield, then the trophy.

Dickens swore to himself, bending the throttle forward. He knew he didn't have the speed to catch Bandfield. He had to hold the Caudron off somehow and take at least second place. He needed the money, to live, to eat, to fly.

Dickens looked in his mirror again, saw the Caudron's prop between his wing and elevator. Dompnier was gaining—his engine must have cleared up. Dickens forgot about Bandfield, forgot about anything but the blue Caudron moving in to steal second place, steal his livelihood from him. He moved stick and rudder in short abrupt slamming movements, glancing back at Dompnier, who was gaining inch by inch. He had no choice; he had to fake this Frog out even if he hadn't fooled that fucking Bandfield.

Dickens viciously flicked his ailerons, kicked the rudder, jigged the Cessna right, then left.

Dompnier's face compressed to a tight smile. "No, my friend, not this time. You didn't fool Bandfield, you won't fool me."

Desperate, Dickens flicked his controls again, harder, jolting unseen molecules of air, scraping loose their grip on his tapered wings. The little Cessna shuddered in a high-speed stall, snapping directly into Dompnier's path.

The Cessna blotted out the sky before Dompnier, a bright red wall centered with the terrified white smear of Dickens's face. In the split second before the collision his hands automatically moved to jettison the canopy and unbuckle the safety harness. The two airplanes merged, disappearing in a thudding explosion that rocked the field. The French racer bored through the Cessna, propeller chewing Dickens and cockpit before lofting the engine away in a high arc as the Caudron disintegrated around Dompnier.

Thrown brutally from his shattered cockpit, Stephan was pain-gouged to a clear untrammeled consciousness by the midair splintering of his shredded body. Turning flat, arms and legs outstretched into a cross, he saw the ground spin beneath him. He did not scream. His last thought was that Patty would not bear his son after all, before he dropped to bounce like a skipped rock on the grassy stubble.

It was a second before the stricken crowd could comprehend what had happened, before the low, dolorous moan concealing the shock of blood-bitten pleasure rolled out.

Coming around for the last lap, Bandy took the checkered flag wondering where Dompnier and Dickens had suddenly gone. He pulled up to five hundred feet and brought the power back, letting the Rascal coast down to 150 mph. His left hand was trembling from the grip he had on the throttle, his muscles sore from the strain and the G forces. But he had the $15,000. They had the factory.

The other racers were spreading out to forge a landing pattern, Dompnier and Dickens not among them. He dropped down to take a slow victory lap, fifty feet above the course. The flame and smoke puzzled him until he saw Patty running toward the wreckage.

7

Sayville, Long Island/April 21, 1933

The sudden arrival of spring threw color everywhere like rice at a wedding, plucking blossoms from the sleeping branches and splashing reds and yellows in every patch of sunlight. Innocent flowering shrubs burst forth, unaware they were sacrificial victims to the frost that was sure to follow. It was wonderful to be alone—Charlotte was at the plant, Bruno off on another of his tours of Germany and France—and Patty sat on the chaise placed near the open French doors so she could drink in the broad, sweeping grounds. For a moment Patty indulged herself in a flight of sympathy for the new blooms, whose happiness was certain to be nipped off early as her own had been.

She poured another cup of coffee with a shrug, saying aloud, "That's nonsense, straight out of an Ouida novel." Sipping, she admitted again that the sadness of Stephan's death, tragic and unnecessary as it had been, was accompanied by some measure of relief. He had become increasingly possessive, and his implacable preoccupation with siring a son—he refused to consider the possibility of a daughter as adamantly as he refused to acknowledge that he might be the one who was sterile—had made him terribly defensive. Their last two years together had been miserable. There was no other word for them.

Yet she missed the early days, when they were content with themselves, and he was not yet distressed by a lack of children.

Their rollicking good times, wonderfully romantic and sexual, were more than most people ever had in a lifetime. Stephan had been marvelous to travel with, adaptable to the ordinary discomforts of foreign lands, amiable with the natives. He had taken her on an eight-week aerial tour of French colonial Africa in their own Caudron cabin plane. It was an unforgettable time, hazarding the parched deserts watching the rich herds of game, enjoying the simple amiability of the natives that Stephan said concealed a valiant warrior discipline, savoring the rough camp fare, impossibly delicious. Then, always, there was the uninhibited loving under the canvas.

But it was over. Charlotte had been astute, giving her correct care—comfort when it was wanted, solitude when it was needed—but even she was beginning to suggest that it was time to get busy. Bruno, direct as always, had told her one afternoon to "stop drooping around and go to work."

She had been to France twice since the crash. Once to bury him in the family plot, a request he had made before the races "in case anything happens." At the funeral, Pierre Dompnier had been a broken man, totally destroyed by the death of the last of his sons. Madame, quite unexpectedly, had been by far the stronger of the two, buoyed by her strong religious beliefs and perhaps hardened by their earlier losses. Monique had been stoic.

Then last month she had gone again, meeting Bruno and Charlotte in Orléans. It was a world turned upside down. The business had made the Dompniers prosperous, and Pierre was determinedly jovial. Monique had assumed the airs of a bank president, aloof, crisply businesslike—except when she thought she was alone with Bruno. Then she became Monique the coquette again. Something was probably going on.

In a dozen unconscious ways, never intended, the family somehow made it clear that they rejected and resented Patty, while they accepted and even enjoyed Bruno. It made sense to her only when she separated events and looked at them dispassionately. She had interrupted their plans and taken Stephan away from them. Bruno had intervened with new plans that in some measure let the family carry on despite the loss of their sons. She understood, objectively; subjectively, she felt a bitter resentment compounded by a sense of personal failure.

A magpie, wings feather-edged in white, whirled in flight above the lawn, then fluttered down to pick up some morsel. Its image plucked a clear vision from the roiling mass of her confused emotions: she intended to go on flying. In part it was a fall-back position—she really knew how to do nothing else. But in the main it was a visceral desire to experience again the joys of flight, the swift transport from the complexities and frustrations of the ground to the serene beauty of the sky.

She had genuinely mourned Stephan, but now it was time to get on with her life. He probably would not have wished her to fly, knowing the danger as he did so intimately. But he would not have forbidden it either.

The resolution stirred a sense of well-being in her, and she began to plan her path of action. She would start over with some instruction at the plant; then a few cross-countries, perhaps some aerobatic work. Then she could see if she could do some racing, appear in some air shows. On the side, there would be flying to do at the factory.

In the long run, this wouldn't be enough. Flying, marvelous in itself, demanded recognition. She had a responsibility to other women flyers to do well, to break down some of the barriers. A few record flights, perhaps, and then a shot at the Bendix Trophy.

Not even realizing it, she had stood up and moved to the mirror, pushing her hair into place and checking her makeup. She could get someone to check her out in the company Waco this afternoon. No sense in wasting any more time.

She was changing into her flying clothes when she became aware of the warmth of a deep sexual stirring. Except for some sad sweet dreams of Stephan, it was the first since the accident, and it shocked her. She sat on the edge of the bed, one leg in the jodhpur-like flying pants, and remembered one of Stephan's deep beliefs. The joys of flying—dawn flights, the panoramic views of the countryside, the satisfaction of doing well—were heightened by a sweet, biting sauce implicitly and irresistibly tinged with sex . . . and death.

Downey, California/May 16, 1933

The factory had thundered into life with a Stravinski-like overture of clanging sounds. When the long-sealed hangar doors were popped open, the welcome breeze caused the silver-lettered red hanging signs—"No Smoking," "Fire Extinguisher"—to jangle vigorously in their chain traces, as if rolling up tin sleeves in anticipation of being useful again. Bandfield and Roget ex-

ulted in the growing cacophony as the ordinary mechanics of
starting up made the building pulsate with life. From the crackling of the light switches being snapped on to the rumbling
tremors sent from the air compressor, the whole factory stretched
and groaned back toward productivity.

The first real clamor came from the insistent cackle of riveting
machines as cut metal came together, small parts being assembled by men glad to have jobs. Downey's entire community
benefited from the reopening, for almost as soon as the impressive ''Roget Aircraft Corporation'' sign had gone up—Hadley
had fabricated the brass letters himself—two other businesses
had moved in. One was a hopeful flight instruction school, with
an ancient Bird biplane as its only trainer (Hadley offered them
a deal on a Kitten right away) and the other was an auto-body
shop, and they gave the field a sense of promise that had long
been lacking. Bandfield had purchased a Kodak Brownie camera for $2.50 and was keeping a day-to-day record of the prog-
ress.

An argument had slowed them down temporarily. Hadley and
Bandy were both working too hard, Roget driving the men on
the floor with an obsessive demand for quality while Bandfield
bent over the drafting board. Late at night, when everyone was
gone, Bandfield would sometimes slump over the table and feel
twin red spots drilling mercilessly through his closed eyes into
his retinas, afterimages of the engineering room's bright incan-
descents. Between the engineering and the financial worries,
both men needed a vacation. They had survived Roosevelt's
bank holiday only because the local suppliers were totally dependent upon them and kept them afloat, fulfilling orders far
beyond the usual credit limits. There were damn few dollars
coming in and every day a new, surprise demand for dollars
going out.

A major rupture almost occurred in mid-April. Bandfield had
forced his eyes open to stare at the two top drawings of the
proposed bomber in front of him, the one Hadley Roget preferred, and his own version.

''Look out the window there, Bandy. We can't screw around
forever waiting for you to make a decision. You wanted to be
president, and presidents make decisions.''

Bandfield pushed his slide rule aside and glanced out the
grimy window to the assembly-bay floor. Work on the wing had
stopped, awaiting a decision. A swarm of men in gray coveralls

were busy fabricating the elevators and rudder, while others were finishing up on the retractable landing gear installation.

Bandy's instincts told him they needed a super-lean aircraft, with an oval fuselage that minimized drag, and the main bomb load carried externally. He figured that you had to have the extra drag only on the trip in; coming off the bomb run you'd be cleaner, and faster. Hadley wanted a bigger fuselage, one that would hold more fuel as well as bombs, accepting the cost of the extra drag.

He was certain Roget was wrong. They'd argued for days, and the time had come to make a decision. The wing was almost complete, waiting for them to decide where the fuselage-attachment fittings would go.

All the calculations resolved down to a simple table. His airplane could carry two thousand-pound bombs externally. It had a top speed of 190 mph, and could fly for about 600 miles. He insisted that the extra drag of the externally mounted bombs was more than offset by the savings in weight and the reduction in frontal resistance of the lean fuselage. Hadley's design offered the same bomb load, carried internally with more room for fuel tanks. The top speed was only 180 mph, but the range was 890 miles. Other than the size and shape of the fuselage, the two designs were identical, both using 630-horsepower Pratt & Whitney R-1860-11 engines.

"Okay, Hadley. Let's decide. But first let's talk about hiring someone to handle the production end. Do you think Howard can do it?"

Roget grunted. "Sure, easy, but I doubt if he's interested. He's learned about as much from us as he can." The older man flopped down in a chair and propped his leg on the drafting table. "Besides, he's not realiable anymore. He's either off working some movie deal or fiddle-fucking with that little Boeing biplane he bought. He's talking about building a racer of his own. Anyway, I'm not sure he can keep his mind on the job and his pecker in his pants. Even when he is here, he's gone half the day, either chasing that cupcake down at the café or dragging his own beauties around. He must have the name and address of every starlet in Hollywood!"

Bandfield avoided grinning. He sometimes went out with Hughes's leftovers, some of the most beautiful girls he'd ever seen, and Roget knew it.

"But before we hire anybody, we've got to decide which airplane to build. We've waited too long already."

Bandfield accepted the rebuke resignedly. Hadley was all get-up-and-go, never willing to stop and reflect. The delays in deciding had bothered Bandy, but were killing Roget.

"No, we haven't lost too much time. A week maybe, no more. I think my design is right, even though you've been building airplanes a long time. The main thing is that I think I know how the Army thinks. They're going to be impressed by top speed more than anything else. It's just like in Peru. Santos was only going to be impressed by the dogfight, no matter what else happened."

When Roget disagreed, he had a way of snorting, tossing his head back, and rolling his eyes that infuriated Clarice; it was beginning to get on Bandfield's nerves as well.

"Doesn't make sense, Bandy. They're not going to race the airplanes. They'll probably never fly at top speed. They need range and bomb load. You forget I spent a little time at Wright Field. And remember—I was responsible for most of the wing design, and I think I know what will work best with it."

Bandfield didn't say anything, and Roget continued, "Either one is okay by me, but let me know what you want, now. It'll make a difference in what we buy, and how we build."

The younger man motioned toward the window. "Look out there, Hadley. We've brought part of this plant back to life. If we get a contract, we'll have the whole place jumping. Forty people depend on us now for paychecks, but we'll employ ten times more if we make the right decision."

"I agreed that you'd be the boss, Bandy, so I'll do whatever you say. But let's decide."

Bandfield felt the familiar sense of compulsive rightness descend on him. He tried to shake it off, to be totally objective, but the feeling came through. "I've got to do it my way. The competition is in June. Can we make it?"

Hadley jumped up grinning, glad to have a decision even if he didn't agree with it. "We'll make it. We'll roll it out the first of May, test it for three weeks, and fly it to Dayton at the end of the month."

The thought of actually having an airplane he could fly instead of a mass of jumbled metal sustained Bandfield as he slogged through the last of the engineering paper shuffle. Most of the remaining design work was now in the small fittings whose needs were previously unforeseen, and the two young engineers he'd hired were doing well with these. Building airplanes was a funny game. After what seemed like weeks without any progress, the skeleton was stop-framing along like a hesitant animated cartoon, and the fuselage was now solid and even beginning to show a few wear marks from the people climbing over it. The slender ovals of the formers had been linked together with aluminum stringers, and then, like shingling a roof, were covered by the specially shaped sheets of thin aluminum skin. The completed wing was on a parallel assembly line, its anodized metal surfaces protected by a paper wrapping until it was mated with the fuselage.

Despite the usual strain of building a prototype—parts that don't come in on schedule, drawings that don't get changed so that other parts don't fit, totally unforeseen problems in routing of controls and cables, the whole complex of things that could go wrong going wrong—Bandfield drew strength from little niceties that counted. The windows in the old Smith plant were positioned exactly right for the natural illumination of his drafting table. There was a small but eager and efficient staff already on board, like Grace Davisson, who had moved from secretary to office manager three weeks after she was hired. She had taken an enormous load from his shoulders, running everything with a cheerful efficiency that automatically picked up his morale.

And there were big things as well, the most important being the bank's establishing a strong line of credit for them, based on the acceptance of their preliminary design by the Air Corps. Design acceptance was a long way from winning a competition and signing a contract, and Bandy suspected that Howard Hughes might have had a hand in influencing the bank to lend him the money.

He sat rubbing a pencil back and forth between his palms. All the things he enjoyed, all the work he did, were poor palliatives for the loneliness that gnawed at him. His dreams—night dreams and daydreams—had changed subtly in the last year. He still dreamed of Millie, but now her face was that of Patty Dompnier. It was totally stupid. Howard had more leftover women than the average man could use, and he was always willing to fix Bandfield up. He had gone out a few times, even found himself tumbling happily in bed with some of them, but nothing permanent had developed. He was looking for someone who didn't exist—Millie—and someone he couldn't have—Patty. Or could he?

Maybe it was just a defense mechanism, an excuse to stay single and avoid the responsibilities of marriage. It didn't matter much: for whatever reason he was desperately lonely.

Even as he thought of Patty, Bandfield was uncomfortably aware that his heart had picked up the trip-hammer rhythm of the riveting machines outside, wondering what she was doing. It had been eight months. How long did young women mourn nowadays? Could she be seeing someone else already?

He shrugged the thoughts away. He had more than three strikes against him. She surely must resent his having won the race in which her husband had died. And then there was Hafner! How could he even think of courting the stepdaughter of a man he hated, and a dangerous business rival at that!

He went back to work, wondering what Howard's plans were for the evening. Maybe he'd have a spare.

Wright Field, Ohio/June 15, 1933

Wright Field had quite by chance turned into one of those blessed anomalies, a military base where civilian scientists and military officers worked in almost perfect harmony. Their activities had the extraordinary benefit of being considered too complicated for investigation by Congress, which in large measure gave the appropriations and didn't attempt to manage the programs. The result was a fertile hothouse of innovation, where manufacturers, inventors, geniuses, and crackpots all intermixed to create new and better aircraft. England had a direct counterpart at Farnborough, and France, to a lesser extent, at Villacoublay, but there was probably nowhere else in the world where science, business, politics, and service matters melded together in so efficient a manner.

There were plenty of fights, ranging from polite arguments to fist-slinging brawls, and the test pilots were often prima donnas, jockeying to get the most record flights. But the combined effect of tradition and the great good fortune of having several excellent commanders in a row made the place work. It even made it possible for flamboyant showmen like Bruno Hafner to be tolerated.

Hafner Aircraft was there for the bomber competition, but Bruno had pulled off an unprecedented stunt. He had flown the bomber in himself; on its right wing was the new transport, flown by Dusty Rhoades. There had been rumors at Wright Field about the transport, but the big surprise came with the third plane in the formation, a beautiful low-wing amphibian racer. Charlotte Hafner had flown it from Long Island in record-setting time, climaxing the trip by arriving precisely as the two larger planes appeared over Wright Field and doing a barrel roll around them before joining them in formation.

The inevitable result was a complete scoop for Hafner in the local newspapers and the wire services. The Wright Field brass, who liked to keep the competitions as low-key as possible, were furious, but said nothing. Charlotte, legs crossed and the top two buttons of her blouse unbuttoned, was sitting on the wing of the amphibian, holding court for a flock of reporters, half blind from the flash cameras but loving every minute of it.

It didn't make the Air Corps feel any better when Hafner announced the humiliating fact that both the bomber and the amphibian were faster than the hottest Army plane at the station, a Boeing P-26 pursuit. This was headline material, particularly when a blond "It" girl was doing the most spectacular flying. Then as a throwaway line, Charlotte commented that the transport was "only just as fast as the P-26"; it was frosting on the cake for the reporters, hemlock for the Army.

Yet they couldn't deny the scope of Hafner's accomplishments, and the German ace was jovially expansive as he led Major Henry Caldwell's troupe of grim and tight-lipped engineers around.

Hafner, his face a broad grin, was shouting his familiar chorus, boasting, "I've more goddamn Russians working for me than Stalin. Every time Sikorsky loses a contract, another dozen show up at the door. I'm going to have to start borrowing his samovars to keep up with the demand."

, Charlotte wondered if anyone had noticed the difference in Hafner's appearance. For years he'd worn the Teutonic skinned-sideburn haircut that had been stylish in his cadet school. Then one evening at the movies, watching *The Dawn Patrol* (he loved it when the Germans won at the end), he rebelled at the sight of a captured German officer wearing the same style haircut. He had let his hair grow and then gone to see "Arlie the Barber" in Manhattan for a conventional haircut.

It went well with his new corporate manner. He had intensified his supervision when he returned to New Jersey, and had submerged himself in the project for the last few weeks. Charlotte tagged along behind the group, talking to Dusty Rhoades, but listening to Hafner with cynical admiration. The business in France was booming—a good way to put it, since they were selling guns—and Bruno was going back and forth to Europe regularly while still keeping close tabs on everything in the

States. There was no doubt that he was in charge. His technique was to delegate important projects to people he trusted for a while, then return and take them over himself again. Spreading himself thin enabled him to get a lot done, but it was disruptive and hard on morale. It was especially difficult for Armand Bineau, who didn't mind taking instructions, but hated Hafner's going around him directly to the engineering and production staff.

After the preliminary inspection, the stone-faced Army officers were obviously impressed, even as Caldwell saw to it that they were arm's-length formal.

"We're not in a position to evaluate any aircraft but the bomber, Mr. Hafner. Other manufacturers might think you were gaining a competitive advantage."

"I understand, Major. But I invited a few friends down to see them—airline presidents like Eddie Rickenbacker, C. R. Smith, Patterson, Ted Mahew, Trippe, a few others. I hope you don't mind."

Caldwell turned several shades darker red. His voice was tight and compressed when he said, "It's highly irregular, Mr. Hafner, but so is almost everything you do." Struggling to end on a graceful note, he added, "They are all friends of ours, so we'll be glad to see them."

A hundred yards away, Hadley Roget and Bandy stood under the wing of their Roget Raider bomber.

"My God, Hadley, Hafner's airplane looks just like your design—the same big fat belly."

"It sure does. Let's hope you were right on what the Army wants and I was wrong."

"How in hell did they pull off three airplanes? We busted our butts to get one done on time."

"Well, the transport's just the bomber with a different fuselage. But the amphibian is really something, with that funny gear. I'm going to nose around and find out how they did it."

Caldwell waved them over to his group. "I believe everyone is acquainted?" They all shook hands except Hafner and Bandy, who didn't even nod to each other.

"Since you're all friends, I'm sure you want to look at each other's products. We'll meet you in base operations in half an hour, and we'll go to the officers' club for lunch." Caldwell marched rapidly off to get ratification from Washington on his handling of Hafner's three-airplane ploy.

Dayton's deadly dullness was reinforced by a savage early

blast of Midwestern heat. The sweat-dampened days passed quickly enough as they stayed with the Army inspectors doing their precompetition inspection of the aircraft. The planes were measured, weighed, and photographed while the plans were pored over in brightly lit conference rooms.

The humid nights, sullen with the soiled heat bounced back from street and building, were endless. Work ended promptly at four-thirty, leaving a lot of time to clean up, dress, and eat. Once the local movies had been exhausted, there was not much to do but drink.

After the opening lunch, the Army personnel stayed away from the contractors entirely, not wanting even to have a cup of coffee in private, for fear of someone's complaining about a competitive advantage. Protocol called for the two companies to maintain a friendly but distant relationship. There was very little mixing between the Roget and Hafner people until Wednesday night in the dining room of the Van Cleve Hotel, where Bandfield found Charlotte sitting with Patty at dinner.

He stepped back behind one of the marble columns of the entrance as he debated whether or not to go over to them. He found himself staring at Charlotte, avoiding looking at Patty the way as a child he had saved the best morsel of food for last.

Charlotte was no longer as slender and didn't seem to pay the same attention to her appearance, but she was somehow even better-looking, having a composure and a serenity he'd never seen in her before.

A narrowing of vision and a constriction in his throat told him he'd better breathe again. He did, shifting his gaze to Patty, who was even more beautiful than he had remembered, the golden glow of her skin set off by her simple white linen dress. She wore a single strand of pearls. She was obviously talking about a serious subject, for she was alternately staring at her plate and glancing quickly up into her mother's eyes, while her fingers tapped against the side of her glass.

He walked over and said hello. Both women jumped up, genuinely pleased to see him.

"I just wanted to say how sympathetic all of us were to your loss."

Patty nodded, thanking him with equal formality. "It was a great tragedy for us all, and for aviation. Stephan was a wonderful pilot."

Breaking the awkward silence, he asked Patty, "Did you fly out?"

"No, I'm ashamed to say I took the good old Baltimore and Ohio. I had a lot of paperwork to do."

Charlotte beamed at them. "Bruno keeps her busy. He's been spending a lot of time on the arms business, going back and forth to France."

"Yes, he keeps me busy at everything but flying."

Bandfield tried to judge what the tone of her voice meant. She obviously wasn't angry with her mother, but her comments were tart and tense.

"Will you be doing any of the demonstration work?"

"No, that's what I was just complaining about. Bruno says it would dilute the impact Mother has on the press if we both flew."

Charlotte excused herself to go to the powder room.

Patty reached over and squeezed his arm. "Bandy, I'm so glad to see you. I wanted to get in touch with you, but just didn't know how to go about it."

"Really?"

"I want to ask you a favor."

Bandfield knew that if souls had eyes, his had just rolled them heavenward.

"Shoot."

"For some reason, Bruno is really holding me back. I don't know whether he doesn't have confidence in me, or if he thinks it is too soon after Stephan's death, or what. But all he lets me do is standard production or maintenance test flights."

Bandfield nodded. "Maybe he just doesn't want anything to happen to you."

"Maybe, although that is awfully altruistic for Bruno. Anyway, will you help me?"

"Anything you want. Just ask."

"I want to have someone build me a cross-country racer, and I want to start shooting for the absolute records. Not the women's record, but the record."

Bandfield glanced around. Was he kidding himself, or was Charlotte deliberately staying away so they could have some time together? It didn't matter; they were alone.

"What did you have in mind?"

"Well, I can't afford to design something from the ground up. But I thought maybe you could figure out a way to soup up some stock airplane, a Northrop Gamma, maybe a Lockheed Air Express."

"You're talking thirty or forty grand, just doing that."

"Rats. I was hoping to keep it down to about twenty thousand. I finally inherited a little money from my father's—my real father's—family."

"And you want it kept secret, no doubt."

"Has to be. Charlotte and Bruno aren't getting along any too well, and something like this could really be trouble."

"Well, I'll have to think about it. Do you ever get to the Coast?"

"Not often, but I'll make a point of it."

Charlotte came back, and the two women excused themselves. Bandy had mixed emotions on the way things had gone. God knew that Roget Aircraft could use the extra money, and it could be an interesting project. On the other hand he sensed that his real motivation was simply to be with Patty, and he wasn't sure that it was the time for that yet. It had taken him years to get over the tragedy of Millie's death. Could he expect Patty to forget Stephan so soon? Or was he being stupid, imagining that she had any but a professional interest in him? Still, she had squeezed his arm. Perhaps if they worked together on a racer, they could find out more about each other, and see if there was any future for them.

His sober assessment didn't inhibit some heady fantasies about Patty, and these helped Bandfield endure the disappointment of the anticlimactic flight tests of the two competing bombers. Even before the company pilots had finished their demonstration routines, it was clear that the Hafner Skyshark's cleaner fuselage design and one hundred extra horsepower made it superior on every point—speed, range, and bomb load—to the Roget entry. The actual judging would be based on a complicated table that awarded points for performance, ease of maintenance, price, and other factors. But even the normally optimistic Hadley Roget knew that it was no contest.

When the flight activities were concluded, everything sank in a welter of paperwork. The one area that the Roget airplane excelled in was maintenance. The two years Hadley had spent at Wright Field were apparent in the way he'd planned to make changing the engines and wheels fast and easy. But both men knew it was not enough, and they knew Hafner would be quick to adopt similar methods.

They sat in the little saloon next to the Van Cleve, morosely drinking whiskey with beer chasers, as down as they had ever been.

"You know, Bandy, if that fucking Hafner came in a revolving door after you, he'd go out first. He is some slick customer."

"Yeah. And it's my fault. I insisted on using my design. Jesus, Hadley, I guess this is it. Even if they buy the prototype, we're about out of business. I hate to go back and tell the guys they're all out of work."

"We have no choice, Bandy. I don't see how we can even keep them on board until the official results come out. It's just money down the drain."

Consolation came the next morning, as unexpectedly as a June freeze. In the hope of seeing Patty again, Bandy had agreed to attend the briefing on the transport that Hafner was to give the airline executives in the Van Cleve Hotel. Hadley came along just to show the flag.

The German had prepared carefully, putting out the news quickly for days in advance that he was going to make a sensational announcement. The reports that had come out of Dayton, the daily press releases on the performance of the transport, had made their mark, and not a single major airline executive felt he could afford to miss the meeting. Each man, anticipating that Hafner was going to announce prices and delivery schedules, had brought along his chief engineer and top accountant.

There was a short sound film showing the Hafner factory and Charlotte flying the transport, along with some obviously fake indoor shots of smiling passengers being ecstatic over their inflight lunches. Charlotte and Patty, dressed in identical hostess outfits, passed out red-velvet-covered brochures that extolled the Skyangel's virtues.

The audience was filled with old pros, men who'd been promised the moon by many a manufacturer, but Hafner's presentation had them at fever pitch. Bandfield watched them slide from a glassy-eyed indifference into a febrile, intense mood, itching to buy. As much as he disliked Bruno, he admired how he handled them. The squarehead had just won the bomber competition, and now he was selling transports as if they were Model As.

"I can't quote an exact price, gentlemen, until we know the quantities involved, but I can tell you that we expect the airplane to come in for about sixty-five thousand dollars."

A murmur roared through the group. It was an unbelievably low price for an airplane that made all the Fords and Fokkers totally obsolete. No passenger would want to fly in a noisy hundred-mile-per-hour trimotor when he could bask in the luxury of the Hafner airliner. It was not a question of whether they should buy the airplane, but how soon they could get it. Every airline man there—executive, engineer, accountant—was completely sold. The normally tight-lipped Rickenbacker stood up. Out of deference, the others grew quiet.

"Good presentation, Captain Hafner. When can we expect delivery of the airplane?"

Bruno savored the moment. Here was an old enemy, Captain Eddie Rickenbacker, the American Richthofen, a famous racing driver, a car maker, and now an airline executive, asking him for a favor.

"Well, Captain Rickenbacker, gentlemen, we thought you would like the Skyangel. We feel it will revolutionize the air transportation system here and abroad. Naturally, we plan to equip our own Federated Airlines with the first sixty planes, and then we'll be offering others the first deliveries in the spring of 1935."

There was a stunned silence. Hafner was obviously trying to establish a stranglehold on the market. In two years, Federated would have established itself as the dominant airline.

A cataract of invective broke over Bruno, washing him to the back of the podium in a defensive posture, totally unprepared for the intensity of the reaction. Rickenbacker, normally very gentlemanly in the presence of women, lost control and yelled, "You Kraut son of a bitch, go fuck yourself." He strode from the room, bald head bouncing, lips tightly set, his people following him in a cluster. Allied Airlines' gigantic Ted Mahew, so big that he towered over both Rickenbacker and Hafner, had to be forcibly restrained from hitting Bruno.

"You arrogant bastard! You invited us down here to see the airplane, knowing you weren't going to have any for sale for two years. This is outrageous."

Hafner scurried around, apologizing and explaining, but it was too late. With a despairing look at Charlotte, he watched the airline people stalk from the room.

Bandfield's old friend from Western Airways, Corliss Moseley, signaled to him. The crowd had left in angry, tight little groups, and he and Moseley followed a still-boiling Mahew back to his room. Roget came after them with Mahew's staff from Allied Airlines.

Over the course of an hour, and half a bottle of Johnny Walker Black Label, Mahew calmed down. "What's the old saying, don't get mad, get even? Let's get even. Hadley, can you deliver me a prototype airliner with better performance than the Skyangel, at least eighteen seats, two hundred miles per hour cruise, by the end of the year?''

Hadley shot a quick glance to Bandy, who bobbed his head in agreement. ''May we caucus for a few minutes? I'm sure we can do it, but I want to give you a best estimate.''

The few minutes dragged into an hour and a half as Bandy and Roget sat making gross calculations of weight, drag, and material lead times.

''Can't be done, Bandy. We'd need a full year, at least, and then it would be close.''

''We can't say that. Let's compromise, say two hundred and seventy days. If we get them excited, get them on board the design, they'll give us an extension. I hate to promise something we can't deliver, but I'm not leaving Dayton without a contract for something.''

The old crafty-codger look came into Hadley's eyes. ''A prototype in two hundred and seventy days, eh? Let's shoot for it. Lots of overtime, get the engine and propeller people on board early, subcontract a lot of things—landing gear to Cleveland Pneumatic, instrument panel to Bendix.'' Roget's face was ecstatic. ''We can do it, by God, we can do it!''

Back out with Mahew, Roget once again assumed the diplomat's role.

''Jim, we can give you the airplane you want, one clearly superior to the Hafner job, in two hundred and seventy days. Figure three months for flight test and production setup, and we'll be able to deliver the first ten airplanes by August 1934, with ten per month after that for whoever wants them.''

''Hadley, I want you to stick it to Hafner, bad. He's been running wild for a long time now, and it's time to stop him. If you deliver, Roget Aircraft has a rosy future, believe me.''

Bandy and Hadley spoke simultaneously. ''We'll deliver!''

''It's my turn to caucus, now,'' Mahew said, waving the two of them out of the room. They stood in the hallway, not talking, but filled with excitement. Hadley was walking up and down, ten steps in one direction, ten back, and Bandfield was standing tracing the intricate designs in the hall runner with his toe. Both men knew that this could be the big break, the benchmark design that would save Roget Aircraft.

Mahew stuck his head out in the hall and motioned them inside.

''Just to show you how serious we are, I'll guarantee you an order for sixty for Allied Airlines, with deliveries spread out over three years. But one other thing. This has to be shared with the other airlines. I want the first ten positions on your line, but after that, make sure that the others get a chance. Understand me?''

"Understand. Are you willing to put up any development money?''

Mahew's natural business caution intervened, and he hesitated before saying, "Let's say a million for openers, and you let me know what you need. I'm going out to the industry for the money, but I'll get it. I'll confirm all this in writing. Better make the airplane a trimotor. The pilots are used to them.''

Hadley and Roget went to their room, to work all night, big silver carafes of rotten hotel coffee propping their eyes open. They argued and laughed alternately, and by seven the next morning, both groggy, they shook Mahew's hand again and presented him with two sketches. One was for a trimotor, the other for a twin-engine transport.

"Let us work out the specs, Ted, and we'll send you a final recommendation. A twin-engine plane means fewer engines to buy, fewer spares, better visibility.''

Both men saw the irony in their return journey home on a railroad train. They had just pulled off the biggest airplane deal in their life, and would have plenty of time to reflect on it as the train chugged toward their Chicago transfer point. Four Roses whiskey swirled over ice cubes in the big cut-glass tumblers in the club car as they began to fill in the details of the design possibilities as if they were dots to connect in a puzzle. Dead tired from the tension of the week, both men dozed intermittently, dreams punctuated by the clatter of the rails. The pleasure of winning the impromptu design competition for the new transport evaporated as Bandfield thought about the future.

"Hadley, I'd like to see Bruno's face when he finds out about this.''

"Forget about Bruno. Just think about his airplane. I want to have our transport's design parameters laid out by the time we get back to L.A. No mooning about—let's get cracking. It's a damn good thing the racer is finished and I can work full-time on this.''

A week later, Bandy and Roget were in the factory early, installing a huge paper poster on which was drawn the outline of the now-famous Hafner Skyangel. Beneath, in bold black letters, was written: "LIKE THIS, ONLY BIGGER AND BETTER!!!!"

Buffalo, New York/June 22, 1933

The Heidelberg Hof restaurant had prospered during Prohibition, when discreet payoffs to local politicians had enabled it to run a full bar without any problems. Now it was a little on the tatty side, with peeling prints of wholesome peasants frolicking in the fields and tonsured monks tippling at their wine casks.

Ernst Udet hardly fit the image of Germany's leading living ace. A survivor of the war, an aerobatic champion, a filmmaker—the chubby-cheeked flyer sat poking at his plate, trying to separate the gristly slices of smoked pork loin from the greasy sauerkraut, his normal cherubic smile vanished. He picked up a stack of white bread and thumbed through it as if it were a deck of cards.

"Well, it's not Horcher's, is it? My God, Bruno, how can Americans make millions of cars and not be able to make decent bread? How do you stand it?"

Bruno laughed. "I never eat it, just as I never drink the cold piss they call beer. If you stick to steaks and lobster and scotch, you can get by."

Udet's movements were mongoose-quick, in odd contrast to his soft, wryly humorous manner of speech. Underneath his courteous manner, he watched Hafner closely, trying to determine if and where he could fit into the scheme of things. Germany needed airmen now, but Udet did not require any more rivals. It was difficult enough just getting along with Goering and his cronies.

He patted his pockets for matches, pushing the earthenware bottle to Hafner as he lit his cigarette. "Can't fly on one wing; have another Steinhager." Hafner poured the clear liquor into the tall thin-walled double shot glasses.

Udet tossed his back and smacked his lips. "Just like the good old days, eh, Bruno?"

They had been good days, even in late 1918, when to their amazement they found that Germany, victor over Russia, was suddenly losing the war. "But times have changed. Then I was thin and had hair. Now, ach." He ran his hand over a balding dome just fringed with hair.

Hafner smiled. Erni was heavier, but that was not the big

change. In 1918, he had been a little gamecock, sure of himself, netting trophies of aircraft and women with equal abandon. And even with sixty-two victories, Udet had been by far the best-liked ace. Von Richthofen had been aloof, a taskmaster, a visionary battle leader who seemed to know that he was doomed to die soon in combat. Goering had been a tyrant, perhaps of necessity, for he had taken over the Richthofen *Geschwader* when the German air force was short of everything but courage. But Udet—everyone had loved Udet, who had taken seriously flying and killing only. The rest—squadron discipline, dress, saluting—had meant nothing to him. The enlisted men particularly, already beginning to be infected with Bolshevik ideas, had respected him.

He was changed—aged and uncertain. He seemed to be unsure of what to say and how to say it.

Hafner watched him closely. He thought he knew why Udet had asked to see him. The Nazis had always said they would rearm Germany, and judging from the inquiries for arms his warehouse in New Jersey had been getting, they had already started.

"Remember how we had to put wooden wheels on the airplanes on the ground, and change to rubber tires before a flight? Or fly out to drain the oil and scavenge the copper from a crashed British plane?"

"It's different now, Bruno. Things are looking up. We'll be flying new planes in a few years, with plenty of tires and all the oil and copper we need."

The flicker of Hafner's eyebrows showed his skepticism. Udet caught it, and tried to analyze it. His slow and sometimes hesitant manner gave him a chance to think before he spoke. He fiddled with the matches again, to gain time. A smart fellow, he thought; I didn't remember him that way. He was always charging out to get the enemy, going into combat every day. Even gave some victories away. That was suspicious!

Udet spoke. "I'm sorry I missed you last year in Germany. I was shooting a film in Greenland. *SOS Iceberg.* You saw it?"

Hafner shook his head. "Sorry. Has it played in the United States?"

"No, and you are lucky. It is a terrible film, almost killed me. I had to crash a Moth into the freezing water near an iceberg. I damn near drowned."

Udet snubbed his cigarette out, lit another, and poured more Steinhager. He pulled a long, slender green leather folder out of his coat pocket and put it on the table, along with a pen. Udet was an inveterate doodler, a caricature artist. He sketched an enormous fat man, bulging out of the cockpit of an airplane, pudgy fingers bejeweled, his arm extended in a Nazi salute. Tossing it over to Hafner he asked, "Did *unser* Hermann take good care of you?"

"*Ja*. Good likeness, Ernst. God, is he fat! I wouldn't have recognized him if he hadn't been all decked out in a general's uniform, with poor stupid old Loerzer at his side."

Both men knew that it was only fair that Goering kept Bruno Loerzer at his side. In 1915 arthritis had crippled Goering, reducing him from a dashing infantry lieutenant to a convalescent, destined to be a supply officer in some garrison town. Loerzer had gotten him into flying, first as an observer, then as a pilot. From that point on, they had been inseparable, managing to get assigned to the same unit, if not the same aircraft, until their successful combat records made them commanders of different fighter units—Loerzer had *Jasta* 26 and Goering *Jasta* 27.

Udet and Goering had been more rivals than friends, and Loerzer always took Goering's part. But all three men had liked Hafner, and he had provided a friendly link among them.

"Apparently you are some sort of fair-haired knight with Goering. He often talks about you, which is rare; he usually talks about himself. What's the story?"

Hafner smiled to himself. The story was simple: he had made a hero out of Goering and never mentioned it afterward. It was just after the war had ended on that bitter November 11, when the politicians had sold the soldiers out, and Goering was ordered to surrender their aircraft, their precious, hoarded Fokkers, to the French at Strasbourg. Goering, already shaken by a brush with a revolutionary "Soldiers' Council," was uncertain how to comply. Hafner had pulled him aside and said, "Let's go—and everyone crash on landing. We'll comply with the terms of the Armistice—but give them shit."

The Fokkers had whirled low across the field in impeccable formation, wheels just brushing the grass, wingtips interlocked, to show the French that these were not amateurs arriving. Then a soaring chandelle climb and they had landed like clowns, crashing their airplanes one by one. Hafner had dug in a wingtip, sending his Fokker cartwheeling and destroying it. Others ran into each other or into the line of trees that edged the field. When they were finished, the furious French had nothing but kindling on their hands.

The act had made Goering a hero anew, at a time when Germany sorely needed new heroes. But Hafner's role was still a secret. It would remain that way. "We just got along. He needed friends; I was one."

"*Ja*, even now, even with all his phony charm, Hermann is not easy to work with." He thought to himself, And he needs friends more than ever, more than he knows. "But he's doing a good job even if he eats and drinks too much, and . . ."

He moved his hands as if he were shoving a hypodermic needle in his arm.

"Dope? Does the Fuehrer know?"

Udet laughed, dragging deeply on the cigarette. "There's not much Uncle Addie doesn't know, because those swine around him tell him everything. They're like a ladies' sewing society, all gossip. I hate them."

Hafner was unsettled. He'd gone to Germany last year to meet the leading men in the German military because Udet had sent him a message pleading that he do so. Udet was sending a mixed signal, telling him of deficiencies in the leadership he was expected to support. Was he trying to confuse him deliberately? Testing him, perhaps? Well, he thought, I've nothing to hide, I'll tell him what I think.

Udet went on. "Goering was badly wounded in the Munich putsch," Udet explained, "and picked up the morphine habit while he convalesced. He controls it, and even with it, he's the best of the lot. God, you should see some of them—crazy Hess, that filthy Streicher."

Hafner decided to call the bluff.

"If you hate the Nazis, Ernst, why are you here? Why are you working with them?"

Udet let the cigarette smoke roll out of his nostrils in a long, lazy stream, eyeing Hafner steadily, as if the remark made profound sense.

"And what was I to do? I don't hate Germany. And how long do you think I can go on making a living picking up handkerchiefs with my wingtip and flying under bridges?" He was quiet a moment, and then said, "And especially doing this." He drank a Steinhager, and poured another.

Hafner was proving to be a little too sharp, a little too smart. He could be dangerous. But he could also be a good ally. In all the turmoil of the emerging air force, allies were absolutely necessary. With Hafner's connections to Goering and Loerzer, he could be invaluable.

"Goering has promised me the rank of colonel when they announce the new air force, and he'll put me in charge of aircraft selection."

Hafner felt his interest quicken. He had his own ideas on the airplanes a great power needed, and they were a break with past thinking. Perhaps Udet could be convinced.

Udet said, "That's why I asked you to come here. After two years of trying, I'm finally getting to buy a Curtiss Hawk, the dive bomber. They call them Hell Divers, and they are like flying artillery."

Hafner was silent, absorbing all of Udet's remarks, analyzing the quiet fury that was now obviously blazing beneath the genial surface. They had both been hammered in the fires of war. He wondered how Udet had been affected. He knew that his own standards of judgment and morality had been forever changed. He had probably killed forty or fifty men in the air, and perhaps twice that many ground strafing. He could not be sure about the number, but he was very sure that he had enjoyed doing it. Once you operated on that level, once you had established an internal ethic that killing was a pleasure, almost nothing else in life fit in. He remembered his boyhood days, when he would go to church on Good Friday, convinced that his sins were going to pull the thunder and lightning directly down on him. During the war he realized there was no one looking down, no God to judge him. You could do whatever you could get away with. Was Udet the same?

Udet was staring at him, wondering where his mind was.

Hafner snapped back to the present and said, "I know the airplane. It must be obsolete, or the U.S. government wouldn't have permitted its sale. It doesn't compare with my own A-11."

"Ah, maybe so, but as an aircraft type it is superb! There was an American film last year, *Hell Divers*, a good film, showing how the American Navy uses dive bombers. I had it shown to the Fuehrer, and finally got permission to buy some demonstrators."

Hafner had seen the film; it was excellent, but hardly a basis on which to make state armament decisions. He filed the remark away. If he was ever in a social situation with Hitler, he'd bring up his own film-flying with Howard Hughes.

"We'll build our own, of course. I have already talked to Henschel and to Junkers. But the Curtiss is a start. I don't think the Americans know what they have."

The fat waitress, her dirndl riding up over huge thighs, had been hovering, happy to have real Germans in the restaurant. Udet pleased her with a lewd grin and then waved her away. He decided to be direct.

"Tell me, what did you think about our new Chancellor?"

"If you asked me last year if he ever had a chance to be elected, I would have said no. He is terribly impressive, messianic—but so common."

A mixed expression came over Udet, successively reflecting humor, fear, and embarrassment. He was both a commoner and common himself, and so was Hafner for that matter. But Bruno was like so many Germans, enamored of the Hohenzollerns who had done them so much harm, just because they'd been invited to dine with them, or spent a weekend hunting in some baronial preserve. It was a medal mentality.

"Ach, Bruno, don't be too quick to judge. It's hard to like Hitler and too easy to underestimate him. That's why he's Chancellor. They underestimated him." He looked around quickly and said, "And that's why I'm here. You can laugh about Addie and *unser* Hermann all you want—but they are going to rearm Germany, and in a way that will make the world tremble."

Udet watched Hafner closely, trying to gauge his reaction. He could offer nothing in the way of money or luxury to compare with what Hafner could enjoy in the United States. But the old martial drums, the banners, the combat, they might snare him.

Even sitting, Hafner towered over Udet like a huge gorilla. He looked skeptical, openly testing the smaller man.

"Do you think the other politicians will let them? Christ, the Nazis are riffraff, brawlers! They won't last six months in civilized society. They are good only to protest, not to wield power and have responsibilities." It was the party line he had heard from his relatives; he thought differently himself.

"They've already lasted six months, Bruno, and Hitler is taking complete control. Goering's put twenty thousand people in concentration camps. There will be more. They burned the Reichstag and had Papa Hindenburg suspend the constitution. Don't worry about this bunch lasting—Hitler will only leave the Chancellery feet first!"

Bruno tossed the Steinhager down and poured himself another.

"But it's not all bad. You've been living well over here, and I've been doing well, too, even though Germany was on its arse! Hitler's our Mussolini. He's getting things moving, pumping money into the economy."

Udet looked up at the huge man looming over him, deciding to turn the tables on him. "If you dislike the Nazis so, why did you agree to work with Goering last year? I'm here to talk business, and I have to know if you are sincere. I know that you are an American citizen, you have an American wife, a big factory, lots of money. It's hard for me to believe you are serious. I'm not sure what I would do in your position."

I'm very sure what you would do, Hafner thought. He then backed off, relaxing so that his bulk seemed slowly to diminish as a frightened cat finally lets its hair settle down.

"You said it for me. I'm a German, first and last. I think Hitler will get things into shape in Germany and then bring back the monarchy. We fought for the Kaiser once—we'll fight for him again."

Udet's voice was determined. He had to be sure that Hafner understood, that he would be dependable. "No, there will never be another Kaiser, there will be no stupid bag of Napoleonic pretenders like those the French tolerate. Hitler will use the aristocracy for as long as he has to, another year perhaps. Then, all of them, princes, nobles, they are all kaput. And after the aristocracy, the Jews."

Hafner nodded. "That's part of it for me too. The Jews destroyed us in 1918, when they bought up Germany during the inflation." The Steinhager had eroded his reserve. "My family lost everything. I went by my house last year, and do you know who is living there? In my house?"

Udet noted with approval that Hafner had grown so intense that he'd forgotten himself. Good. A fanatic was easier to manage.

"A Jewish doctor and his fat wife, an ass like an apple barrel! There was a little hook-nosed yid coming out the gate on a bicycle. Out of my gate!"

Udet relaxed. The commoner was taking over. He had Hafner. Over time, he would make an ally of him. If not, he could be disposed of. It was important to use him—or at least prevent Goering's using him.

Steinhager and the memories of his house stirred the old patriotism in Bruno. "What am I supposed to do, crawl back in a Fokker D VII?"

"No. We want you to stay right where you are."

"We?"

"Right—we, Hermann and I and Milch and Kesselring, and yes, even Hitler. We want you to keep doing what you are doing, but keep us informed. You don't have to be a spy and put on a false mustache and steal secrets from safes. Just be a pipeline for technical information—new airfoils, new alloys, trends in what is going on, assessments of strength. We can get most of it out of the magazines, but we want you to be the filter, the judge of what we interpret.''

Hafner was nonplussed. He could do this for a while, but even now Charlotte was asking questions about his trips to Germany. And the Air Corps people were not fools—they could track the source of most ideas that were really supposed to be kept secret. It wasn't what he wanted to hear. The way Goering had sketched it out last year, he would sell his businesses and go back to Germany to live. With his money and a commission, it would be better than during the war. He could perhaps be a lieutenant colonel for starters. And sooner or later, he'd buy up his old house, live like a king, do some decent flying. It was time to bargain.

''What's in it for me?''

Udet paused, then told him a long, involved joke about a *Fraülein* who didn't need anything because she didn't drink, didn't smoke, and had her own pussy. ''You don't need any money. You don't need any women. But you do need to be a soldier.''

Hafner felt the hook ease in, secure him. Udet was quite correct. Besides, there was the matter of Charlotte and Rhoades, which severely needed rectification.

''Germany is ten years behind in the air. Versailles crippled us. We're gaining, but Goering wants you to act as an overseas research laboratory, as we did in Russia at Lipetsk, where we built a factory and trained people. You can use American dollars to experiment, to design airplanes, and get the results to us.''

''No, Ernst, I don't like it. I don't want to be some kind of *verdammt* spy, pussyfooting around, pretending. Besides, how long do you think I could get away with it? The Air Corps is not stupid—they could smell out any technology I got to you.''

Udet, his head nodding yes as it always did, said, ''You don't have to do it for long. We'll have to come out in the open with the Luftwaffe next year or the year after. By then we'll have the new airplanes on the line. You can come back then and run an aircraft factory.''

''No! I'll be a technical adviser, but I want a *Geschwader* to command. If there's going to be any combat, I want to be in on it.''

"*Ja*, Bruno, I know what you mean. But let me tell you something. Like Hitler or not, he's a smart bastard, too smart to start a fight with America. He was a *Frontsoldat*, he knows what it's like. He's going to demand that the Rhineland be reoccupied, get the African colonies back, get an agreement with Poland for a corridor."

Having disposed of Europe, Udet drank. "But the main thing is Russia. He hates the Reds as much as he hates the Jews, says they are the same thing. So you won't be doing anything to be ashamed of in America. You'll be helping it, really."

Bruno sat back. It wouldn't matter. The old loyalties came first. Russia. There would be a hunting ground! They could shoot airplanes as the English shoot grouse, spend all day potting and then lay them up in rows at night. He pounded his knee.

Udet's voice was becoming increasingly military, crisper, more demanding.

"We'll start with Curtiss." An order, not an offer.

"What do you mean?"

"I'll get you a private demonstration, let you fly one of the Curtiss dive bombers. You can put a five-hundred-pound bomb in a pickle barrel dive bombing. As I said, it's better than artillery, cheaper, more flexible, faster. You'll see."

Udet's hands sent his pen flying.

Hafner blurted out his real thoughts. "*Jawohl*, but it's not the answer, Ernst. You need big bombers for England. You couldn't fly the Hawk across the Channel and then back with a bomb load."

Udet handed Hafner the sheet of paper. It showed Hafner, huge, his nose an eagle's beak, straddling the fuselage of a diving Curtiss Hawk as a cowboy straddles a horse. There were crosses on the fuselage and a huge swastika on the rudder. He had even remembered Hafner's personal insignia from the war, a winged sword. Bullets were pouring in a stream from the nose of the Hawk and a bomb was being slung from its belly. Down below was a target, a circle of concentric rings. In the center was a word in tiny print. It was "Boredom."

Hafner nodded his head. "Good, Ernst. You know your subject."

He folded the drawing and put it in a breast pocket. "But you don't know your bombers! You should be building big airplanes, with four engines, and maybe four-thousand-pound bomb loads. That's what I'm going to do next, though nobody knows it."

Udet shook his head slightly, mild as always in his disagreement. He preferred to charm his way out of arguments.

"You sound like our purist, Colonel Wever! Big bombers are expensive. We don't want to fight England, or France for that matter. We just want dive bombers to fly along with our tanks, to break through in Russia. No more trenches! And if France and England just leave us alone—and Hitler is sure they will—we can settle matters in the east."

His voice was slurred. "You and I, Bruno, we will be the new Junkers, the new ruling caste. We'll have the estates, the forests. You'll see."

Hafner sat back. That would be decent. An estate in the country. Maybe he would be von Hafner after all! It had amused him when Dusty Rhoades used to call him "Baron." Maybe Rhoades wasn't so far off at that.

The two men got to their feet, Udet stumbling a bit. Hafner put a $5 bill on the table and winked at the fat waitress.

She had been pleased and surprised to have two real Germans drinking in her restaurant until she glanced at their plates. Neither man had eaten much. She palmed the fiver and then shook the Steinhager bottle. It was empty, and it comforted her. Maybe they were old war comrades who just wanted to drink.

8

Downey, California/July 17, 1933

Ted Mahew's blessed out-of-the-blue order for the new transport was a lifeline to solvency. The order meant the bank would talk to them and that they could offer people meaningful jobs instead of part-time work.

They had decided to call the airplane the RC-3, to take advantage of the publicity Douglas had already gained on its competing DC-1. The new contract meant that they had to triple their production-line employment immediately, and double their engineering staff. From the instant their first small help-wanted advertisement was phoned in, before it ever appeared in the paper, they were deluged with applicants.

The outpouring made Bandy feel like Midas. He had known that California was a pool of talent, but he had had no idea that he could choose from the very best talents—engineers, stress analysts, engine men, production-line workers. It was hard not to hire them all, but he kept it down to a minimum, phasing them in over time, so that they were needed badly before they came on board. He got his greatest pleasure from sending wires to the good people he'd worked with in the past and offering them big salaries and bigger responsibilities, a surefire approach.

The small crew of veterans who had started with Roget Aircraft at Downey were nervous at first, but then welcomed the newcomers when they recognized their talent. The joy of having in hand a contract that promised work for at least two years and maybe more sent morale sky-high, and long hours meant nothing. A few of the older men, transferring from other industries, were interested in forming a union, and were amazed when Bandfield was sympathetic to the idea, his father's old politics surfacing. He had watched many other factories live off the substance of their workers, devouring their overtime, only to dismiss them all summarily when a contract went sour. Roget Aircraft was going to be different. Hadley wasn't convinced that it was a good idea, but Bandy gave the new union every encouragement.

The factory had a sharpened sense of vibrancy and discipline as parts came down the tributary aisles to join other parts in the general march to the main assembly line. The staccato banging of the riveters, the shrill rise and fall of the drill presses, the continual reciprocal movement of the lathes all had new tempos and new meanings. Bandy felt a kinship with a symphony orchestra conductor, who played no instrument but made everything happen.

Another plus was that Howard Hughes was drifting away more and more. He had asked early on to help in designing the cockpit layout, and he'd done well, seeing to it that the instruments were grouped sensibly for two-pilot use. The problem was that he became too proprietary, too insistent on having the final word. To get some relief, Bandy had sent him on a survey trip, to check out what was wrong with the current fleet of airliners that they might be able to fix in the RC-3.

Still traveling incognito as Charles Howard, Hughes came back bubbling with ideas. Mahew's airlines operated both Ford and Hafner trimotors, and Bandy had asked Hughes to make the thirty-six-hour trip from Chicago to Los Angeles on the Allied line, just to see if he could get any ideas.

"Bandy, I learned as much on the train trip out as on the flight back. On the trip out I learned that I like to eat and drink and sleep in comfort. On the trip back I learned I didn't like the noise, the heat, the cold, or the rubber chicken."

Even Hadley, pretty fed up with Hughes for some time now, seemed amused.

"You know what they give you when you get on the trimotor? A kit that has cotton to stuff in your ears, smelling salts, and a paper bag to throw up in! Damn near needed it, too. It was so hot on the ground in Chicago that a woman fainted, passed out right in the aisle. Then between Denver and Salt Lake it got so cold my hand stuck to the metal chair edge."

Hughes ruffled through the drawings and glanced out the window at the floor.

"Listen, you get out there and tell those guys that we're not just building an airplane, we're going to build comfort and stick wings on it. We want heaters that heat and seats that don't blister your ass and insulation to cut the noise down. The Ford is bad, but the Hafner trimotor is worse. I was sitting in the second seat, on the leg from Salt Lake to Sacramento, and the propellers felt like they were driving lag bolts into my eardrums."

With a "mission accomplished" nod, Hughes left, bounding out to his latest hobby, a huge Doble steamcar. He was talking about setting up a company to build the steamers and running General Motors and Ford out of business, right after he finished setting some records in the new racer he'd conceived. Hughes had learned all he could from Bandfield and Roget, and he wouldn't be with them long. He had sketched out what he thought a racer should look like, and he served notice that he'd be calling on them for help when the time came. Even though he'd become an enormous pain in the ass, he'd get whatever he asked for, having saved Roget Aircraft's bacon more than once.

They spent the afternoon going over the production schedule, marking up the existing drawings to make the conversion from bomber prototype to transport as easy as possible. There wasn't a massive amount of rework, but Bandy thought it worthwhile to call Mahew and warn him that Roget Aircraft might be asking for a two-week extension for delivery of the first plane.

The call to Chicago went through surprisingly fast—too fast—as it turned out.

"Not a goddam day, Bandfield!" Mahew's explosive temper was legendary, and Bandy pulled the earpiece away to protect his hearing.

"You people got a sweetheart contract because I was pissed off at Hafner and you were handy. Now my board of directors is all over my ass because I didn't compete it with Douglas or Boeing or somebody. I've been saying you could do the job, and you goddam well better. If you don't, I'll get fired and Allied will tear up the contract."

There was a pause as Bandy tried to think of a graceful way to close.

Mahew roared again. "Another thing. We've hired Lind-bergh as a consultant. He's going to be checking over the design, and the board insists that your airplane have the capability to take off with a full load from the highest airport on our route with one engine out. You might want to consider a trimotor again."

Bandfield took a pencil and drew a mustache on the smiling calendar girl drinking a Coke on the wall near his desk.

"That's one hell of a change in the contract, Mr. Mahew. We'd want to negotiate some money and some schedule differ-ences for that."

"Negotiate hell! Take it or leave it. It would take one phone call to Douglas to get them started. The DC-1 they're building for TWA will do most of what I want. Any questions?"

Bandy said no, gently returning the phone to the table.

"Back to the drawing board. Mahew wants an engine-out capability with a full load from Denver."

"Holy shit, Bandy. I'm not sure it's possible."

"Let's see that slide rule smoke, Hadley. I'll call Hartford to see where Hamilton Standard is with their new propellers."

Late that afternoon, they pushed the papers back. With split flaps and the new controllable-pitch Hamilton Standard props, they could just do it.

Bandfield's mind was churning. He'd decided that they had better figure on three shifts a day to gain some time while Hadley designed the flaps. The wing modification alone would take three weeks just for the flaps. If worst came to worst, they could extend the wingspan another ten feet or so to lower the wing loading.

The worst effect was the complete demolition of the budget. They had planned to be breaking even by the tenth production aircraft. Now they wouldn't make a dime until they sold forty airplanes.

Forty airplanes. The most Roget had ever built of one kind before was the five Rockets, one of which had become the com-pany plane because they'd never been able to sell it. Spread out over the years, that was hardly a roaring production rate. Forty airplanes!

Farmingdale, Long Island/July 17, 1933

Bruno Hafner motioned Murray to sit down while he continued his business discussion with an associate.

"You fucking guinea! I paid you a thousand dollars to burn that warehouse."

Tony Bonaventure squirmed. "It was impossible, Bruno. For Christ's sake, ask Murray! There were people all around, and the goddam cops were having some sort of a meeting in the building next door. You ought to be glad I saw what was going on."

"Do it tonight. That place is filled with obsolete parts that will never sell, and I've got to get rid of them. There's lots of thinner and paint there, and a lot of fabric. It'll burn like a torch once you light it off."

Bonaventure left, glad to have gotten off so lightly, and Murray cleared his throat to speak.

Hafner interrupted him. "What can I say, Murray? Nobody's got balls anymore."

Murray was no more comfortable with the new Bruno, the airline executive, then he'd been with the old Bruno, the gunrunner. He knew better than anyone how fast his moods could shift, how fine the line between the conservative businessman and the killer. Today, after an almost eight-year association, Murray still sat on the edge of his seat, sweat staining his collar.

"I hear that Rhoades is going to the Coast to work for Hughes."

"He is. Howard wants him to do most of the procurement for his racer. He actually expected me to go! All he ever did for me was let me risk my neck in a movie he was making. At least he's cut out the crap about calling himself Charles Howard. He never fooled anybody, not in this country, anyway."

Murray tried not to look pleased at Rhoades's departure; Dusty had gotten too comfortable in his relationship with Charlotte, and it bothered Murray very much. Bruno, smile fixed and eyes burning, sat as still as a hawk on the hunt watching Murray. Bruno speculated whether in his long devotion Murray had ever gotten even a quick tumble from Charlotte. No, probably not.

Bruno went to the bar and gestured with the bottle. "Sometimes I wish it was like the old days, when we were just pushing rifles and machine guns, before we got into planes and airlines and all the rest. You've done a good job with the arms sales, Murray.''

''It's hard to miss, boss, with wars flaring up all over the world. The communists are blowing things up all over Spain, Sandino is still raising hell in Nicaragua, after all these years, the natives are fighting the Dutch in Java, there's another rebellion starting in Cuba . . .'' He paused. ''I counted them up this morning—there's at least half a dozen. The Japs are scaring the hell out of everybody. I've had three Chinamen in buying everything in sight. And every time this new guy Hitler makes a speech, I get calls.''

Hafner spilled his whiskey at the name Hitler. He mopped the bourbon up, and moved to shift the topic.

''Did the Chinks ask about airplanes?''

''No, but I'll ask them. They're coming in again tomorrow.''

''Give me a call when they come in. I'd like to size them up, see how they behave.''

''I even had some Paraguayans—can you believe it, I didn't even know where the goddam country was—wanting to buy everything, for a war with Bolivia. They came right out and said they could pay in cocaine. They got no idea what it's worth. We'll clean up.''

''Is it any good?''

''I don't know. I'm having the doc test it, but even if we have to refine it somehow, it will be worth it.''

Bruno was concerned. ''Jesus, it's a good thing Dusty's going to the Coast; he'd burn a hole right through his nose. The problem with cocaine is that the Feds will get really involved if they find out about it. Let's think about that one.''

''Okay, will do.'' He gauged the other man to see if he could get by with some flattery, then make his exit.

''You know, Bruno, we couldn't have done half as well without the warehouse in France. I could smuggle Mount Everest out of that port, and no one would be the wiser. That was one of the smartest deals you ever made. And old man Dompnier was a real help at the start; he spread the grease around like an artist. I've seen the gendarmes stop traffic for us when we're bringing in a big piece, a 105 or something.''

Hafner laughed, scratching Nellie behind the ears.

''But since Stephan was killed, he's turned into a rummy.''

''And how is Monique?'' Hafner studied him closely. He had been tempted by Monique, but decided he wouldn't share yet another woman with Dusty. There were already too many scores to settle there.

"Monique is fine. She's as smart as the old man and tougher. The spics and the wogs and the people like that don't like dealing with her at first, you can tell, but she soon sets them straight."

"Is she a decent lay, Murray?"

"Man, I wouldn't know, but there's a lot of hoochy-kootchy action going on all the time. She's got the office fixed up with a couch the size of a football field."

Murray was lying, and they both knew it, but it was the right answer. After Stephan's death, his compunction about the family relationship had vanished. But it was nothing to talk about even now.

"If that's it, boss, I got to get back to the shop. I brought back a big antique grandfather's clock on the last trip, and I got all the parts laid out. I want to get it back together before I forget how it came apart."

The big man sat twirling the ice cubes in his glass with his finger, satisfied that things were working well. Hafner had an acute sense of distance and timing exceptional even for a pilot, an ability to relate things spatially that gave him an edge in combat and aerobatics. In a twirling aerial combat, his ability to integrate his own position and attitude with that of his opponents meant that he could instantly compute the deflection necessary for a quick snap shot in a churning dogfight. He had somehow transferred this to business practice, and it was part of the secret of his success, an almost uncanny knack of judging how things were progressing, as well as how and when they would come together. He mentally calculated the things that were on the way, the things that had to be done, and the people concerned that would be involved in his going back to Germany. He'd be an officer again, but wealthy this time, not having to live on the tiny salary.

The single most difficult problem was Charlotte. A divorce was out of the question; it would ruin an officer's career. They had been ardent lovers, and done well in business together. Charlotte would have been irreplaceable in any normal situation, with her business acumen and her ability to get along with the Army procurement people. It was typical of her to have insisted that the plant needed more professional engineering support for Bineau. But the curious fact was that neither had ever liked the other. They had probably loved each other at some point, but they were always more attuned to each other's vices than to their virtues. The infatuation with Rhoades was obviously a serious thing, something he hadn't counted on. At first it had turned out to be very convenient; it might have been awkward if she had fallen for someone else. But they had not been discreet. The antlers Rhoades had hung on him were increasingly visible, and circumstances had forced him to endure it. He still needed them. For a while.

Hafner pulled a daily diary from his desk drawer and leafed through the future-year calendars in the back. He selected a red pencil, and put a small X through June 1936. Things would have to be resolved by then. It gave him a little leeway; he could leave earlier or later, depending upon business conditions. But June 1936 would be perfect.

The Brown Palace Hotel,
Denver, Colorado/October 17, 1933

Bandfield had planned the operation from the moment he entered the lobby and gazed up the nine stories, each girdled by a hall and railing, to the ceiling. Asking for a room on the ninth floor, he'd spent twenty minutes at his desk, carefully drawing the plans. Folding the paper, he made a minute adjustment, then moved swiftly out of his room and down the hallway to punch the elevator call button. When it arrived, he stepped to the railing, took a quick look around, and launched the glider.

The elevator ride down was interminable, but when he reached the lobby, he saw the glider making a wide circle at the fourth-floor level, riding some internal thermal.

"Jesus, that's the first goddam airplane that's worked right for me in years."

Bandfield walked over and sank into the deep couches that were set with military regularity across the huge floor, brass nailheads punctuating the glossy maroon leather. After a day with Mahew, fending off his incessant demands and trying to get a few dollars in progress payments, he was looking forward to the evening. The glider finally made its last turn, having a midair with the back of a clerk's head at the registration desk. Bandy turned the other way.

Things were really breaking right for once. Mahew had scheduled the meeting in Denver purely for the convenience of his local staff—and because he had a mountain home in Colorado Springs. The very next day, Patty had written, saying she would like to come out to California for one final discussion of the racer. He'd suggested that they meet in Denver instead, so he could get completely away from the problems of the plant and have her entirely to himself, away from the Rogets and Hughes and everyone else.

Stretching out, he parked his crossed legs on a throw rug made from a sad-eyed brown bear who'd seen better days. Tonight he was going to make a move. Twice before he had met with Patty on the racer, and each time she had been very friendly and open. Some insane sense of reserve, an exaggerated regard for propriety, had kept him from trying to kiss her. Their conversations were always convoluted. She talked freely and openly with him in a way that invited a response; instead he had kept her at a distance each time. The truth was this meeting wasn't necessary—it must mean that she wanted to see him. Tonight she could be the one to keep the distance—if she wanted to.

He rose when he saw her coming, noting with pleasure how heads bobbed as she went by. She was wearing a beige blouse and a dark tan skirt, her long legs flashing as she walked. She came up to him and put out her arms. He embraced her, and they kissed with a precisely measured tenderness that mixed correct appearance and a promise of things to come.

She was carrying the roll of plans.

"Let me park these at the desk. We can have dinner here, then go to my room to study them."

They ate hurriedly. Bandfield, a man who usually scrimshawed Porterhouse bones with his teeth, sent most of the enormous steak back to the kitchen uneaten.

Her room, unlike his own, was immaculate. He had a faculty for immediately turning any living quarters into a Hooverville slum within thirty seconds. They put the plans on the bed and drew up two small chairs to sit on.

It had started on the usual crisp engineering note.

"Remember now, a standard Beech Staggerwing with a two-hundred-and-twenty-five-horsepower engine has a top speed of about one seventy-five. With the seven-hundred-and-fifty-horsepower Cyclone, you should be able to hit two-forty, maybe two-fifty, and cruise at two-twenty. You don't have to be that fast to set the women's record. A two hundred cruise would do it."

"That's the point, Bandy—I don't want to set women's records. I think that's a mistake for women and for flying. The airplane doesn't know whether the pilot's a man or a woman."

Bandfield's expression didn't change. "I think it's a mistake to try to set an absolute record. But if you insist, don't put the big engine on it right away. Learn to fly it with the standard engine, then work up to the big one. It'll cost a little more, but that way you'll know the airplane, and it will be safer."

"I'll do whatever you say on the training. We have a little time."

As they leaned over, their arms brushed together. The hairs on Bandy's arms stood up, static electricity directing them toward Patty.

She noticed and, laughingly, said, "Look at those little devils, all trying to get hold of me."

She touched her finger to his arm, and a spark jumped.

"It's just my electric personality," he said, as other stirrings gathered heat. "Did I tell you I changed the gear-retraction mechanism from pneumatic to electric? Takes a little longer to go up and down."

He moved closer to her and put his finger back and forth on the plans, tracing the arc of the retraction cycle. "It takes longer, but it's a lot more reliable."

"That's good in an airplane or a man."

She was obviously not trying to be subtle, and whatever ambiguity or restraint he had felt dissolved in the sure knowledge that they wanted each other. Still, he wanted to be smooth, not to appear abrupt and as greedy as he felt.

Patty felt a sense of relief; he had been stubbornly missing or ignoring her hints until she had been embarrassingly obvious, but now he had taken command, and she was prepared to relinquish the lead and herself.

They moved closer together now, playing to each other, enjoying the mutual restraint, not wishing the little engineering loveplay to end just yet.

He tapped the color-specification block on the plans and said, "Yellow is a sexy color for an airplane. You'll look good in it."

She was looking at him, not at the plans, the slightest bit of moisture beading on her brow.

"Will I look sexy in it, too?"

"Sure. Is it getting warm in here, or is it just my imagination?"

"It's warming up."

"Let's put a red stripe of trim down the side, something dramatic." He glanced away to sketch a broad red arrow, the feathers ending at the tail and the head spread across the cowling.

She ran her long fingers across the arrow, then moved in closer.

"Do you ever think how symbolic a marking like that is?"

"Symbolic? Of being fast, of being dangerous?"

"Sure, a fast sex symbol, that's what I want to fly, that's what I want to be."

What the hell, he thought. He turned to her and they gently guided themselves into bed.

Their first kisses had the awkward gasping quality of a thirsty man at a slow fountain, a sort of rasping, sucking urgency that shot Bandfield's testosterone gauge past the red line. He would not surrender her lips. She backed away to grab a breath, and he held her face forcibly to his, beginning to unbutton her blouse. She tried again to move away, and he fastened to her, mumbling, "Don't stop, don't stop." She realized he wanted to strip her of her clothes without letting his mouth part from hers.

Her hands worked his buttons, and their lips began to pain from the pressure, but he was unremitting, not willing to let her have a second to herself, yet gentle, taking her clothes with care. She was not wearing a corset; when he removed her slip, with her help, he moved his head away for the first time.

She gasped, light-headed, her eyes rolled back.

"I was making up for lost time."

She started to unfasten her brassiere, and he stopped her.

"No, stay like this for a minute." He shucked himself out of his own clothes like a hot dog squeezed from a bun, and knelt beside her.

"This is pretty fancy underwear. Do you wear stuff like this all the time?"

"It's a treat for you. I want all of me to be a treat for you."

He moved her bra slightly to kiss the lines left by the elastic, then did the same with her step-ins, then began kissing her in a continuous stream, working from one ankle across her middle, tongue gently flickering under the silken cloth, and back down to the other. Then he rolled her over. "My God, you have a beautiful bottom." He kissed her thoroughly, his fingers unfastening her bra.

Her breath was coming fast, and he removed the rest of her clothes. He held her cradled in his arms, kissing her lips in a Rodin statue pose. Then he eased her to the bed and kissed her brow, her eyes, her nose. Their mouths merged for a long moment, then he pulled away, starting a line of kisses at her chin and ending it with his head tucked between her thighs.

"Come inside me," she called. He moved and covered her, her legs grasping him tightly.

"This is heaven." She nodded agreement, her eyes closed.

He was surprised at his control. He had wanted her for so long, and was almost irrepressibly excited, yet he managed to be restrained, moving easily with her, their bodies fused, the undulations steady but not frantic, both equally enjoying the long deferred moment.

Her breathing changed, and he sensed the passion tearing away her control as the tempo of her pelvis quickened. They stopped kissing and her head moved beside his ear, he could hear her breath coming faster and faster, little low moans telling him that she could not wait. He felt his own rush, and they moved more swiftly, climaxing together, she with triumphant little murmurs, he with a gasping joyous cry of relief.

He collapsed upon her, maintaining himself within, nibbling at her earlobe. After ten minutes of murmured love words, he leaped up, saying, "Stay there."

He returned from the bathroom with three towels, one very warm and moist, one cool, and one dry. He put the warm one between her legs and wiped her body down lovingly with the cool one. Then he threw both towels by the side of the bed and gently patted her dry.

"I could get to like this."

"You're going to get a chance to. I'm never letting you out of my arms again. I'm just going to send out for club sandwiches and milkshakes, and keep you here forever."

They made love again; he let her be the aggressor, kissing him erect, then maneuvering until he covered her again. After they had climaxed, she got up with the towels.

"My turn."

Later, lying nude together in the fully lit room, she said, "You know, this was your last chance. If you hadn't kissed me in here, after I had set everything up, I was going to give up."

"You don't realize how intimidating you are. You are so goddam good-looking that you scare the hell out of me."

She looked at him quizzically. "No, it's not that at all. The big thing is that you knew Stephan. You felt funny making a pass at the widow of a friend, particularly a pilot."

"That's part of it."

She sat bolt upright. "Is there someone else? Are you going with someone now? It's okay, of course, you have every right—"

"No. There was. You probably heard about it. Her name was Millie Duncan."

It took a moment for the name to register.

"The girl on the airplane in the race to Hawaii?" He nodded. "Bandy, that was six years ago. Are you still carrying a torch?"

He felt foolish. "It's not exactly that. It's just that I made a promise to myself that I'd never fall in love with a woman who flew again."

He was startled at what he'd said.

"What about me? After Stephan died the way he did, I should fall for a preacher, or a doctor, somebody who plays it safe."

They both stopped, each afraid that they had gone too far too soon, that talk of love and marriage was premature.

"The problem is that ever since Cleveland, before Stephan's death, I was attracted to you. You replaced Millie in my dreams, in my fantasies. Then there was the accident and you went away, back to France for a while, I guess, and I just couldn't forget you."

She put her finger on his lips. "Let me shock you completely. If you had made a pass at me in Cleveland, before Stephan died, I could not have helped myself. I would have come to you. That's a terrible thing to say, but it's true and I want you to know it."

She had rolled away to face the wall. He began kissing her back.

He thought about what she had said. What would have happened? Where would they have been now? It didn't matter—he'd used good sense. If they had fooled around, and then Stephan had been killed, it might have ruined everything.

He browsed her body, nibbling behind her knees, lifting her breasts with his nose and kissing the soft, untanned flesh underneath, pressing his face into the back of her neck. "Do you know you have a lot of tender spots I want to kiss?"

"I hope so. I'll let you know if you forget any. And you've got a few I've noticed, too. I'll get to them."

He marveled at the suppleness of her lean body. Heredity had worked perfectly for her, letting her retain Charlotte's full figure, refined to a taut perfection in a marvelously toned body. Her breasts were large, with a ripe-melon firmness that kept them full even when she was lying on her back. Her nipples, roseate buttons when she was not excited, would grow in length and size to great luscious grapes as her passion built.

All their reserve had disappeared, and he explored her body at length, eagerly, with a puppy-love ardor. He caressed and kissed every inch of her, sniffing her so deeply to pull out her very essence that she laughingly called him her little Hoover vacuum. After midnight, the peaks of passion came at greater intervals, and she said, "Was I too obvious with the 'sex symbol' remarks?"

"No, I was being such a dodo. Normally I'm not a slow starter."

"No, most pilots aren't. Mother says most pilots have this stupid mixup between penises and airplanes and flying and fucking, and they tend to jump on a woman the way they jump into a cockpit."

He stared at her. He'd seldom heard a woman use the word *fucking* before in casual conversation. The fact that they'd been clawing at each other like hungry hounds for five hours didn't diminish his surprise.

"Excuse my French, Bandy. I've been around flyers—and Bruno and Charlotte—too long. Does it offend you?"

"Yeah, a little, but it makes me hot too. Let's try saying it in another context."

"Okay, but only if you promise to do that little trick again."

"Trick?"

"Yes, you know, where we're really passionate, and you think I'm just about ready, and you roll over and put your toe in the electric light socket. That's a real treat."

Laughing, he said, "That's what I call my patented toe-in-socket sex—pretty shocking, huh?" The joking made them easy and considerate with each other, already familiar now, eager to be inventive still, but enjoying just the closeness, the penetrating intimacy. They would doze, then talk, then love, then talk.

He asked, "Is setting a record some sort of symbolic thing for you?"

"There's no sex symbolism in setting records. It's ego, pure and simple. I want to be the most famous woman flyer in the world."

"What does your mother say about that?"

"She understands, but she doesn't approve. She thinks that Bruno has put a jinx on us with the press, that neither one of us will ever get the kind of recognition that Earhart gets."

She ran her fingers through his hair. "You know, as much as I enjoyed making love to you—as much as I needed to make love to you—I like this part best. Let's get a little sleep, and then talk some more."

"It's three o'clock. I'd better get out of here."

"No, stay. To hell with the maids. We're paying for two singles; if we decide just to use a double, it's our business."

Her head fell to his chest, and in seconds she was snoring gently.

Cupping her bottom in his hand, he sighed, "I am one lucky son of a bitch."

Downey, California/July 4, 1934

Roget had insisted on delaying the first showing of the new RC-3 until the Fourth of July, to take advantage of the patriotic publicity, and he was angered when a ripple of laughter went through the crowd of reporters. Bandy had signaled the ground crew to open the hangar only to find that the massive sliding doors, rust hidden by huge American flags, were bolted together by a strange square padlock.

"It's that goddam Hughes!" Bandy muttered to Hadley. "That smart-ass was over here fooling around this morning. Send somebody for a bolt-cutter."

Bandy went over and talked to the small group of reporters, who were grinning broadly over the doughnuts and coffee Clarice Roget had provided.

A snap like a rifle shot signaled that Hadley had dealt with the lock. On each side four men pushed the sliding doors rattling back on their bent iron tracks. Inside the hangar, ancient parachutes, patched and yellowed with age, hung like theater curtains to block the view; red-white-and-blue bunting gave a wistful holiday air to the scene.

Herb Hines, from the *Los Angeles Times*, said, "Getting pretty Hollywood, aren't you, Bandy?"

The curtains parted and the gleaming silver Roget RC-3 rolled forward into the sunlight for the first time, propelled by the hands of every worker who could find a place to shove.

The normally vocal reporters went into a shocked silence, broken by Hines's subdued voice: "Holy Christ. It's a flying hotel."

The tall nose of the RC-3 towered over the crowd of newspaper people, who swarmed around an airplane bigger, sleeker, and shinier than any they had ever seen. The passenger door opened and a short ladder was extended. Ted Mahew stood proudly filling up the center aisle, and passing out press kits, with photos, specifications, and the kinds of words he wanted to read in the papers.

"When's the first flight?"

Mahew's confident pose concealed his raging anxiety. "We're going to begin a very leisurely test program—start with taxi tests, a few lift-offs, and take everything very easy. There is so much new on this airplane—retractable landing gear, landing flaps, controllable-pitch propellers—that it is going to revolutionize the aviation industry. We want to make sure we don't rush it.

Bandy smiled to himself at Mahew's words. Privately the Allied president had been clamoring for a rushed test program, with delivery of the test airplane to the airline in thirty days. Bandy had calmed him by promising to let him fly in the right seat on the initial test flight.

Bandfield retreated to the cockpit to avoid the rush of questions, but more to glow in the pleasure of at last having built an airplane exactly as he'd always wanted to do, scientifically and systematically. The competition to supply the engines had been fierce, so Bandy had a white line painted down the middle of the engine bay, and let the two engine manufacturers, Wright and Pratt & Whitney, have a contest right on the factory floor. They had worked for weeks, customizing the engines to the RC-3. For the time being, it looked as though Wright had won.

Mahew hung around for as long as he could after the press conference, fretting while the normal tuning process delayed the first flight. The brakes needed adjustment, the cowl flaps weren't working right, and there was a shimmy in the tail wheel on the taxi tests. It was all perfectly normal, but each delay jacked Mahew's blood pressure up another few points.

"You're just trying to outwait me, Bandfield. You know I have to get back to Chicago for a meeting with the board, and I know damn well you'll fly this thing the day after I leave." He stormed off with a flurry of threats, furious because he had to take the train. All the airlines, his own included, were grounded because of weather over the Rockies.

Downey, California/July 11, 1934

At noon on the day following Mahew's departure, the entire staff of Roget Aircraft—four hundred strong—lined up to watch Bandy and Hadley taxi out to put everyone's career on the line.

They went through the checklist twice, everything checking perfectly. The engines delivered full power, the propellers changed pitch on cue, and the controls all operated properly.

The usual pretest nervousness gripped Bandy. He turned and said, "Well, Hadley, I guess I can't put it off any longer. We've got a lot riding on this. I hope it'll go okay."

Hadley gave a thumbs-up sign, and Bandy advanced the power. The RC-3 accelerated smoothly, the factory force cheering as it roared by. It broke ground and began to climb at ninety miles per hour.

Bandy and Roget had agreed not to retract the gear on this flight, but when the left engine backfired and billowed black smoke, the planning went out the window.

The usual "Oh shit, it's happening" thoughts went through the crew's mind as Bandy barked out orders.

"Pull up the gear, Hadley. What's going on?"

The right engine coughed, and the power fell back on both engines. The airplane staggered uncertainly, as if a grabbing hand were pulling it to earth. The leaden feel was spelled out on the sagging needles on the manifold pressure gauges. The tachometers surged, fell back, and then stabilized at 2,400 rpm. On the ground the crowd suddenly went silent. One reporter muttered, "It's going in."

Bandy fed in back pressure, caution tempering need, as he kept the nose high and the airspeed hovering around eighty-two miles per hour.

"For Christ's sake, Hadley, what is it?"

The big transport staggered toward an open field. Two pairs of hands flew like fan blades around the compartment, repositioning the controls, checking again and again.

"We got fuel pressure, Bandy, and I dipsticked the tanks myself, I know the gauges are okay. The only thing I can think of is contaminated fuel—and I can't believe that. It came out of the same tanks we always use."

Time took on its familiar dual dimensions in the emergency: hours since the emergency started, only seconds since takeoff.

"How about putting her in that field?" Hadley nodded at an angular open area coming up on the right, nestled between an irrigation ditch and an abandoned farm building.

"Not if I can help it—there's a gully that will tear it in half. I'm going to try to keep it flying long enough to get back home."

Sweat poured down his face, and his wet hands fought the wheel to keep the airplane away from the ragged edge of a stall that would snap them and the Roget Aircraft Company into a smear of burned blackness on the landscape.

His mouth was dry and his words garbled together. "Don't know how accurate the damn airspeed indicator is. This thing could pay off any second. We're too low to jump, so strap yourself in good."

Hadley glanced out, saw that the ground was no closer.

"Keep it as level as possible, Bandy. When it's level, the engines pick up power and we gain a few miles per hour on the airspeed."

Bandfield nodded and began a delicate stepladder dance, edging the RC-3 up foot by foot until they were three hundred feet off the ground, alternately flying level to let the airspeed build a little, and then trading a few miles per hour for ten feet more altitude. At three hundred feet he began a shallow turn to the right. As soon as the right wing lowered in the bank, the left engine barked a series of savage popping backfires. He hurriedly leveled the wings and the engine smoothed out. He tried again, a five-degree bank, and the turn became like the climb, a slow ragged edging toward his goal, the north end of the runway.

"How long will it take for the gear to come down, Hadley?"

Roget, face ashen, thought before saying, "About fifteen to twenty seconds. Better allow for thirty, though."

"Okay. We're lined up. Drop the gear. I'm not going to use any flaps."

The gear came down and Bandy trimmed the nose up to get the eighty-mile-an-hour approach speed he planned. Both engines backfired.

"Put in thirty degrees of flaps."

Hadley started to protest, then ran the handle down. The engines smoothed out as the lowered flaps rotated the nose down, and Bandy was able to add power to keep an even seventy-five miles per hour. The engines seemed to be running right for the first time since takeoff as the runway rushed toward them.

Bandy touched down with both wheels, bounced, held back pressure on the wheel, and let the RC-3 dribble down the runway, sweat sluicing off him in the California sunshine. He let it roll straight ahead, then shut the engines down.

"So much for first flights!"

Roget said softly, "And thank God Mahew wasn't here. If he didn't have a heart attack, he'd have eaten us alive."

The airplane was towed in and the engineers swarmed over

it. Two hours later, the Wright engineers came to him, red-faced.

"Our error, Mr. Bandfield."

Bandfield felt sorry for the engineer who poured out the tearful apology. They had installed the float valves in the carburetors with the hinges on the wrong side. When the nose went up, the floats closed. It was a factory modification and they just hadn't picked it up.

"Thank God you didn't crash. And thank you for not letting it crash."

Bandy slumped down, speechless, as the enormity of the error hit him. A stupid error, the worst kind, had almost killed them, and wiped out the company. He didn't reproach himself—there was no way in the world he could have known about the carburetor float valve if the Wright people didn't.

He thought of all the people he'd known who had been trapped and killed by such a pointless mishap. With all his experience, with all his skills, he was totally vulnerable to some distant mechanic's improperly installing a part. In part it was the growing complexity of aircraft. No matter how many hours you worked, you could no longer do everything and check everything yourself.

Bandfield had no illusions about himself, no false modesty, knowing his virtues as well as his limits. One virtue was an ability to be utterly emotionless about engineering problems, to see them in a clear light. It was impossible to feel the same way about human-error problems.

An urgent need to see Patty came over him, an almost childlike desire to flee and bind himself in her arms. The feeling shook him. He had never needed anyone before. Never had anyone been able to barge in emotionally when he was having practical flying or engineering problems, not even Millie. He had loved her, but now he realized how entirely different it had been. He had always wanted to protect and take care of Millie—with Patty he wanted to share, to discuss, to sort things out. She offered a kind of resilient strength that he had never known before—but now that he recognized it, he needed it, and badly.

Thinking about her shifted the whole perspective of the near-accident. She was the important thing in his life, and the racing airplane they were planning had to work flawlessly. He realized that his entire future happiness was bound up with an engineering problem far more important even than the RC-3: Patty's flying the racer.

She had come to California to help with the design—at least that was the excuse they used. They had spent every possible day together since the wonderful night in the Brown Palace, and he realized that they had formed a strong partnership that could endure almost anything—even marriage. If everything went well, she could handle the airplane easily. If she had some sort of unusual emergency, she would probably be overwhelmed. In an airplane as tricky as the Beechcraft, the accident would probably be fatal.

He realized again that he did not handle personal problems with the clinical precision with which he attacked engineering difficulties. She had made it perfectly clear that if she married him, he would have to let her do exactly what she wanted to do about flying. The only solution, the only middle ground, was for him to stay with her, to train her and prepare her for the flights as if she were a boxer getting ready for a championship fight. Maybe, after they were married, after they had started a family, she would have a change of heart.

It was the best solution he could come up with to bridge the twin personal and engineering problems. He felt better and was turning his attention back to the recalcitrant carburetors when he thought to himself, I've got to tell her about this, about how I feel. It might be important to her.

The next flight of the RC-3 went off perfectly, and Bandy decided he'd raise and lower the gear on purpose this time. The rest of the testing passed so smoothly they were able to double up on the test objectives, and by the end of the month, Bandy felt they could take their "final exam," the route test with Mahew.

Denver, Colorado/August 6, 1934

The Brown Palace seemed far less comforting than it had last year during the first three days of his visit to Denver. Instead of being locked in Patty's energetic embrace, Bandfield spent his time showing the Allied Airlines brass and their wives through the airplane, and listening to Mahew complain about everything.

"Charles Lindbergh is coming in tonight about six; I'll want him in the copilot's seat tomorrow."

Bandfield nodded; he would have preferred Roget, but only

because he was familiar with the airplane. Lindbergh would do well.

Bandfield had raced out to buy Patty a present. He went over-board and got her a $35 Elgin watch, particularly enjoying it because there had been a time when all he had in the world was $30 to get him to Paris. He paid cash for the watch, even though there was a time-payment plan available. At the cash register, there had been a display of Mickey and Minnie Mouse watches, $1 apiece. He'd bought a Minnie Mouse and asked for a big box. When he gave them to her, he would put the Minnie Mouse on top of the Elgin, just for a gag.

The evening wasn't promising. He was going to have to be pleasant to Lindbergh without appearing to trade on their past relationship. And it wasn't going to be easy to be pleasant. From the press, Bandfield had discovered how versatile his old flight-school friend had become. He had already made many flights as important as the one to Paris, and now was busy in some very scientific activities, far removed from the world of stick and rudder. Lindbergh was working on something called a per-fusion pump as a step toward an artificial heart. His experi-ments, done with some French doctor, had been written up in medical journals and the popular press.

Perhaps even more surprising was his political clout. He hadn't been afraid to take on President Roosevelt when the big air-mail scandal erupted. It was all politics—Roosevelt had can-celed the air-mail contracts with the airlines and assigned the Army to do the job. Initially, the Army hadn't had the training or the equipment, and a lot of deaths had resulted. Eddie Rick-enbacker had called Roosevelt a murderer, and gotten away with it. Lindbergh had been less dramatic, but his voice carried more weight, and his direct confrontation with Roosevelt had been strongly criticized. It was as if the public wouldn't allow a hero to be controversial. He was always going to be "Lucky Lindy" on his way to Paris; publicizing his political points of view didn't sit well.

Bandfield was too honest not to admit to himself that much of the problem was jealousy. Lindbergh's successes had been a too-sweet coating over the bitter pill of Lindy's failure to help Roget Aircraft when it desperately needed it. He knew that if the positions had been reversed, if he'd made the famous Paris flight and Lindbergh was struggling to sell airplanes, he would have helped Lindbergh.

Maybe that was one of the prices of fame—maybe you couldn't

help your friends. And Lindbergh had paid another terrible price, the loss of his baby. Bandfield looked over at the framed picture of Patty on the hotel dresser and gave a little salute. He tried to imagine what it would be like to live with her someday, to have babies. The thought of losing their child to a kidnapper was impossible! His heart went out to Lindbergh as he went downstairs to the dining room.

The evening started with mutual congratulations, to Lindbergh for his pioneering survey flights with his wife and the radical "artificial heart" he was working on, to Bandfield and Roget for winning the contract. Lindbergh was obviously more interested in the medical matters than he was in flying.

He had changed dramatically, the gangly charm of youth gone lupine-lean. He was so tensely alert that his ears seemed to twist and turn to sense the always present enemy. Where he had once been reticent, shyly diffident, he was now actively angry when he felt the conversation was drifting away from what he wanted to talk about. His brittle, argumentative conversational tone revealed his thinly veiled annoyance at having to be in public at all, even with some old friends. Bandy could not believe that this rigid, almost fanatical politician—there seemed to be no better word for him—was the same man who had put itching powder in the first sergeant's shorts.

Yet he was gracious about Roget Aircraft's winning the Allied order, telling Bandy that the new Roget transport was clearly superior to the Hafner aircraft.

"You're on your way now, Bandy. If you can hold Douglas off, you can get more orders than you'll be able to fill."

"We're going to try, Slim."

After the initial round of ritual kidding, Lindbergh was subdued, almost uninterested, unless he was vociferously directing the conversation into political channels.

He started on Roosevelt. "The man is a criminal. I think he's a Bolshevik. Look what he did to aviation when he canceled the air-mail contracts. He ruined the lives of honest businessmen and killed ten Army pilots."

Lindbergh's voice took on an evangelical quality, as if he were addressing a huge audience. Used to being the center of attention everywhere, Lindbergh was unaware that people at every table were looking at him, a few supportively, but most astounded at his ferocity.

"Eddie Rickenbacker was right! Roosevelt is a murderer! He

sent those Army pilots into the weather with poor equipment, and they died! We've got to get a Republican in there.''

Bandfield wanted to be still, but couldn't. ''Slim, I can't agree with you. I knew people in California who were down to picking out of restaurant garbage cans to feed their families. After Roosevelt came in, they got some relief. It seems to me that he's trying to get the country back on its feet by providing jobs for the ordinary man.''

He could tell that Lindbergh was angry, resentful that he'd taken issue with him, but he continued, ''Hoover was only interested in the rich guy. When I talk to the workingmen in the plant, I can tell they are for Roosevelt one hundred percent. You'd never see Roosevelt using Army troops to throw out veterans, the way Hoover did.''

''Bandy, you always were just about half a communist yourself. I remember how you talked about your dad. But make no mistake, Roosevelt is a disaster for this country. You only have to make a trip to Russia to decide whether you want the country run by people who work in the factory, or by people who have achieved some success. It's almost a biological thing, a survival of the fittest.''

Lindbergh's voice had risen, and he was gesturing with his hand, the index finger pointing, underscoring his remarks.

Bandfield shut up. They had a flight to make tomorrow, and it was one that had to please Lindbergh. He wondered if his old friend was thinking about running for office. Slim's dad had been in Congress; it would make sense. But he ought to be more prudent about Roosevelt.

Stapleton Field, Denver, Colorado
August 7, 1934

The next day, the crisp blue sky seemed to march the mountains right up to tidy, carpenter's-square-straight city limits. Bandy was glad it was cool, but didn't like the twenty-knot wind blowing from the right of the runway.

Lindbergh spent an hour familiarizing himself with the cockpit and discussing the engine-out procedure with Bandfield and Roget. He regained his former friendly personality as he became more absorbed in the engineering of the aircraft.

They started the engines and taxied out. Just after the pretakeoff checklist was completed, Mahew came forward and edged Roget out of the way to stand just behind Bandy and Lindbergh.

"I'd rather have Hadley stand there, Ted, for the takeoff."

"Not this time. Go ahead."

Bandy shrugged and pushed the throttles forward. Denver's mile-high altitude drained the engines' power, and the RC-3 accelerated slowly toward its 75-mph lift-off speed. Bandy cranked in aileron to lower the right wing into the crosswind and keep the plane from drifting off the runway. He felt the left wheel lift off, then the right.

Mahew's huge arm reached up and switched the left engine magneto off. "Now crash or fly, Bandfield. Let's see how good this fucker is."

The airplane swung sharply to the left, responding both to the roaring power of the right engine and to the drag of the windmilling left propeller as the plane drifted off the runway. Bandy pushed in hard on the right rudder, slamming the propeller and throttle controls forward simultaneously. The relentless wind drifted them toward a line of hangars.

"Gear up, Slim, and engine-out check," he shouted.

The gear was going up as Lindbergh, his features set and eyes flashing, feathered the left engine and "cleaned up the cockpit," putting all the switches and valves in their proper position for the emergency. The RC-3 nuzzled the thin air as its speed crept to ninety, then ninety-five, climbing strongly.

"Wahoo! You just sold me a whole bunch of airplanes, Bandfield," Mahew yelled.

Bandfield nodded grimly, thinking, Thanks for nothing—you fucking near killed us all.

When they landed, Lindbergh grabbed Bandfield's arm. "Bandy, I swear I didn't know he was going to do that. It was inexcusable."

Then he pursued Mahew down the long aisle and backed him up, crouching, against the rear bulkhead. Lindbergh put his finger in Mahew's face and dressed him down quietly and ferociously. Bandfield couldn't hear what was said, but he wished he knew the words that were turning Mahew from a strutting bully into a nodding yes man.

The past few weeks had changed Bandfield's view of the world. Patty was as absorbed in airplanes as he was—when they were working on them. When they were not, she insisted on an absolute exclusion of airplanes, aviation, aviators, and anything to do with flying from the conversation.

"You're a monomaniac, Bandy, do you know that?"

"Most pilots are."

"I don't sleep with most pilots, and I'm sleeping with you. You've got to broaden your horizons, and I'm just the girl to do it."

They had started with a concert. Bandy had heard of Leopold Stokowski before, and knew that the three Bs were Beethoven, Brahms, and Bach, but that was about the extent of his musical knowledge. He had agreed to go only because she insisted, and because he thought he would sleep through most of it.

Stokowski's magnetic presence changed his mind. Bandfield had no basis for comparison, but when the night was over, he was aware that he liked classical music, something he couldn't have been persuaded of the day before. The conductor, with his leonine shock of white hair, had led the Philharmonic in the Berlioz *Symphonie Fantastique*, and Bandfield was hooked.

It was the same with travel, which he had always considered before only in terms of time en route. The scenery below was often interesting, but few flights were pleasure trips—he was either on his way to a meeting, his mind filled with what had to be done, or he was hauling people or parts that had to get from Point A to Point B in a hurry. Patty dragged him to a Burton Holmes lecture series, and he found himself actually panging with the desire to see London, Paris, all the great capitals, to take Patty to the South Seas, to go to "darkest Africa."

Patty watched the transformation with approval bordering on glee. She loved this man, and was going to marry him, but she wanted his full potential developed. Flying had stunted him; she would change that.

She changed him in many ways. He was naturally conservative when it came to public behavior; she was wildly daring, unorthodox, equally willing to picnic or make love in a public park.

She had amazed him again on this training trip to Dayton. Twice on this trip out they had almost crashed. The second time was due to the rotten weather at Wright Field, when a wild ring of blue-black lightning-laden thunderstorms had almost blasted them out of the sky. At the last second, with the radios completely jammed with static and the turbulence threatening to break up the Beechcraft, Bandfield had spotted the Wright Field runway through a hole that had opened as quickly and as fleetingly as a sea anemone in a tidal pool. Patty had cut the power and sideslipped the Beechcraft into a perfect landing. He was proud that she hadn't ground-looped and not at all sure that he would have done as well.

The first near-crash had been more fun. After slow-timing the 450-horsepower Wasp they'd installed to upgrade her training, Patty had volunteered to fly Bandfield back to Ohio. Roscoe Turner had set a new transcontinental record on the first of the month, flying from New York to Los Angeles in ten hours and two minutes. Patty wanted to see what she could do on a west-east run.

The trip was in response to Henry Caldwell's peremptory summons to Bandfield. His wire said only: "Urgently request your presence Wright Field earliest possible date." When Bandfield had called Caldwell, he wouldn't discuss the matter on the phone.

After a long day at the plant, they had taken off at 10:00 P.M. from Downey, anxious to take advantage of strong tailwinds. The night climb out from the Los Angeles area had been easy, with the bright light of the moon turning the mountains into sharp relief. Following her custom, Patty had slipped her hand into the fly of Bandfield's trousers right after takeoff. She had begun the practice on their first encounter in Denver, routinely holding his penis with a firm grip at every opportunity, when they were driving, in the movies, everywhere she could do it without a too obvious risk of discovery. He rather liked it but was initially curious, asking, "I'm not complaining, but why do you do this? We've had about as much loving as you can cram into three days."

"All loving is not fucking. This is quiet loving. Besides, it's something Charlotte counseled me about."

Bandfield had laughed, thinking that conversations between Charlotte and Patty were probably a little different from most mother-and-daughter talks.

"She said the sure way to a man's heart was not through his stomach but his groin. If you grab hold and don't let go, you can be sure his attention doesn't wander."

It seemed reasonable to Bandy.

"Besides, Stephan played around a little, and that was probably my fault. This way, if I feel any signs of life at all, I'm going to be on the spot to take care of it."

So far it had been a good arrangement. The flight across the Kingston mountains had been gorgeous, single lights here and there from lonely miners picking out the ebony blackness of the ground. The sky was a star-bathed smoked crystal, blanched into a shimmering transparency by the full moon. The Beechcraft flew effortlessly, hurtling across a sleeping countryside as if it had been protectively slipped into a transparent pneumatic duct that would whoosh it to Dayton unassisted.

They were crossing Kingman, Arizona, as their mutual response to her soft squeezing grew. She withdrew her hand and began disrobing, bit by bit, leaning over to sing garbled intermixed snatches of "Anything Goes" and "I Only Have Eyes for You." Her voice was terrible, but he didn't care as she peeled down, doing as good a takeoff on a burlesque stripper as the confining cockpit permitted. She'd somehow removed her bra without his noticing; when she unbuttoned her blouse the moon caught her breasts tumbling out in an avalanche of beauty.

Bandfield frantically trimmed the airplane to fly hands-off as she reached over and began undoing his belt.

"Look, we don't have room to really fool around here. If you don't watch it, we'll be singing 'Tumbling Tumble Weeds' on the desert down there."

They had not been together for a week, and he was burning. She was as determined to be funny as she was to be passionate, and she reached over and bobbed her breasts in his face, before kissing him deeply. The airplane also began to bob and weave.

She leaned forward and yelled in his ear, "When we go up, you really go up. And when you really go up, I really go down." Her head dropped to his lap, affording him both pleasure and a chance to check the instruments.

"Okay, that's enough, I can't stand it. Let's try it."

He moved his seat back as far as it would go, and she swung her right leg up and over, facing him, her breasts pushed into his face, her efforts to mount him reminding him of the carnival game in which you try to throw a hoop over a slanted pole. There was just room for her left leg between the seats, while her right was pressed up against the side window. Trying to retain control by glancing over her shoulder, he felt the airplane's gyrations increase as hers did. His attention to his instrument crosscheck began to wander.

"Got you!" she yelled when they finally fused in a potion of blind passion brewed by lust, love, and strange places. He climaxed as the airplane nudged its red line in a screaming spiral, their breathing matching the rising scream of wind across the wings. Putting his head under her arm, gasping, he brought the instruments back into a normal range, and struggled back to straight and level flight.

"Promise me not to do that again. Not till New Mexico, anyway."

Patty had pulled a notebook out. "How high were we when we started?"

"About eleven thousand feet."

She wrote it down. "I'm going to keep track of this. We may as well set a few private roistering records of our own."

Major Henry Caldwell was watching out the window of his second-story office when the yellow Beechcraft landed, seemingly by magic from the heart of the towering thunderstorms. The landing coincided with the familiar twinge of mixed anxieties. He was worried about the appropriation, about the new fighter competition, and about his wife's complaints about his tiny salary. He spooned Bromo Seltzer into one glass, then poured water into another. There was comfort in the fizzing as he splashed the mixture back and forth from glass to glass, gathering his strength from just the sight of the fizzing white foam. He drank it, then raced down the stairwell, two at a time, to meet the Beechcraft on the flight line. On the way he thought of the pride he'd feel in owning an airplane like the Beech, and snorted. With a major's pay he was damn lucky to own the old Hupmobile that had given up the ghost on him this very morning. He'd caught a ride out to the field with a friend, his wife's angry argument ringing in his ears. She saw him making decisions for companies involving hundreds of thousands of dollars, and he wasn't making enough to buy a house, get a new car, or even be sure their son would have a college education.

But there was an even bigger problem, that of Europe, where it seemed that every air force, including the Italian, was forging ahead of the United States Army Air Corps in performance, numbers, and productive capacity. The final item was the real unknown. The air attachés could comment on airplanes they had seen—often, in the case of the Germans, anyway, specially prepared ships whose performance might not be carried over into operational types. But there was no one who could look at the factories and tell him what the production potential was.

He knew where the United States stood—almost destitute. The country was producing less than two thousand aircraft a year. In a pinch, the present factories might double that amount, but it would take time. There were only a few hundred combat-ready airplanes in the inventory, spread from Panama to the Philippines, not enough anywhere to really fight.

The European problem had a troubling component. Hafner Aircraft, one of his most promising companies, was under suspicion. Bruno Hafner was building bombers for the Air Corps, and supposedly had something revolutionary in his experimental shed. Yet in Caldwell's safe there were three separate assessments from the American air attaché in Berlin that Hafner was involved in some kind of espionage work with the new German air force. It seemed incredible that a supplier to the U.S. Army Air Corps could also be a traitor to his adopted country. When he considered that he personally had awarded Hafner Aircraft contracts for the A-11 and the Skyshark, he paled. He didn't expect to be much more than a major when he retired, but he'd like to do that without a court-martial.

Caldwell had selected Frank Bandfield as a means to solve both problems, if he could. He was certainly wise enough in engineering and in manufacturing to tell what was going on in Germany and elsewhere. Caldwell remembered from the days of the bombing competition, when Hafner and Bandfield had refused to shake hands, that an enmity between the two existed. By asking around, Caldwell learned that Bandfield nursed a deep and abiding hatred of Hafner, going back to the days on Roosevelt Field, just before Lindbergh flew to Paris. Hafner obviously reciprocated.

Unable to dissemble, Caldwell met the Beechcraft and pulled Bandfield aside brusquely, with a bare nod to Patty, saying, "What is it with you, Bandfield? You smell like a French whorehouse! Are you wearing some goddam perfume?"

Bandfield checked the wind sock and moved downwind.

"Jesus, Henry, you sure are an old smoothie. What a cordial greeting."

Caldwell's wattles turned a brighter pink. "Goddammit, Bandfield. Don't screw around. I invited *you* out here, not her."

"Jesus, you didn't invite me, you ordered me. I don't even know why I'm here. I'm not working for the Air Corps anyway, and I sure as hell haven't sold it any planes. What the hell business is it of yours who I bring with me?"

"Look, it's nothing personal." He thought for a moment,

weighing whether he should proceed, then plunged ahead. "Frankly, we're worried about Bruno Hafner. We're not sure where his loyalties lie."

"I'll tell you. They lie with Bruno Hafner and nowhere else."

"Yeah, that's what I'm afraid of. I've got some official word that makes Hafner look pretty suspicious."

"You thought enough of Hafner to buy a whole bunch of airplanes from him. You didn't buy any from me."

"*Touché*. But a lot has happened since, and that's why you're here."

Caldwell furrowed his brow. "I'm going to have to talk to Patty personally, to reassure myself about her. Hafner is just her stepfather, I know, but it could lead to problems. I've got my neck on the line on this. But lemme give you some background, first. Then I'll tell you how you can help us."

They did it Army-style. Sitting in a top-floor office of the Matériel Division headquarters building, at a highly polished dark oak table, Bandy listened while a series of sharp young lieutenants and captains brought him up to date on all the trouble spots in the world, each man an expert with maps, pointer, and overhead projector. While he was getting groggy from the lectures, Caldwell spent the time getting to know Patty, gently interrogating her.

Bandfield was astounded at how weak the United States was militarily, given the critical world situation. If you believed the briefing officers, everything was apparently going to hell everywhere, and all Roosevelt seemed worried about was the Navy and the National Recovery Act. Maybe Lindbergh was right.

The Congress wasn't providing much money to the military, the Navy got the lion's share of what was given, and the Army kept a tight rein on Air Corps spending. Every major country in the world, including Russia and Japan, was getting ahead of the U.S. militarily, especially in the air.

Bandfield had promised Patty dinner at the officers' club, but Caldwell had asked him to come by his little house in Dayton first, to tell him what the whole trip was about. Patty, weary with the interviews, and not anxious to see Caldwell again, had gone directly to the club.

When Caldwell opened the door, Bandfield laughed openly. The major, never spic-and-span, was scruffier than ever in a workman's cap and a set of coveralls with a big Sinclair Oil sign with its familiar brontosaurus insignia. Underneath was the legend "Mellowed a Hundred Million Years." Old Henry Caldwell would take longer than that to mellow.

"What the hell is this, Henry? Are you working as a grease monkey part-time?"

"Sorry, Bandy, but my old Hupmobile burned out a main bearing and I'm overhauling it. Tonight's one of the few times I've had to work on it. We can talk while I work, if you don't mind."

In the tiny wooden garage at the back of his lot, lit by a dangling bare bulb in a white porcelain socket, Caldwell had rigged an A-frame to pull the Hupp's engine from the hood.

Caldwell reached inside the brass-buttoned coverall and pulled out a standard Army manila folder carrying large red SECRET markings.

"Bandy, it's all right here. It got delivered to me by a courier straight from Air Corps headquarters. They tasked me to pin a rose on you, and I'm pinning it. If you'll let me."

He wiped his hands on a greasy rag, then delicately pulled out a file and said, "And I learned a little bit about you. I never knew you and Slim had a midair or that you were a washed-out cadet."

"Being washed out is not the first thing anybody wants to talk about. Yeah, Slim ran into me one day down in Texas. He came out of it pretty well. He got to Paris, and he's made colonel already."

Caldwell laughed. "Well, we can't do that well, but how would you like to be a captain and maybe go to Berlin and Rome? Or maybe China and Tokyo?"

Bandy raised his eyebrows. "I didn't even make second lieutenant. I stopped at buck-ass cadet."

"They want you for a special project. They need somebody who has a reputation as a pilot, is an engineer, and knows how to build airplanes. You fit the bill perfectly."

"Really? I don't know how much of a reputation I have outside of a pretty small community."

"You'd be surprised. Anyway, to use you legally, we'll need to commission you a captain in the United States Army Air Corps. I can have the paperwork here tomorrow if you'll agree. Of course, you won't be able to tell anybody about it, or about the project for that matter."

"What am I supposed to do?"

Caldwell's voice dropped to a conspiratorial level.

"We'll arrange that you get some official tours, at the highest level, of some foreign air forces. Some will be friendly, some not so friendly. The not-so-friendly ones are our real interest, of course.''

''I thought that's what the Army and Navy attachés did.''

''They're supposed to, but they don't have your experience. Mostly they see what the host country wants them to see.''

Bandfield hesitated. ''Tell me a little more about it. What does it have to do with Hafner?''

''Well, I'm not sure. I just think you might be able to confirm something about him on your trip to Germany. You'll be entertained, you'll meet a lot of the top people. Maybe you can sound something out.''

''I don't know, Henry. I've got a lot of responsibilities back at the plant. And I don't want to leave Patty.''

''Take her with you. And Hadley can run the plant, can't he?''

Bandfield's mind was racing. Actually, the timing was not bad. Douglas had outsold them across the country, and it seemed certain that the production line for the RC-3 wouldn't run much beyond the original order from Mahew. If he left, went on the Air Corps payroll, it would make it that much easier for Hadley to survive.

Caldwell seemed to be reading his thoughts. ''You know, Hadley came to work for us once when things were quiet at the plant, back in the early thirties. You were off trying to sell airplanes, and the money he was making kept Roget Aircraft going. Maybe it's your turn to pull a tour of duty and let Hadley run the plant.''

Bandfield nodded, wondering how Patty would feel about being married to another Army captain.

''When would I start and how long will it take?''

Caldwell looked at his watch. ''Well, it six P.M. now . . .'' His voice changed from the joking note. ''We'd like to start right after the first of the year.''

''Let me talk to her. My inclination is to go along with you, but I want her to approve.''

''Bandy, did you ever hear of the draft in the last war?''

''Yeah, sure.''

''Well, think of this as your private draft. You can talk it over with Patty, and think it over all you want, but come the first of the year, you are going.''

Bandfield bridled, then subsided, knowing that he wanted to

go, and there was no point in arguing about being forced to do what he wanted to do.

"Go on back to Downey and get Hadley squared away with the plant. The sooner you get started, the better, because we want to send you through a few quick schools before you go."

"Schools?"

"Yeah, the fighter tactics school. We want you to spend a month or two here at Wright Field, flying all the different airplanes we have, so you'll have some basis for comparison. And they're bringing in some guy from the East Coast to give you a crash course in German."

Bandfield looked bewildered.

"This is a long-term project, isn't it, Henry? You're not investing all that time and dough in me for a one-month trip on the continent."

Caldwell nodded. "As I said, a lot depends on you. But yeah, they're looking to call on you in the future. It's sort of like reserve duty, you know—you're called up for a while, then get sent back to civvie street."

"Jesus, tell me, Henry, what the hell is going on? The Nazis are building subs, the fascists are marching in England, the communists are trying to take over China, there's fighting in Spain, Mussolini's talking about going to war. Finland seems to be the only country with any sense. Are we going to be strong enough?"

"Shit no, Bandy, that's the problem. We're worse off than we were in 1917. The Army's got only a few thousand men— Rumania's got more men under arms than we do!—and you know how bad off we are in the air."

"And I'm supposed to fix it?"

Caldwell laughed. "Well, it'll be a start, won't it?"

Bandfield knew that he would agree, and looked for some quick rationalizations.

"Well, it could actually help the business to see what the competition is doing. Would the Air Corps have any problems with that?"

"Hell no. We won't be paying you much, just a captain's pay and expenses. Anything you get out of it you'll deserve."

Caldwell figured he'd let out enough line, so he set the hook.

"The beauty of it is that you and Patty can travel at government expense. She'd have to keep her eyes and ears open, but from what I've seen of her, she'd be a real asset."

"I'll think it over."

Caldwell's face creased into three parallel lines as he grinned. "You already have. But talk it over with Patty and Hadley, and let me know. For the time being, don't tell anyone else. Okay?"

"You're on!"

Burbank, California/September 28, 1934

The crazy working habits of Howard Hughes were a match for his career. He turned everything upside down, from hours of work to return on investment. The money that flowed endlessly to him from his Texas tool company and his oil investments were poured into the film and aviation industries with equally lavish abandon. He was filmmaker, airplane designer, and playboy, all rolled into one, and if he'd had a candle he would have burned it at both ends and the middle as well. Yet the situation was exactly right for Hadley Roget, giving him the time needed to keep his own plant going. Hughes rarely surfaced until after nine in the evening, so Hadley was able to keep on top of things at Roget Aircraft and still be on hand when Hughes needed him. It meant sixteen hours a day, seven days a week, but that was the way he'd worked all his life, and if he began spending some time at home, Clarice would have been suspicious.

He had been Hughes's "boss" for years; it felt funny to be working for him. But Hughes's unusual way of dealing with people seemed to work. He'd pick the best people he could find, tell them what he wanted, then leave them alone. Usually the results were better than he could have expected.

It was a weird world, though. The pay was wonderful—Hughes doled out salaries as if they were all movie stars—and the other people were first-rate. The racer was beginning to take shape, and it was clearly a winner, a sleek low-wing monoplane with the smoothest finish he'd ever seen. The fuselage was all-metal, with every plate butted into the next and flush-riveted so it was smoother than glass. Hadley had been asked to build two wings, one short for the speed-record attempt and a longer one for a transcontinental record.

The only puzzle was Dusty Rhoades. Hadley was shocked by his appearance. In the past, he had been husky, almost over-weight, dressing as fastidiously as Adolph Menjou. Now he was rail-lean and dressed like a scarecrow, his long hair uncombed and his manner strange. He had been a great pilot, and apparently still flew, but most of his work with Hafner had been administrative. Hughes seemed to be using him as a general handyman. In his usual bluff way, Hadley asked, "Dusty, what the hell are you doing here? I didn't know you knew Hughes."

"Yeah, I knew him, but I'm here because Hafner couldn't come."

"Are Bruno and Howard old buddies?"

"Yeah, Bruno flew in *Hell's Angels* for him, and then Howard got him some other roles in other films with other studios—*The Dawn Patrol*, *Aces of Aces*. Anyway, Howard figured Bruno owed him, and wanted him to come out. Hafner's involved in the bomber contracts and sent me instead."

"You earning your dough?"

"No more than usual. How about you?"

"No more than usual."

Rhoades watched the older man turn back to work. His life was so simple. He had been married to Clarice for probably thirty years, loved airplanes, and worked day and night. And that was it.

It was different for himself. First, always, there was the habit, the goddam chains that bound him to Hafner. Bruno had introduced him to cocaine back in Long Island, just as an embellishment to the booze-and-broad parties going on all the time. He had found heroin for himself. Yet Hafner made everything so easy—a constant supply, medical attention, lots of money. He could do what few addicts did—live a relatively normal life, working at what he loved to do. In return, all Hafner demanded was that he be a slave.

He'd started the business with Charlotte just as she had, light-heartedly, a romp, a finger in Bruno's eye. Then it changed. She'd developed a need for him. It was odd, but although he didn't need her as a woman—there were always plenty of women available—he needed her to need him. It somehow canceled out his dependence on Bruno.

It was amazing that they were able to enjoy each other so much, knowing that Bruno was aware of what was going on. So far, he had tolerated the situation, seemingly content that he could control them both, Charlotte through the flying and the freedom he gave her, Rhoades through the dope. Yet Bruno was not a tolerant or forgiving man. Someday, sometime he would render his bill. That's why he was going to work with Charlotte on kicking the habit. She'd promised to take care of him, to see him through all the pains of withdrawal. It might work.

In the meantime, he had to go on with this rotten spying on

Howard Hughes. He was sure that the only reason Bruno would want him to do it was to supply the information to Germany. Hafner was obviously enamored of the Nazis now; every time he came back from Germany he was more secretive.

Rhoades shrugged and banished Hafner from his thoughts, thinking about his last bittersweet meeting with Charlotte. He knew that he no longer satisfied her sexually, for the dope had made him almost impotent. She had matured and didn't seem to mind. They had drifted into a mothering relationship that served them both well.

He had lain with his arm around her, her breasts warm against his chest, as she said, "Dusty, you've got to break out of this. I've got some money. Let me take you to the Mayo Clinic, where you can get some help. You're killing yourself."

He'd tried to fight off the suggestion. "And how about you? You're insisting that you'll fly the new airplane. It's a lot riskier than these damn needles."

She had nuzzled into him. She was heavier now, no longer youthful, but that suited him. He wanted her comfort, not her sex. "I'm going to fly it. That goddam Amelia Earhart has never flown anything but those itty-bitty Vegas. When I fly a four-engine bomber, that will be something."

"What do you care? You have so much that she'll never have, a beautiful daughter, a business reputation. She's a creature of the press."

"You and Bruno don't understand, you can never understand."

She reached down and rubbed his arm. "Dusty, just as you have to keep cramming that stuff in your arm, I have to keep cramming some records in my system, to keep my sense of worth. When I think about Earhart, I die inside. It's an obsession, I know, but that's the way it is. With the big bomber, I can do it all—speed, altitude, distance—in a year. After that, I won't have to think about Earhart, and I'll let Patty do the flying."

He had given in. "If you promise to stop flying after you demonstrate the new bomber, I'll go to the clinic. Deal?"

"No. I want you to start as soon as you come back from California. Deal?"

"Deal." They had slept long in each other's arms, two misfits fitting together perfectly.

Rhoades watched Roget again, envying his simple, happy life. God, he missed Long Island. There he was productive at the factory, and Charlotte was nearby. Here he was simply and plainly a spy, and there was no one.

Air Ministry, Berlin/September 30, 1934

The meeting place had been selected with special care. It was a small conference room, furnished only with a highly polished oak table, four chairs, and a wall of locked filing cabinets. There were no decorations, not even a calendar, on the two-tone gray walls, except for the obligatory picture of a stern-faced Adolf Hitler.

Hermann Goering, Reichskommissar for Air, Minister-President of Prussia, Reich Chief Forester, head of dozens of commissions and committees, his tanned face surely the result of a sunlamp, put his ham-sized arms on the table. He spoke to the two men facing him with none of his usual bombast, for they were the trusted instruments of his policies.

"Gentlemen, the Fuehrer has informed me that we will announce the Luftwaffe formally in March of next year. By then we must have parity—or at least the appearance of parity—in airpower with England."

It was a simple order made to the men who would have to carry it out. Milch, the State Secretary for Aviation, waited. It was usually best to let Goering finish if you wanted to get his attention, particularly if you had to tell him anything he didn't want to hear. At Milch's side, sitting in the correct position of attention, shoulders back, hands placed on the legs, was Colonel Walther Wever, chief of the Air Command Office, his mind as sharp as his features.

An aide came in and whispered in Goering's ear.

"Gentlemen, excuse me. The Fuehrer is calling. I'll be back as soon as I can."

Milch pulled a folder from his briefcase and began to thumb through its pages. Walther Wever gazed out the small window that opened onto a brick courtyard, considering the options available to him in shaping an air force.

They were spread so desperately thin, and the leadership was so eccentric. In the old Imperial Army, before the war, there had always been a surplus of men and materials. The whole system had been designed for expansion when a war came—the old regiments would go off to the front, leaving cadres to form replacement groups with the never-ending classes of young soldiers. Now they were expanding even faster, without the necessary base, creating whole new units on paper with no one to man them. The expansion was going on so swiftly that there wasn't enough talent to go around, especially with the capricious way the Party had infiltrated the army.

He looked at Milch. The man was a merchant. In the old army he'd never gone past the rank of sergeant. Goering, at least, had been an officer from the old school, but he was power-mad now, demanding results without providing the resources. He expected Wever simply to conjure trained airmen from the ground, like the dragon's teeth, and airplanes were supposed to pour forth from factories that hadn't been planned, much less built. And there was so much catching up to do. The Versailles Treaty had brought aviation to a halt in Germany.

He cleared his throat, and Milch looked up. "Have you and Udet made any progress with Hafner in the United States?"

"Yes, it's working better than we could have thought. Hafner has sent the first sets of drawings for his aircraft. It looks like it might be what you're looking for. I'm not sure we can afford to build it, but it looks splendid on paper."

"Hafner's factory is like having a research facility without having to pay for it."

"I'm not sure how long we can go on. We've had some indications that Hafner is under suspicion. We may have to bring him back here."

"I knew him during the war. He would make a good *Geschwader* commander."

Milch snorted. "Hardly! We'll need him more as a technician, someone to run one of the new factories."

Goering returned, obviously pleased to have the summons from Hitler reinforce his importance. "My apologies, but the Fuehrer needed some information that only I could supply." He put his gloves on the table, arranged his jacket carefully, and got down to business.

"I know that you both read the Knauss memorandum. It will be the basis for the first expansion. But it is not enough."

Major Robert Knauss, one of the earnest staff toilers who generated the ideas that shaped the path of the army, had written a paper outlining the advantages of secretly building a fleet of four hundred heavy bombers. When they were ready, they were to be unveiled as a "risk fleet," as Knauss called it, an inexpensive weapon with which to threaten other powers.

The army high command had dismissed Knauss's ideas out

of hand, but Milch had gotten them to Hitler, who saw at once the benefits. It would take years for Germany to build up an army as large as France's, decades to even begin to match the English navy. Four hundred bombers could be built at the cost of five infantry divisions, or perhaps two battleships. Even more important, no one, not even Russia, had a striking force of four hundred bombers. Used as a shield, they could check the talk of a "preventive war" being heard in France and Russia, and give the Nazis time to rearm Germany adequately.

"Herr Reichskommissar."

"Yes, Colonel Wever, go ahead."

Wever's voice had a pedantic quality, a lecturing tone that made Milch wince. You didn't talk to "Der Dicke" like that.

It was a subterfuge. Wever could barely suppress the energy coursing through his frame, and had to be sure what he said was measured for impact.

"We are now standardizing on the combat aircraft for the Knauss risk fleet." Wever paused for effect.

"You forgot yourself. It is the Goering risk fleet." It was a gentle, genial reproof. Hermann was in too good a mood to be angry.

Wever took the bait, converted it to flattery.

"All the more reason, then, to make sure we have not selected the wrong aircraft to build. If this risk fleet is to have credibility, it must have capability. The airplanes we are planning—single-engine and twin-engine bombers—are inadequate. We must have heavy, four-engine bombers that can carry two tons of bombs for a thousand miles, as far as the Ural Mountains, if we are to bluff—much less fight—the Soviet Union."

"Wever, I came here to tell you the good news about announcing the Luftwaffe. I didn't come to get bad news about our aircraft types."

Wever and Milch stiffened in their seats.

"However, your point is not without merit. But listen to me." He became affable Hermann again, their confidant, their leader.

"This is just the first round. The Fuehrer assures me that there will not be a war until 1943 at the earliest. By then, we will have introduced our second generation of aircraft, and, Colonel Wever, you can be sure that it will include your Ural bomber. We'll let our 'experimental station' in the United States develop the first round, and then we'll be prepared for the second."

He paused and nodded genially to Wever. "I'll pass your

comments on to the Fuehrer." Goering went on with the other points on his memorandum, items concerning the new uniform with which he was almost inordinately concerned, cooperation with Italy, and the possibility of using political prisoners in factories. He didn't ask their opinion, he simply told them how it would be. When he'd finished, he stood up and the meeting was over.

Milch punched Wever lightly on the arm. "Good job. You salted the idea for the four-engine bomber. He'll spring it on Hitler and take credit for it. That's the way we have to work it."

Wever's reply was stiff. "It's a pity when the general staff has to adopt the sycophantic tactics of an advertising firm. In the old days, you were paid to say what you thought—or else!"

Milch laughed. "Thank God these aren't the old days, Wever. I'd be grooming some Hohenzollern's horse!"

9

Like an aging high school beauty queen primping for a reunion, the distressed Beech Staggerwing sat in the back of the Roget hangar, its dignity destroyed. The firewall was festooned with wires and tubes, and an asbestos blanket covered the windscreen to fend off the sparks that flew as Frank Bandfield welded up a new engine mount.

Hadley slipped on dark goggles and watched approvingly as the torch left a perfectly smooth bead. The deep blue shade of the goggles was a perfect complement to Hadley's sad, reflective mood, the goggles turning the torch's flame into a mirror reflecting all their efforts of the past. It seemed like only yesterday he'd watched Bandy doing exactly the same work on the original *Rocket*, sweating to get it ready to fly to Paris. So much had happened since then—the races at Cleveland, the first flight of the RC-3, the deliveries to Allied Airlines—yet financially they were headed back almost exactly to where they had started.

The euphoria of the sixty-plane order Mahew had given for the RC-3 had led them to expand the plant and its work force too rapidly. Ironically, it was the very size of that initial success that was now giving them problems. They had created a full manufacturing plant to deliver aircraft at the rate of ten per month, but had not since gained any other orders for the airplane. Douglas Aircraft had quite simply trumped their ace with its DC-2, sewing up the marketplace, and Roget Aircraft was trapped in the classic aviation dilemma: a large work force, a huge payroll, and no backlog of orders.

No outsider could have guessed this by looking at the plant, for the aisles were still filled with planes in the process of being built. But the simple truth was that unless there were some sizable orders for new aircraft in the next few weeks, they were going to have to start laying people off as they began the process of shutting the plant down.

It had startled Hadley to find that success was far more difficult to deal with than failure. Before the "big order," Roget and Bandfield had been able to keep body and soul together with the survival techniques they'd learned over the years. They would do odd jobs, charter flights, and repair aircraft and cars. Now the focus was shifted entirely away from themselves onto the work force which depended upon them for its livelihood.

Hadley roused himself from his uncharacteristic reverie and said, "Your pay runs pretty high for doing a welder's work, doesn't it, Bandy?"

Bandfield's nod showed that he had heard. He didn't interrupt his fierce concentration on the job at hand. Working at night on the Beechcraft was a relief from the frantic pressures of the day. As he watched, the blue-black metal glowed red, then white as it fused. He remembered all his father had taught him about craftsmanship. George Bandfield had been a wild-eyed dreamer, but he played machine tools the way Paderewski played a piano. Even as the two pieces of metal merged into the stout angle he sought, he recalled how closely his father had supervised his work, rejecting any that wasn't perfect. Like any smart-aleck kid, he'd resented it at the time; now he knew it had paid off. Recognition sparked like the torch; it wasn't only craftsmanship his dad had taught, but philosophy, probably shaping his attitude about selling safe, well-proven aircraft as much as Millie's crash had done. So Slim Lindbergh was probably right when he had said his dad had influenced his political arguments.

Finished with the bead, he snapped up his welder's mask and grinned. "I've had a lot of good times in this bucket." The thought of Patty's athletic sex-at-altitude program stirred him. "And I'd never forgive myself if something happened to my girl in an airplane I'd worked on."

He flipped his mask down, then up again. "You know this airplane is twice as fast as the Nieuports her dad flew in the war? Who'd believe a woman would be flying something like this?"

"Yeah, lots of progress in airplanes, but none in business. If we don't get some more orders we'll be starving to death again. I thought we'd broken out of that rut."

Bandfield nodded, sharing Roget's sorrow and anxiety over the roller-coaster ride of the aircraft business.

"Well, maybe I'll learn something at Wright Field that will help. And maybe you can sell Howard on buying an airline and outfitting it with Roget Aircraft planes. I know he's wanted to get into the airline business for years, ever since he flew for TWA."

"I think that's part of our problem, Bandy. We depended too much on Hughes in the past. That's why I'm willing to take the time to work on his racer. But I don't think we can depend on him now. The only thing to do is come up with another design, something smaller that doesn't take a big work crew to build in quantity. We could afford to design a fighter, maybe, or a trainer. Henry Caldwell was always trying to get me to design a trainer for the Air Corps."

"Well, Hadley, we'll swing something. Right now, though, I've got to get back to work. Patty is on my ass all the time to get this thing finished. She's not too happy that I only work on it after hours."

Hadley examined the bright yellow Beech appreciatively, letting the beauty of its lines restore his humor. He asked, "Which engine are you installing now?"

"It's a six-hundred-and-ninety-horsepower Wright Cyclone. I'll tweak it a little bit until it delivers seven-fifty, and Patty will have the fastest biplane in the country, maybe the world."

Roget ran his hand over the bulldog-jawed lower wing, which gave the Staggerwing its name. "Will she be able to handle it?"

"No problem in the air, and any Staggerwing's a problem on the ground. She's got about fifty hours in it, and is doing a good job. She'll be all right. If there was a problem, I wouldn't let her go."

Roget laughed. "Yeah, I know how much attention she pays to what you say—about like what Clarice does to me."

The older man turned and bounded off to the tool room. He doubted if Patty would really be able to master the airplane. It would be bad enough if Bandy lost another woman in an aircraft accident, impossibly worse if he felt he had been the cause.

Bandfield turned back to his torch. As with any task, he approached the welding with a single-minded intensity, a tidal wave of concentration that swamped the event and usually any-

one associated with it. When he could not be exactly focused—
in the bath, walking to work, driving—he tended to wander mentally through a portfolio of ideas, setting them in order, shaping
them to be a task that could then be done. It was another legacy
from his father. They would sit in the woods, waiting for a deer
to come by, and his father would whisper to him all the things
that needed to get done, what they were going to do with the
deer, how they would cook it, and, always, with whom they
would share it. Not a Christian, George Bandfield had nevertheless always more than tithed his possessions, taking care of
anyone who needed it.

Patty had been waiting for thirty minutes when she saw Bandy
appear at the door, wiping his hands on a handkerchief, brow
furrowed. She honked the horn of the cream-and-red Auburn
Speedster, a car whose curves suited her own perfectly.

"Hey, ye old absent-minded professor, over here."

He looked up, genuinely surprised, then glanced at his watch.
"God, honey, I'm sorry I'm late. Been waiting long?"

"Just the usual half hour."

A familiar surge of pleasure washed over him. He was content
for the first time ever with his love life. Patty's highly charged
eroticism matched his own, and they enjoyed an intensity of
lovemaking that continued to surprise him. Their life was spiced
by wild arguments that led to name-calling, dish-throwing, and
door-slamming, and almost always dissolved into a quick, heated
tumble right where they were—the kitchen, the car, wherever.
And when it was over—the fighting or the loving—they could
talk endlessly about everything.

A bursting hot whiff of the local White Castle's greasy fried
onions bubbled around him as he walked to the car, whacking
his appetite as a jockey whips a horse.

"Let's eat. How about a steak at Pancho's?"

She pointed to a bag of groceries. "I've got a two-inch-thick
Porterhouse and a box of mushrooms. Forty cents a pound for
the steak, but so what. It's been a bad day—a letter from my
mother worrying about all sorts of things."

"Like what?"

"Like will the airplane be too much for me, am I getting
enough sleep, and if your intentions are honorable."

"The answer to all three is no. But I could make an exception
for the last one."

Laughing, she turned left toward Santa Monica.

"Where are we headed?"

"To the beach. I've borrowed a cabin for the weekend. I'm giving you one more chance to see if you like playing man and wife with me. If you do, we're going to see a justice of the peace pretty soon."

"A JP? We ought to have a big wedding, invite everybody."

She winced, remembering the wedding in Orléans. "No thanks. I've done that once too often. Let's just get Hadley and Clarice to be witnesses and do everything quietly."

"What about your flying?" He meant: Are you going to give it up, as I want you to do?

She took her eyes off the road only long enough to look at him and say, "What about yours?" It was a complete message.

The weekend had gone predictably well, and two weeks later they were married in a simple morning ceremony in Riverside. Clarice Roget insisted on her Episcopal priest conducting the ceremony in the St. Francis Chapel of the Mission Inn. The inn, done in traditional Southern California–Spanish formula, had come to be a gathering place for both military and civilian flyers. The custom had begun with a series of rollicking wakes, when saddened comrades would gather to toast the latest death. In time, the inn was adopted by flyers as the appropriate place to drink, have a romantic rendezvous, or, less frequently, to get married.

Clarice was terribly pleased with herself for choosing the little nondenominational chapel, for she knew that its decorations included a gilded wooden altar and nine genuine Tiffany windows. In good times and in bad, no matter what Hadley had earned, Clarice had lived an impoverished life. Aviation had drained their finances like a major illness, and she had watched all the money go for "necessities" like tools, parts, and payrolls. For years she had lusted for a Tiffany lamp, to her a glowing symbol of luxury and taste. She knew she would never have one simply because Hadley would never understand how it related to airplanes. Having Tiffany windows in the chapel served as a substitute, and was in its own way a personal victory for her.

There was a small reception, during the course of which Hadley managed to bring Bandfield back through the stuccoed archways of the inn to the fabled Flyers' Wall, where famous and not-so-famous flyers were honored.

"Come take a look at this, Bandy." The beige stucco wall was covered with ten-inch-long copper wings, each one signed by a well-known aviator. Other walls were filled with signed photos of flyers from the early days of aviation in California. All the aviation greats and near-greats were there. Roget ran his finger along the wall, calling out the names—Glenn L. Martin, Lincoln Beachey, Hap Arnold, "Doc" Young, Jimmy Wedell, Jimmy Doolittle. Half the photos were marked with a simple black ribbon slanted across the upper right-hand corner.

They were bantering back and forth when Roget pointed to the picture of Millie Duncan, standing with Jack Winter near the *Golden Eagle*, cute as a button in her fake military outfit, looking up at the stars.

Bandfield was visibly staggered—he'd heard of the Flyers' Wall, but he'd had no idea that Millie was included. His jaw dropped as he flushed with irritation; the photo was the same one that had been run in the *Oakland Tribune*, the one he had reproached her about.

Roget was relentless. "Most of these guys were good. And most of them are dead. You've survived pretty well. If you let Patty fly, the odds are against her, no matter how talented she is. You ought to put your foot down."

Bandfield walked away, shaken. Though tactless as a shark, Roget was right—but there didn't seem to be anything Bandy could do. He sat down at a table, wondering where Patty had gone.

She was with Clarice, Roget's faithful teammate, who pulled her to the same wall, the same picture. In an affectionate, caring voice, Clarice whispered, "She put him through hell. He never stopped blaming himself. You've saved him. Don't let it happen to him again."

The effect was different. Patty was not shocked, just angry, wondering if Bandy had put Clarice up to it.

The Rogets were traditionalists, from the rice they had thrown after the wedding to the tin cans Bandfield found tied to the back of the Auburn and to the tail wheel of the Roget Rocket they were to fly to San Francisco. He had arranged with the Army to land at Crissey Field, and they had splurged on a room at the St. Francis Hotel. Patty had been upset all the way up, and they hardly spoke through dinner. As they undressed unenthusiastically for bed, Patty said, "Great start for a honeymoon, isn't it? I'll bet Clarice is a scream at a wake."

"They meant well. And I happen to agree with them. You don't have to prove anything."

"I know you agree with them. Did you put them up to it?"

She could tell by the look on his face that he had not. In a kinder voice, she said, "How can you be so understanding about most things, and miss this completely? Stephan was right. You men flyers have flying and sex so screwed up you think women feel the same way."

"I thought you said they did."

"If I did, it was because we were courting, and I didn't want to argue about it. Why can't flying be a challenge, like painting or music? Why can't a woman pursue something she's good at?"

"It's not natural. A woman is supposed to be the homemaker. Why are there so few women doctors or lawyers? It's the same thing, it's just not right."

She turned rigid with fury. "You're making my point. There aren't many women in the professions because you men won't let them in. And that's why I'm going to have a flying career. Mother is all wrong about Amelia Earhart. She does her flying for a larger cause."

"I'm not worried about any goddam larger cause! I'm worried about you and I'm worried about having a family."

He stopped, appalled at his echo of Stephan's discontent, biting his tongue in dismay at the cold, hard look that came over her. He reached over and stroked her arm.

"Get your hands off me and get the hell out of this room. I'm no serving cow, waiting for the current King Bull to jump me."

After a few apologies, he stayed in the room, ruefully remembering that they'd had a lot better honeymoons before they were married.

Sayville, Long Island/December 18, 1934

Charlotte Morgan Hafner was rarely sentimental, but tears welled as she realized that this snow-drenched Christmas was going to be the worst since the awful years after her first husband had been killed. Bruno was off on another of his trips to Germany and France; Dusty, poor bedeviled Dusty, was sequestered in Burbank working for Howard Hughes; and Patty was apparently determined to go on flying no matter what anyone said.

When she'd first realized that she'd be alone, she'd been delighted, imagining that she would have a permanent wave, lie about in bed, and generally take it easy. Then she thought about the factory. Bruno had been systematically excluding her from work at the plant, and she used the opportunity to try to get back into the thick of things. Sometime in the last year he had completely revised the accounting department, hiring all new people. They were polite, but they followed his instructions to let no one look at the books. Not even a first-class Charlotte Hafner tirade with an aria of curses and a coda of tears had budged them. They were properly cowed and apologetic, and their manner told her that Bruno was doing something unorthodox. But they were adamant, and whatever it was would have to wait until Bruno returned and she could dig it out of him.

She was unsettled by it. When Bruno had begun to become obsessive about the business, a few years ago, it had pleased her, for she was tired of the work, just as they had mutually tired of their sex life. She welcomed the chance to divert his interest, leaving her more time for Dusty. The irony was that Dusty too had long since become an indifferent lover.

I must be some hot number, she thought. Losing an American husband to the Germans, a German husband to boredom, and an American lover to dope.

She curled up on the couch, listening to Russ Colombo records on the Victrola, putting the squeeze on a box of chocolates to find the nuts and caramels. Once she had been addicted to sex and flying and chocolates. Now she was down mostly to chocolates.

Charlotte tossed the box of candy across the room, knowing only too well that her real distress stemmed from the burning desire to somehow excel over Amelia Earhart, to get the recognition that the ''Lady Lindy'' got so effortlessly. Despite all Bruno's warnings, and her own very clear insight, it had supplanted everything else in her life save her love and concern for Patty, and her determination to help Dusty break his habit.

She knew that helping Dusty change was by far her most difficult task. They had made good progress before Bruno sent him to California; Dusty was going longer between injections, and had begun to put back on a little weight. Now his latest letter admitted that he had relapsed. He romantically blamed it on his need for her, and there was probably some truth to the idea. As long as she was with him, nagging him for his own good, Dusty had the strength to quit. The problem was the close association with Bruno, who kept Dusty supplied so conveniently with drugs. The only real way out for them would be simply to leave, to start a new life somewhere away from Bruno.

In some respects it would be easy. Patty was mature, and

Charlotte no longer loved flying for flying's sake. The days when a flight above the clouds or aerobatics close to the ground had given her a near-sexual satisfaction had gone forever, vanished in the irritation over the adulation that Earhart had received for her flights across the country and from Hawaii. Bruno had explained to her time and again that Earhart had an advantage with her fragile delicate looks and vulnerable manner that was almost insuperable. Her husband, George Putnam, had a genius for promotion, and made Amelia unbeatable in the press.

Bruno had tried to reassure her, telling her, "Among the professionals, you are the best—but you'll never beat her in the newsroom." But now, she had a story winner in her grasp—the new four-engine bomber. To her knowledge Earhart had never flown anything bigger than a Vega. Initially, Bruno was against her flying the bomber—said it was too big for her—but he yielded quickly to her argument that it was the one sure way to sell Congress. There was a strong Congressional sentiment, fed by careful briefings from the Navy, that anything bigger than the twin-engine Martin B-10s would be "too difficult for the average Air Corps pilot to fly." It was baloney, but it suited the battleship admirals perfectly. They wanted the Air Corps relegated to close infantry support and coast defense.

Even within the Air Corps, there was a powerful faction that wanted smaller airplanes, simply because you could buy more of them. When Bruno had told her that he was entering a four-engine plane in the bomber competition, she saw the possibilities for herself at once. She would demonstrate the plane at Wright Field, and then get one on loan—or have the company build one especially for her if necessary—and set all the women's records for speed, distance, and altitude. She could probably do it all in two or three flights. Then she could put her helmet in the locker and concentrate on the chocolates—and on curing Dusty.

The only genuine difficulty was persuading Patty to quit her own career. In the end she gave up and simply promised to support her every way she could. Maybe Patty could be her copilot on the bomber—that would be something, a mother-and-daughter team setting records. Having a daughter was one thing that damn Earhart couldn't do, for sure. Charlotte had always wondered if Amelia wasn't a man in disguise.

Downey, California/February 15, 1935

Bandfield glanced over his *Los Angeles Times*, covertly watching
Patty planning her flight, her desk awash with maps, plotters for
drawing the course lines, and tables to predict her fuel consumption. He loved her deep absorption in any flying task. Her
lips would compress as tightly as a recalcitrant clam and her
ordinarily smooth brow would furrow into ivory corrugations
as her whole body became a tightly wound coil of total concentration.

The quarreling honeymoon had set the tone for most of their
first month of marriage. She made it into an elaborate game of
marital diplomacy that left her in complete possession of the
field. Their compromise had been that she was going to manage
her own flying career, doing exactly what she wanted to do when
she wanted to do it, and he was going to help her to the exact
degree that she required.

Beyond that she was now a perfect wife, still very eager in
bed, maintaining their little ranch house without help, and cook-
ing well enough but not so expertly as to prevent making eating
out a regular pleasure. Tonight, she was planning her record
transcontinental run, doing all the figures herself, refusing to let
him help until she was finished. Then she was glad to have him
make any corrections.

He went back to the *Times*. The newspapers were filled with
gloom and doom, at home and abroad. The Depression was
getting worse instead of better, and things were heating up in
Europe. Mussolini was claiming that ninety thousand Ethio-
pians were massed on the border of Italian Somaliland, threatening to invade! The newsreel scenes of *Il Duce* strutting and
posturing were laughable, yet the League of Nations seemed to
buy his preposterous claims.

"Did you see that they convicted Hauptmann? I wonder if
Slim will come back from Europe now."

She looked up, pensive. "He would if the press would let him
alone. Sometime I'd like to meet his wife."

Yeah, me too, Bandfield thought. He had corresponded with
Lindbergh over the past few years, mostly about the RC-3, but
always with a little personal stuff mixed in. Lindbergh seemed
to be drifting rapidly to the right—unless it was himself drifting
to the left. Bandy had written something about the purges in
Russia not being much different from the arrests Hitler was
making in Germany, and Lindbergh had taken violent offense,

claiming that the differences in scale and cause were enormous. He maintained that Stalin was eradicating whole sections of the country because he felt they were a political threat, while the Germans were simply solving some of the problems caused by the war.

Bandy felt a little guilty, because he knew he was at least in part baiting Slim—he realized it was bad practice. The situation at Roget Aircraft was critical now. Douglas was simply eating up the market, so that even mighty Boeing was giving up on commercial aircraft. He might need Lindbergh to give him the nod in some domestic competition.

It was probably a forlorn hope. He hadn't helped in the past, and with all their arguments, it was even more unlikely that he'd help in the future. Fuck him.

He put down the paper and reached for his Spanish text. Major Caldwell was insisting that he have a reasonable proficiency in German and Spanish. The Spanish came easy, but the German was tough. Thank God they'd decided he didn't need to bother with Chinese.

Farmingdale, Long Island/May 8, 1935

The final assembly bay looked like a disaster-area dormitory, with iron cots and surplus Army mattresses and blankets lining the walls. Fully clothed workers were asleep in some of them, oblivious to the glare of the overhead lights and the machine-gun rattle of the riveting guns. At the far end, an improvised kitchen served three hot meals a day, with coffee and sandwiches at all hours.

Armand Bineau, arms aching, forced his wheelchair past the desk where he had spent almost eight years serving Hafner Aircraft as chief engineer. In the old days, Hafner used to let him alone to do his work, rarely making a suggestion. For the last two years, though, Bruno was into everything, always wanting documentation, always insisting on "improvements." Hafner knew just enough about aircraft design to be dangerous. He'd never had the engineer's capacity to keep the entire concept in mind, to see that good ideas, perhaps even great ideas, sometimes didn't work as a part of the whole.

Ironically, the reverse was true with the present airplane. When Wright Field had announced the competition for a "multiengine" bomber, it had been Hafner who had insisted on interpreting the specification to permit four engines. There had been long arguments—in the past, "multiengine" had meant only two or three engines, and that was how Martin and Douglas were interpreting it.

As the plane took shape on Bineau's drafting table, as the figures began to add up, two things became apparent to him. One was that his health was going, his heart unable to take the hours and Hafner's harassment. The other was that Hafner had been right about building a four-engine plane. They'd heard that Boeing was following the same path, but it was only an industry rumor. Both companies had clamped tight security on the work areas.

The heart attack had not been a surprise—his doctor had been predicting it for years—but it came at an awkward time, just when he was forcing Hafner to face reality. All of the engineering changes had boosted the new airplane's weight by more than two tons—equivalent to the bomb load—and every ounce of it could be attributed to Hafner's insistence on change, on "improvements."

When Bineau confronted Hafner with the overweight problem, the German had flared up in a wild fury. Bineau remembered for the hundredth time the insane look in Hafner's eyes. Years before, Bineau had polished a single stainless-steel propeller blade and placed it in his office as a decorative sculpture. Hafner had seized the propeller and walked to the case where models of all the aircraft designed by Bineau were stored. He had raised the propeller blade and smashed it into the cabinet, sending glass flying and mashing the jewellike models into dust. Bineau was powerless to stop him, and the pointless destruction had triggered his attack, sending him to the hospital.

Bineau patted his breast pocket in frustration. The cigarette pack that had been found there for more than thirty years was gone, a victim of his doctor's new regimen. No smoking, no drinking, and no more than ten hours of work per week.

He pulled a sheaf of drawings off the desk, sighing. They were of the control locks, a typical example of Hafner's interference. Historically, the Army had always used external control locks on the surfaces of big airplanes. Simple blocks of wood with felt protectors, they kept the ailerons, elevators, and rudders from banging around in a high wind. Hafner had insisted on installing internal locks, operated from the cockpit, saying that the airplane was too big for the standard locks to be used.

The installation took a lot of engineering man-hours, and added more than a hundred pounds.

He put the drawings back, aware that none of it mattered now. The airplane was ready to fly, with Dusty Rhoades and Charlotte as the test pilots. Bineau had pleaded with Bruno to hire professional test pilots, but he had refused.

"Look, Armand, the Navy has already got the attention of Congress about how difficult big airplanes are to fly. If we have Charlotte fly it right from the start, we'll gut their argument."

Any hope that he might have had of persuading Bruno was undercut by Charlotte's own insistence on being the pilot. "If I can fly a Gee Bee, I can sure fly this," she said.

A summer storm threatened to delay the first flight, but the day dawned bright and clear, a fresh, salt-tinged breeze caressing the field. The airplane was enormous, towering over the swarming ground crew, more than twenty people absorbed in their individual tasks. Bineau watched enviously as Rhoades reached up to grab the sides of the belly hatch under the cockpit, swing his legs forward, and ease into the fuselage; a decade ago he could have done the same thing, but now he'd never see the inside of the airplane. Charlotte was right behind him, swinging up like a trapeze artist.

"That woman is a miracle," Bineau whispered.

They were comfortable together in bed or in a cockpit. Dusty motioned her to take the left seat.

"You make the takeoff. I'll be here to help if you need me."

To her surprise, the big bomber handled easily, needing only a firm hand on the controls. The takeoff and climb-out had been very little different from the transport's, and it stayed in the turns she made, steady as a bowling ball in the gutter, until it was time to roll out.

They flew conservatively for thirty minutes, and Charlotte made a perfect three-point landing.

When they got out, Charlotte pulled Hafner aside. "It's a great airplane. Give us a few hours of takeoffs and landings, and we'll dazzle Wright Field with this thing. The papers will have a field day, and you'll turn Congress around."

He said, "You win. And I guess you'd better let me know what records you're planning. No sense arguing about this."

Bruno's emotions were obviously mixed. "You charmed them out of their boots with the A-11 and the transport. You can do it again. It's sort of a tradition now." He wondered how they'd feel about it in Germany if the Air Corps wound up buying the airplane.

The bomber turned out to be the worst-kept secret in military history. A vacationing newsman had watched the first flight in disbelief, and turned out a feature about "the Hafner Aerial Arsenal" that made the wire services. By the time the test program was well underway, the field was clogged with reporters and newsreel men. The initial comments from Washington were adverse because Congressman Dade from Nashville pilloried the Air Corps for intruding on the Navy's mission. But by the end of May, the "Aerial Arsenal" had accumulated more than forty relatively problem-free test hours and the best press backing any American warplane had ever received.

In Downey, Bandy, Patty, and Roget sat through a double feature to watch for a second time the Paramount newsreel which showed Hitler and what seemed like all sixty million Germans saluting, shots of nubile starlets traveling on the *Queen Mary*, a fashion show, and the big Hafner bomber. There were only about ninety seconds of it on film, but they were absolutely devastating. The huge silver plane, with its finely tapered fuselage and four slender nacelles, flashed by in a high-speed low-level pass, then peeled up to land and park with light planes perched under each wing to emphasize its size. At both showings, the audience broke into spontaneous applause when the announcer said, "And here's a surprise—the giant Aerial Arsenal is flown by a lady pilot." Charlotte dropped down out of the cockpit and embraced Bruno Hafner as the scene faded out.

The three were silent as they drove back to the factory, terribly aware that Hafner Aircraft's fortunes were rising while Roget Aircraft's were declining. Patty felt awkward, falling between the stools of pride in her mother and concern for Bandy. Finally Hadley said, "Has anyone heard how Armand is doing?"

"He's recuperating. Charlotte wrote that Bruno pretends to be so worried about him that he won't let him hang around the factory at all. My guess is that he just wants to ease Armand out, for some reason."

Bandy said, "Caldwell's asked me to spend June and July in Dayton, flying the new crop of fighters. I'll be there during the bomber competition. I'll try to get a line on it, and let you know how it looks."

Patty froze. "Two months! I thought this was going to be like a reserve assignment, a few days every year. What gives?"

"I don't know. If we don't get some more orders for RC-3s, I may apply for active-duty status."

Bandfield's comment wasn't offhand. Roget Aircraft was once again hanging in the balance, its once blue skies tinged with red ink.

Sayville, Long Island/June 22, 1935

Bruno Hafner put the last suitcase into the Duesenberg's trunk and yelled: "Come on, Charlotte, we're late. Half the newsreel industry is waiting at the field for us to leave."

Charlotte ran out, a blond Myrna Loy dressed in white whip-cord jodhpurs and jacket, a matching white helmet in her hand. She was wearing her favorite red leather boots. Murray followed her with two more suitcases.

"Jesus, we're only going to be out there for a week! You didn't need to bring the whole wardrobe."

"The hell I don't. You'll have me set up every day with the papers, and I'll have to wear something different all the time."

"Murray, you take care of things here."

"Things" meant mostly Nellie, Bruno's dachshund, and Murray knew it.

"Sure, boss. I'll bring her out on the train with me."

Hafner slipped behind the wheel of his Duesenberg, a brand new Model J with a Bohman & Schwartz custom body. Despite its huge size, there was room only for two; Murray was going to have to drive out to the field in the sedan.

Charlotte climbed in the other side, and Hafner slipped the car into reverse. There was a shrieking howl of pain, and Murray cried: "Stop, you backed over Nellie!"

"Oh my God!" Hafner leaped from the car; Nellie was lying under the huge rear wheel of the Duesenberg, eyes wild, snapping, her back crushed.

"Here, baby, let Daddy—" Hafner screamed as Nellie's frenzied jaws closed on his hand.

"Get a blanket, Murray! We've got to get her to a vet!"

Murray looked at him in disbelief. Hafner was crying, his eyes streaming tears.

"You go on to the field, boss. I'll take care of her."

"Goddam you, get a blanket. Nobody is taking care of her but me."

Murray grabbed the lap robe from the car, and Hafner seized

the bumper in his hand. Exercising a fear-driven strength, he lifted the car so Nellie, now whimpering, could be pulled from beneath the wheel. The agonizing eight-mile drive to the vet passed in silence except for Hafner's frantic apologies to Nellie. Charlotte watched him in the mirror, amazed at the tenderness and the devotion he was showing, emotions he had never shown to her, or to anyone.

Wright Field, Ohio/June 24, 1935

It was six o'clock in the morning, and only two things kept Bandfield from being completely happy: being too far from Patty and too close to the bomber competition, where Hafner Aircraft was getting its mammoth bomber ready to make its first demonstration flight. The rest of his life was pure joy, for Caldwell had put him to work flying the new crop of Seversky and Curtiss fighters.

It galled him to see the bomber on the ramp. His only satisfaction was that he had heard that the Army was clearly dissatisfied with Hafner's paperwork submissions. Henry Caldwell, scrawnier than ever under the pressure of his work, filled him in.

"This bird is way overweight, Bandy, according to the rumors. Hafner says he's 'lost' the weight and balance history."

Bandfield shook his head. The weight and balance of an aircraft was absolutely vital; Hafner couldn't have "lost" it. He had talked to Charlotte earlier, and she had warned him, "Steer clear of him, Bandy. I think he's lost his mind. All he can talk about is that poor dog. When the vet told him he had to put her to sleep, he blubbered like a baby. He's just now beginning to get over it."

The hazy red June sunrise had stacked purple stratus clouds like rungs in a ladder. There was no wind, and the high grass made boots glisten with the heavy dew. Ground crews were checking the aircraft over; the engines were raucous in the dawn calm. Bruno was conferring with Rhoades at the edge of the runway. Bandy was scheduled to fly the Curtiss Model 75 again, and he sat quietly with Charlotte in the operations building, drinking coffee and chatting. Since his marriage to Patty, Charlotte had treated him like a son, and they had grown close.

"Are you sure you want to do this? That's a mighty big airplane."

She grinned at him. "Yes, my junior birdman, that's the whole point. It's about twice as big as anything Earhart has ever flown."

She tapped him on the arm and pointed out the window. "Have you noticed how good Dusty looks?"

"Yeah, I did notice. He's put on some weight."

"Believe it or not, I think I've got him to kick the habit, finally. After this competition, we're going directly to the Mayo Clinic for a full course of treatments. It's taken me years to get him to agree."

Bandy felt awkward about the revelation. "What will Bruno say about that?"

"He says it's a great idea. I think he's even more ready for a divorce than I am, God love him." She giggled and said, "God had better love him, because damn few humans do."

She reached over and patted his arm. "I'm glad Patty has you. I think Dusty and I will move away, go down South somewhere. I want to get him out of the New York environment."

"How about your flying? Are you willing to give that up?"

"Oh my God, yes. You knew I set a New York–Dayton record coming out. Going back I'm going to go for the altitude record, and next week I'll try some closed-course records. That will be enough to have even George Putnam throwing rocks at Amelia. And that will be enough for me."

Bandfield walked with her out to the airplane, sensing her eager nervousness. He could not detect any animosity at all in the discussion Hafner and Rhoades were having on how the flight would be conducted.

"Look, Dusty, don't do anything flashy. This first flight is for the brass, not the papers. Don't pick up the gear until you've passed the point where you can land, don't make any low passes. Just a gentle demonstration. Got it?"

Dusty was smiling. "Got it, Bruno. Don't worry about a thing."

A strange world, Bandfield thought as he did the walk-around inspection on his fighter. He kept an eye on the other airplane. Charlotte swung herself up into the fuselage, followed by Dusty Rhoades, Hafner, and another Air Corps test pilot, a young lieutenant named Joe Teague.

Bandy crawled into the Curtiss, adjusting his parachute and headset. The crew chief was an old friend, who asked, "What's bothering you, Bandy? You keep looking at the Hafner airplane like it's going to blow up.''

Bandy shrugged, and saw Teague drop out through the front compartment. Then Bruno appeared at the rear, his sharkskin suit rumpled, apparently having crawled through the fuselage and out the aft door. It seemed strange to Bandfield; he had been inside and seen how crowded the fuselage was. Hafner would have had to crawl over the center-section fuel tank and around the side of the bomb bay. He probably just wanted to be sure everything was stowed properly.

Bandfield's headset crackled. Radio communications were a new wrinkle at Wright Field competitions, and he was surprised at the clarity of the transmission when he heard Rhoades announce that they were ready for takeoff.

Inside the bomber, Charlotte motioned for Rhoades to lean over. She kissed him and whispered, ''This is the last competition, Dusty. After this we're going to settle down and live like normal people. Well, maybe like almost-normal people.''

Always all-business in the cockpit, Rhoades squeezed her hand and gave her a thumbs-up sign, then completed his checklist and nodded. She eased the throttles forward, and the huge Hafner bomber moved across the grass, the four propellers sending a spray of dew in shining curls over the wing as it gathered speed.

Charlotte said, ''Call out seventy-five miles per hour for me, Dusty,'' just as the nose of the bomber jerked off the ground in a rocketing climb. Both pilots shoved forward on the control column as the airplane trembled, not yet a hundred feet high.

Her voice calm, she said, ''Controls are locked.'' Dusty had placed his feet on the wheel and was pushing forward with all his strength when the airplane stalled. He didn't see Charlotte turn to him, didn't hear her say, ''I love you,'' as the airplane's nose merged with the earth.

Bandfield had watched unbelieving as the bomber broke ground at about sixty miles an hour, pulling up so sharply that he could see the full outline of the wing, the engines racing, smoke pouring back from the exhausts. Bandy heard Charlotte's call about the control locks just before the aircraft shuddered and pitched violently forward to dive vertically, crashing just inside the field boundary. A black balloon of smoke and flame roared up as crash wagons started their claxons. Bandfield was transfixed, noting in surprise that he had seen the crows in the trees lining the field scatter in flight even before he had heard the explosion. Shoving the throttle forward, half flying, half taxiing, he hurried toward the wreck.

On the ramp, Hafner and Murray were hustled into a staff car that raced to the scene. Hafner sat sunk in the backseat while Murray perched forward, tears in his eyes. He turned and drove his fist into Hafner's face.

"You bastard, you killed her! It was the control locks, wasn't it? You stupid crazy bastard, you cared more about that goddam dog than you did about Charlotte!"

He hit him again, and Hafner made no move. A young captain leaned back and grabbed Murray's arm as they pulled up to the site.

Bandy stopped one hundred yards from the crash. By the time he was out of the airplane and running toward the flames, he knew it was too late for anyone to help. The bomber had impacted vertically, and the flames consumed it from the nose to the tail. The only recognizable parts were the wingtips, propellers, and the outline of the rudder.

Murray had rushed toward the crash site. A fireman was restraining him when a secondary explosion knocked them both flat, the wall of flame broiling Murray's face and hands.

Within an hour, the fire had died sufficiently for the crash-investigating team to take a preliminary look. The internal control lock had kept the elevator firmly fixed in the full-up position. No matter how strong Charlotte and Rhoades had been, they could never have broken it loose.

Bandy stayed until the firemen, using their long steel hooks, dragged the charred lumps from the crash. Then he went back into the operations shack to telephone Patty. In the brief time since the crash, the reporters had flooded the news circuits, and the operators were busy, handling the deluge of calls. Henry Caldwell came in and shoved a photo, still wet from the developer, across the table at him. "Our photographer snapped this right at the top of its climb. You can see that the controls are locked."

Bandfield tapped the picture of the elevator with his finger. "Full up. She never had a chance." He paused, then asked, "How is Bruno taking this?"

"He and Murray both acted like they were crazy. Murray was badly burned, had to go to the hospital. Then Bruno climbed into a staff-car ambulance and demanded to be taken into town. He really depended on Charlotte, didn't he?"

Bandfield could tell that something was behind Caldwell's

questions. He nodded his head yes, as Patty came on the telephone line. "Bad news, honey."

There was silence on the other end, then a single anguished sob. Patty's voice was weak as she asked, "A crash?"

"Yes. On takeoff. Nobody had a chance."

The sobbing came more deeply now. Bandfield's heart constricted in sympathy.

"Oh, God. I knew it would happen someday. What was it, engine failure?"

He waited, picturing her as she cried, her eyes closed, tears welling down her face. He said, "We don't know yet what happened. The main thing was that she didn't suffer, honey. It was instantaneous."

There was a silence, and he could feel her gathering herself together, calling on that magnificent inner strength.

"Call me later, will you? I just need to cry now."

"You shouldn't be alone. I'll get there as soon as I can."

"I'll be all right. Call back in an hour. I love you."

He hung up, sorrowing more for Patty than for Charlotte.

Caldwell had stood, head down, during the conversation, thinking of Charlotte in the A-11, of her dash in flying in the amphibian. Now she was gone, like so many others, in an inexplicable instant.

Caldwell cleared his throat and managed to say, "This was awful, Bandy, the worst I've seen. Tough luck, Bandy. She was a great woman."

He took a deep breath and went on. "Apparently Dusty Rhoades had no next of kin. We don't know who to contact. Do you know anyone?"

Bandfield shook his head as a deep inner grief seared him. He'd seen accidents like this so many times in the past. He wondered how often he would have to see them in the future.

Beaten as if he'd run a marathon, Bandfield had just thrown himself down on his hotel-room bed when the phone rang.

"Caldwell here. Come out to base headquarters, right now."

"Jesus, Henry, can't it wait? There's nothing we can do for anybody now."

"Oh yeah? Just get your ass out here, now."

Bandfield drove to Wright Field in a daze, trying to put some reasonable meaning on the day's events. An interminable Illinois Central freight train had kept him stalled as it rumbled past, sparks flying. When it cleared, he charged forward into sharp consciousness when a passenger train, hidden by the freight cars, roared by behind his rear bumper. He stumbled, unshaven and still in his smoke-stained flying suit, past some tight-lipped military police into the base commander's office.

The suspended incandescent lights barely burned through the fog of cigarette smoke, casting long dark shadows like those in a Howard Hawks movie. Grim-faced military policemen stood at parade rest around the walls. In the center, at a brightly polished wooden table, sat Murray Roehlk, one arm pillowing his square head, the other dangling straight down. Bandfield could see that he had been crying.

"What's going on, Henry? What's going on with Murray?"

Caldwell raised his voice. "The little bastard is under arrest. And Bruno Hafner is gone."

"Slow down, Henry, I don't follow you. What's with Murray?"

"The son of a bitch sabotaged the aircraft and murdered two innocent people."

Murray roused himself like a wounded bull seal protecting his harem, shook his head, and shouted, "I didn't. It was Hafner. I wouldn't never have hurt Charlotte. I idolized that woman. She was a living saint."

Time seemed to stand still for Bandfield. He looked at Murray in amazement. He had never seen the man express any emotion before. Now his face, burned and blackened, partially covered with bandages already needing changing, was filled with a bitter mixture of sorrow at Charlotte's death and livid rage that Caldwell was detaining him.

And Henry Caldwell had changed as well. His face was a mask of suppressed fury and blind hate, as if Murray were the one man in the world upon whom he could vent all his frustrations.

"I'll living saint you, you sawed-off gorilla! We've got a witness that says Charlotte had unlocked the controls. Lieutenant Teague says he saw her move the safety lever before he got out of the cockpit."

Roehlk turned on him, his eyes savage with hate. Bandfield felt that either man would have killed the other without a second thought. "Yeah, and that's what I'm telling you. That's why Hafner went out the back. He must have manually reinserted the control lock."

Caldwell's brow furled in fury. "I don't believe you. I don't believe one goddam thing you say!"

"Wait a minute, Henry. I saw Hafner come out the back of the airplane. He might have done it then. Where is Hafner? Why don't we question him?"

"We don't know. He's just disappeared."

Caldwell turned and jabbed his finger in Murray's face. "And he's left Roehlk to take the fall. Somebody is going to fry for this, and it might as well be you." Roehlk turned as pale as the burns and dirt would let him.

Caldwell took Bandfield into the dreary room next door. "The two MPs working him over will get the truth out of him. Would you call Armand Bineau? See if you can find out what might have happened, if Hafner could have done something to sabotage the airplane."

Bandfield let his eyes wander over the room's standard austere Air Corps decor, white-enameled overhead reflectors, painfully plain brown furniture, and dismal beige walls, as he waited for the call to Bineau to go through.

When his voice came over the phone, weak and tearful, Bandfield was almost sorry he had called. After some preliminary commiseration, Bandy asked, "Mr. Bineau, what I have to ask sounds terrible, but you are the only one I can turn to. Was there any way someone could have manually reinserted the control lock after the pilot removed it with the normal system?"

Bineau's voice was almost audible. "Let me think. Yes, perhaps. If one knew the system, one could. There is a connection just aft of the bomb bay. It is a knurled nut, a union. If someone disconnected the push rod there, it would be easy to reinsert the remaining part manually in the tail of the airplane. It would lock the rudder and the elevator, but, of course, not the ailerons."

Bandfield probed, "And the pilots wouldn't have been able to tell, would they?"

"No, they would have been holding the wheel full back, to keep the tail down. They wouldn't have become aware of it until the takeoff run."

There was silence, and Bandfield asked, "In the ordinary course of events, would Captain Hafner have been familiar with the system?"

"Why yes, it was his baby from the start. I didn't want the extra weight and complexity." Suddenly, anxiety strengthened the timbre of Bineau's voice. "Are you saying this was sabotage?"

"I don't know. Please don't say anything about this to anyone. I'll keep you informed."

He hung up the old-fashioned upright phone and said, "God, Henry, I probably gave him another heart attack, poor guy. He says it could have been done, that Hafner was familiar with the system."

"Yeah. After Charlotte had unlocked the controls, Hafner could have disconnected the push rod, then put the end of the rod back into the elevator-control lock. Neither Charlotte or Dusty would have been able to tell it was in place."

"That's why the ailerons were unlocked. The whole thing's incredible. Why would he do it? He tossed away a multimillion-dollar contract."

Caldwell shook his head. "Nothing figures."

They walked back in, and Roehlk snarled, "Jesus, man, don't you see it? How fucking blind can you be? He sabotaged the airplane, he killed Charlotte."

Caldwell set a bottle of Black & White on the desk. He poured a shot for Bandy, and took one himself. He hesitated, then poured a generous measure for Murray. Maybe it would loosen him up.

"What makes you say this? How do you know?"

Roehlk downed the scotch, coughing. "I know because I know what a rotten bastard he is."

Even from across the desk, Murray smelled terrible, a ferocious combination of fear, hate, burned flesh, and unwashed body somehow adding plausibility to his story.

Caldwell said, "Why would he destroy his own airplane, Roehlk? He was sure to win, to get millions in future orders."

"The goddam thing was four thousand pounds overweight. He wanted it to crash. He figured the Army would be impressed enough with the paper performance to finance a second prototype."

He was silent for a moment, obviously puzzling things out in his mind. "It figures for another reason, you know. Maybe he didn't want to win. He's been draining all his companies of cash for the last two years. I don't know what he does with it. He had me doing a lot of the work, but he's siphoned off most of the money and squirreled it away. Hafner Aircraft is damn near bankrupt. After the crash, it probably is."

Caldwell turned to one of the young officers. "See if you can check that out with Hafner's accountants."

Bandfield asked, "But why would he get rid of Charlotte?"

Murray assumed a bulldog look, then put his head down in his hands. He couldn't bring himself to talk about Charlotte.

There was no way they could understand. Murray was pretty sure that Charlotte and Dusty had been planning to run off together. God, that would have hurt. Maybe it was better that they crashed.

Bandfield whispered to Caldwell, "He's been carrying a torch for Charlotte for years. This really hits him hard."

"Jesus, that's creepy."

"Yeah, well, look at him. He's a creep, all right."

Roehlk raised his head, and Caldwell asked, "Where do you think Hafner's gone, Murray?"

Roehlk started to reply, then caught himself. He'd probably already said too much. He was going to need all the information he had to bargain with. If they started checking into some of Hafner's other activities, the trail would lead back to him.

"I don't know. Let me go. I'll find him for you. He probably went to California. Or Germany maybe. He was always talking about how great it was in Germany."

Bandfield tried a different tack. "I don't believe you, Murray. I think you probably sabotaged the airplane. You were more upset about Dusty and Charlotte's affair than he was."

Roehlk reacted. "That's not so. No matter how much I hated Dusty, I'd never do anything to hurt Charlotte."

"No. Hafner had been an officer, he was a prosperous businessman. It doesn't make sense for him to do this. As much as I don't like him, I don't think he would do anything like this."

Roehlk's face contorted, and he let the tears run. "If anyone believes me it ought to be you," he said, turning to Bandfield. "He's done a good job of screwing you over the years."

Murray moved his hand to cover his mouth and became completely silent.

Bandfield walked around the table and grabbed him by the throat. "Tell me what you know, you bastard, or I'll choke it out of you." His hands closed. Caldwell started to move forward, then stopped, signaling the military policemen to stand fast.

Roehlk tried to struggle, then croaked, "If I tell you, what's in it for me? Do I get some protection if this goes to court?"

Bandfield slammed him back in his seat. "I'll tell you what's in it for you. I won't kill you here, right now, if you start talking."

Caldwell waved him away. "Now Bandy, let's be reasonable and listen to what Murray has to say." He adopted an avuncular tone. "If you help us get Hafner, I can guarantee we'll give you full support at the murder trial.'' Caldwell's voice came down so hard on the word *murder* that Roehlk winced.

Murray was breathing heavily. Maybe the angle was to get Bandfield on his side, to make him so angry with Hafner that he would forget about everything else.

Rubbing his neck, he said, ''Jesus, Hafner has always done exactly what he's wanted to do. You were right about your airplane back at Roosevelt Field. He had me make a time bomb— I didn't know what it was for, thought one of the mobs wanted it. He stuck it in your airplane. That's why he didn't try to press charges when you slugged him. He figured you were onto the facts, and so he backed down.''

As he talked, a measured truculence surged back into his frame, and his squat body seemed to absorb power from the smoke-filled room.

Bandfield leaned forward, ''You're not telling me anything I didn't know, Murray. I thought he'd done it right from the start. Why are you bothering me with that sort of stuff?''

''I'm just trying to show you what kind of guy he was. He had no respect for life at all. Look what he did in Oakland.''

Bandfield's breath came in short gasps. He hesitated, then said very slowly, ''You mean in 1927, the Pineapple Derby?''

Murray nodded.

''What did he do then?''

''Well, you know he figured that Jack Winter was his only real competition. He had me make a timer.''

Bandfield felt an iron band constricting his chest, but he kept his voice calm. ''You put a bomb in their airplane?''

''No, it was a little battery-powered magnet. Hafner put it under the cowling, near the compass. A few hours after takeoff, the timer turned on, and gradually built up a current that pulled the compass in the wrong direction. It probably only took them fifteen or twenty degrees off, but it was enough.''

Bandfield snapped. He grabbed Murray by the throat again, shaking him. The MPs had to pry his fingers from Murray's throat.

''Let him go, Bandy. We've got enough on him to send him up for murder.''

''Where the hell is Hafner, then? I'm going to kill that murdering bastard.''

All of Bandfield's long years of frustration and anger poured through him in a tide of hatred, a wild frustrating rage that could only be assuaged with violence. He reached over and sent a fist smashing past the startled MPs into Roehlk's face. The little monster had just admitted complicity in arson and a multiple murder, and it hadn't even dawned on him that he'd done anything wrong.

Murray reeled, spitting blood. His voice was plaintive. "Say, listen, I just did what I was told. He never told me what he was using it for. Most of the time it was for the mob. But I could guess, afterward."

Bandfield realized that deep within he had always thought that Hafner might have had something to do with Millie's disappearance. He forced himself to regain control. He would fix things, once and for all.

"Where is Bruno now?" he repeated.

"I don't know. He kept getting calls from Washington right before the accident. And I think he kept most of the money stashed in his office in Farmingdale. He had a room there in the back with a big safe, wouldn't let anybody near it, not Charlotte, not anybody."

Bandfield grabbed Caldwell's arm. "I'm going after him, Henry."

Caldwell hesitated. Bandfield had his RC-3; he could be on Long Island in three or four hours. "Okay, I'll try to stop him if he's going by train." Caldwell went in the next room and came back with a Colt pistol. "I don't know if you know how to use this, Bandy, but you ought to have something. He's dangerous. Do you want anybody to go with you?"

Bandfield shook his head no.

En route to Farmingdale, Long Island/June 24, 1935

The volcano of hatred spewing within him kept Bandfield's fatigue at bay, permitting him to enjoy the speed of the P-36. He'd kept the throttle forward, and with the help of the tailwind, had been averaging 280 mph ground speed. The fuel gauges, always unreliable, wound down toward zero.

Caldwell was going to be furious when he realized that Bandfield had pulled the Curtiss pursuit out of the hangar, literally stealing it from the Air Corps. It was 80 mph faster than the RC-3, and he knew he didn't have a minute to waste.

Bandfield checked his options. The best thing would be to capture Hafner, to bring him to trial. But Hafner was too smart, and had too much money. He might get off. The only reasonable course was to put an end to Hafner's depravity, to kill him in cold blood.

Bandfield resolved not to give himself the luxury of letting Hafner know what was coming. It would be nice to toy with him, to make him suffer as Millie must have suffered, knowing that death was coming. But Hafner was too tricky, too powerful to play with. He would kill him as soon as he found him, just as he used to shoot rats at the junk pile.

The weather was decent, at least. He wondered if Caldwell was doing any good trying to stop Hafner on the ground. He'd feel pretty foolish having flown across country in the middle of the night if the FBI picked Hafner up in Dayton.

Wright Field, Ohio/June 24, 1935

Henry Caldwell slammed the phone down. He'd contacted everyone he could think of—the FBI, the Farmingdale sheriff's office, the MPs at Mitchell Field—and not one of them had been any help so far. Hafner had vanished into thin air.

The railroads had been the best; they had quickly checked the trains leaving Dayton that Hafner might have boarded, and there was no trace of him. Even using an assumed name, Hafner was such a giant of a man that the conductors would have remembered him.

The police in New York had been friendly, but uncooperative. He had his first stroke of luck when he finally persuaded the local sheriff to go out to the plant. He was waiting to hear from him. Maybe they could at least find out where Hafner was headed.

Caldwell's hunch was that he was going back to Germany, sure as hell. It was the only thing that made sense in the whole dismal mess.

Exhausted, Caldwell looked at Murray and turned to the guards. "Put this animal in a cell and maintain a twenty-four-hour guard. Make sure you take his belt and stuff from him. We'll need him for a witness."

Farmingdale, Long Island/June 24, 1935

Bruno Hafner paused, confident that he had all the time in the world, and trying to be sure he had left nothing to chance. The factory was deserted, except for the night watchman he'd sent off to town on a bogus errand. Sitting outside, just refueled, was the rented Vega he'd had waiting for him in Columbus, Ohio. Between the bus ride to Columbus and the flight out in the Vega, he hadn't had time to eat, and his stomach was growling. He'd grab a bite later.

All he had to do was trundle the little parts cart, filled with diplomatic pouches stuffed with currency, out to the Vega. A quick trip to Canada, to the German embassy in Ottawa, and he was on his way home.

Things had gone incredibly well, except for that cretin Murray's reaction. He wondered where he was. He was too smart to go to Caldwell or the police, but they'd probably picked him up by now. They had nothing on him, and Murray couldn't talk without indicting himself. The *Dummkopf* would probably show up at Charlotte's grave every year with a bouquet, the way the stupid women did with Valentino.

He stowed the pouches and took the cart back to the building. With one last glance around the deserted plant, he said, *"Auf Wiedersehen."*

Bandfield's eyes were heavy, but a single thought of Hafner would send the adrenaline of hate rushing through him. The man had ruined so many lives, for such little purpose. Bandfield shuddered in revulsion when he realized that Millie could have been circling in the Vega, knowing she was doomed, for eight or nine hours after he had landed at Wheeler Field, and for four or five hours after Hafner had been found.

It must have been nightmarish for Winter and Gordon, too, anxiously checking the horizon for any sign of the islands. He wondered if they sensed what had happened.

And now this crazy business. Why had he killed Charlotte and Dusty? Hafner had known about them for years, and seemed to enjoy the relationship in some perverse way. Then suddenly, for no apparent reason, he killed them both, and destroyed his company as well.

Bandfield wished he were more familiar with the Curtiss he was flying; he had just guessed at the cruise power settings, and it was obviously using fuel faster than he had planned for. Band-

field turned the selector which gave readings on the fuel tanks—
two main and two auxiliary—and they read the same as they had
thirty minutes ago: zero, zero, zero, and zero.

He adjusted his parachute. If the engine quit before he got to
the field, he'd jump and let the shiny new Curtiss auger in
somewhere in the countryside, and face Caldwell's wrath later.
Stealing a modern Army fighter shouldn't be worth more than a
ten-year jail sentence, twenty if he crashed. At the moment, a
term in jail sounded rather peaceful.

The fatigue that had gnawed at him as a bulldog gnaws a bone
disappeared when he recognized the outline of Hafner's field at
Farmingdale. It looked exactly like the little chart they'd drawn
for him at the Wright base operations, a rectangle lit on three
sides by roads. He was surprised that the boundary lights were
on.

The field had popped up suddenly, and he was high; with
exquisite timing, the engine coughed and quit as he started his
descent. He tapped the fuel gauges and switched tanks again,
knowing it was useless to do so. Bandfield ran a quick estimate
of his height, his airspeed, and the distance he had to go, wishing he knew which way the wind was blowing.

The Curtiss was silently sweet, a four-thousand-pound glider
reaching down through the stray cirrus clouds to reach a perfect
approach path to Farmingdale. As he passed through three hundred feet, he saw that he had the field made and put the gear
down while sliding his canopy back. Twenty seconds later, he
saw that he was a little high, allowing the luxury of twenty
degrees of flaps. A night dead-stick landing in a strange airplane
at a strange field after almost twenty-four hours of nervous tension—this might be interesting.

At two hundred feet he saw the blur of another airplane pass
underneath him, exhaust torching.

Bandfield's Curtiss touched down, bounced, and rolled to a
stop. He looked back to see in the distance the dim red winking
of a disappearing exhaust.

No one came out to meet him, and he abandoned the Curtiss
in the middle of the field. As he reached the factory, the guard
had returned, rolling through the gate in a Graham sedan. He
was puzzled to find Bandfield there and Hafner gone.

Bandy yelled, "Have you seen Hafner?"

The other man peered suspiciously at the wild-eyed Bandfield, nearly hysterical and staggering from fatigue. Bandfield

had to produce his Air Corps identification before the guard would talk.

"Sure, Mr. Hafner was here. He had a beat-up old Lockheed Vega that I helped him fuel. Then he sent me into town."

Frustrated, Bandfield said, "I just saw someone take off."

"If you saw a plane leaving, it had to be him." It was obviously all he knew.

The sheriff arrived, fuming about the nasty Army major who had cursed him out on the telephone, and they searched Hafner's offices together, finding nothing. Bandfield got a call through to Caldwell in Dayton.

"I'm glad you called, Bandy. I want you to drop whatever you're doing and come back to Dayton. And bring that fighter plane you stole back with you in one piece. If anything happens to it, it will be your neck, and even worse, mine."

"Have you caught Hafner?"

"Forget about him. The word has come down from the State Department that we are to ignore the whole thing. I guess there are wheels within wheels. I don't understand it, but apparently the German ambassador has intervened, and State is anxious to keep him happy."

"How could they know to intervene unless he'd set it up? This proves that man is a murderer, a saboteur, a traitor."

"Can't hear you, Bandy. Must be the line. Is the Curtiss okay? Can you fly it back?"

"Yeah, it just needs fuel and oil. I'll get a few hours' sleep and then take off."

Caldwell hesitated, then said, "No, you stay there. I'll send someone up for the airplane. I talked to Patty, and she wants you to help with the funeral arrangements. No sense in your coming back here."

"Thanks, Henry. But keep me posted on Hafner."

"Right. And don't go off half cocked. The guy from State didn't mince any words about letting things cool down. It's serious, Bandy."

Bandfield said good-bye and tossed the phone across the room, the cord bringing it up short and crashing it to the floor.

"That louse Hafner never loses! I'll get him if I have to go to Berlin to do it!"

Sayville, Long Island/June 27, 1935

Bandfield was surprised at how well Patty was bearing up. She had apparently cried herself out, and was now grimly bent on providing Charlotte and Dusty with a first-class funeral in Charlotte Morgan Hafner style.

Given all the twists of circumstance, especially Hafner's role in the accident and his mysterious departure, Bandy had tried to talk Patty into a quiet burial with a private service.

"Absolutely not! Mother enjoyed life to the fullest, and I'm going to give her a proper send-off."

"Most people won't think it proper to have one ceremony for both her and Dusty. No one is going to think it proper to bury them side by side."

"That's just too damn bad. They wanted to be together in life, and couldn't; they can be together in death."

Part of Patty's defense mechanism involved completely ignoring the existence or the whereabouts of Bruno Hafner. Not only had he ceased to exist in Patty's world, she expunged all references to him from the past. Bandfield had returned to Charlotte's home on Long Island just as a big moving van was leaving. When he asked Patty what was in the van, she replied, "Nothing, nothing at all."

Once in the house, Bandfield knew immediately what she had done. There was not a photo, a single piece of furniture, or a scrap of clothing that had any particular relationship to Bruno. Even the photographic laboratory had been cleaned out. Bruno Hafner had been erased from his own house as cleanly and completely as a wet cloth wipes off a blackboard.

"I want you to make the funeral arrangements. We'll have the ceremony here—I know a Unitarian clergyman who will officiate. He was a friend of Mother's, a 'very good friend,' I think. I've already purchased the burial lots."

"Honey, I'm glad to help, but I think you're making too much of this."

"No, I'm not. I'm her daughter, and I know what she would have wanted."

Bandfield had gone to the stately Kassly Funeral Home, a three-story red brick building with a huge terrace that encompassed two sides of the structure. Inside he met Everett Kassly, a gelatin-mold man seemingly held together only by his clothing and a skin translucent as a smear of vaseline. Thin blond ringlets topped a too-smooth Campbell-soup-kid face that welled up into a purse of pink lips, perfect for a voice that could have oiled the rust off the *Titanic*. He looked as if he had never lifted a finger to help himself or anyone else.

Kassly led Bandfield into the cool chill of the funeral home's basement to a showroom of caskets ranging from plain walnut-colored plywood boxes to satin-lined and organdy-pleated confections that would have pleased Madame Pompadour.

"This is our finest model, the Berkshire. It—"

"Don't tell me about it. Just give me two of the most expensive."

"Two? Of the most expensive?" Kassly's unctuous voice churned from cream to butter.

"Yes. What else do you offer?"

Kassly's face lit up. "Well, we always recommend a protective vault. My personal favorite is the Grant model. I can show you some literature—"

"Is the Grant the most expensive?"

"Why yes, but—"

"Then make it two Grants."

Later in the violet sachet-scented leather-bound comfort of Kassly's office, Bandfield watched without expression as the funeral director ticked off all the things Bandfield had agreed to, from the open floral carriage to the eight limousines to the children's choir. Kassly's hands were trembling, but his eyes sparkled as he said, "You've done a magnificent job, Mr. Bandfield. I know your mother-in-law would be—" He hesitated and raised his eyes heavenward, "—*is* pleased."

Bandfield brought out his checkbook. "The one thing my wife was insistent on was a complete forest of white roses for her coffin, and red roses for his. I don't want just a few floral arrangements, I want both coffins and the background to be a sea of roses."

"Don't worry about a thing."

"Understand me now—there can't be too many, but I'll be upset if there are too few. Lots of roses!"

"Lots of roses."

Two days later, Bandfield stood listening to the Reverend Gerald Robins's eulogy and admiring the way the red-faced prelate tiptoed around the fact that he was praising a woman and her lover in her husband's home. Everett Kassly had taken him seriously. The two closed caskets were covered with white and red roses, and the room was banked with huge quantities done in every conceivable manner, from straight bouquets to woven blankets.

The problem was that the home was far too small. Patty had had no idea of the affection in which Charlotte was held by the work force at the Hafner factory. The crowd filled up the large living room where Patty had insisted the caskets be placed and flowed out past the porches onto the lawn.

Praying was difficult for Bandfield, but he went through his small portfolio of remembered prayers and lifted a few others from some books the Unitarian clergyman had scattered about. His principal difficulty was addressing the memories. Charlotte had been beautiful, lusty, full of life, quick to laugh and quick to anger. Dusty . . . long ago, Dusty had been handsome and strong, with a good Irish wit. Lately he had suffered, but he had been coming back. It was hard to reconcile the two of them with the little bits of burned bone and gristle that he knew were wrapped and folded within the handsome Berkshire caskets. It was a mistake to hold funerals for pilots, he thought; the earth should just be heaped over where they crash, letting them lie amalgamated with the wrecks of their airplanes. He wondered what other profession demanded the steady toll of lives for participation—the police probably, firemen perhaps, a few others. Did people pursue these jobs because of the danger or in spite of it?

Patty squeezed in beside him. He patted her hand. "You okay?"

"Yes, but I've had some more bad news. Eleanor Bineau called. Armand is sinking, and she doesn't think he'll make it."

"God, how awful. Anything we can do?"

She shook her head, and he tried to change the subject. "Charlotte would have been so pleased to know so many aviation celebrities would show up."

Patty nodded. Amelia Earhart was there, clearly as a favor to Patty. There were dozens of other famous flyers—Bernt Balchen, Jimmy Mattern, Bobbie Trout—but Patty was touched even more by something else.

"Look! How pleased Charlotte would have been!" With a small wave of her hand she pointed to the rear of the crowd, where the entire work force of the factory, painfully dressed up in their Sunday best, were on hand.

"She would have loved it!" Bandy replied.

There were dozens of floral offerings which reflected the imagination and taste of the flying community, everything from huge wings made out of blood-red roses to towering horseshoes of flowers that would have flattered a Kentucky Derby winner.

The ride to the cemetery turned into a logistic nightmare when more than a hundred cars followed the hearse. Charlotte and Dusty had been committed to their last resting place together before the last car had parked. The minister had kept the service mercifully brief.

As Patty got back in the limousine she said, "Now comes the fun part, the part Charlotte would have loved."

They returned to the house. While they had been at the cemetery a huge crew had removed all the funeral flowers and replaced them with flowering shrubs in pots. A band was almost ready to play, and huge tables, groaning with food, were already set up. In every corner were tubs of ice packed with Veuve Cliquot champagne.

"Mother always said that there was no place like a funeral to really enjoy yourself, and she always wanted Veuve Cliquot—the widow—served at her own."

Bandfield squeezed her hand and followed her in. The crowd's tone had changed. Gone were the murmured "So sorry" and "You have my deepest sympathy" set-piece speeches. Instead the noise level began its steady rise as glasses clinked and nicknames were shouted in greeting.

"You've done a great job, Bandy. Thanks. She would have enjoyed it."

"You too. I hope it's helped you."

Patty was smiling as she drifted off to work the crowd. Bandfield thought to himself, The only way this could be improved would be to have Bruno's head served with an apple in his mouth.

PART THREE

DESPERATE ODDS

10

Karlsruhe, Germany/March 26, 1936

He was quietly pleased by the respectful glances the old soldiers were giving his Great War decorations. Unlike the new ribbon around his neck for the Blue Max, they were slightly worn and made a handsome contrast with his perfectly tailored brand-new Luftwaffe uniform. Lieutenant Colonel Bruno Hafner settled comfortably back in his seat to watch the master at work once again.

As he had been every night of his whirlwind tour of Germany, Adolf Hitler was engaged in a miracle of oratory. Like a great conductor, he transformed the multilegged, single-voiced animal of an audience into a steaming, sweating pipe organ that exultantly played his new tune: honor had been restored to Germany! The March 7 remilitarization of the Rhineland, conceived by Hitler and carried out over the objections of his military advisers, had redeemed the glories of Sedan and Tannenberg. The guttural voice, so implicit with threat and promise, sank to a low throbbing, a masturbatory keening that crawled into the souls of the bright-faced, cropped-haired Nazis jamming the hall.

Hafner sat in detached amusement. Charlotte had finally persuaded him that daily baths were essential; she would have had her work cut out for her here. He held a cologne-soaked handkerchief to his nose, watching the crowd rather than listening to the speech.

"What I have done, I did according to my conscience." There was a collective sob. The words *honor, honor, honor* came crashing down, turning the shabby potbellied listeners into convulsively cheering knights, ready for the Thousand-Year Crusade.

The moment was coming. Hitler closed, as he had each night, with a pious touch: "And should unnecessary sorrow or suffering ever come to my people because of my actions, then I beseech Almighty God to punish me."

The end came with the characteristic flourish of head and arm, the multiple cheers, the endless volleys of *"Sieg Heil!"* Hafner was on his feet cheering with the rest of them, until the sweat-soaked Hitler broke for the wings. As soon as he did, Hafner hustled outside, anxious to see the next part of the spectacle. Right on cue, mirror-silver in searchlights, the latest triumph of Nazi technology, the Zeppelin LZ 134, the *Hindenburg*, appeared. It hung, silent, phallic, ominous, a great gray dumpling awash in the rain-soaked clouds, threatening not with its weaponry—it carried none—but with an implicit incendiary threat that it, like the Nazis, might suddenly go up in flames.

Joseph Goebbels, knowing the limited deductive capacity of his audience, hammered home the association of the old and the new. The whitewash of the searchlights splashed an iridescent set of circles dancing from the huge dark letters forward, spelling out the magic name of Hindenburg all the way aft to the gleaming black-red-and-white swastika insignia on the gigantic tail fins. It said, more clearly than any poster, that Germany was awake and powerful in the partnership of Reich President Hindenburg's tradition and Hitler's leadership. Yet the cheers became less frantic; with Hitler gone, a more imperious call came from the beerhalls.

Hafner was glad that the Luftwaffe group seconded to the tour would have a night's respite. Hitler was going back to Berlin to orchestrate the plebiscite on his actions in the Rhineland.

As he pulled his boots off in the hotel room, Hafner mused on the whole crazy business. The man the great Field Marshal Paul von Hindenburg und Beneckendorff had dismissed as "the Bohemian corporal" had done what no one else had dared to do—rearmed Germany and torn up the Versailles Treaty. And he had done it with an empty bluff, a few regiments of soldiers, a few squadrons of mostly unarmed airplanes.

He flopped on his bed exhausted. The business of being an expert had turned into an endless day-and-night round of back-breaking work and travel.

Hitler's close-run gamble had turned out to be a personal gold mine for Hafner. On three separate occasions, calls had come in to him, one each from *Generalleutnant* Wever—the little man was on a fast track; he'd been a colonel last year!—from Milch, and even from Goering himself.

The Luftwaffe had fielded three *Staffeln*—two fighters and one dive bomber—to cover the handful of jackbooted troops marching across the bridges into the Rhineland. Hafner had been assigned the task of getting the flying units on a wartime footing. It had been a joke; they were so unprepared that Hitler Youth footing would have been more like it. But when Wever called, worried about ammunition, Hafner had managed to get a truck filled with links for the fighter squadron's guns all the way to the new base near Cologne, Köln-Butzweilerhof. When Milch had called, frantic that the Heinkel fighters of *Jagdgeschwader* 134—the Horst Wessel wing—needed gunsights, he had stripped the training units and had them installed in eight hours. And when Goering called, needing an answer to the Fuehrer's question whether the Junkers Ju-52 squadrons standing by could fly to Paris with a bomb load, he had been able to tell him yes— just barely!

The result had been this plum of a trip, with its unexpected side benefit. Little Dr. Goebbels had opposed the Rhineland initiative initially, but had quickly come around when he saw that Hitler was adamant. To make up for this uncharacteristic gaffe, he had seen to it that Hitler's triumphal sweep around the country was well attended by good-looking young movie ac-tresses.

Hafner had met one, Lili Behrens, and they had immediately fallen into bed and into love. She was not the approved tall blond Nordic type, but instead dark, sinewy, and thoroughly delicious. Now Germany was complete, for she promised to fulfill all his needs. She was as good in bed as Charlotte, and might well prove to be as faithful and useful as Murray Roehlk. Best of all, Hitler himself had pronounced her an "artiste" and was backing her career. Hafner suspected that Goebbels might have provided a little career backing on the UFA casting couches, but that was all to the good. Altogether, a fine week's work.

He took a quick bath and put on a dressing gown, as he tried to sort out whether or not the fast-moving events—the Rhineland, Italy's fight in Ethiopia, Germany's leaving the League of Nations—were good or bad for him. The pyramidal expansion of forces would help, but a war before Germany was prepared would be disastrous. He'd been on the losing side once before. The only thing to hope was that Hitler was as smart as most people said he was, that he'd keep them out of war until 1943. That would be perfect. The big bombers would be ready, and the long-range fighters, not just built, but with crews trained to use them.

Hafner shifted his thoughts from the future to the past. He had never really left Germany, never left the military. Versailles had sent him to America as surely as it had carved western Poland out of German soil. Now that he was back, he could see that it had been for the best. He could never have learned in postwar Germany what he had learned in postwar America. He had kept in the forefront of the Lindbergh boom, and now he had much to offer the Fatherland.

Nor could he have become wealthy in Germany. America had made him rich. He felt a brief sorrow that his parents had not lived to be with him. He would like to have restored their house and their fortunes.

He shook his head impatiently at the remembrance of the American press's pious condemnations of the Nazis. The Nazi tactics had been pioneered in the gangs that ruled Chicago and New York; they were different from the Brownshirts in Munich and Berlin only in motivation. In America it was money, pure and simple. In Germany it was politics.

There was a tapping at the door. Lili.

Downey, California/September 6, 1936

"It's good to have you back, Bandy, even for a little while. How are you finding Wright Field as a place to work?"

"I'd work there for nothing, Hadley, if I had to. The bureaucracy drives me crazy, but the Army people are first-rate. I'm sure you used to feel the same way."

Roget pulled Bandfield over to the window and pointed down onto the factory floor. "It doesn't look much different from last year, does it?"

"No. Same old problems, I guess?"

"Yeah—no money, slow pay from the government, and Douglas beating us out of every order for a transport."

Bandfield shrugged his shoulders. "Nobody ever said that the airplane business would be easy."

"I thought we were getting a little reprieve last year after Charlotte's accident."

Bandfield silently agreed. The Air Corps had awarded Roget Aircraft a contract for eighteen RC-3s to be used for military cargo and passenger service. It was a godsend, but the work was just about finished now and there didn't seem to be anything else on the horizon.

"Take a look at this." Handley tossed a copy of the *Times* over to Bandy. "That's one record Patty didn't make this year."

There was a two-column spread announcing that Beryl Markham had flown solo from England to Nova Scotia.

Bandfield nodded. "Patty knows her, you know. She and Stephan met her when they took a tour of Africa. Patty says Beryl would have raped Stephan if she hadn't kept a firm hand on him."

The thought bemused him. Had she kept the same firm hand on Stephan that she used to keep on him, always tucked in his pants? Probably. Their relationship had changed dramatically since Charlotte's crash, and it was largely his fault. The obsession with Hafner was completely destroying his life.

Patty was offended by his preoccupation, and properly so. She had come to her own accommodation to the idea of her mother's death, had grieved deeply and then bounced back. He hadn't been able to help her at all—quite the reverse. Within a few weeks of the accident—the murder—she had tried in every way to get him out of his frustrating depression.

Their sex life had virtually ended. He was not impotent, they could come together for some banal relief, but the rollicking enjoyment was gone in his own despair.

She had insisted that his obsession with revenging himself on Hafner, and thus avenging Millie's death, was abnormal, and he had agreed to see a psychiatrist. Long, expensive sessions had not helped. Patty was turning from him to her own career, seeking from flying what he could no longer give her.

He shook the thoughts away. "This is the important stuff." He tapped his finger on a headline: "Fighting Intense at Alcazar." "Have you heard about Americans volunteering to go fight for the Loyalists?"

"Get that out of your head, Bandy, that's your old man talking. We have problems here that are more important than a bunch of spics fighting each other."

"It's more than that, Hadley," Bandfield said, ignoring the slur. "Caldwell's been briefing me, and the Germans and Italians are helping Franco out. I've got the urge to shed this paperwork and go do something useful."

Hadley was no dummy. "So that's it. You'll go to Spain and work yourself out of your depression, eh? Bandy, you're nuts. You've got to snap out of this. Don't go thinking about doing any fighting. That's a young man's game. You'd get over there and some square-head would shoot your ass off."

Bandfield turned him out as Hadley launched into one of his endless dirty stories, this one something about the British army wearing red coats so that the blood from wounds wouldn't scare people, and the Italian army wearing brown pants for a similar reason. Roget was annoyed when he didn't get the customary pro-forma laugh, and raised his voice.

"If you want to do something, sell one side or the other a whole bunch of airplanes. We've gone from bad to critical here."

The remark brought Bandfield back to the sorry present. "Who would have believed it, Hadley? That accountant guy came with a résumé from the bank that was good as gold, and references from some of the best people in town."

"Yeah, they should have been good—the schnook wrote them all himself."

During the last year, Bandfield had acquiesced to the new arrangement with Patty, submerging himself in a flurry of work attendant to the tidal wave of publicity that had deluged Patty's record setting. The good part was the income—she had contracts to make more money in 1936 than Roget Aircraft was going to earn. Every magazine carried pictures of her, usually dippy-looking pastels, enthusiastically endorsing Ivory Soap, Congoleum floors, Johnson's wax, and Auburn cars. She had refused to do cigarette advertisements, despite an offer from Camels that had made both their heads swim.

He had resigned himself to trailing his wife around, answering questions about her life, her breakfast-food preferences, whether she really drove an Auburn, or if she really used Pond's. He also had to ward off the handsome male would-be movie stars who had swarmed out of their back-alley dormitories just to get photographed as background in her publicity tours, and who all tried to interest her in their "careers."

To help out, he had hired a bright young man, Gerald Rosson, three years out of Columbia University, as their "chief accountant.'' That meant he supervised two clerks and took the load off Bandfield's back.

He'd also taken approximately $62,000 in cash before departing for parts unknown.

Roget grunted. ''I told you we should never have hired that guy. He was too damn polite.''

Bandfield pointed to the stack of correspondence on his desk. ''Well, he politely left so much fucking bad news that I can measure it with a ruler.''

Rosson not only had departed with the cash, but apparently in his brief two-month stay had run a brisk business ordering tools and materials and reselling them, neglecting to pay the vendors. Roget Aircraft's credit rating, which had taken so long to establish, went sour in a six-week period. Bandy, who had spent years watching every nickel he had, had let his preoccupation with Hafner and Patty's new career goad him into turning the place over to Rosson in blind faith.

Hadley leaped in, anxious to make a point. ''It's not all that crook's fault, either. Look at these!'' He picked up a handful of letters and pawed through them. ''The union is talking crazy— our labor rates are already higher than anyone else's in the industry, and they want a five-cent-an-hour raise!''

Bandfield agreed with him inwardly. A nickel an hour didn't sound like much, but even with the reduced work force, it would cost $250 a week, almost $13,000 per year! And Douglas was walking away with every sale that came along because of their prices. It didn't make sense and shook his faith in unions. The country's unemployment rate was nearly 20 percent—and his people wanted a raise.

''I told you we should never have let them in the shop.''

''Hadley, do you realize how fucking helpful it is for you to tell me all you told me, when the goddam business is coming down around my ears, and I'm acting like some sort of water boy for my wife?''

Hadley nodded with some satisfaction as Bandfield went on, ''If I'd always done what you said, we'd never have gotten big enough to go bankrupt. We'd have just gone bust in your old barn, the way we always did.''

It was true. Old Roget's mistakes would have kept them from getting big. Now they were so large that they had to have new contracts as an addict had to have drugs. Every contract that came in was immediately sent to the bank for discounting, and they lived from hand to mouth, scraping just to meet the payroll.

The $62,000 that Rosson had embezzled was the steel beam that broke the camel's back.

"We've been down before, Bandy. We'll get back up."

"Maybe. I don't know if it's worth it. You might have had the right idea, just building airplanes you liked to build for yourself, and fixing cars on the side for expenses."

Bandfield sighed. "I don't see how we'll survive much past the end of November. We're going belly-up unless we get a contract from somebody."

They moved to the window that overlooked the assembly bay. Compared to the days when they had started building the RC-3s, it seemed empty of workers. The rampant competition from Douglas had eaten up the market. They had to get another order for at least ten RC-3s, or they were out of the manufacturing business for a while. The worst thing, of course, was letting the people go. They might be able to get some subcontracting work from somebody, but there was damn little of it around. The staff could see what was happening—the better engineers and foremen had already left, picking up jobs where there were some live contracts.

The only bright spot was the tour the Air Corps had set up for him in Berlin. It offered the prospect of encountering Hafner, and was the one thing besides Patty that made life worth living. He had had enough of managing and running an aircraft factory to last a lifetime. The Air Corps problems were challenging, and for some reason the Air Corps listened to him.

Bandfield smiled painfully at the irony—the worse business got, the more famous he became and the more people paid attention to him. His old English teacher at Salinas had seen an article he'd written for *Popular Flying* and had written to compliment him, not hesitating to point out a few grammatical errors. Caldwell had invited him to Fort McNair to speak to the War College.

Much of it was a rub-off from Patty's success. In the last six months, she had completely eclipsed Earhart, Ruth Nichols, the whole lot of women flyers. God, after years of struggle, to wind up being his wife's spear-carrier. Still, the money wasn't bad.

Berlin, Germany/August 23, 1936

Sunday in Berlin. Lieutenant Colonel Bruno Hafner, anxious to get away from the Olympic hoopla, walked dejectedly along Unter den Linden, the wash of heat offset by the shade of the trees. It was hard to believe that the year that had begun so well was ending with such a totally shocking, impossible turn of events. Everything at the beginning—quietly removing his company funds, causing the crash, the furor roused at Luftwaffe headquarters by Howard Hughes's setting the speed record in the racer—seemed to have been orchestrated solely for his benefit.

He had embraced Nazi Germany, and the Fatherland had seemed intent on returning the favor. Symbolically, he had discarded everything he had ever owned from America. Over time, as he was able to replace them, he had shed all his clothes, wallet, cigarette cases and lighters, shoes. Everything was gone. In their place he had purchased the best of everything from the shops along the Kurfürstendamm.

And the house, a villa in Berlin-Zehlendorf! He had made arrangements to pick it up very reasonably from an emigrating Jewish couple. Udet had said it was too showy, that it would cause jealousy. Good. In his experience, for every jealous person there were four or five sycophants anxious for any crumbs. As a counterpoint, he had not bought a Mercedes; instead he'd acquired a little BMW 315/1 that would have fit in the trunk of his Duesenberg. A Mercedes would come later, perhaps a 500K *Sportwagen*. The advantage of having money was enormous; he could entertain on a scale far beyond his rank. And not needing to be promoted for economic reasons, he didn't have to conform so slavishly to the Luftwaffe's viewpoint. He could take an outsider's view, and get promoted even faster.

The difficulties had started almost at once. After initially welcoming him and getting him established, Udet became infuriated when then Colonel Wever arranged for a private interview. He had not wished to alienate Udet, but events made it necessary to go around him.

Ah, Wever! There had been a man! He had been quick to see the value of the bomber plans. Hafner selected a Monte Cristo cigar from the leather pouch he carried, cut it carefully, and lit it reflectively as he let his first conversation with Wever run again through his mind.

At the outset he had been nervous. Wever was an upright general-staff type, the best of the breed. Hafner wasn't sure how he'd regard a man who had left Germany after the war, when it was in such terrible distress, and then betrayed his new country.

It was a pointless worry. Wever clearly thought of him as the German patriot he was. He had the detailed drawings for the Hafner bomber spread out in front of him.

"Ah, Hafner, these plans can be the basis for our Ural bomber! It is exactly what we need. But that is not the only reason you are so welcome."

He had leaned forward, anxious to learn what this little man, with his nose and chin like a Punch and Judy doll, wanted.

"Please understand that this is not a criticism of our leadership." It was a remark that clearly forecast a criticism. "Unfortunately, most of them are fixed on the continent, bound up by Haushofer's geopolitics. Not one of them has traveled very much. I don't believe Hitler has been farther than the front lines of France. Goering went to Sweden for a while. Udet, God bless him, has traveled the world around, but has never seen past his cockpit or his barstool."

Wever had leaned forward and rapped savagely on the plans with the flat of his hand.

"But you have seen the United States, know how vast it is. You understand what it can produce. What we need from you is a sense of scale, to break us out of this Thirty Years War mentality."

The rest of the conversation had gone even more pleasantly. Hafner was to have the best of both worlds, a *Geschwader* to command, when the time came, and influence with the staff.

Characteristically direct, Wever came right to the point.

"Udet is out of his depth. I'm going to depend upon you for advice. He views the dive bomber as if it were a universal panacea! He even wants twin- and four-engine types to be able to dive-bomb."

Hafner was genuinely surprised. A twin-engine dive bomber was stretching it; one with four engines was quite absurd, even for Udet.

Wever had brought him to see Milch and Goering almost immediately, and then later, in November, he had had a short private audience with the Fuehrer in Munich. Goering had been thoroughly charming, attributing to him at once the crash-landing tactic they had used at Strasbourg. Altogether everything had been most satisfactory. Hitler had been friendly, amazingly well informed, and positive about both the need for the four-engine bomber and the new fighter. Either the man was brilliant or he had been carefully briefed. It didn't matter—either case boded well.

Hafner carefully dusted one of the benches that were placed in profusion along the sidewalk and sat down. His was provided in honor of "Corporal Anton Dietl, 1899–1917." Some wet-behind-the-ears *Lander*, dead before he was aware of life, memorialized only by the ass of anyone who cared to sit down.

He slammed his fist into his hand. Everything was coming to pieces. Poor Wever, killed in a crash, and Udet was already circling like a wolf, trying to scuttle the big-bomber concept.

He reached down and felt the small cylinder in his pants pocket. He never went without it, never left it anywhere. In it were the photos and the plans for the Hughes racer. There was a duplicate hidden in the garden shed of the house. The plane would make a good fighter and be a perfect encore to the bomber when it was underway. And if it didn't, if that *Schweinerei* Udet sabotaged him, he would offer the fighter to someone, Focke-Wulf probably. He had flown the Messerschmitt—a fine plane if they were always going to fight within the borders of the Reich! It had no legs, no range. The Hughes racer, scaled up slightly to carry military equipment, would be a far better bet when he found the right company to build it.

Hafner yawned and stretched, scratching himself under the arms at length. The truth was that he wasn't cut out for political intrigue. He considered himself a simple soldier. He had asked for combat duty in Spain, a squadron of fighters. The lust for combat roared through him, sitting him upright. He anticipated the old rush of pleasure in the headlong attack, the clattering guns, the bucking airplane ahead of him, shedding parts, bursting into flame. That was what he wanted, that was what he'd craved so long. And then Udet would be hard put to attack him. And his thoughts about modern warplanes would have a greater authority, enough perhaps ultimately to undermine Udet. He was far better qualified for the job than Erni. Despite the rapidly growing war in Spain, he'd been kept out of sight for the last three weeks, while the great Lindbergh had been conducted on a triumphal tour of the resurgent Reich. Apparently Lindbergh had accepted everything at face value. Each night, Hafner had gone over the recordings of all of Lindbergh's telephone calls, to see what opinions the famous flyer had formed. Lindbergh was clearly impressed by most of what he'd seen, but had said things about Goering's girth that had to be deleted in the official transcripts that went to "Der Dicke" each morning.

A pain crossed his stomach; he belched. If he didn't watch it, he'd be catching up to Goering. The German food was as good as he had remembered, the beer even better. He'd put on five kilos since he'd arrived, but the wise German tailors had made provision for a little gain in all his trousers.

The bellyache caused him to notice that his hands were locked together, almost cutting off the circulation. "Too tense," he muttered. "That's what's wrong with my gut." He forced himself to think of America, to think what he missed about it. Not Charlotte. He had not missed her for a moment; Lili Behrens more than made up for her. Not the work; his aircraft factory had become a zoo, with Bineau, before his illness at least, always a problem. The stupid competitions, the arguments with the airlines, were always annoying. The U.S. Army was difficult to deal with, but a *Dummkopf* like Mahew even more so.

He stood, snuffed out his cigar, and carefully placed it out of sight beneath a pile of leaves. He felt a sudden poignant sadness when he realized that in recalling America, the only thing he missed was Nellie, his darling Nellie. As soon as he was settled in, he'd get another dog. The Kaiser had kept dachshunds; he would too.

Washington, D.C./November 10, 1936

Sitting in the hard oak-bowed chair outside Lieutenant Colonel Caldwell's overheated office, Bandfield squirmed apprehensively in a little pool of sweat. Just off a long series of flights, he hadn't had a shower in two days, and his skin felt as crawly as the pit of his stomach. In the past week, he had managed to antagonize his wife even further, annoy the Army, and apparently infuriate his old friend Charles Lindbergh.

An imperturbable white-haired warrant officer, his stained tan shirt sleeves ringed with perspiration, said, "It shouldn't be too long now. With the business in Spain, the colonel's been on the phone all day."

The American embassy in Madrid had been abandoned two days earlier, and the military had been put on a conditional alert. The German Condor Legion, all "volunteers," had been bombing the city every day, and the Loyalist government had fled to Valencia. According to the briefing Caldwell had given him the week before, when he presented his report on his trip through

Germany, Americans were fighting for the Loyalists in the International Brigade.

That's what I ought to be doing, he thought. Anything would be better than the way things had gone the last six months. On the Coast, Roget Aircraft, in what had almost become an American aviation business tradition, had closed its production line, and was staying in business on a small scale only by subcontracts for parts from Douglas.

At first, Patty had leaped at the idea of a trip to Europe, hoping with him that it would put some life back into their marriage. He had ruined it by his insistence on pursuing the subject of Hafner's whereabouts. Instead of being a grand tour of the bright lights, a sort of early second honeymoon that might have brought Patty closer to him, it had turned into an endless, frustrating series of receptions and dinners, broken only by his forays into the field to look at airfields and factories.

The Germans had recognized Patty in her own right, and seen to it that she was fêted by the German women flyers, led by Hanna Reitsch. Hanna was a tiny woman with a great wide grin and a fanatical belief in the Nazis; she soon wore Patty into a propagandized frazzle. Patty had endured the first few days, then lapsed into a stoic acceptance.

Only the idyllic flight back on the *Hindenburg* had briefly restored their good humor. Initially ill at ease on the gigantic airship with its softly undulating motions, she had quickly taken to the quiet, attentive service.

They had cast off into gray skies from Frankfurt at five in the morning and followed a course that passed over sleeping Germany, across Belgium, and down the English Channel. Patty had moved from side to side, watching first the French, then the English countryside unfold. He had sat holding her, and toward evening, as the light dimmed, he had cupped her breast in his hand, softly rubbing her nipple through the folds of silk and cashmere.

They had a wonderful dinner in the airship's dining room, so sparingly decorated that it might have been Japanese. Fueled by good German wines and his earlier caresses, Patty insisted on going to bed early. Their cabin, separated from others by walls of light-weight aluminum and fabric, had an upper and lower bunk.

She kissed him passionately when they entered.

"I don't think we can make love, honey—our neighbors will hear us."

"I don't want to make love. I'm too hot to make love. I want to have sex, silent sex, silent, sloppy sex, silent, sloppy, sucking, sensual, toe-in-socket sex." She pushed him toward the lower bunk, whispering, "Take off your clothes," as she shucked herself out of her own.

"Lie back." He did so, and she put her lips to his ear. "No talking. No gasping. Just kissing till we come."

It had never been harder to be silent, but the restraint added a bizarre surrealistic dimension to their loving. They were floating over the Atlantic, separated from the water only by a few inches of aluminum and fabric, working quietly and assiduously to gratify each other, slowly transforming the entire compartment with raw, heated sex. Then, as always, they transitioned into lovemaking, slow, ecstatic, and still totally silent.

Later, they lay whispering in each other's arms. "What's happened, Patty? Why are we so different now, since the crash?"

"We're not any different. You're just going through your male revenge mode, your silly pilot's need to win."

He didn't answer. She said, "I was jealous for a while. I thought you were still in love with a dead woman. But that's not it. Hafner's beaten you—or you think he has—a few times, and you can't stand it. It's so stupid. He's a criminal, a killer. How could you and he ever compete on any equal terms?"

"We did in Peru, and you're right, he beat me again."

"Equal terms? You were flying with two broken legs, and he was an ace from the war. Equal terms?"

The words gave him comfort—but not relief.

The next day they realized that they might not have been as quiet as they had thought. The crew was unusually jolly and friendly, and the airship commander, Dr. Hugo Eckener himself, made a point of stopping by at breakfast and inquiring how they were enjoying the trip. Later he gave Bandfield a personal tour of the *Hindenburg*. The more the grand old man of dirigibles explained how safe the gigantic Zeppelin was, the more convinced Bandfield became that the ship was a floating bomb, depending entirely on a superb crew and benign weather to keep from blowing up. The *Hindenburg* had been far more comfortable than any plane, train, or surface ship Bandfield had ever ridden, but he knew he wouldn't have another peaceful moment until they had disembarked in Lakehurst, New Jersey. He didn't tell Patty about his worries until the trip was over.

The phone rang, jarring him from his romantic recollections.

He turned back again to thoughts of his mission, trying to anticipate what Caldwell and Lindbergh would have to say.

His one abiding impression of the trip through Germany was that his hosts, from Udet down, had been consummate actors. He had asked Udet's aide, a bright-looking young lieutenant named Helmut Josten, if he knew what had happened to Bruno Hafner. The aide had blushed slightly, saying that he'd never heard of the man; it was obviously a *verboten* subject. Even Udet, always so cordial and correct, had simply looked blank and changed the subject abruptly.

Josten, speaking perfect English with an American accent, had taken him for a tour of the well-built factories, paternally laid out with housing and recreation for the workers. Modern aircraft were moving swiftly down the assembly line at a rate much faster than in America or England.

At one plant, Josten had brought him to a "secret door." They had gone down a flight of stairs piercing a good six feet of concrete, and there, totally idle, was a complete duplicate of the factory above. All the machine tools, the conveyor belts, everything stood ready for a work force to begin. Josten had pulled him inside one of the empty glass-windowed offices that lined the factory side.

"And look," he had said, pointing toward a drafting table. "Sharpened pencils, one hard, one medium, one soft. We are prepared for anything!"

It was impressive, but too slick. Bandfield had seen immediately that the electrical cables for the machines were all too small to carry the current they would have required. It was obviously a Potemkin factory, good for impressing visiting dignitaries and for storing machine tools until they were needed.

Slim hadn't spent much time working in a modern factory. The discrepancy wouldn't have been obvious to him. He was probably better able to analyze the personalities of the German leaders.

Patty had her own ideas about them. As soon as she and Bandy had arrived in Berlin they had been invited to a reception that sent her antennae twirling like a bumblebee at a honey tree. Standing in the reception line, she had kept up a running *sotto voce* commentary on their hosts. Patty saw—as he had not—that underneath the cordial smiles of the young Luftwaffe and foreign ministry officers was an agonized need to be correct.

As they worked forward in the line down the handsome marble halls, the usual high-decibel level of cocktail conversation declined. Most of the group were military, the men with frozen smiles, their wives looking anxious. As the group moved along the receiving line, the tense silence was broken only by the mumbled introductions that passed the guests from dignitary to dignitary. At the end of the line, they could see Goering, jovial in a well-cut uniform of the new Luftwaffe blue. He was of medium height, his rather long hair combed back, and not so much fat as heavyset. Behind him, shorter, beautifully dressed in formal civilian attire, Adolf Hitler was chatting casually with a young woman, holding her hand to detain her, gazing directly into her eyes as he spoke. Behind each man stood an interpreter.

Patty squeezed Bandy's hand and whispered, ''These men are dangerous! They have cobra eyes!''

Yet Lindbergh and his wife had found them charming. The American air attaché had shown them a photo taken at a luncheon, Goering in one of his wild chamois hunting outfits, Frau Goering decked out in a gorgeous floor-length dress, the Lindberghs obviously enjoying themselves. What had they seen that he and Patty had not—or what had they missed? To know would help in the meeting today.

The warrant officer's discreet cough brought Bandy back to reality, to the prospect of the imminent battle with Lindbergh. His reports had differed significantly from those that Slim had rendered, and an apparently outraged Lindbergh had demanded a face-to-face meeting. Caldwell wouldn't permit either to read the other's report, but gave them a brief summary that told Bandy that it was as if they had visited two different worlds.

''You can go in now.''

Bandfield snapped out of his reverie and walked into Caldwell's office. Lindbergh stood up, but did not extend his hand.

''Well, Captain Bandfield, I wasn't aware that you were a foreign affairs expert!''

''Wait a minute, Slim. I'm just saying what I saw.''

Lindbergh sat down, looked directly at Caldwell. ''Let's get this over with. I resent having someone sent to check my work. You asked me to go to Europe, and I went. My report stands as written. If you don't believe it, that is your privilege.''

''Look, Colonel Lindbergh, I'd like to keep personalities out of this if I can.''

''You can't. Bandfield has always been a minor Bolshevik, ever since cadet days, and I suspect that has conditioned his report.''

"Slim, that's not fair or true. What the hell has gotten into you?"

"It is both fair and true. Besides that, you don't have a basis for comparison. You haven't been out of the country except for a trip to South America."

"And Hawaii." It was a stupid correction, and Lindbergh's smile was tightly superior.

"Ah yes, Hawaii, the famous industrial center."

"That's enough, gentlemen. Let's get on with it."

Caldwell referred to some notes.

"Let's talk about aircraft quality first. You both flew the Messerschmitt and the Hurricane. I wish they'd let you fly the Spitfire. Slim, which was best?"

"The Messerschmitt, by a large margin."

"Bandy?"

"I'd agree that the Messerschmitt was perhaps a little more modern than the Hurricane. But the Spitfire was clearly superior to them both."

"That's the sort of amateur response I resent. You can't tell anything about any airplane unless you fly it yourself!" As Lindbergh argued, he seemed to draw more into himself, to grow taller and leaner. His mouth was set and his eyes almost shut with the intensity of his anger.

"I disagree entirely! The RAF showed me the performance specs. The Spitfire is a winner."

Shaking his head in mock exasperation, Lindbergh assumed a quiet, diplomatic tone. "One cannot always believe performance specs!" Then he rasped, "Look, you saw the Heinkel factory. They are demonstrating four prototypes—a bomber, a fighter, a dive bomber, and a reconnaissance plane—all first-class. I defy you to name another manufacturer in the world capable of such a display of technology."

Caldwell sighed. This was getting to be like a kids' fight. "What about strengths and production figures? Slim?"

"My report is clear on that. Germany probably has six thousand first-line combat planes today, and can produce, in wartime, at the rate of fifteen thousand or more per year."

"I strongly disagree, Slim. The training base wasn't there for an air force that big. I'd say they had half that number now, and no more than a four thousand annual production rate even in wartime."

Lindbergh's voice grew colder still. "Captain Bandfield, I saw things that you were not privileged to see. I saw a duplicate underground factory, complete with equipment, offices, everything. There were even three pencils on each desk, sharpened, one hard, one medium, one soft.''

''Jesus, Slim, they show that fake factory to everyone! It's a con game.''

The taller pilot stiffened with rage, infuriated both at being opposed and at the possibility that he had been duped. Once more Caldwell intervened. ''The difference in production estimates is really crucial. Can we agree on something in between?''

Bandfield asserted himself. ''I've run a factory, and I know what can be done. I stand by my estimate.''

''You are wrong. And events will prove you wrong. Germany has done in four years what it took the United States nineteen years to do, what hasn't yet been done in England or France. They will roll over France and then defeat England from the air! You mark my words.''

Caldwell was not enjoying the tension, and he decided to end the meeting soon. ''Just a few more questions. What do you think of the overall leadership, Colonel Lindbergh?''

''Goering is deceptive. He is genial and personable, but he is a hard-hitting executive, the kind who could run General Motors if he had to. Hitler is initially off-putting, but the more one sees and hears of him, the more impressive he is. Udet is a brilliant flyer, well qualified to run the technical development.'' He went on down a list of officers, most of whom Bandfield had not met, commenting favorably on almost all of them.

''Bandy?''

''It's hard for me to say; I only saw Hitler once, briefly. Goering I met twice, but he didn't impress me as a businessman. I have to say that my wife was distressed by what she saw in each of them—hired killers.''

Lindbergh was pained. ''Now your wife is the expert, is that it? It's utter nonsense to say that the German people would elect killers. The Nazis didn't stage a revolution, you know, they came to power legally.''

Bandfield spun. ''Did you see the signs warning people about shopping in Jewish stores? Did you see, as my wife and I did, a gang of Brownshirts beating up a Jewish couple?''

''Straight Communist Party line, Bandfield. We have more problems with Negroes in the South than the Germans do with Jews. Have you ever heard of a Jew being lynched like those colored boys in the South? Besides, Hitler is right when he says that the Jews have an unreasonable representation in the professions, in banking, in commerce. They have a stranglehold, and he's going to break it. I don't blame him at all.''

Bandfield looked at him. There was no doubting Lindbergh's sincerity or his patriotism. But he was so far off base, Bandfield wondered what his real politics were—not Democratic or Republican, for sure.

Caldwell pressed on, weary, relentless. ''And Udet?''

Bandfield hesitated. ''A charmer, but technically incompetent. He is out of his depth, and knows it very well.''

Lindbergh stood up.

''That is poppycock! Udet test-flies the aircraft personally! He shot down sixty-two airplanes in the last war. Do you think for one moment that General Goering would put Udet in charge of something if he was not competent?''

The tall pilot's rage was translated into a nostril-ripping snort that surprised and embarrassed him.

''Excuse me.'' He drew himself to his full height. ''Colonel Caldwell, if you are weighing Captain Bandfield's testimony equally with mine, I'm afraid I'll have to ask to be excused. He is obviously unaware of what is going on in Germany. My personal feeling is that Captain Bandfield is attempting to take some petty kind of revenge because I failed to buy an aircraft from his factory.''

Bandfield's contained anger and resentment oozed out the seams.

''Jesus, Slim, you know that's not so. And since when are you an expert on factories? You've been a hero so long you've forgotten what it is to actually do some work. You—''

''That's enough!'' Caldwell's voice jarred them both. ''I thought we'd get some benefit out of a face-to-face meeting. I was wrong. You are both excused.''

Lindbergh nodded and strode out. When Bandfield reached the door, Caldwell said, ''Just a second, Bandy. Sorry about the argument. Can you stay another five minutes to talk about another subject?''

''Yeah, if I get to talk about one myself.''

They eyed each other in the growing discomfort of his crowded office. The building's ancient coal-fired heating plant had failed again, and while they had argued a haunting graveyard cold had seeped through the poorly fitted windows of the ''temporary'' buildings put up in 1917.

Bandfield's anger began to subside. ''I'm sorry I got sore,

Henry, but the crack about the business really hurt." He grinned. "Partially because he's not all wrong."

"You have to remember he's been through hell with the press, Bandy. You have to make allowances."

"I guess, but the thing that worries me is that they fooled him! He's a smart guy, and if they can fool him, they can fool most anybody."

Caldwell watched Bandfield's quick fuse gutter out. "How's married life?"

"It's okay—we've got some problems, but who doesn't?"

"Well, I hate to tell you, but you're going back to Europe. And this time Patty can't come."

"Jesus, Henry, she'll kill me. Where am I going, back to Germany?"

"No, Spain. You're going as Jorge Trego Gómez, a Spanish expatriate. You're going to fly with the Loyalists, check out the Russian equipment they're getting."

"Come on! I speak a little Spanish, but no one will believe I'm a Spaniard. And why me? Don't you have anybody else?"

Caldwell laughed. "Well, I sure as hell can't send Lindbergh! Besides, you've seen the German aircraft; it'll help you to evaluate what the Russians are using."

He paused, then went on, "Don't worry about the language. You probably won't have to speak much Spanish, and it won't make any difference if they know you're American. Few of the Americans volunteering for the Loyalists speak Spanish. It's just a dodge to get you into Spain. Once you're there, nobody will care whether you're Greek or Chinese. Everything will be greased, don't worry about it."

"No sense in arguing, is there?"

"None at all. I want you to go to New York, stay at the Waldorf just like you had good sense. They'll get in touch with you there."

"Well, I've got no job, and damn little money. Might as well." Bandfield tried to sound indifferent; inside he pulsed with excitement at the prospect. He thought about his father— he would be pleased that his son was to fight on the Loyalist side. The way the world was, it was a wonder they didn't have him flying with the Germans!

"Any chance that Hafner will be there with the Nationlists?"

"No idea. He'd be a natural, but we don't have personal reports yet. I'll keep you posted if we hear anything."

Caldwell grinned and said, "Okay, that's my nickel. What's yours?"

"What is all this business about Patty making some sort of a secret flight with Earhart?"

"Beats me. The only thing I know about the caper is not to know anything at all. If I were you, I'd just butt out."

"Don't stall me, Henry. There's damn little that goes on in the Air Corps that you don't have a finger in, one way or another."

"Look, I'm telling you I don't know." He looked at Bandfield, and grinned. "Ah, shit. Here it is. This is secret—don't talk about it with anyone, not even Patty. Amelia asked for her. Amelia is a great fair-weather pilot, I guess, Bandy, but she knows her limitations. She wants Patty along to help with the navigation and the radio work, and to make the heavyweight takeoffs."

"What kind of airplane are they supposed to fly?"

"They'll use her Lockheed Electra, specially modified."

"I don't like it, Henry. It's too much responsibility for Patty—and Amelia will walk away with the credit, no matter how nice she is about it. She is the pearl of the press's oyster."

"Publicity has nothing to do with it. This is a serious mission, just as yours is. You'll be getting back from Spain well before she's ready to go; you can help out."

"You're really getting your money's worth out of a captain's pay, aren't you, Henry?"

Caldwell laughed. "We've always got to think of the taxpayer—you know the government always wants a bargain for its money."

Downey, California/November 25, 1936

It was only six in the evening and he had spent two hours watching the disaster develop with a clinical clarity, ringside at his own anointment as a prize jackass. He tried to concentrate, to listen to announcer Boake Carter's velvet voice coming over their Philco radio, saying something about a pact between Japan, Germany, and Italy against the communists, but it was too petty compared to the hole he was digging for himself. Once again he had backed himself into a foolishly bull-headed position in a domestic argument, saying too many extravagantly mean things that obviously had no basis in truth, casting totally spurious aspersions on Patty's flying ability, denying all his own faults, and then, in truly fatal error, saying some things that were absolutely true. As Hadley had always said, only the truth hurts, and when he told Patty that she was undertaking the Earhart flight not to honor her mother but to upstage her, he knew he had lost game, set, and match, as well as the battle and the war.

But even so, some internal nugget of incredibly stupid hubris made him realize that he had not yet reached the stage of humiliation when he could admit his mistakes. He raised his voice to raise the stakes, bluffing once again that he was fed up and tired of her nonsense, that he was leaving, that a divorce was the only option, that she could get on by herself. He prophesied how happy he'd be and how miserable she'd be, when in fact all he wanted was to throw himself at her feet and then at her sweet round ass.

She looked at him with that hard little fighter's look, the sweet smile of victory lurking on her lips, fully realizing that he had said something for which he was now sorry, that she could move in for the kill and ram home a few hard truths before he caved in.

"Yes, and my little smarmy Wobbly, my smart-ass Nazi-hater, guess who's going to go to Spain to show his daddikins that he's a big communist and a fighter for freedom, and is going to save the world? What thirty-six-year-old has-been pilot is going to gird up his rapidly tiring loins and save Spain for its noble peasants?"

She had him, he was spinning on the spit of her insight, each side roasting evenly in the truth of her words.

"Not so. I'm going because I'm ordered."

"Weak comeback. If they ordered you to fly for the Nazis, to be in Franco's air force, you'd stand on your stubborn ideals and refuse to go. No, you're just being Daddy's boy, one more time. You're going to hunt for Hafner, to revenge Millie. Bandfield, you're nuts!"

It hurts so bad, it was so true, that he laughed and grabbed her, planting his open mouth around hers, forcing her lips open, probing her somewhat in fear, for she had been known to bite, but confident that he could get another set of hormones going simply because he was admitting that she had won.

She responded as she had that night in Denver long ago, sucking him in, tearing at his clothes. They kicked the coffee table over as they fell to the floor, Boake Carter's fluid baritone still singing over them, fumbling and feeling and tussling to get merged, to push into each other with every ounce of energy, to jam tongues and fingers and noses and organs into any handy orifice, plunging and bucking and finally coming in a wild relief that signaled not only sexual release but the end of their argument.

They walked amiably naked into the bedroom, arms linked, hands stroking. He ran back out to the kitchen to get some ice and some whiskey. She brought warm moist towels to the bed, and they comforted each other.

"Bandy, I know you're right. I won't go."

"No, I was wrong, you have to go, you said you would."

"No, let's not either of us go. We've each given so much to flying—our lives, our lovers; I even gave my mother. We don't have to do any more. There are other people who can take our places. Henry Caldwell would understand."

"I don't think we can get out of it—at least I can't."

"You can, and you will. You've got to get over this Hafner business. He killed my mother, Bandy, and I don't hate him as much as you do. He'll get his. But he's ruining us. This is the best—almost the first—lovemaking we've had since the *Hindenburg.*"

He watched her moving about. Lately she had become compulsively neat. She gathered up their garments from where they had been strewn and walked around the bedroom hanging up their clothes, placing their underthings in neat little piles, knowing that he was admiring her, that her movements were arousing him again. He watched her breasts bobble as she moved, her hips lifting as she bent over to smooth the sheets. He pulled her to him, began kissing her again, murmuring in her ear that he loved her, that they wouldn't go, that they would get out of flying, and she responded once again.

They were lying contentedly together, fully agreed that they would start over, that neither one would leave, no matter what anyone said, when at nine o'clock, the phone rang. She ran into the living room and talked briefly to Rose, the woman who lived next door.

When she returned, she said, "I've got to get dressed. Rose's child is sick and she wants me to look at her."

He nodded.

She looked around the room, under the bed.

"Where are my step-ins? I had them right here."

He shrugged.

She looked at him closely.

"What have you got in your mouth?"

She jumped on him, plumped his cheeks. He coughed, laughing, and pulled the shell-pink step-ins out.

"Delicious, as always."

"You absolute goof! When I get back, I'm going to ravish you again."

Seville, Spain/December 10, 1936

The war gushed over Spain like a rising tide, the angry rivulets of flame and fire destroying fields and homes alike. What had begun as localized uprisings, sporadic militant relics of the monarchy, had coalesced into a major upheaval when Franco had brought in the savage Moroccan tabores, troops whose color, skin, and reputation for artful dismemberment boosted hate and fear to hysterical levels. The positions plotted on the maps shifted rapidly, as Spaniard battled Spaniard and the Loyalist government forces were shoved to the east. The coming of costly friends—Italians and Germans to the Nationalist "rebels," Russians to the Loyalists—changed the black internecine bitterness into a miniature world war.

"Sunny Spain my arse! I was warmer in the backseat of a Rumpler over France in the winter of 1918 than I was in that Junkers!" No one spoke; if Major General Hugo von Sperrle, commander of the Condor Legion, said it was cold, it was unquestionably cold. A brutal face—eyes like oysters sunk in a soufflé—and a harsh, insistent laugh that demanded agreement, not humor, made him frighteningly formidable. He stamped his feet and swung his arms: "Well, Richthofen, whom have you got to talk to me? I want to hear the bad news directly from the source."

He moved with surprising grace to the battered table that served as a desk. Behind him was the obligatory picture of Hitler. On the wall opposite a crucifix hung, a withered bit of palm still curled behind it from a long-ago Palm Sunday.

Sperrle's chief of staff, Colonel Wolfram von Richthofen, had shot down eight Allied airmen flying in his famous cousin's flying circus in the World War. For Sperrle, he had more than the usual pilot's contempt for an observer. Silently, he took in Sperrle's bulk, the "mark of the Prussian" curl of fat about his neck, the diamond-studded signet ring sinking in an ocean of flesh. Worst of all, Sperrle was crude, with deplorable table manners. But von Richthofen was more ambitious than fastidious, and he had the delicate task of informing the general that the principal German fighter in the Luftwaffe, the Heinkel He-51, was outclassed by Russian airplanes.

"I've asked Colonel Hafner to brief you, Herr General."

Von Richthofen had not so much chosen Hafner as had him thrust upon him.

"Hafner? He's Udet's pretty boy, isn't he? I knew him in the last war."

"I don't know if Udet likes him or hates him. This assignment could be a plum or a death sentence. It doesn't matter—he knows his airplanes."

Von Richthofen's uncertainty was compounded by Udet's own ambiguous status. One heard one moment that he was Goering's right-hand man, another that he was on the way out. So von Richthofen elected to treat Hafner at arm's length, as just another fighter pilot, ignoring all the political implications.

There was another very good reason for choosing Hafner to brief Sperrle—his huge size. This very important meeting could grow unpleasant, and Hafner was as tall as Sperrle and twice as muscular. It wouldn't come to a shoving match, of course, but Sperrle was a bully, and bullies preferred smaller men as victims.

He signaled to his orderly to bring Hafner in. They went through the formalities, discussing where they had flown and fought in the World War. Then Sperrle said, "Hafner, tell me straight out. Is the problem the Heinkels or the pilots? Don't try to cover for your friends."

"Herr General, the pilots are superb. But the Russians are flying a better airplane."

"Nonsense, it's just a copy of an old American Curtiss fighter. I've read the intelligence reports about it."

"Herr General, you have read the reports, but have you ever seen one on your ass, with four streams of bullets coming at you? Have you ever seen our shitty seven-point-nine-millimeter bullets bouncing off their armor plate?"

Sperrle's monocle popped off. Von Richthofen stepped forward as Hafner continued, "It is quite stupid to say that it is a copy of a Curtiss. The Russian I-15 is also a radial-engine biplane, but those are the only similarities. It is a far better airplane than the Heinkel, and we are soon not going to be able to cross the battle line unless we get something better. You'll recall that the airplanes were shipped in packing crates marked 'Furniture.' We'd have been better off if there had been furniture inside, rather than the Heinkels!''

Von Richthofen was appalled. He wanted Hafner to be frank, not belligerent. His time in America had made him undisciplined.

''And, for the last month, they've been using a monoplane fighter with a retractable landing gear, very fast. We can't even engage them.''

As Hafner spoke, Sperrle replaced his monocle, realizing that his only way out was to laugh, to treat this swinish behavior as a joke.

''Ah, enough, I believe you. And what about the Russian pilots?''

''They are quite good, not as well trained as we are, but with those airplanes they don't have to be. The Spanish are flying them as well. We'd better get some Messerschmitts down here, and soon, or borrow some Fiat CR-32s from the Italians.''

Sperrle's monocle popped again. He could see Goering's reaction if he recommended borrowing Fiats from the Italians.

''Very well. All the 109s we have are experimental aircraft so far, as you know. But we'll bring three of those down, until the production deliveries start. It's not much, but it's the best we can do. Dare I ask you about the bombers?''

''The Ju-52s are slow, but as long as we can protect them, they'll do the job. But we won't be able to fly protective formations for long. The Russians are too powerful.''

Von Richthofen leaned forward. ''Will the Messerschmitts be adequate?''

Hafner turned to him. ''I think so, against their biplanes, of course. I'm not sure about their monoplanes. They are very fast, but don't seem to be too maneuverable. The Messerschmitts will help only for a year or two, anyway, until the Russians bring down something better.''

He turned and stood at attention, thumbs placed precisely on his trouser seams, eyes riveted just beyond Sperrle's bulbous head. ''Herr General, what comes after the Messerschmitt?'' he asked.

Sperrle shot a look of warning to von Richthofen. Enough was enough! Von Richthofen smoothly intervened, ''Thank you, Bruno, for your customary frankness. You may be sure that what is coming after the Messerschmitt will be quite adequate. You may go.''

Hafner saluted and did an about-face. On his way out he raised his eyebrows to the aide holding the door, as if to say, "Court-martial or promotion—who cares?"

"The remark about what comes after the Messerschmitt, von Richthofen! What did he mean by that? The 109 is brand-new, not even in squadron service yet, and he's talking about what comes after?"

"*Ja.* It's a problem that Udet has as well. He's quite right— something should already be on the drawing boards. The problem is that Hafner has an interest in a certain airplane, one he's shown Focke-Wulf. He is a somewhat entrepreneurial lieutenant colonel!"

Sperrle shrugged and told his adjutant to arrange for him to speak to Kurt Tank at Focke-Wulf. Tank was as much of a genius as Willy Messerschmitt; he'd tell him what to make of this Hafner fellow.

Over New Mexico/January 3, 1937

She was a fury, wrapped in passion concealed in rage, and hidden by hubris. Patty Morgan Dompnier Bandfield leaned forward in the cockpit of her Beech racer, trying to will the recalcitrant instruments into proper order.

Bandy had broken his word, leaving the morning after the night they first had the violent argument, then made violent love. He had said he had to go to some secret briefings at Wright Field. Now she knew that he was somewhere in New York. She didn't know where, but she would wring the truth from Caldwell and find him. He was going to Spain, after he had promised— sworn!—not to, and after she had promised to remove herself from the Earhart trip.

She would have killed him easily, if she could have loved him to death. In her heart was an ominous fear that he would not return, that he would cross the ocean to die in Spain, to be left a burned and jumbled mass, crumpled in the wreckage of an airplane, just as Stephan had crossed an ocean to die in the race.

And to ice the cake, the flight was going sour. She had been averaging 240 mph. Now she was at sixteen thousand feet over New Mexico, between cloud layers, deliberately slowed down to 150 mph. A sinister quiver running through the yellow Beech-craft exactly matched the oscillation of the tachometer, now nervously buzzing from 2,200 to 2,300 rpm every thirty seconds.

She'd left Los Angeles, intending to confront Bandy and set a transcontinental record in the process. Until twenty minutes ago, the flight had been perfect. Patty corrected course angrily, unhappy that she'd allowed her preoccupation with the tachometer to let her drift twenty degrees off. She reduced power a little more to bleed the airspeed back to 140 mph. The record was out of the question, but she still had to be in New York by the 5th, if she was to see Bandy before he left. She would stop him if she could; if she could not, he would go warm with her love. As much as she needed to see him, she now needed a hole in the undercast even more, a brief blessed spot of light where she could let down if she had to.

There was a faster surge, and the tachometer picked up to 2,400 rpm, before subsiding to 1,900 Patty reached up and pulled the propeller level back. She hated to touch it, afraid that any change would make things worse.

Nothing happened until she reduced power again. The engine sagged, then surged, the rpm bobbing back and forth, until the pointer pegged itself at 2,600, the sound of the freewheeling propeller singing back through the windscreen. She glanced down at the map, then back out the windscreen, desperately trying to spot a hole in the clouds.

The propeller whine went up an octave and culminated in a shuddering jolt that jerked the airplane almost sideways and sent her head clattering against the cockpit wall. Half the prop sailed into the New Mexico skies. Unbalanced, the massive engine lunged convulsively, wrenching away from the mounts Bandy had welded with such care. The big Pratt & Whitney's lurch to the right sent the cowling whipping back over the wing, tearing the yellow fabric into shreds. The now useless engine dangled halfway to one side, a massive derelict forward rudder.

Don't let me die! Let me get to him! she thought, instinctively pulling the throttle back and switching the magneto off, pointless reactions since her horsepower had just been transformed to junk metal. The Beechcraft, normally so stable, began an aimless yawing descent, instrument readings on the panel spinning wildly.

"Mother," she said, the image of Charlotte fighting the controls of the bomber adding to the choking fear gripping her throat. She forced herself to try to save herself as her fear turned into an insistent anger that the full force of her left leg was not enough to halt the biplane's relentless skid to the right. The agonized airplane wanted to plunge straight down, despite her full back pressure on the stick. She had already run in all the available trim, and there was nothing she could do that would bring the disfigured nose up. The airspeed increased to 160, then 170. At the higher airspeeds she regained some control authority, and the rate of descent stabilized at seven hundred feet per minute.

Her arms were aching and her left leg quivered from the strain so badly that she brought her right leg into play, standing with both feet on the left rudder pedal. The corkscrew spiral moderated to a wide, skidding turn to the right.

Patty reached over and pulled her chute toward her. She was wearing the harness, and forced the connecting rings of the pack into place. She swung over in her seat, forcing the door open. The Beech swung downward with a dreamlike intensity, a maddened runaway creature determined to scrub her off against a mountain as a horse rubs a rider off against a tree. The hands on the altimeter rushed through ten thousand feet. She knew the ground below was at least five thousand feet high, and the mountains might reach to nine. Her legs still held full left rudder, slowing the turn to about two degrees per second. The cloud layer engulfed her momentarily in mist, then dissolved. She sobbed in relief when the snow-dusted mountain peaks appeared below. They seemed to reach up beseechingly even as they spun in a flat circle around her.

Patty slacked off pressure on the rudder, and the airplane whipped to the right. She let it turn a full circle, then led in with full two-leg pressure on the left rudder pedal. It straightened momentarily and she forced herself out the door into the slipstream, which pulled her away and free.

Don't know how high I am, she thought, pulling the ripcord, and accepted gladly the wrenching pain of the opening shock. Moments later, she saw the bright glow of the Beechcraft exploding as it struck the ground. Her legs hit pine branches and she hurtled through, hands crossed over her face, wondering where she was, if she would survive.

The grasping hand of the parachute canopy enfolded the top of a pine tree. She sensed the tree's indignation as it bent almost double, then jerked her upright like a broken marionette. She bounced up and down, not certain if she was alive, where she was, or if she would spend the rest of her life tucked in some New Mexico pine tree like a forgotten Christmas ornament.

None of it mattered. Bandy would be gone to Spain and never know that she had sought him, that she had tried to stop him, that she had forgiven his going.

She looked around in the darkness. There was a glow not far away, a farmhouse. Then she saw headlights coming, someone probably looking for the airplane. The lights grew larger, and a truck came around the curve, skidding to a halt as its headlights illuminated her.

An Indian got out.

"Are you alive?"

"Yes. Thank you for coming."

"I'll get a ladder. Are you hurt?"

"I don't know. Thank you for coming."

He went back to the truck, and then stopped and yelled, "Don't go away. I'll be right back."

She laughed until it hurt to do so.

11

Valencia, Spain/January 11, 1937

The braying of donkeys awakened him from a troubling dream; he thought for a moment that he was back on the farm in Salinas. He lay quietly, trying to figure out what was different. Then he realized that he'd slept the night through for the first time since his arrival in Spain, not kept awake by a solid lump of beans and *chorizo*, the inevitable main dish served to flyers at the Loyalist training station. The dream had been a puzzle—Patty and Millie had been with him in a New York restaurant. Then it clicked into place. The incredibly inedible soup last night, made of equal parts of oil and garlic, had reminded him of the onion soup at Orteig's restaurant.

The news of Patty's crash had just reached him. Thank God she was safe. He thought wryly of the Great War term "blighty"—a minor wound just serious enough to get you out of the trenches and back to England. Her injuries—burns and bruises—sounded like a blighty that would keep her from flying with Earhart. He hoped so.

And he hoped she would have time and charity to forgive him for leaving without telling her. There was no way to explain to her, as Caldwell had "explained" to him, that failing to go would result in a court-martial. Caldwell was a friend, but a soldier, and he expected Bandy to honor his bargain. Bandfield had filled Roget in, and he hoped he would have time to talk to Patty, and perhaps convince her that his going was necessary.

So far, he had been safer entering combat than she had been at home. The great Spanish adventure had been one anticlimax after another. He had waited in the Waldorf as Caldwell had directed him to do, expecting someone like Erich von Stroheim or Peter Lorre to contact him. Instead, an attorney sought him out. Dan Schecter was a mousy little man, more clerk than spy, and he quietly gave Bandfield his passport, tickets, and a contract that said that he would be paid $1,500 a month, plus $1,000 for each enemy plane shot down. One paragraph specified that he had to take a check flight in Spain to prove his flying abilities.

He had been the only Loyalist volunteer on the ocean liner that carried him to France. A Spanish captain, Augustín Sanz Sainz, who insisted that Bandy call him Augusto, met the boat and took the American by train on a long circuitous journey to Valencia. Before leaving, the captain brought in an old friend from the Roosevelt Field days, Bert Acosta. Acosta was returning to the United States, disgruntled with the Spanish and incensed that Bandy was going to be checked out in fighters.

"Fred Lord and I were sent to Bilboa to fly Breguets on coastal patrol! We're probably the two best pilots in Europe, and they made us fly something that should have been scrapped ten years ago!"

Bandy didn't say anything, figuring that Acosta's age and drinking had worked against him. He didn't know Lord.

"Frank Tinker got fighters, too. How are you supposed to get a bonus for shooting down people when you're flying Breguets?"

Augusto later indicated that the Loyalists were less than pleased with the work Acosta and Lord had done, intimating that they expected rather more from Bandy. They lived on sour red wine and bread on the train, a trip that would have been interminable if it had not been for the ever-changing panorama of beauty and pestilence that rolled by. It was as if Peru had been superimposed on California, arid browns pressed against sudden verdant foliage. Bandfield loved the closely built homes, the shrouded women walking to get a loaf of bread as secretly as if they were sneaking from a seraglio, and everywhere kids playing soldier with sticks for swords and rifles.

Augusto took him to the Air Ministry in Valencia. The processing was simple, and the next morning Bandy left for the Escuela de Caza, the fighter school at San Javier airfield.

Bordered by straight rows of stunted, moisture-starved trees, the rough flat field stretched like boring company endlessly to the horizons. The broken remains of landing crashes, sad airplanes angled into bloody junk, were strewn haphazardly around the former military parade ground. His initial check ride was in a well-maintained Caudron Aiglon. The check pilot, a dour lieutenant named José Torres, said nothing from start to finish. While they were walking back to the long low frame building that served as an operations shack, Torres grunted and said in English, "Report for Chato training at six in the morning."

The next day, the atmosphere thawed in the dingy flight shack. Torres helped him get fitted in a beautiful Russian-issue leather flying suit, then took him into a classroom where a cockpit from a wrecked aircraft was propped up by rough boards.

"This is from a Polikarpov I-15. We call it the Chato, because of its flat nose. I'm going to show you what all the buttons and gauges mean."

That afternoon, Bandfield had his first flight in the gullwing Russian biplane fighter. Painted a dull dark green, with red wingtips, it handled like a Boeing P-12, but was forty miles an hour faster. To his surprise, it was powered by an American-built Wright Cyclone engine. In the next week, he flew twelve hours in the Chato, including some practice gunnery.

The instructors liked him because he was proficient, unlike the typical Spanish student. The Loyalist government was trying to lure more native pilots into service, and the carnage was devastating. In the week he was checking out, the Spaniards lost three pilots on the base and one at sea during gunnery practice. One had ripped his wings off, pulling out of a high-speed dive too close to the ground. Two others were lost when a Chato landed on top of a Caudron, a falcon raping a duck. The man at sea had become target-fixated and flew single-mindedly into the water. The Spanish instructor pilots were furious and frustrated. There were too few Spanish pilots already, and the Russians were assuming a preponderant role that would give them power at the peace table. The losses shrouded the field with gloom.

Torres called Bandy in. "You've passed your checks. I'm recommending you to the Escuadrilla de Chatos at Las Alcazares. You will be flying with American and Spanish pilots. Your commander is Andreés Lacalle. Serve him well. He is one of the loyal ones; almost all of the other officer pilots joined

Franco. And remember, if you weren't flying for him, you'd have to fly for some bastard of a Russian."

Bandy received word to report to the Air Ministry in Valencia before going to Las Alcazares. When he got there, an American dead ringer for Charlie Chase was waiting. He introduced himself as Harold Lowe and made small talk until they got back to his hotel room.

"Henry Caldwell sent me, Bandy. He said everything is fine at home, and gave me these." He handed Bandy a packet of letters from Patty.

"Read them later. She's doing just fine, has even been flying once."

He saw the look on Bandy's face and hastened to add, "I haven't been reading your letters. Caldwell just passed the news along."

Bandfield nodded, and Lowe said, "I'll be your contact here. The Spanish have accepted me as the advance party for a group of Red Cross volunteers forming in New York."

"Why would they believe that?"

"I don't think they do. My impression is the Loyalists are trying to do anything to ingratiate themselves with the United States, and if we send a few spies over they expect it. They hate being so dependent on the Russians. That's probably why you're being sent to Lacalle's squadron—they hope it will have the same effect on public opinion as the Lafayette Escadrille did in the World War."

"How did you know I was going there? I just found out myself."

"You have to hand it to the British. They've had an intelligence network in Spain since Wellington, and probably have a contact in the Air Ministry itself. And they have a pretty good radio intercept service working. We don't need to know how they do it as long as they share it. Anyway, Henry will be glad that you're going to Lacalle, but he really wants to get you in a Russian unit if he can. And he wants you to try to get into the I-16 as soon as possible. It surprised the hell out of everybody."

"I haven't seen one. Torres says they're tricky devils, but fast, almost five hundred kilometers an hour."

"Look, we'll try to work a transfer if there's any way we can. In the meantime, you do the best you can in Lacalle's group, and see if there's any way you can volunteer to fly with a Russian unit. They tend to keep to themselves, so it may not be possible."

Bandy shrugged his shoulders. "Say, if I get lucky and shoot somebody down, do I get to keep the thousand dollars?"

"I don't know. Never thought about it. But knowing the good old Army, probably not. Let's wait till it happens."

"How long do I have to stay here?"

"Henry says they'll bring you back as soon as you think you know enough about the I-16, or get to fly with the Russians, or preferably both. But he also told me to tell you to be ready to leave instantly."

Lowe had popped his hand in his fist for emphasis, a laughable gesture for a man who appeared about as pugnacious as a parakeet.

"We have to assume the Russians know about your status, and are just accepting it. You have to be prepared for a change in attitude at any time. If they decided to, they might execute you on the spot."

"Jesus, great. Now you tell me."

"In any event, if I tell you to go, or if you become suspicious yourself, just go. Take an airplane and go to France, or Portugal, or fly out to sea and land by a neutral ship."

"I'm not sure a captain's pay is worth this. I'm not cut out to be a spy, and from now on everything I don't understand will worry the hell out of me. What kind of place is this?"

"We're all in the same boat. I've been surprised myself at the amount of espionage and counterintelligence going on. Spain is a war bazaar, a coming attraction. All the people are getting killed just so Europe can practice for the next world war."

Lowe looked around the shabby room, and inclined his head for Bandy to lean over.

"This may be of interest to you. Bruno Hafner has been identified as commanding a fighter unit for the Condor Legion. He's in the Madrid area right now. You may just run into him."

"Are you sure?" Bandfield was galvanized by the prospect, almost too good to be true.

"The radio-intercept teams have it pretty well nailed down. I know you have a special interest in Colonel Hafner. I'll keep you posted."

Ordinarily, Bandfield let the world spin to a halt while he read Patty's letters. This time he put them aside unread, thinking about the satisfaction he would have in nailing Hafner's ass in combat. Hell, he would pay the Spaniards $1,000 just for a shot at Hafner. There were so many things to get even for. He had been prepared to execute him in cold blood in the States, if he had caught him. Now, if he shot him down here, it would be revenge sauced in patriotism, a tasty dish, cold or hot.

It might be an even fight for a change. Hafner had a lot more combat experience; Bandfield remembered too well the debacle in Peru. But he had a hole card, a big wild ace. The Russian planes were superior to the Heinkels the Germans were flying. It would more than even things out. He would fight him, he would shoot him down, and end this ten-year-long battle.

When he turned to Patty's letters, they surprised him. After the usual expressions of love and concern, as well as the usual stern reproval from having left without telling her, she went into her own fall from faith. There was no hint of apology; she simply said that she was going to make the "big flight"—she avoided using Amelia's name, referring to her as "my friend." She was already training "her friend" intensively to teach her the techniques of taking off in a heavily loaded twin-engine airplane. "Her friend" had some sort of mental block, and they had reached an agreement that while she would always get in the left seat and taxi out from whatever terminal they were flying from, Patty would make all the heavyweight takeoffs. It was just as he had figured—Patty was going to do the work, and Amelia was going to get the credit.

Bandfield stared at the wall. What on earth had they got themselves into? They were as much in love as any two people he'd ever seen or heard of, and they seemed to spend half their time building obstacles to being together. Then the thought of Hafner hit him, the sweet prospect of revenge like hot wine in his mouth. There had to be some justice in the world. Maybe this would be worth it. And things would be different when he got back.

Guadalajara, Spain/March 12, 1937

Bilious gray clouds had spewed rain for four days, turning the front into a sucking sea of brown mud and compounding the protracted depression engulfing Bandy. They were grounded, locked into the grimy field boundaries. Without the anodyne of flying, the Spanish war was more impossible than ever. Not even the rattling purr of El Rojo was comforting. The orange cat, ears tattered and skin flecked with lesions, had so far survived both the war and the hungry peasants. Bandfield had befriended him by picking out the solid pellets of fat from the sausage and feeding them to the cat. El Rojo never permitted Bandy to pet him, but always turned up in the room after Bandfield had gone to sleep, matching purr for snore.

After a breakfast of coffee and bread, Bandfield slumped in the operations room, listening to a scratchy radio playing a Russian station, convinced that Caldwell had forgotten his existence.

Absolutely nothing was going well. He hadn't heard from Patty in three weeks. There had been further news of Hafner from other sources. The German had six or seven victories now, and was apparently commanding a special unit. In contrast, Bandfield had flown in six combats without scoring and had almost been shot down twice. Captain Lacalle had given him two serious dressings-down, one public, and a more scathing one in private. He hadn't quite accused him of cowardice, but the inference was there if Bandy wished to take it.

Lacalle was wrong. Bandy had no doubts about his own courage. Twice he could have killed. He had the pretty Italian Fiat biplane fighters in his sights, at close range, and didn't shoot. Killing someone besides Hafner in a futile war like this was simply murder.

At the beginning of the month, he'd hoped he'd get some insight into the insanity thanks to some unexpected idle time when an extreme shortage of gasoline had forced a general squadron stand-down. He had gone out into the countryside to try to talk with the people, to see if he could understand how they could fight so well with so little.

He was appalled. He had not expected to find a happy countryside, but there was no song in Spain, no joy among the children, no casual look of happy indifference. Instead, there was universal guilt and fear, and an uncanny, pervasive impression of bitter sin, a feeling he'd never encountered before. The sins weren't of the flesh, not drunks in bars nor whores sitting in doorways; instead, there were the sins of torment, of ugly, unrequited hatred. Most people would not talk to him about anything political, as if they feared what he would do with their opinions. For the most part, the endemic bitterness had nothing to do with the Loyalists or the rebels. Instead, it was a deep, dolorous, fratricidal resentment of the landowners and the aristocracy. There was a curious division of feeling about the church. Even the most avowed communists spoke in terms of God and blessings, using all the usual Catholic turns of speech. He had talked to one quiet man—he gave his name only as Pablo—for an hour, asking him about the land, and the church, and what the outcome of the war would be. Pablo was reasonable and intelligent; he felt the Loyalists would win, but that it would take years, and when it was over the country would be forever impoverished. Only a few minutes later, Bandy was told that Pablo had killed at least four priests in cold blood, stabbing them to death in the street without warning, deliberately denying them the chance to cry out a last act of contrition. He had sworn to do the same to as many more as he came across.

On a tip from Harold Lowe, he had searched out Bob Merriman in Muricia. A captain in the Abraham Lincoln Brigade, Merriman was recovering in the hospital. Bandy brought him a bottle of wine and was surprised to find his pretty wife, Marion, with him. Merriman had been wounded in the left arm and shoulder while leading untrained infantry in a pointless attack. Yet Merriman was boyishly enthusiastic about the cause, about the war. Bandfield had looked to him for guidance, for reason, and found only a sophomoric idealism that had nothing to do with Spaniards killing Spaniards. He talked to him about Pablo and the priests he had killed, and Merriman just shrugged it aside as a picaresque anomaly suitable for Spain.

The fellow flyers in his flight were worse, sitting like five little Indians around the depressing, laundry-strewn hovel that they used as a ready room. What a bunch! Whitey Dahl, whose passport read Hernando Díaz Evans, was Army Air Corps–trained and had flown the airmail in 1934. Something had happened—a drunk-driving rap, a scandal—and he had been thrown out of the service. He was aggressive, but Bandy thought he lacked judgment in the air. He'd been sick for weeks, some kind of dysentery, and was scheduled to go in for treatment soon. Ernie Hopper was asleep next to Dahl. Hopper was an ardent communist. Bandy had spent time talking to him when he first arrived, but the man was exhausting, always wanting a conversion to the cause on the spot. He wouldn't say where he got his pilot training; wherever it was, Bandy didn't think it was adequate to be flying combat. Next to Hopper, George Reid was carving a stick figure from a slat from a wooden crate. Reid was quiet, and inspired confidence. The story was that he had hijacked a Nationalist Cant seaplane and flown it to the harbor in Valencia. When the Loyalists came on board, they found the rebel crew, throats slit, laid neatly in a row on the floor, dressed tallest to shortest. He was their kind of man.

Then Lacalle came in. Tall and slender with a jet-black pompadour of oily hair, he was affable on the ground, a martinet in the air. Bandy shuffled to his feet as Lacalle called the group to attention; the similar scene in the Richard Barthlemess film *The Dawn Patrol* flicked through Bandy's mind.

"The weather is supposed to improve around eleven o'clock. All the aircraft will carry bombs. The Italians are retreating along the road from Brihuega to Trijuque. The mud is keeping them on the road, so we'll attack in trail."

The room was quiet; no one took notes, they all just stared at Lacalle. "Hopper, you'll lead the attack. I want you to drop from no higher than five hundred feet, and no lower than four hundred. Got that? Reid, you follow Hopper, and Bandfield, you go next. I'll bring up the rear, to check on how you are doing. Dahl, you stay at altitude until we recover, then make your own attack. After the drop we'll strafe as long as we have ammunition. Any questions?"

There were none. Bandy knew the attack method was devised for his benefit. Ordinarily Whitey Dahl, with his greater experience, would have led the attack, and Lacalle would have flown top cover for them. Lacalle had eleven victories, and was clearly the best shot in the unit. Hopper was only a fair pilot and Reid didn't have much time in the Chato. Lacalle was checking on Bandfield.

Great wet bags of clouds bullied the little spots of clear air, squeezing in and coalescing, insolently changing shape and color as they picked their way through to the front. The Chatos were sluggish with the weight and drag of the two twenty-five-pound bombs carried under each lower wing. Hopper leveled off just under the cloud base and led them directly to the line of retreat. From one thousand feet, Bandy could see derelict armored cars and light tanks pushed off into the mud, the road choked with streams of brown ants occasionally illuminated by a white up-turned face. After nervous hand signals to Lacalle to make sure he was properly positioned, Hopper peeled off, his wings flashing up as his nose came down in the classic attack mode, and the rest followed at twenty-second intervals. He saw Hopper's bombs hit well to the right, and then Reid's bracket the road perfectly. He dropped, hoping that he'd miss but be close enough to satisfy Lacalle.

They formed up, watching out for Fiats and Heinkels, as Dahl made a textbook dive that tore chunks of men and rock from the roadway. Lacalle waved his hand in a circle and they dove again, Hopper leading them down to race just above the road, firing their machine guns at any target. Details swam into view, lodging in the mind and becoming distinct only long after Bandy was past. He saw a tank, hatch open, a body hanging out; a horse, down, broken, but terribly alive; two men, carrying a third between them, falling simultaneously to the side, dropping their comrade facedown in the mud. The images simply poured in, he could concentrate on nothing; oddly, no one was shooting back at them, no one at all. The long stream of fleeing Italian soldiers divided into purled lines on each side of the road, as if a comb were running through them instead of bullets.

They exhausted their ammunition and flew directly back to the field. Even before Lacalle had hoisted himself from his cockpit, his adjutant handed him a congratulatory message from the Russian commander of the counterattack. The mechanics refueled and rearmed the airplanes while the pilots ate thick sandwiches of coarse white bread and sausage and gulped scalding black coffee. Lacalle came over to Bandy. He had evidently carefully planned what he was going to say, because for once his English was flawless.

"You were just adequate on this mission. I'm tired of your talking about a transfer, about flying I-16s, about joining a Russian unit. If you don't start getting some victories in the air, I'll have you transferred to coastal patrol, flying Breguets."

Bandfield stiffened into a position of attention. Lacalle went on. "Now you lead this attack. The weather's breaking, and we can expect to see some action." He paused, then reached out and grabbed Bandy's shoulder. "I expect to see some action from you, or I will shoot you down myself."

The American had no doubt that the Spaniard was serious.

Bandy led the takeoff, the other four Chatos quivering in formation just off his wings. They began a standing patrol over the line of white cloth the infantry had laid out to mark its farthest advance. He climbed to six thousand feet, grateful that the first bright sun in weeks had elbowed the clouds out of the way, adding to the warmth of his leather flying suit. Without the bombs, the little fighter felt like a different airplane. Lacalle suddenly slid over into the lead position, signaling with a machine-gun burst. He pointed down and to the north.

Six Junkers Ju-52s, slow trimotor bombers, were coming in V-formation, two flights of three. Above them a squadron of Fiats circled like hornets. Bandy laughed in excitement. The Fiats, CR-32s, were from the La Cucaracha Squadron—what a name to call yourself! Lacalle began an immediate climbing turn to the left, gaining an additional altitude advantage and posi-

tioning the flight between the bombers and the front line. Lacalle glanced across at Bandy, pointed to the enemy, and sliced
his finger across his neck, a clear message to produce or die.
Then he waggled his wings and dove, the other Chatos stringing
out behind him.

The five airplanes plunged through the Fiats and toward the
bombers. Bandy caught the Junkers in his sights. It was a curious airplane, with corrugated metal surfaces like the Ford Trimotor, but with its engines mounted wall-eyed on the low-set
wings. They moved into view slowly, the details making them
somehow less real than when they were dots in the distance. He
fastened his sights on one, huge, ponderous, death-laden yet
dancing lightly on the wind. The camouflage was distinctive, an
earth gray-green covering the center section of wings and fuselage, followed by a band of beige. The tail and wings were
chopped up in diagonal colors, with an all-white rudder marked
by the huge black X. At one hundred yards, he began to fire,
stitching a line of bullets through the fuselage and into the cockpit. A burst of smoke came from the center engine, and with a
dreamlike grace the Junkers slowly peeled up and out of formation, its arc like the hand of an opera diva taking a final bow.
Two men jumped from the rear, their parachutes opening immediately, jerking them alone to a halt in an otherwise constantly moving universe. From the front, a third tumbled, his
clothes on fire. A Chato, probably Hopper, sliced across, firing
at the men in the parachutes.

He was watching the slow tumbling of the bomber when his
instrument panel disintegrated, spraying glass and wood splinters instantaneously past him. Scorching hot wind-driven oil
burned his face as he kicked the rudder and shoved the stick
into the opposite corner. The Chato snapped and the Fiat followed, pumping 12.7mm bullets into him. Anger superseded
fear as the Italian pilot pursued him through every maneuver,
cooly firing snap shots as if he were on a target range: a tough
fighting cockroach. Bandfield knew he had only seconds to live.
He looked back and saw Lacalle on the Fiat's tail; there was an
explosion and the Fiat disappeared into a thousand pieces. Lacalle had saved his life.

He turned and caught sight of the remaining bombers, four
of them, pressing their attack. There were no instruments left
to check, but the engines were running and a quick burst showed
that the machine guns still worked.

He put the Chato's nose down and dove below the bombers,

pulling up sharply under the lead aircraft. A gunner, suspended below the fuselage in the ridiculous garbage-can open turret, fired at him. The war was suddenly personal. He could see the gunner plainly, his face covered by goggles and scarf, shoulders hunched to force the machine gun against the slipstream. It seemed strange that he was aiming at Bandy, shooting, trying to kill him. Indignant at the hostility, Bandy kept the Junkers in his sights and walked his rudder back and forth, spraying bullets across the wing center section. Orange-red flames poured out as an explosion tore the right wing away. The airplane rolled rapidly to the right. He wondered if the gunner could bail out of his suspended bucket, now whirling around the axis of the falling Junker's flight.

Above him a Fiat, engine smoking, was gliding down. Its pilot stood in the cockpit and pulled the ripcord of his parachute; the billowing chute jerked him backward and out, like toast out of a toaster. He saw three Chatos descending in a fast glide, and the Fiats were forming up in a loose formation as they departed. God, they could maneuver. The Italians in the air were apparently far different from the Italians on the ground.

He glanced around his airplane, saw the fabric flapping, thought he could hear the wind whistling through the bullet holes in his windscreen. The engine was running rough, but he knew it would get him back. When he turned his head forward again, he saw Lacalle's airplane boxed in by three Fiats. Lacalle was turning but not firing—his guns were jammed or he was out of ammunition. Bandfield dove headlong, pulled in behind the lead Fiat, and hosed it with a long shattering burst that sawed the Italian pilot in half.

Bandfield turned left to get on the tail of the next Fiat, which went inverted, diving away in a split S that might or might not clear the ground. He turned right and pressed his firing buttons, only to hear the pneumatic chargers hammering away. He was out of ammunition. The remaining Fiat hung in behind Lacalle, firing short bursts.

Bandfield could see the pieces flying from Lacalle's airplane. Almost without thinking he hurled his Chato at the Fiat, felt a *crump* as his gear tore through the enemy's wings. The Italian pilot sheered off, quickly establishing a gentle descent, obviously trying just to stay airborne in one piece.

Bandfield tucked his wing next to Lacalle's, and they flew back in formation. En route, Lacalle signaled that Bandfield's right gear was damaged. He brought the Chato in on its left wheel, letting it slow almost to a halt before the broken right wheel touched down and spun it in a sharp circle.

Lacalle came running over.

"Bandy, forgive me! You saved my life. That dago bastard was a good shot—another minute and he'd have had me."

Lacalle embraced him and took him inside while he got headquarters on the field phone and demanded a decoration for Bandfield.

Bandfield was happy, almost for the first time since being in Spain. He had fought and killed and they had turned the bomber attack back. Even better, he had saved a patriot's life, a life worth saving.

The fight transformed Lacalle's attitude. He was now as friendly to Bandy as he'd been distant before, and in the next few weeks, Bandfield felt closer to Lacalle than he did to any man except Hadley Roget. More important, Lacalle took him aside for long talks, and into the air for mock dogfights, passing on to him all of his experience. It didn't make sense in instructional terms; much of what he passed on would have been more helpful when Bandy started flying combat. Yet he was indebted, for Lacalle was a master flyer, and expert in the airplane.

He taught Bandy some things he thought he already knew, but which seemed richly different when explained by Lacalle. The mode of attack in the Chato was "always from above—rarely from the level—and never, never from below," he said.

"The Fiat has a better ceiling than we do and is more maneuverable, so we have to attack them when we can dive, shoot, and run." Lacalle's hands flashed in mimic combat, his eyes deadly serious.

Bandy thought he'd been flying the Chato well enough, but the insight Lacalle brought from his own experience could easily have made the difference between life and death. Lacalle advocated always cruising in the combat area with the mixture slightly rich. If combat occurred suddenly, you could apply full power, advancing the throttle and the mixture simultaneously, without risking a momentary cut-out. It cost a little more fuel, but Lacalle insisted that the flights back to the base be conducted with maximum fuel economy, no stunting, no flat-hatting, and this more than made up for it.

"That engine is your great mother's tit, and when it comes time to suck on it, you want it to be ready." He called the Chato the "good communist God's gift to Spain," and said he wouldn't trade it for anything on the Nationalist side. Bandy didn't believe him, but it raised his morale to hear it said.

Lacalle took him as a protégé, called him his *compañero*, and Bandfield began to believe that he'd survive the war.

Luke Field, Hawaii/March 20, 1937

The only thing missing in the poster-perfect scenery was Ukulele Ike. Everything else—the soft morning light, the song of brightly plumed birds, an invigorating ocean breeze—called for relaxation and romance. She wished Bandy were there—or that she were with him, wherever he was.

Patty watched Amelia Earhart lower herself into a distinctly different, unforgiving environment. Her metal seat was covered by a hard leather pad, and she was surrounded by hundreds of gallons of gasoline in an aircraft that seemed totally hostile to her.

Amelia Earhart had almost mastered the Vega; she felt different in the Electra. It seemed to her malevolent, with twice as many engines, throttles, props, rudders, everything. She hated it, sensing a lurking evil that promised to reach out and get her.

Patty reached down and helped Earhart with her straps.

"Feeling okay?"

"No." Earhart hesitated. "You know how I'm always quoting Hamlet, saying he wouldn't have been a good pilot because he worried too much?"

"Yes?"

"Well, I'm afraid I'm being the Hamlet on this one. I'm worried about everything. I wish you were coming along. I'm sorry it wasn't possible."

"Me too."

The wan look on Amelia's face prompted Patty to say more than she would have.

"Look, you've had plenty of instruction. You've done well! Don't let this takeoff spook you—it's no different from those we practiced in California."

Patty hoped her voice carried conviction that she didn't feel. Takeoffs were critical, with the weight of the fuel pressing the Lockheed's landing gear oleo struts down, flattening the tires, slowing the acceleration that would pour a blast of air back to give control authority to the rudders. She had made Amelia practice the initial seconds of the takeoff roll time and again, insisting that she bring the power up gradually, keeping the aircraft straight with differential throttle, and not using the brakes. Time after time she had said, "The brakes will just slow you down, get you in trouble! Control it with the throttles."

Patty had shown her how the brakes induced a twisting movement that could shear the gear, while the engine power gave the rudders something to bite on. The problem was that Amelia felt that the reaction of the brakes was positive, instantaneous; to use the throttle and rudder, you had to anticipate, to begin the corrections almost before a problem developed.

But it was difficult for Amelia, almost as if she were reluctant to really learn, as if she were reaching out a hand to Patty, calling for help, not for flying, but for life. She bitterly regretted that fate had intervened, that Patty was not going to be able to make the flight with her. She had finally convinced her husband that it was safer to share the flight with Patty, even if it meant sharing the credit. Then, in the end, Patty couldn't go. Instead of a capable pilot, there were two navigators, Fred Noonan and Harry Manning.

All of the formalities were over; Manning and Noonan were aboard and waiting. Patty knew by the way they had checked the quick-release pins on the safety hatches that they were nervous about Amelia's ability.

Patty moved back to the edge of the runway and gave Amelia the thumbs-up sign. Mutely, she responded, her face drained of emotion, and pushed the throttles forward, the serenity of the Hawaiian breeze broken by the burbling sounds of the two engines.

Amelia was anxious to be off, to have it over with. As the Electra gathered speed, it began an implacable drift to the side of the runway. Earhart glanced blankly at the throttles, trying to decide which one to pull back to counter the turn; when she looked up the edge of the runway was coming close and she jammed on the brakes to counteract the drift.

The airplane began to turn rapidly, twisting on the inner wheel, flattening the tire further, the outer wing rising and throwing more weight on the tortured landing gear. Shuddering, metal screaming, Noonan and Manning yelling, the Electra whirled in a ground loop. Earhart gripped the wheel tightly, standing on the brakes, letting the engines run wild until, with a snap like a broken limb, the gear folded. There was a shrill knife-sharpener scream as the propellers smacked the ground and the airplane halted in a twisted heap. Sick with fear and relief, Earhart switched off the magneto switches and threw the hatch open. She could hear Manning and Noonan scrambling out behind her.

At the edge of the runway, Patty closed her eyes, praying the airplane would not explode.

Alcala de Henares, Spain/April 2, 1937

The new Russian squadron commander, Kosokov, taught Bandy in three days all he needed to know about the Russians, personally demolishing the idealized vision his father had provided him. Kosokov was as hard and treacherous as a rusted saw, totally pragmatic, and ruthless in a way that made Bruno Hafner seem like Florence Nightingale.

Now the blond six-footer stood perfectly erect, surveying his pilot-victims. His eyes were slits watching with the expectant cruelty of a savage chow, blinking back the smoke from the cigarette that always dangled from his mouth. Kosokov ran the squadron with an iron fist. When the Popular Army beer wagon first pulled up, its sides decorated with signs saying ''Bar'' and ''Free Service,'' he had driven it away with a burst of fire from his rifle. He permitted no drinking on the field at any time; woe betide any pilot who smelled of liquor before a flight. Even Lacalle was deferential to him.

Lacalle's squadron had been moved nearer to Madrid during the early part of April, coming under the Russian's command. Kosokov insisted on flying with each pilot to check his skills, including Lacalle. It was a calculated insult, administered in front of the squadron, that the proud Spaniard could never forgive.

Bandfield was glad that his victories, and shooting the Fiats off Lacalle's tail, had induced Lacalle to be his friend. The Spaniard was now deeply depressed, and needed someone to talk to. Not only was the tide of battle shifting against the Loyalists, but the communists were becoming more and more powerful. Lacalle took Bandy into the village, got a bottle of rough red wine, and told him about how his people had hated the bourgeois, how cruel the landowners had been. ''When the Marxists took power, they forced collectivization, put all the land to work. I thought it was a good idea, that the rich wouldn't live off the working-man's labor. The harvests were all going to be centralized and distributed fairly.''

They were sitting in a peasant's hut, a rough wooden table between them. Lacalle drank from his tin cup, poured again.

"Now it was the communist committee men who stole the harvest; the workers wound up exactly as before, with barely enough to live on through the winter."

"If you are disillusioned, if you don't believe, why do you keep on fighting?"

"Simple. As bad as the communists are, the fascists are worse. And I think the communists are less efficient. If they win the way, the people will be able, someday, to get out from under them. If the fascists win, we will live under Franco's thumb for life."

Bandfield's heart went out to him; Lacalle would have been a leader in any air force in the world, and he was forced to fly and fight for a cause he didn't believe in.

"There are other reasons, too."

Bandfield was silently, waiting.

"The fascists have killed two of my brothers, and one of my sisters. Thank God my father and mother were already dead."

The next few days brought news that sunk Lacalle deeper into his depression. The war was going very badly in the north. The Loyalist territory was shrinking daily, meter by meter. Contact had already been cut off from France, and there were no means to reinforce the Loyalist forces from the South. Lacalle could no longer learn what was happening to his wife and two children at his home in Bilboa, a garden city gradually being reduced to rubble by the daily bombing.

Bandfield was depressed too, despite his victories. He had shot down four airplanes; he wondered if they would pay him in dollars, as they had promised. He couldn't believe they would.

He was doubly glad now to be Lacalle's friend. It would have been a bad thing to be in a squadron where your immediate supervisor didn't like you and the squadron commander, Kosokov, didn't like your immediate supervisor.

Any doubts that he might have had about Kosokov were dispelled in their first encounter. The Russian took Bandfield in his turn on a checkout flight, thoroughly besting him in a mock dogfight. But the real lesson came afterward. They had been shooting landings when Kosokov whipped away in a violent bank, sideslipping in to land at the far end of the field. Bandy flew at three hundred feet as the Russian walked over to where a sentry was lying. The American, circling with the left wing of his Chato pointed at the pair, saw Kosokov kick the apparently sleeping sentry. There was no response. The Russian pulled out a pistol, shot the man in the head, and went back to his airplane. When they landed back at the operational end of the field, he took the measure of Bandy's expression.

"Drunk on duty. *Kaputt.*"

Bandy made up his mind not to drink on duty.

The following day Kosokov led nine Chatos into a fight over the Brihuega-Valdesor-Pajares sector. Three Savoia-Marchetti trimotor bombers, pretty fabric-covered airplanes with a distinctive humpbacked look, were scooting in, escorted by a flight of five Fiat CR-32 biplanes. It was a beautiful sight, the eight aircraft and their shadows leaping like dolphins among the marshmallow clouds.

Kosokov gave the attack signal and the Chatos hammered into the formation, Lacalle leading four into the Fiats and Kosokov taking the rest against the bombers.

Bandy was lucky. The dive took him directly behind the last fighter. It was at top speed, quivering in its mottled sand-green-and-ocher camouflage, blue-black smoke crackling from its exhausts. The upper wings had three black bands on each tip, followed by a large white X. The Italian pilot, a novice probably, was concentrating on maintaining his position in formation, and Bandy's four machine guns tore holes from the engine back to the cockpit. The pilot slumped forward, and the Fiat went into a dive, flame curling from the engine.

A Savoia had broken from the formation, the right engine smoking from Kosokov's attack. The gunner in the humpbacked bomber's top began firing as Bandy closed in a diving attack from the right rear.

Like imminent danger, combat split time into two dimensions. In one, everything happened instantaneously. In the other, all of the events were indelibly recorded in slow motion. He ignored the bullets going over his head, and fired. His first burst went through the insignia on the aft fuselage, a black circle with a white chicken inside. Cockroaches, chickens, he thought, the Italians have funny ideas about heroic insignia. He pulled back on the stick and fired again, edging the four streams of bullets into the bomb bay. The Savoia blew up, and he flew through a cloud of smoke and metal.

The Chatos formed up; there were six left. He wondered how many of the Italians had gone down.

Lowe was waiting for him when he returned.

"Bandfield, we're in trouble. The word is that we've both been slated for execution."

"Jesus, great. What for and when?"

"The Russians figure we are American spies. I'm not sure when they plan to act, but we can't afford to wait around. I'm leaving the country tomorrow. You should too."

Bandfield listened, nodding. He was ready to go back for every reason but one: Hafner. Somewhere, the bastard was flying, and he wanted to nail him.

"And I have news from Henry Caldwell. He'll be in Paris during May and June, working out details for a sale of aircraft to France."

"What kind of reception will I get when I land in France?"

"They'll just shuttle you to the embassy in Paris, and you'll be smuggled home. There won't be any problems. When will you leave?"

"I'm not sure."

"Look, don't screw around. Go the next time you fly. Just peel off and head for France. Maybe I'll see you back in the States. So long."

Bandfield watched Lowe leave, wondering if he'd make it, feeling a mixture of relief and anxiety well through him. Time was running out on him. Sooner or later, some Nationalist pilot was going to get in the first shot, and that would be it.

That night at the field, Lacalle bounded in, grinning widely.

"How would you like to fly an I-16, a Mosca?"

Bandfield, suspicious, hesitated to reply. This was just the sort of thing the Russians might do to put him off-guard. But he had fulfilled most of Caldwell's requests, learning about the airplanes and flying with the Russians. Flying a Mosca was the one thing he hadn't done. Besides, if he could not trust Lacalle, he could never trust anyone.

"What do I have to do?"

"Come with me tomorrow. I have permission to take one pilot and two I-16s and fly to Bilboa. They are down to their last two Chatos. We'll have to leave early in the morning, and fly directly over Nationalist territory."

Bandy hesitated. He had tried to find out where Hafner was— the only thing he could determine was that he wasn't on the same front. Maybe he was in the north.

The chances for it were admittedly slim. Kosokov had kept all intelligence reports to himself, and gave out only the minimum information at the preflight briefings. The front was hun-

dreds of miles long—meeting Hafner in combat would be pure
chance.

He felt a wild enthusiasm at the thought of leaving, of getting
away from the misery that was Spain. His life had become a
wretched aggregation of hours in his miserable hut and brief
terrifying moments of combat. But there was a pang when he
thought about deserting Lacalle when he needed him. That, with
his gambler's obsession about finding Hafner, overcame his good
sense.

He tried to think what Patty would be doing back in the United
States. She was probably spending her last days before the flights
with Amelia started again. Going with Lacalle would delay him
only a few days at most. And he'd be able to indulge the pilot
in him by flying yet another type, getting the information Caldwell wanted.

As he thought about it, he realized the delay was risky. But,
he reasoned, why would they let him take a modern aircraft, a
Mosca, if they were going to kill him? Lowe was probably
wrong. His spirits soared again. Bilboa was less than an hour's
flying time from France. He'd fly the Mosca to freedom. As
tired as he was of the killing, as disillusioned with "the cause,"
he still wanted one last chance to find Hafner.

And this was it. If Hafner wasn't in the north, if their paths
didn't cross, he would forget about him. He would never leave
Patty again, never experience again this deep-seated loneliness
and longing for her.

Lacalle was matter-of-fact. "We won't have a formal checkout. You've flown planes with retractable landing gear before,
haven't you?" Bandy nodded. "This is no different—you just
have to keep on the rudder on takeoff. It's hotter than the Chato,
but probably less difficult than the racers you flew. And thank
you for coming with me. My days with Kosokov are numbered!"

Mine, too, Bandy thought.

Vitoria, Spain/April 24, 1937

The entire business in Spain was crazy, but von Richthofen
thought the most insane event so far was bringing this new committee form of warfare to the front. It was on Udet's orders, and
Richthofen had been furious.

For his part, Bruno Hafner was happier than he had been

since the palmy days of March 1936, when he had impressed his new bosses with his management skill.

Reentering combat had been like a passionate encounter with a lover from the past. He realized how pale any other stimulus was. He'd tried cocaine, when Dusty was getting so involved, and it meant nothing. He drank for the oblivion, not the pleasure, it brought. Women were the next best thing to combat, as Charlotte, and more recently Lili, had proved, but he was older and his juices were drying up. Ah, but combat! There was nothing that gave him the consummate, fulfilling sensation of the slashing dive into an enemy formation. To fasten like a bulldog onto someone's tail, to sense and savor his terror, and then, with simple pressure from the fingertips, to erase him. It was an exquisite pleasure, as good now as in 1918. In his brief time in Germany, he had met the Japanese attaché, who had described the pleasures of eating blowfish, apparently a combination of delicacy, intoxication, and danger. Combat was that and more, hardly delicate, but so laced with danger overcome as to be magnificent. It was all he had remembered it to be, and more. He had scored seven times, three fighters and four of the ancient observation planes the Loyalists flew. Each time the old familiar rush of pleasure had returned, the biting sense of absolute and final control and superiority, the glowing sense of victory.

Combat changed life's ordinary wine into vintage champagne. And life in Spain was good, especially after the idiocy of Germany and the hectic self-imposed pressures of America. The Spaniards treated the Germans well, as they bloody well should have. Franco had controlled Vitoria longer than almost any other city, and had been able to provide the Condor Legion a convent—sans nuns—in which to quarter their officers. Hafner had a comfortable room, and the food was excellent. And Udet had arranged for the pilots to look at the plans of the Hughes racer, as the Focke-Wulf company had modified it, to judge its worth. He could not have asked for better treatment.

They were in Richthofen's headquarters in the Hotel Frontón. Lieutenant Josten spread the plans out on the table, big rolls of three-view drawings, smaller drawings of details, and sheets of tables showing the predicted performance.

The pilots, none of whom besides Hafner had flown anything hotter than their Heinkel biplanes, were ecstatic. "Look at the wide tread on the landing gear! You could land this airplane on any field and not have the gear come off." The Heinkels and even the new Messerschmitts had vicious takeoff and landing characteristics that had killed many a pilot.

Hafner tried to refrain from commenting, but could not. "And look at the armament. Two guns in the cowl, and three in each wing. The British are building eight-gun fighters, and we'd better have them, too."

Even von Richthofen became enthused. The airplane would make an excellent ground-support type. He turned and, in his clipped Prussian staccato style, said, "Lieutenant Josten, please tell General Udet that this is what should come after the Messerschmitts! I will inform General Sperrle of my opinion."

At the end of the evening, Josten sent a wire to Udet saying that the pilots approved. The following day, a copy of a wire to the Focke-Wulf aircraft company came in. It was a single word: "Proceed."

Hafner weighted the consequences of his coup. If he judged Tank correctly, the whole matter of the Hafner and the Hughes racer plans would be forgotten. It would be a Kurt Tank design from now on. That was acceptable. The people who counted— Udet, Goering, Milch—would know the truth. Now if it was only possible to get the big bomber back on track. If he could see Hitler personally, he could probably sell the idea. But that was almost out of the question; in the last year the Fuehrer had become even more unapproachable. Perhaps when the Condor Legion returned there would be a victory parade. He would be one of the leading aces—only two men were ahead of him now— and Hitler would undoubtedly decorate them. That would be the time to spring it, before Goering or anyone else could interfere.

He held two envelopes in his hand. One was of heavy, cream-colored paper, richly embossed. It contained a personal message of congratulations from Adolf Hitler himself. The other was made of the cheap yellow-glazed ersatz paper used by every government office. It was by far the more important of the two. Udet had sent it—again, why, Hafner did not know. He was still unsure how he stood with Erni. But he had sent it, and inside, on his personal note paper, was a little combat scene. A Heinkel, with Hafner's head bulging out, was shooting at a Russian Chato biplane. Udet had not tried to do the pilot's face in the Chato—he'd covered it with a helmet and enormous goggles. But there was a little arrow from a circle in which was written: "Your old friend Bandfield." At the bottom of the letter was the message: "He's near Madrid. I'll keep you informed."

It was almost too good to be true. Good Christ, to have a

chance to down Bandfield. Hafner recalled the flight to Hawaii, when he had perched in a perfect attack position behind Bandfield, unable to do more than watch. Not this time! If he could catch him in the air, the American was a goner.

Hafner rubbed his hands together. If Udet could pin down where Bandfield was exactly, Hafner knew he could arrange to be transferred to that area. He wondered how good Bandfield was in the Russian plane. It might be a problem, one that he'd have to look at carefully.

Less than a hundred yards away, relieved at last to be alone, von Richthofen riffled through the neatly mounded paperwork on his desk. The meeting with Josten and Hafner had been far more productive than he'd expected. The little war in Spain was proving to be quite fruitful, even as it became routine. He looked at the schedule. On the twenty-sixth, they were scheduled to bomb Guernica. It was a short mission for the bombers from Burgos, and the Loyalist air force had just about been shot out of the sky. He might just lead this one personally.

Bilboa, Spain/April 25, 1937

Bandfield was continually surprised at how the sharp shock of war was so quickly worn into ordinary depressing poverty. The streets and houses of Bilboa had been bombed and shelled into shattered masses that seemed to defy reconstruction. Immediately after the bombs hit, the broken buildings stank sharply of flame, cordite, and, all too often, burned flesh. Within a few days, the odors had given way to musty wet-mattress smells, overladen with the deep, sickening dead-dog scent of decaying bodies. Tired from the shelling, the poor food, and the inevitability of surrender, the local people were sullen and unfriendly.

And Lacalle was furious with himself. He had ground-looped his Mosca landing on the polo field the Loyalists were using as their last-ditch airfield in the defense of the north. It had been in the makeshift repair shops—abandoned stables—ever since, and in the meantime, the last of the Chatos had been shot down.

By midafternoon on the twenty-sixth, Lacalle's airplane was finally repaired, just as reports began to come in that an Italian bomber, probably a Savoia-Marchetti, had bombed the Renteria bridge east of Guernica, with little damage. A few minutes later, a Heinkel He-70 had bombed the railroad tracks at Guernica, then machine-gunned the town square. The methodical Condor Legion always followed a similar pattern. If another Heinkel showed up on a reconnaissance mission—the "before" picture for intelligence purposes—it usually meant that a full-scale bombing raid would be on within the hour. Bandy decided he would follow Lacalle through the initial attack to gain the combat information Caldwell wanted on the airplane, then return. When Lacalle landed, he would make a break for France. He felt no remorse about leaving. His mission was accomplished, and he was tired of killing, tired too of the Loyalist cause, and absolutely exhausted and disgusted by the communists. War had become so totally repellent that he was ready to give up everything but his quixotic crusade to find and engage Hafner in combat.

Lacalle ran out of the operations shack. "Full-scale attack on Guernica. We just got word that three flights of Ju-52s are en route."

They walked out to the stubby little green I-16s. Lacalle punched him playfully on the arm. "At least fuel is no problem. We're the last airplanes the Republic has left in the north. We'll get the best of everything."

Bandy carefully preflighted the Mosca, aware that this would be his last combat flight. The stubby little Russian plane reminded him of Hadley's racers, small, short-winged, lethal-looking. Methodically, he checked the fuel tanks with his own dipstick. They were full. He calculated that he could fly to France with half tanks, even if he had to ditch in a field or on a beach. It would be over then.

Burgos, Spain/April 26, 1937

Von Richthofen had settled into the narrow cockpit of the Junkers Ju-52 when an orderly ran forward with a message. He read it and cursed. "You take it, Baumer; I've got to go back to the office."

After von Richthofen was safely out of the cockpit, Captain Werner Baumer threw up his hands. "I thought we might actually get him into combat today, and let him see what a hopeless dog this airplane is as a bomber." Baumer resented the way the high command thought the Ju-52, designed as a transport, could do any job. In the past, they had even had them going low, ground strafing, where any Spanish child could shoot at them without missing. He signaled that he was ready to start engines. On either side of him, ground-crew men dressed in dusty black coveralls went through the final checks to see that the bomb safety pins were removed, the chocks pulled, and the runway ahead clear.

Baumer saw the green flare ascend and pushed his hands forward, the movement of the three throttles adding power, while simultaneously releasing the brakes. The Junkers moved sluggishly ahead, and Baumer settled down on his hard metal seat, sensing the adrenaline coursing through him, as it always did, even on an easy mission like this. In the back, gunner Erich Tauber ran his hands over the 7.9mm MG 15 machine gun, sighting down it and making machine-gun noises with his mouth, an eighteen-year-old delighted to be at war.

Guernica, Spain/April 26, 1937

The heavy bell in the church tower began to peal. The Basques were crowding the streets, drivers forcing their ox wagons through the densely packed crowd of buyers and sellers. Monday was market day, rain or shine, peace or war.

On the hillside, Father Alfonso Miravittles stopped to catch his breath. His finger, still moist from the oil of extreme unction used to slip poor dying Arturo Consados through the gates of heaven, crept down into the heel of his boot to comfort the blister. He realized what he had done and wondered if the Lord would consider it a misuse of a sacrament.

In the distance, he could see the crumbling ruins of the ancient Basque parliament building in the north end of town, now decked out with multicolored rags, washing hung out by the refugees to dry. Since the refugees had swelled the population, everything was made to serve as housing. His own work had tripled.

He began to move again, slowly. On the way to old Arturo's hut this morning, he had passed the famous Guernica oak tree. Six hundred years old, cut to a stump during the Napoleonic wars, it had flourished since, and become Guernica's symbol for Basque resistance. But this year it had come into leaf early, a sign as ominous as the trembling rumble he sensed in the air, a low guttural growling that was causing the magpies to fly in quick calling circles. He crossed himself, and hurried on.

* * *

Baumer's Ju-52 was the lead aircraft. He flew it precisely, anticipating maneuvers so that it seemed to fly as crisply as a fighter, rather than the lumbering truck it was. His observer, Lieutenant Henke, was suspended below in the archaic bombardier's position, exposed to the wind that he was busy calculating. They were flying at four thousand feet, secure in the knowledge that there would be no enemy flak or fighters.

Above the bombers, Lieutenant Adolf Galland watched the Junkers roll on. He and his fellow fighter pilots were delighted to be flying an escort mission in their Heinkel He-51s, instead of the usual dangerous attacks against ground targets. And circling above the Heinkels, unable to fly in formation with them because they were so slow, essing back and forth in easy turns in his brand-new Messerschmitt Bf 109 drafted from the test group at Rechlin, was an elated Lieutenant Colonel Bruno Hafner.

He had pulled strings to get the airplane assembled swiftly, flying the test flights himself, driving the crew overnight to get the special paint job completed. The bright red paint was totally unauthorized, as was the large white winged sword behind the cockpit. But this was wartime, and the authorities winked at the deviations from discipline that signaled high morale.

Hafner patted the intelligence report in his flying-suit pocket. Two I-16s had reinforced Bilboa; one of the two pilots was an American volunteer. Hafner grinned to himself. It had to be Bandfield, it *must* be Bandfield!

Five thousand feet below, Baumer muscled the Ju-52, keeping the airspeed and altitude constant, aware that a deviation would bring a rocket from Henke. The observer's signals to turn right or left were marked by a red or green light on the panel. At the beginning of the war, the bombardier had sat in a hole chopped in the floor and dropped the bombs by hand. Things were improving a little, bit by bit, as they learned their way. It would be better in the next war.

Behind Baumer, three other flights of Junkers, all loaded with 550-pound high-explosive bombs, were readying to drop. The big bombs would break the buildings into kindling, open the gas mains, prepare the way for the fires. Then they would return in the third wave, carrying incendiaries.

Unheard below the bombers, the church bell ringing the air-raid alarm sent a few of Guernica's population into the crudely built bomb shelters. More crowded into the church, with contradictory hopes. The first hope was that they wouldn't be hit in a church; the second was that if they *were* hit, their death in church would assure salvation.

Lacalle had led Bandy to the north to gain altitude, then back in a sweeping climb to ten thousand feet. Flying the Mosca was like balancing a marble on a pencil, and Bandy was not yet comfortable in it. Below them lay Guernica's houses, built wall to wall so that streets meandered through them like water through a rocky field.

Unaware of the approaching Russian fighters, Baumer felt a sense of quiet satisfaction. All of the long efforts—the trips from Germany, the training, the sweat and hard labor—all were made worthwhile at the press of Henke's bombardier's button that sent the bombs hurtling toward the town. It was a signal to the other planes, whose bombs cascaded down, tumbling from their vertical storage to course clumsily into alignment.

Henke's string of bombs, falling in pairs, hit the Hotel Julian, then walked explosion by explosion across the street to the railroad station. Erich Tauber depressed his gun as far as he could and fired a burst into the streets.

Father Alfonso stumbled as he watched the bombs from the second wave of bombers smash into the church, crumpling the steeple and throwing the altar forward across a line of kneeling women, turning prayers into screams. The priest's eyes were streaming tears as he raced to his church, his people.

Lacalle signaled and dove, accelerating to five hundred kilometers per hour before firing. Lacalle aimed for the number-two man in the formation, Bandy for the lead airplane. As he dove, he knew the only thing that would make being here worthwhile would be finding Hafner in one of the German planes. He was too tired to feel fear anymore, too jaded to enjoy a victory.

Baumer was surprised by the controls jumping in his hand in concert with the metallic clatter of the heavy Russian machine-gun bullets cutting through his wing. He banked his Junkers into a gradual turn to the left, trying to keep the formation together as he saw the two green Russian-built single-seaters chandelle up ahead. He felt the vibration of Tauber's gun—the youngster's bursts were too long, he'd burn out his barrel.

"I-16s," he called to no one.

Lacalle's target started to smoke. He turned to the left and attacked its wing man. Bandy dove to attack the lead plane again. The Junkers grew big in his sights, and he put a line of bullets across the corrugated skin of the fuselage. He still had respect for the German gunners, having seen more than one of his comrades go down from their fire. The Junkers's top gunner was huge, sticking much farther up into the slipstream than usual.

Where are the damned fighters when we need them? Baumer thought as he jerked the Junkers into a shivering right-hand turn. He wondered if Erich, for all his talk of fighting, was hitting anything. Even if he didn't, just the act of firing would be a deterrent. Where were the fighters?

Below, Galland was pulling up; even in a full-throttle dive the Heinkels couldn't catch the I-16s. He was going to have to climb, and try to cut them off from their base in Bilboa.

Hafner circled above the fight, choosing his time. He could not tell which airplane Bandfield was flying, but he had ammunition enough for them both. When the lead Mosca dove again, Hafner swung down in a tight arc that pulled white trails of condensation from his wingtips. The ugly little Russian fighter grew in his sights. He raised his nose, fired, saw the hits registering directly in the cockpit; smoke and flames erupted in a violent wind-lashed stream.

''Kaputt,'' he said, and arced back into a roller-coaster climb to his perch above the combat. He would have liked to stay on the Mosca's tail, following it down, pumping more bullets into it. But there was still an enemy—and it might be Bandfield. He would get them both and be sure.

The fight had drifted away from Bandfield after his first attack, and he was sitting at altitude, seeking the next target, when the cameo battle unfolded beneath him. He had seen Lacalle's masterful attack, smashing the Junkers and then deftly disposing of the defending Heinkels like an aerial Cyrano de Bergerac, a fencing master sliding in and out among the Germans. Then Bandfield watched the red blur of metal scything down to attack. It was a Messerschmitt just like the one he had flown back at Augsburg.

He saw the quick burst—no more than ten seconds—that shredded Lacalle's airplane, and swore as the Messerschmitt converted all the speed and energy of its dive into altitude.

Lacalle's smoking airplane straightened out and began to fly level. It was surrounded by Heinkels driving in and firing as leisurely as if it had been a target sleeve. Below, flames were already boiling up from the city.

Bandfield's thoughts came clattering like bullets even as he reacted. The Messerschmitt was faster and could climb more rapidly. It didn't matter; he was plunging headlong into the Heinkels, trying to save his friend Lacalle if he could, to draw the Messerschmitt down on him if he couldn't. It was the worst way to engage—low, in an inferior airplane, against a host of enemies—but he had to try.

Hafner watched the Mosca dive, irrationally sure now that it was Bandfield. He saw the streams of smoke from its cowling and wings. He waited, letting the Heinkels engage the enemy as it went past, each little biplane turning and darting to fire either at the first Mosca, now burning brightly, or at the second one, which had just broken through the melee.

The German hunched forward. There was a line of Heinkels behind him now, ready to cut off the Mosca if he missed. He would not miss. He shoved the Messerschmitt's nose forward and dove, seeing the Mosca turning towards him.

One of the Heinkels had been good, turning behind Bandfield to shatter his windscreen, punching a line of holes across his instrument panel that terminated in a wide pulsing wound in his hand. He pushed his bloody fingers against the throttle, blood squirting against the windscreen. He glanced at his ammunition counters—they read zero. He checked an impulse to test the guns—if there were any bullets left, he wanted to put them into the Messerschmitt.

The gleaming red Messerschmitt came dropping down in a vertical arc, curving in for the attack, an all-white winged sword gleaming behind the cockpit. In a surge of pleasure no different from instant, urgent sexual arousal, Bandfield leaned forward, anxious to fall on the neck of his foe. He had smelled it, he knew that it was his old enemy Hafner, and the insignia confirmed it. Bandy raised his nose, worrying about losing airspeed, but unable to turn away. He could see a bright winking on the cowl of the Messerschmitt, felt the slugs ripping through his fuselage. Bandfield mashed on his gun button, heard the clatter of air as the pneumatic charging system pulsed the empty guns. The Messerschmitt's fuselage flashed by overhead, and Bandfield turned instinctively to follow, knowing that he could not dive away with the German pouncing on him like a leopard.

Hafner pulled up and rolled over to look down at the battered Mosca. This was Bandfield, no question. A flight of Heinkels appeared. He whirled on his wingtip to fire a warning burst in their direction. They understood, pulling away to the north.

This pigeon belongs to me, he thought. Bandfield was below, slow, hurt, and apparently out of ammunition. Hafner felt a glowing sense of excitement, a realization that it was going to be better than he had planned, better than he could have dreamed. He would snip at this upstart American like an Oriental torture master, slicing bits from him until he flew him into the ground.

Bandfield watched the Messerschmitt ease in next to him, flying in formation. He lolled his head to the side as if he were wounded. Jesus, he thought, the bastard is going to whip me again. Patty is really going to be mad at me about this.

Hafner's Messerschmitt disappeared behind him. Bandfield had turned to stare to the rear when a shadow blanked out the sun. He looked up, and smiling down, just as he had so long ago in Peru, was Bruno Hafner's huge head, with its hooked nose and its fleshy lips stretched into a smile.

Hafner looked into Bandfield's shattered cockpit, smeared with oil and blood. Bandfield glanced up and pushed away, but a hint of pressure on the Messerschmitt's controls let Hafner follow. This stylish victory would do him no harm. The younger pilots would talk about the quick kill of one Mosca, and then this complete domination of the other.

He checked his fuel gauge; not enough remained to fly Bandfield into the ground. It would have to be an execution, better than he deserved.

I'll drop back now, he thought, and gave him two twenty-second bursts. He waved a slow salute—flip, not correct; Bandfield wasn't worthy of a correct salute—and reached down to check his gun-charging handles.

Bandfield gazed up at Hafner's coarse and heavy face distorted by the helmet and the strain of combat. There was not much he could do. His hand crept to the side, moved the lever; the heavy landing gear, screaming in protest, thundered down into its extended position, slowing him abruptly. Simultaneously, Bandfield chopped his throttle, raising his nose a hair. The Messerschmitt shot forward, and Bandfield's propeller nicked through the light metal of Hafner's fin and rudder. In the milliseconds in which it sliced through frame and formers, the exploding effect of the 250-mile-per-hour wind blew the Messerschmitt's rudder off at the stump.

Hafner's first sense was that the Mosca had somehow disappeared, his second that his rudder pedals were slack. The Messerschmitt snapped, then spun crazily, pinning him to the cockpit side. Above, two of the Heinkels milling in amazement locked wings and began an earthward plunge that matched the Messerschmitt's. Hafner pushed against the canopy, trying to overcome the G forces pinning him inside. He snapped his seat harness loose, straining to get out, his thoughts kaleidoscoping to match the whirling brown and green of the land below. Spinning in his mind were images of Germany, of his father's house, of Charlotte, of the Bristol fighter he'd shot down in 1918, of Charlotte again and Nellie, and of the Bristol again and the Bristol again and the Bristol, Nellie, the Bristol, he was merging with the Bristol, spinning down, locked with the Bristol.

Bandfield's aircraft shuddered and bucked as the damaged propeller threatened to tear the engine from its mounts. He shrugged, popped the throttle full forward, and dove for the sea, for France—and for Patty.

EPILOGUE

Paris, France/May 1, 1937

Only nine years and 345 days too late to win the Orteig Prize, Frank Bandfield woke up in the American embassy, his first conscious thought of Patty, his second that this was surely not the room Lindbergh had slept in.

He passed his throbbing hand over his forehead. He had crash-landed on the beach near the village of Saint-Jean-de-Luz, out of fuel and anxious to be on solid ground. The local doctor—if he could be called that—had poured cognac into the hole in his hand and bound it up with a cheap gauze bandage. The doctor stationed with the embassy had gasped in horror and spent the afternoon snipping at the wound with scissors and muttering about blood poisoning and French medicine before sewing it up.

Henry Caldwell had used the time he'd spent with the doctor profitably, firing question after question to Bandfield about the Russians and the Germans. Caldwell had been apologetic about the shabby treatment from the embassy—officially Bandfield did not exist, was not in France, had never been to the embassy. The ambassador was not worried about what the Germans would think, having this ''mercenary'' on the premises, but the French were, and it had taken two days to get custody of Bandfield, and another to have him transferred to Paris.

One more interrogation was scheduled for this morning. After that, Caldwell had promised a quick trip to Le Havre and then a luxury voyage home on the *Normandie*.

After washing up, Bandfield peered up at the single window near the ceiling of his dingy room. Last night, he had propped himself on a chair and looked out over the rooftops of Paris, wondering how it had looked to Lindbergh in May of 1927. Roosevelt Field was an eternity away in time, a universe in distance. So much had happened. When he landed on Long Island, primed to be the first to fly from New York to Paris, he'd felt he had the hottest airplane in the world, the original *Roget Rocket*, good for 125 miles an hour. A few days ago, he'd abandoned an airplane that could fly twice as fast and was already obsolete.

It had started out the Lindbergh decade; it was winding up the war decade. Aviation had promised an El Dorado of riches in 1927—you simply had to fly faster or farther or higher, and money would flow in an endless stream. A few people had made money; many times that number had lost their fortunes and often their lives. He started to count the friends he had lost. The number grew too high, and he shook the thought away as morbid, grateful that Patty and Hadley had survived. He jumped nervously at a clatter in the hallway; some scurrying maid dropping a tray of dishes had thrown him back to the puffy skies over Guernica on his last mission, the mission he'd flown repeatedly in his dreams since his landing on the beach. He remembered the bitter frustration of being once again at the point of defeat at Hafner's hands, his screaming outrage at losing again to a brutal traitor who had destroyed so many people close to him. In a single desperate move, renouncing life, Patty, the future, everything, he had lowered his gear to brake his airplane and send the smug, grinning Hafner slashing over him. He'd felt his prop claw through the Messerschmitt's fin, severing it cleanly. The German fighter had shot in front of him like a car accelerating from a stop sign, then begun its wild, snapping spin to the earth around Guernica.

He had felt no elation, only a sense of being clean and free. He had beaten someone who had deserved it badly. If the Heinkels had not been there, he would have tried to follow Hafner down, to watch him impact. He doubted if Hafner could have bailed out of the wildly gyrating airplane. But Bandfield's sluggish Russian fighter had almost been blown to bits around him, and the drumming, clanking noises had told him that he could not fly for long. He had dived, ignoring the vibrating engine,

the propeller screaming a banshee accompaniment to the bag-
pipe songs of the wind whistling through holes left by German
bullets.

The remaining Heinkel fighters had been disorganized, unable to react. One flight of three had anticipated his line of
retreat and dove, firing at him, but their bursts had fallen far
behind. Far out over the Bay of Biscay, he had flattened out,
racing along the ocean's surface for the first thirty minutes. Then,
cautiously, he had throttled back, afraid that the engine would
quit, trying to understand the meaning of his new freedom,
oblivious to the beauty of the Mosca's shadow hurtling over the
bright blue waters, and to the surprise on the faces of the sailors
on the small sail boats. His fuel gauges had long read empty
when he had seen a spit of beach that he knew must be French
soil. He had flown low over the sand once, to be sure there were
no idling lovers in his path, then bellied in, the I-16 sending a
spray of sand and water geysering behind it.

Two stoic French fishermen had watched him crawl out of the
cockpit, bleeding and throwing up in response to the release of
tension. When he had finished, they had launched their boat and
sailed away, still staring. For the first time, his hand had begun
to hurt, and he had waded out to rinse it off in the surf, letting
the bite of the salt water act as a counter to the pain. In a few
minutes, a black Citroën *traction avant* had pulled up, driven
by two members of the gendarmerie. After an hour of voluble,
incomprehensible French, windmilling arms, and accusations
of everything from invasion to smuggling, they had impounded
the airplane and taken him to their local clinic. Three days later,
he had reached Paris.

His propeller had sawn through his obsession as cleanly as it
had through Hafner's rudder. He felt free for the first time since
the confrontation with Murray Roehlk back in Dayton, when all
the suspicions, all the dark thoughts, about Hafner had been
suddenly turned into reality. Now all he wanted to do was return
to Patty, to some semblance of a normal life.

A knock on the door brought him back to France. It was
Caldwell, carrying their breakfast on a tray.

"Sorry about the service, Bandy, but you know the ambassador is in a bind about this. He was good to let us use the
embassy at all; he's under a lot of pressure from the French
government to get us out of here."

Bandfield picked up a croissant. "This will never replace ham
and eggs."

Caldwell nodded, munching. "We've just about finished, but I've got some good news for you. I think I can swing some contracts for Roget Aircraft from the French. They're ready to buy anything the United States will send them, and your transports would be a godsend."

"God, that's great! Old Hadley will have to get a new stock of jokes for the French customers."

"Better than his American ones, I hope. Say, Bandy, you've been coy about how many victories you had. Give me the straight story, now. I'm going to propose that you tour all the Air Corps pursuit units and talk to the pilots, and that's the first thing they'll ask."

"Henry, with the exception of the last fight, I hate to think about it. Let's say it was nine, counting Hafner. Have you been able to get any confirmation that he was killed? It would be just like that bastard to bail out and land in some Spanish whorehouse."

"No, the Germans have clammed up on this, and even the Brits haven't found anything out. There's such a stink brewing about the way Guernica was destroyed that we may never know."

"How bad was it?"

"Totally destroyed. The Nationalists are saying the Loyalists blew it up, the Loyalists are calling it a massacre. That's what's making the French so nervous about having you here."

"I'll be glad to go."

"Sorry I couldn't get you on the *Hindenburg*. I know you liked the last trip so much. It's leaving the day after tomorrow and getting into Lakehurst on the sixth."

"I know you're joking. The Germans would love to get their hands on me—and I'm frankly scared to fly in it."

"Well, let's get started. We can talk on the boat train. I wish I were going back with you, but I'm due to brief the air attaché from Berlin on Lindbergh's next visit."

"He's going back?"

"Yeah, he's even talking about taking a house there and living in Berlin, if you can believe it."

"Jesus, I wish he would live in Germany for a while—that would bring him around. And I wish you could have known him when he was in flying school, or at Roosevelt Field. He was a prince." Bandfield was sadly reflective, then went on, "For a long time I've tried to tell myself that success spoiled him. It wasn't that. I think the press drove him crackers."

"He's not crazy—just has a defeatist outlook."

Bandfield took a shot in the dark. "Henry, it looks like Patty isn't going to fly with Earhart when she tries it again. If you had anything to do with her not going, I sure appreciate it."

"I had nothing to do with her going or not going, Bandy, although I don't think you believe me. Anyway, you can get the whole story from Patty when you get back."

Aboard the *Normandie*, New York Harbor
May 5, 1937

Frank Bandfield was fit, rested, and hot as hell to see Patty. He had spent five celibate months since their argument had turned into a sexual romp. He was ready. For the past four days, he'd done nothing but eat and sleep, making up for all the lost meals in Spain. Caldwell had told him apologetically that he wouldn't be getting his bounty money, the $1,000 for each airplane shot down, and had arranged instead for a first-class cabin. Bandfield had done little more than go back and forth from his stateroom to the dining room for the whole trip.

The crowd pressing the dock reminded him of the stands at the National Air Races, a sea of upturned faces, waving arms. Most of the women were wearing wide white hats—he knew he could pick Patty out because she wouldn't be.

The ship was finally warped in and the gangways rolled into place. He saw her, and he felt his excitement grow. She waved, her arm coming up through a cluster of happy, excited faces.

He bumped his way through the pack of people on the gangway, forcing himself forward. Patty was forging ahead to him, and their hands reached out to touch, their bodies buffered by a group of celebrants hugging and kissing each other.

The crowd parted, and they embraced, arms wrapping around each other, mouths firmly intersected. He hugged her, trying to drive his pelvis against hers, unable to do so because there was something in the way—her belly.

The crowd closed in around them as they both dropped their hands down.

"My God, you're pregnant?"

"Either that or I'm going to have to go on a hell of a diet."

"When is it due?"

"It had better be no later than August, or I'm in big trouble."

"*Now* I understand why you didn't go with Earhart."

"There wouldn't have been room for the three of us."

Bundling the luggage through customs took forever, and in between the catching up and kissing he asked her, "What happens to our sex life now that we have a star boarder?"

"Well, you'll see soon enough. We're going to the St. Moritz. I've already checked in and gone to the room. I've got three towels ready—one warm, one cool, one dry—and an extension cord with a two-toe socket running to the bed."

He kissed her again.

Author's Note

In nonfiction, no matter how hard one tries to validate every fact, errors are still made. The soul-saving grace is that in making errors the author provides pleasure to the ardent buffs who love to set you straight. The author has more latitude in fiction, where you can make necessary changes in people, places, or events to suit the requirements of the plot.

I've taken some small liberties in this regard, changing the real Dole Derby to a fictional Pineapple Derby, and creating some special races, planes, and paint schemes for the Cleveland Air Races. For the most part, however, I've tried very hard to convey the true flavor of the times in both civil and military aviation, and would hope that the buffs might find pleasure in recognizing in fiction what they know so well in fact.

I would like to express my gratitude to Crown Publishers, Inc., for the tremendous support they have provided me in creating this book. My most profound thanks go to Senior Editor Mark Gompertz, whose inspirational help has been crucial. It is a privilege to work with Mark, who is a wonderful editor, a great friend, and a marvelous human being.

About the Author

Walter Boyne, a retired Air Force colonel, has been a director of the National Air and Space Museum in Washington, D.C. In addition to co-writing the novel *The Wild Blue*, he is the author of ten books on flight, including *The Smithsonian Book of Flight*. He is presently at work on the sequel to *Trophy for Eagles*.

He lives in Reston, Virginia.